AND ONE RODE WEST

"This fast-paced . . . romance sizzles with everything we have come to expect from this extraordinary writer."

—Romantic Times

"For the exciting conclusion to this story and the trilogy, pick yourself up a copy, take the phone off the hook, and indulge in sheer reading pleasure."

—Rendezvous

LORD OF THE WOLVES

HEATHER GRAHAM

A DELL BOOK

LORD OF THE WOLVES
A Dell Book

PUBLISHING HISTORY
Dell mass market edition published October 1993
Dell mass market reissue / February 2009

Published by Bantam Dell
A Division of Random House, Inc.
New York, New York

This is a work of fiction. Names, characters, places, and incidents
either are the product of the author's imagination or are used
fictitiously. Any resemblance to actual persons, living or dead, events,
or locales is entirely coincidental.

Dell is a registered trademark of Random House, Inc., and the
colophon is a trademark of Random House, Inc.

ISBN 978-0-440-24549-0

Printed in the United States of America

www.bantamdell.com

OPM 10 9 8 7 6 5 4 3 2 1

A Note from the Author

I have always loved historical romance and started with it myself when I was reading a special history of Ireland, given to me by my mother, who was from Dublin. I found a fascinating true story about a Viking prince named Olaf the White, who came to the very doors of a great Irish king named Aed Finnlaith. Aed held his own against the Vikings, yet in the midst of the fighting the high king called a truce, formed an alliance with the Viking, and gave him his daughter as his wife. I found the same reference later that day in a different history, and from that point on I was completely intrigued. My Viking was born, and he married his Irish princess, and my first historical romance, *Golden Surrender*, was written. I loved the research. I loved what could be seen so clearly in hindsight—the Vikings had indeed dominated the seas and plundered and pillaged far and wide. But they had also given back to each of the lands they had raided, and in the end many of the seafarers found new homes in those lands. As time passed, the Vikings who had stayed behind became as much a part of their new lands as the people they had so harassed.

Olaf the White came to Ireland with his Viking raiders. Alfred the Great went up against them in England, and so I later gave Olaf and his Irish princess a son to join in that fray—on Alfred's side!—in *The Viking's Woman*. I wasn't ready to let go of the family yet—I had become very fond of Olaf and his lady and their large brood, children with a heritage from both the savage sea raiders and the great golden civilization Ireland was at the time. In *Lord of the Wolves* another son takes to the seas, this time finding his battles must be waged across the English Channel. It was a tempestuous time in history: countries battled within, and the greatest of rulers sought to ally with Viking princes or hire them against their enemies. I hope that Melisande and Conar can take you back to that near-mythical time in history, a time when the world could be wild and savage, and yet compelling and beautiful still!

Dedicated to old friends with thanks for the warm memories, the great slumber parties, and all the stories we used to tell, and the dreams we used to weave.

To Patti Hill McVay, Patti Barbara Holland, Debbie Coule Dombroski, Marsha Wagner Penna, and especially to Ann Dulaney Ahern—who has always kept the laughter going.

To Sherri Adair Tatum, Brenda Hunt Causey, and Carol Zebrowski Thompson, with special thanks for always being so wonderfully supportive.

Most especially, to Debbie Durfey Craig. If old friends are truly gold, she is twenty-four karat.

Prologue
The Blood
of the Wolf

A.D. 865
The Coast of Eire
Land of the Scotia

The tall boy was rigid, his young soul in a tempest of indignation. Golden blond, already strong beyond his years, he withstood the wind well as it whipped around him, almost as if he drew more strength from the force of it.

His mother had rued his behavior and told him he was acting like a *Viking*.

Well, he was a Viking!

"Look to the sea, my son!" his father told him, and the king's hands set upon his son's shoulders. "Look out to the whitecaps, breaking on the water. Imagine them our ships! So many of them, lean, sharp ships, ships that slash the water and can best any storm out there! See the great dragon prows, my son, the bared teeth, the mouths drawn back in snarling grimaces! See the carving of them, the excellent way they are crafted! We are the masters of the seas, and that cannot be denied."

He smiled up into his father's eyes. "Vikings, Fa-

1

ther. We *are* Vikings. And we still sail such ships from here!''

''They are the best ships, as most of the world has seen. It is a world in which we are often under attack and a world in which we often make alliances, and so we need strong ships,'' the king commented thoughtfully. ''And yes, we are Vikings, or Norsemen, in one way, Irish in another. Sometimes, son, it is not so wise to remind your mother of that fact.''

The boy grinned. His mother was every inch the Irish princess. She had taught them all the great Irish laws of hospitality, and the Brehon laws that made the people so civilized. She had seen that they were taught art and history, languages, and religion. But he did not know if his mother really so much minded his father's being a Viking. Whatever else his father might be, he was a great man who had perhaps invaded once, but then had stayed to fight for the land—and the people.

His mother had been the one to send him to his father now.

He had gotten in trouble, for Leith had teased him, taking his newly hewn sword, the very handsome one that his grandfather had fashioned for him.

Leith always had everything, or so it seemed. But then Leith was the eldest son. Leith was their father's heir. He would rule here, in this place that was so rich and green, so beautiful, that they all loved so much. He knew that, he understood it. He even loved his brother who had been trained to be a king, who was older, wiser, dignified, and, like his mother, very thoughtful and very fair.

But today he had tried to take the sword!

The worst of it had been that it had all begun in the chapel during mass. His mother had taken his hand and led him from the church, and her emerald eyes had looked upon him with a deep anger.

''Leith took my sword!'' he had told her, his small

jaw set, his eyes blazing. He should have been sorry, of course. He loved his mother deeply and was sorry to disappoint her.

But he would not back down.

"The land is his! Dubhlain is his!" The little wooden sword had been in his hand, and so he had lifted it high. "I will defend his right to it to the death against any invader!" he had vowed passionately. "But *this sword*, Mother, *is mine!*"

The words were so sure and so passionate, the queen had thought. Her son was so proud, so determined!

A pain had clenched at her heart, for despite his youth, she had suddenly realized, he would be like his father. He would love his brothers and sisters, honor the land of his birth.

But he would need more, crave more, *fight* for more.

She'd bitten her lip. Indeed, he was like a miniature version of the great *Wolf of Norway,* as were several of her sons, but perhaps none so much as this one! His hair was pure gold, his brows were high arched, his face was a little *man's* face, finely, ruggedly hewn.

His eyes were that cold Nordic blue of his father's people. Bright blue, direct blue, impaling blue. He was a boy, but it was so very hard to look away from those eyes! He stood like his father, tall already, nearly her own height. His shoulders gave promise of great breadth.

And his will . . .

Was one of steel.

He had waved in the air the wooden sword he had so determinedly retrieved. "I am a younger son, Mother," he had explained impatiently. "But I will not have *everything* taken away from me!"

"You are the younger son of a king known round the civilized world," she had reminded him shrewdly, "And—"

"I will make my mark upon that world!" he had said defiantly.

She had thrown up her hands suddenly. "Your behavior today is horrid! You're acting just like a Viking—"

"But my father is a Viking, Mother.

She had inhaled and exhaled, trying to control her temper. She'd already survived this temperament once. Was she going to have to do so again?

"A very Irish Viking, my son. Tamed by the land, tamed by—"

"You?" he had suggested impishly.

Her emerald eyes had widened as she started, then she laughed. "Nay, I think not! And don't you dare say such a thing to him! He is a Viking, but a *civilized* one. One who reads, one who thinks, one who judges and is fair, one who *learns* everything about a people."

"Still a Viking."

"Fine, fine, my young Lord Wolf! Your Viking father has gone to the cliffs, so, my love, go bring your complaints to him!"

Standing very tall and very straight and angry all over again, he had started to walk away. "My son!" she had called to him.

He'd turned back. "I love you!" she'd called softly.

Some of the anger had gone out of him. He had smiled in return and run on, outside the walls of his home, and across green fields to the rise of cliffs, and there he had found his father.

Standing there, the ultimate warrior, one booted foot set high upon a rock as he stared out to sea.

"Do you miss it, Father?"

The king turned to him. "Never, son, for I have found my place in life." He sighed. "They accuse us—Vikings—of evil deeds, and of so many we are guilty! But, my son, I never came to ravage the land. I came to take it, aye, but always to build upon it. I brought it strength, and it brought me . . ."

"Aye, Father?"

"It brought me beauty and peace. A place to call home. It brought me your mother."

The youth smiled. He stood next to his father, one doeskin-booted foot high upon the cliff, his arms crossed over his chest, his blue eyes out upon the sea. It called to him, just as the legends of his father's gods called to him, the great warriors feasting in Valhalla, the angry Wodin riding his eight-legged horse across the skies.

"It can be good to sail," his father said softly. "Good to seek. Good to go a-Viking. To lift your sword for another, perhaps, to find your rightful place."

He met his father's eyes. "I *will* sail the seas!" he vowed passionately, small golden head thrown back, wooden sword facing toward the heavens, toward those gods of his father's people, Wodin and Thor, toward tempest, thunder and lightning. His cloak flew in the wind behind him. He closed his eyes and felt the sea air.

"I will sail the seas," he repeated more softly. "And I will find my rightful place upon this earth, and rule there! I will be the law, and I will bring the peace. I cannot be king of Dubhlain like my father, but I will be his son. They will call me *Lord of the Wolves*, Father, like the great Wolf of Norway! Indeed, Father, I will fight for right—"

"And for what is yours?" the king mentioned shrewdly, amused, yet knowing that this was the way it would be.

"And for what is mine, always! Fighting is how one acquires land, Father, isn't it?"

The king grinned. "Well, son, there's that. And then, one can marry for it, too."

"Marry for it or fight for it," he mused.

The king laughed. "And sometimes, son, it's really quite one and the same."

The golden-haired boy looked out to the sea again. "I will go a-Viking, I will have my rightful place, however much I must fight for it—others, or my wife!"

A crack of lightning tore across the sky. The king looked up to it.

Mergwin would call it an omen, the Norse king of Dubhlain thought. Then he felt something, he didn't know what, not unease, but a warning. He knew, without turning, that Mergwin himself was behind him, staring at the boy, and looking to the heavens.

The king sighed. "All right, magician. What is it you're about to tell me?"

Mergwin, long white hair and beard flying in the wind, stared at the king, affronted. "I am not a magician, Olaf of Norway."

"Druid, aye, and rune master!" Olaf said wearily. The boy turned and flashed a quick smile to the old man, then stared back at the sea, his eyes intense.

"Do you mock me?" Mergwin asked. "After all these years, king of Dubhlain?"

Olaf smiled. "Tell me, then. You vowed once that Leith would live long and well, and rule wisely. You promised a tempest for Eric upon his birth. Now . . . what say you about Conar?"

"Well, I don't know, milord Viking, what would you have me do? Slay a lamb and pray to the ancient gods? Ah, but then I am like the boy, half Irish and half Norse. But it is the Norse I see in him today. Close your eyes, great king. Imagine the man!"

Olaf wasn't sure he really closed his eyes at all. For a moment he was convinced he saw his son as a man, regally tall, golden, a man of taut muscle and sinew, a warrior to defy any enemy of god or man.

"Aye, great king, this son will travel, too!" Mergwin prophesied softly. "He will be a mighty power, strong and shrewd. And he will sail . . ."

"Sail where?" the king asked.

Mergwin hesitated, frowning. "His journeys will take him south across the channel, he will quickly claim what it is that he seeks . . ."

"Then?" Olaf demanded.

"Then he will have to fight to keep it. And . . . *it*, and *her*! It will not be easy. Vast hordes will come, a battle as has never been imagined must in the end ensue."

"*Her?* Mergwin, who is the *her*?"

Mergwin shrugged, looking to the boy who stood so tall, straight and proud, blue eyes trained out to sea.

He sighed, eyes twinkling as they met those of the king of Dubhlain.

"No sacrificial lamb in the ancient Druid way, eh, milord? Nay, nay, that wouldn't be right!" He clutched a bag that hung from his robe belt and shook it slightly. "Remember, my king, that I am like the boy, partly Viking, partly Irish, and that is why I am so strong! For a Viking lad, then, I must cast Viking stones!"

Viking! Olaf closed his eyes, suddenly certain that his son would go a-Viking, cross the sea to distant lands.

And there he would find a woman, one to battle, one to marry, and their lives might well be at risk again and again, for they would be at odds, and fighting one another . . .

He had wanted peace for his sons. But it was not a peaceful world.

He looked to the boy, and he saw himself, and he knew that whatever sorrow it caused him, he would have to see him go.

Mergwin suddenly stooped, shook the bag, and cast his finely carved wooden runes upon the earth.

The wind howled. Lightning slashed against the sky again.

"Indeed, like his father, he will be called the Lord of the Wolves!" Mergwin said.

Olaf stared at his son, then back to the ground, looking at the symbols upon each of the little wooden squares, Mergwin looked up to him, grinning. "Indeed, it will be so, the lightning has decreed it so, just as if Wodin himself had etched the words across the sky!"

"Umm," Olaf said, crossing his arms over his chest. "And pray tell, old man, just what else has Wodin etched across the sky. Where will he sail? Who is this woman, this—*her*?"

"Patience, milord, patience!" Mergwin advised, and grinned mischievously. Arching a brow, he looked to the tall boy upon the cliff, then back to Olaf. "Let's look to the stones, Wolf of Norway, let's look to the stones! The Viking way, for a Viking prince . . ."

"And the woman?" the Wolf demanded.

"Aye! And the woman!" Mergwin agreed. "She's very beautiful . . ."

"But troublesome, I imagine."

"Like a tempest!" Mergwin agreed, laughing. But then the laughter faded from his eyes and his voice grew thoughtful and grave. "Aye, indeed, tempests whip ahead, the enemy will number in the thousands, and to best them all, they must survive . . ."

"Survive what?"

Mergwin rubbed his beard. "Themselves, I believe."

"Read further!" the king commanded.

And there, on the rugged, windswept coast, *their* future was foretold . . .

1

The Lady
and the Land

Battle Thus
Engaged

1

Spring, A.D. 885
The Coast of France

"Melisande! Melisande! *His* ships are *here!*"

Melisande had been a flurry of motion. The words brought her to a dead standstill in the center of the tower, a sudden cascade of both fear and anticipation sweeping through her.

She had not believed that he would come!

But with Marie de Tresse crying out the warning from the wooden parapet beyond her open tower door, Melisande could no longer doubt his promise that he would have his due.

She stared at Marie's anxious face for a moment, dropped the tunic of delicately crafted mail she'd held, then tore through the doorway from the high tower chamber and ran out along the stone wall to stare out to the sea from the parapet.

Indeed, he was coming.

Dear God, it had been a day like this when he had first come. It seemed so long ago now! Was he always to catch her in adversity such as this? Would she always be left to wonder if he had come to her aid—or to destroy her completely?

There was no question today, she told herself. He had come for what he considered his.

She felt suddenly hot and cold at once. She pressed the back of her hand to her face. Her face felt like fire, her hand like ice.

God, he was coming, he was coming. Wave after wave of tremors shot through her, sweeping her up. It seemed so long since she had seen him. As if it weren't enough that a thousand Danes under that loathed Geoffrey were at her door! Now, *he* was coming, too. After so long. Maybe there was a lot he had forgotten.

And maybe there was a lot he had remembered.

And God, how ridiculous! She wasn't half as afraid of meeting the Danes as she was of meeting him!

Not *afraid* . . .

Yes! Afraid, after all that she had done.

And surely, with what his coming must mean!

Dear Lord, he was almost here. She could see his ship, see the man!

It was an extraordinary ship with its huge dragon prow. He rode his ship just as he had those many years ago when she had first seen him.

One booted foot was high upon the helm. His great arms were crossed over his heavily muscled chest.

A crimson mantle, broached at his shoulder with an ancient Celtic emblem, flew wild behind him with the whip of the sea wind. His hair, as golden and rich as the sun, also flew back.

She couldn't see his eyes yet, but she didn't need to see them. She could remember them all too well.

God, yes, she could remember their color! Remember that astounding, piercing blue. Sky blue, sea blue, deeper than cobalt, brighter than sapphires. They were eyes that looked at her, and through her, stripping her bare to the soul.

"So, he will not come, eh?"

She heard the taunting question spoken from a rich

masculine voice at her rear and spun around quickly. Ragwald was there on the walkway with her, as ancient as the moon, as nagging as a fisherwife. He wagged a finger at her. "Milady, you cannot turn your back on a bargain with such a man!"

"I made no bargain! You did."

"I bargained for our lives!" Ragwald reminded her with great dignity. "And thank the good Lord! It does appear that you might have need of the man again. Then again, perhaps the young jarl is angry and not in the mood to be very helpful, eh?"

"You—" Melisande began, ready to tell him that he was the adviser, *she* was the countess, and therefore, hers was the final word. But she broke off, biting her lower lip. There was a more immediate danger. When she stared down from her vantage point on the fortress wall, she could see her men already engaged in battle.

Odd, how things came around! They'd made these very enemies they fought now that long ago day when *he'd* first come, and now they were embroiled in battle again, even while *his* ships sailed through the seas, their great dragon prows slicing the water.

Strange that the day was gray, that lightning ripped, that thunder drummed. Strange that he had a penchant for coming in such a tempest, as if he were one of the gods himself, casting down his fire bolts as if he cast out his fury.

"Which shall it be?" Ragwald mused. "Has he come to slice and dice us—or has he come to the rescue once again? A Norse Viking—to fight these Danish Vikings!"

How could it be that they lived in such a lawless land? Melisande wondered for a pained moment. She used to love to hear her father talk about the great King Charlemagne, and about his love for the arts and astrology—and peace!

But Charlemagne, like her father, was dead. He had

ruled nearly a hundred years ago, and many things had changed since then. Charles the Fat was king in Paris—except that he wasn't in Paris, he was off somewhere in Italy, and the Danes had been ravaging the coast, heading for Rouen, forever, or so it seemed.

Melisande's enemies had joined with the Danes once again to attempt to take what was rightfully hers.

She'd gone against them before. Ever since that day years earlier when her father had fallen dead, she had learned to still her cries when she watched men die by the sword. She had learned not to shiver before the war cries, and hardest of all, she had learned *not to run!* She had been all that was left to lead her people, and she had learned how to lead.

Not that *he* had ever intended that she should, but then again, that first meeting had been a long time ago. So much had happened since then.

So much for which he must surely long to wind his hands around her neck. His very powerful hands. She could almost feel them.

That thought again made her hot and cold, and incredibly weak. She had vowed to him that she wanted no part of him, yet even the thought of him made her tremble.

Ah, and there was the rub! For she dared not show the man weakness, dared never let him know her mind, her heart! Never let him know that thoughts of him filled her days, her life, always.

Most definitely not now! She couldn't be weak. She didn't even dare think about herself at the moment.

Or fear him or his touch. Think about it, loathe it, anticipate it, loathe it, ache for it. Hate him, love him, despise him, long for him . . .

Her men were in trouble, she realized suddenly. Deep trouble. From the parapet she could see the changing position of the warriors below, see the promise of defeat when they could not.

"Sweet Jesu above us!" Melisande cried. "Pray God someone has come for our side! I must hurry out there, Ragwald. Our forces are being split, there, see!"

Ragwald caught her arm. "Let it be! Don't go! Let the Viking come in! One of them will have it—the Danes or the Norwegians. Let them battle it out, you remain here safely this time!"

Melisande pulled from him, angry at first, and then with sorrow.

Ragwald loved her. In these dark days love was hard to come by.

"I remind you, my dear adviser, you first sent me out in armor. I am the countess! I will hold this place. You are right about one thing—let them battle one another. But I must lead our men from the trap that is beginning to divide them now!"

"Wait!" Ragwald called. "See—his ships are beaching!"

"I cannot wait! See, Ragwald!" She dragged him to the edge of the parapet, pointing out the shore far below. Her father had built an exceptional fortress. A motte and bailey work, a castle. Such structures had become very prominent here in the last century since the Vikings had started their constant raids. Theirs was a truly fine example of all that such a fortress might be. They were located upon a mount with a safe harbor and beach directly in front of high stone walls. Most castles or mottes and baileys were wooden—her father had seen the great benefit of stone. It did not catch fire. Within the high walls there was the promise of safety. There was a great courtyard with room for men and animals, space for smiths to work, stables for the great war-horses, craftsmen's shops, kitchens. To the left and to the right of the walls high precipices with forests mounted great cliffs that rose above the sea. The view from the parapets seemed never ending, and it was possible to gain infinite information here. Indeed, the fortress's cunning placement had kept it standing when the troops left to defend it were minimal.

Now Melisande took full advantage of her bird's-eye view. "See, Ragwald, there's Philippe, and there's Gaston, their forces being split, and they are so fierce in their combat that they cannot see! I must go."

"Melisande, no!" Ragwald repeated. He gripped her arms when she tried to run past him. She stared into his eyes, and for once Ragwald could see a glimmering of fear there.

In Melisande? Melisande feared nothing.

Except the Viking, Ragwald thought in silence. She always had. He had both infuriated and fascinated her. Perhaps she had good sense to fear him now, as well as pray that he had come to defend them. After all, she had quite directly defied him in everything.

And now she meant to take her sword and ride out and do battle on Warrior!

"*Don't do this!*" he warned her, holding fiercely to her once again.

"I have to!" she cried back, her voice husky, tinged with a certain desperation now, her eyes wide and wild with the tempest of her emotions.

"No—" he began again, but she had wrenched herself from his arms. "Melisande!" She ran from him down the parapet and into the tower.

"Melisande!"

Her name rose on the air and seemed to echo at him in a long taunt.

It didn't matter. She was gone. Tensely he paced the tower parapet, the highest point of the fortress. He could see the courtyard below, the wall, the outer parapets; the field beyond the gates, and even to the sea.

Ten minutes later he saw her. His old heart leapt to his throat.

She was mounted upon Warrior, before the gates. She was clad in the gilded mail he had first seen so many years ago.

Clad as she had been when she had gone to war before.

Ragwald could see that the Viking ships had beached. From his distance he could see their leader donning his conical war helmet. The horses were being loaded off the ships. His majestic Thor, a huge horse, muscled like his master, but as agile as his master in every movement, came, too.

The Viking needed no explanations. His men were ready, striding straight from their ships into hand-to-hand combat on the shore, or leaping atop their Viking mounts, horses that had withstood their daring sea voyages time and time again.

Instantly they were within the fray.

Ragwald's hands tightened around the edge of the parapet. Melisande was in the melee, too. Away from the new arrivals she was circling groups of fighting men, her sword extended and waving high in the air as she ordered her forces to regroup. The Danes—with their treacherous Frankish allies—were after her men in much greater number, perhaps a thousand of them to a mere two hundred of hers.

There were more coming, Ragwald had heard. Thousands more. They meant to lay siege to Paris, it had been rumored.

But they could care little about Paris here today. Melisande had gathered her troops. He could hear a cry going out. She was bringing the men back behind the walls of the fortress. Some sign had been given to the guards. Great caldrons of boiling oil were being brought up to throw down upon the invaders should they follow.

The gates opened. With Melisande in the lead, the defenders came rushing through.

"Strike!" Philippe shouted to the men above them on the outer wall of the fortress.

Ragwald closed his eyes. He heard the sound of agonized screams. The first of the invaders had been driven back by the boiling oil that had cascaded down upon them.

And there, dead still, hearing the screams as he did, was Melisande. So very pale and straight as she sat atop Warrior, she had just ridden into his sight within the courtyard, the men streaming in around and behind her.

She hated it, he thought. *She hated the battles, she hated warfare. She had seen everything the day her father had died, and she dearly cherished peace since then.*

But what if she lost?

Well, that consequence would be clear enough if the Danes were victorious. They would rob and pillage, murder and rape, and be done with it.

And the land and the fortress would be left to Geoffrey, just as soon as his raiding allies thought that they had taken their fill of the spoils.

And Melisande's fate would be dire.

And if the Viking won?

She might consider *her* fate every bit as dire! But the people would live, the fortress would stand. Dear God, no matter what *her* fate, it would be much better for her people if the Viking were to win the day. There would be no pillaging, no robbing, no raping—no murder. Melisande would know that and accept her own fate, no matter what the consequences for her.

"The girl!" Came a cry from beyond the walls. "Give over Countess Melisande! Then will there be peace!"

Ragwald, from the tower parapet, could see everything so clearly! It was Geoffrey himself calling out. He had been in pursuit of Melisande, yet now the guards from the wall parapets held him off with their threat of death from the pots of burning oil. He sat on his own horse, fury contorting his features. Paused there just beyond the wall as Melisande's men struggled valiantly to stream in behind her. Soon, enough of Geoffrey's men would be with him so that more would be forced to brave the walls.

Some would perish.

Some would surely make it through.

There was not twenty feet now between Melisande and her enemy, but the great stone wall of the fortress separated them.

Yet the situation remained grim. The gates were not yet closed and bolted. The threat of the oil would not hold Geoffrey or his Danes long, not when a prize was nearly within their grasp.

"It's Geoffrey!" Philippe, reining in his horse near to Melisande's, cried out to his countess. "The bloody bastard, making the same demands as his father before him!"

Melisande could not see the troops beyond the walls as Ragwald did, but she could hear the cries clearly enough, and equally well she could hear the prancing of the war-horses, impatient as they waited. More and more of Geoffrey's men gathered closer and closer to the walls. Soon they would rush the gates in such a multitude that nothing would hold them back.

"The walls will fall!" came another shouted threat. "Every man here will perish and die!" Geoffrey promised. "Melisande, you are outnumbered!"

"I was outnumbered!" she cried back. "No more!"

"The Viking comes! But can he save you in time? I've men of yours out here, Melisande. We pluck them up even as they try to escape us. You'll seek to burn us—but you'll burn them as well. Even now I have a knife at a man's throat!"

Melisande stared up to Ragwald, high atop the tower parapet. Ragwald looked down at Geoffrey. Next to him one of his men did hold a prisoner, a razor-sharp blade thrust against his throat.

Ragwald looked to Melisande and saw in her eyes that she demanded the truth.

He nodded.

Melisande looked quickly to Philippe. Anguish touched her eyes. "I must go out there. There's nothing left to do—"

"Men perish in battle, lady! For the fate of just one warrior—"

"Philippe! In seconds they will surge forward. We will kill our own people to press their's back. More and more will die. If I ride Warrior out and give myself over—"

"No!" Philippe shouted.

She started to urge her horse forward, toward the gate. She despised Geoffrey. More than anyone in the world, she hated him deeply and fiercely. Even as her horse moved ahead she denied with all her heart that she could go to so despised an enemy.

His father had slain her own. To take the fortress.

Her teeth chattered suddenly.

No, she couldn't go to Geoffrey. No matter what. Because the Viking was out there. And if he were ever to know that she had given herself over willingly, no matter what the circumstances might be . . .

She needed to buy time!

She reined in and stared up from Ragwald on the inner heights across the courtyard to her guards, stretched out on the outer wall parapets. Most of her guards were grimly ready with their caldrons of oil, but several of the best archers still held their weapons.

She met one man's gaze. "Can you hit the enemy who threatens one of our own?" she asked softly.

"Lady, aye!" he swore.

She nodded. "Do it then. When he is free, command our men to rush. See that they enter—even with what enemy they drag in with them. Then *close the gates. Fast!*"

Her archer turned. Swiftly he raised his bow and took aim.

She heard a scream. "Men, move now!" One of her captains shouted from the parapet, and there was an inward streaming at the gate, men fiercely battle men there.

"Close it!" she ordered.

"Melisande!" Ragwald cried down suddenly. "Hold fast! *They* are with us now!"

Then she heard a cry—a deep, rich cry of rage and surprise. It came from Geoffrey himself, she thought, and for a moment she savored the pleasure.

The Viking had reached her enemy . . .

She heard the awful sound of clanging, clashing steel. She heard the worse sound of steel sinking into men.

"Nay, Melisande!" Ragwald called out suddenly.

From his vantage point upon the inner tower parapet, Ragwald saw what she did not. Yes, the Viking had come. Geoffrey himself had gone into retreat, swiftly riding from the scene of the fray, yet leaving his men—and a multitude of Danes—to battle there.

Too many of them, for the Viking had split his forces, having brought half of them in the reckless dash forward that now saved Melisande's forces, while the others had remained behind to battle the rear. His first wave of men were nowhere equal in number to the Danes there. He had meant to swell the ranks of the fortress guard, then find harbor to renew the battle from within the walls.

But Melisande had ordered the gates closed . . .

Right upon him, and his men.

"Sweet Jesu!" Ragwald prayed, looking to heaven, swiftly, then back to the battle that was unfolding before him now.

Perhaps there was a chance . . .

For he could see the warrior who had come to their defense now.

They called him the Lord of the Wolves, as Ragwald had heard they called his father before him. Now Ragwald knew why. Confronted with insurmountable odds, the man showed both incredible skill and incredible courage. Sword whipping from side to side, he rode straight into the worse of the fray, downing his enemies before most saw what hit them. There were berserker cries from the Danes, and some charged him, near frothing at the mouth, as berserkers were known to do. But one and all alike, they fell beneath the sheer force of his charge. There were more and more men upon him. He called out something that Ragwald didn't understand, but then Ragwald saw what the order had been. While he battled, his men brought forth a ram. The Danes were kept busy while others of the Viking's men went to work upon the gates—so recently slammed upon them—with their ram.

Ragwald realized suddenly that he had been staring at the battle open-mouthed. "Melisande!" he cried. But she couldn't hear him above the din of battle. She was shouting out her own orders. He pushed away from the parapet and came running through Melisande's tower, racing down the length of the stairway, then bursting out into the great hall. Out in the yard within the palisade, men, women, and children, cows, ducks, and pigs, all scurried to safety against the far walls, mothers grabbing their infants, farmers clinging to their precious livestock. A donkey brayed, chickens screeched and squawked flying everywhere. Ragwald, clad in his old comfortable gray cape, looking like a giant, ragtag bird himself, hurried toward Melisande and the troops who were now dismounting from their horses, preparing to man the walls.

"*He's* there! He's the one ramming the gate! Doing battle with the Danes. You—you locked him out!" he cried.

He watched the swift light of realization that came to her eyes, then the sinking horror within them.

She hadn't meant to lock *him* out.

He would never believe it.

"The gate!" she cried, but it was too late. The heavy wooden ram broke through the weakened area of stone.

The Vikings knew their business. Aye, *Lord Conar* knew his business.

She saw Philippe, still mounted, riding hard to meet the new horde that burst in upon them.

"Call Philippe back!" Ragwald commanded quickly.

"He won't come!"

"Tell him *you* need him—he will come. Don't let a fighting man meet your Irish Viking first. The Viking will know *I've* not come to do battle. Call Philippe, quickly!"

"Philippe!" Melisande shouted his name. He turned, hurrying back to her. She quickly saw the wisdom of Ragwald's words, for the old man himself went hurrying over to the broken wall, his arms flapping wildly.

It looked as if one of the Vikings meant to slice him through as he crawled atop the rubble. Melisande choked back a scream as she saw Ragwald halt.

He had come through the rubble himself. Mounted upon his great ebony stallion, wearing that helmet that hid all thought and made his eyes all the more piercing.

"They've beaten them! Geoffrey flees even now!"

Philippe cried out suddenly. He started to laugh, the sound deeply relieved. "There—we've some of his men trapped within the fortress. I need to bring you quickly away, Countess. And finish this thing. Though, Lord God! Now we are under new attack since—"

"No, Philippe, no!" Melisande said softly, touching his arm. "Ragwald has reached the Wolf."

"Then we are spared the evil of the Danes!"

Melisande was silent, convinced at that moment that there was no evil greater than the Viking who rode with such confidence and arrogance into her fortress. The man with the searing blue eyes and rock hard shoulders. The one who had come to lay claim to everything, who did as he chose, brooking no opposition.

A moment's guilt tugged at her heart. *She owed him!* Yes, she had owed him, for a battle fought long ago. Yet he had been paid, and paid well. It was only the foolish bargain Ragwald had made with him so long ago that brought her to this moment now.

A bargain that might well have saved the day, she reminded herself.

None of that mattered. The guilt could not outweigh the fear that seemed to have risen to a storm within her. She couldn't still the trembling within her. She had never been able to do that when he was near. Never been able to fight the tremendous heat, nor the cold, his nearness evoked. The feeling of shivers racing up and down her spine.

What difference did it make? she wondered. One bastard or another! But she didn't really believe that. Geoffrey was as cruel and ruthless and cunning as his father had been.

As for *him* . . .

Him!

He merely wanted to slit her throat!

Oh, she could never abide his arrogance. Then there was the matter of the very elegant blond woman who traveled with him wherever he went. There was also the humiliating matter of all that he had commanded of Melisande . . .

The simple fact that he demanded, took what he would, gave orders.

Among other things, she reminded herself, was the way he must feel now. Now, when she had so defied him. Now, when he so nearly had his hands upon her again.

Warmth assailed her. She closed her eyes, promising herself that she would not think about him, that she would not consider what was to come.

Impossible. He was here. Memory was flooding the length of her as if her blood had become molten steel.

She inhaled deeply, mentally straightening, seeking strength. She was the countess. She had become so upon her father's death. The land was hers. The fortress was hers.

And, so help her God, she would keep them!

"Jesu, lady! How many has he with him?" Philippe demanded at her side.

Mounted, the men were as striking as they had been in their dragon-prowed ships. They were men trained by Satan himself, so it seemed. Huge fellows, trained with axes and maces, knotted with muscle, reckless, fearless, dangerous.

They had saved her once. She knew how they fought!

And at the head of them . . . *him*!

"I must take you to the tower," Philippe murmured, watching the action. It was evident that Geoffrey's men must surrender or die, but there was still fighting in the yard. It did seem the safest course for her to be out of harm's way now that she was no longer needed to rally her men.

"I can take care of myself, Philippe," she assured him. "Hurry, see to our men."

Philippe did not look comfortable with her decision, but Melisande did not give him time to argue. She hurried to the steps leading to her tower and began running up them as swiftly as she could with the weight of her mail upon her. She desperately needed some time. How did she greet him? Did she actually *have* to greet him? Wasn't there any possibility at all that she could just run away?

Did she really want to? Maybe their time had finally come.

Some of the steps were broken. A battle-ax had fallen against the stone with such strength that it had cracked and broken. Melisande leapt across the gap and hurried onward to her tower room.

She paused, then ripped the mail quickly from her body.

It was a cowardly thing to do. But she thought that perhaps he hadn't seen her on the battlefield and then wouldn't think that she had intentionally closed the gates against him.

Fool! she charged herself. Coward! *She was countess here! He was just a younger son of a king, seeking his fortune, and trying to make it from her rightful inheritance! She needed show him no fear, and certainly no humility!*

She had dropped her sword with her mail. Now she clutched it again and looked uneasily about the room. Her eyes fell upon her bed with its cool, clean linen sheets and bear fur rug. A shaking seized her and she swallowed hard.

She didn't want to be caught here! She hurried back out to the parapets and looked to the yard below.

Her heart seemed to stop completely. The shivers took hold of her again, hot and cold, fire and ice. She stood dead still and met his gaze.

2

Melisande. . .

Mounted upon his huge war-horse, Conar Mac-Auliffe returned her scrutiny.

Ah, he thought, at last!

There she was, the little vixen, in all her fantastic glory.

He couldn't wait to get his hands on her!

In the midst of the melee that was dying around him at long last, he could finally set his eyes upon her. Smoke from burning oil and fiery arrows was lifting now, and she appeared on a high step to the parapets, staring down at him. He had never seen anyone look upon him with such contempt, and he wondered that she would dare do so now, when the stone of the castle had come to mean nothing, when he had proven his right to the fortress, and when it seemed that he must be the victor.

She did not tremble. Perhaps she thought that the distance between them was her safety, though he could have reached her easily with just a few steps. All he had to do was dismount from his stallion and leap upon the stone stairway leading to the tower.

But it seemed that his proximity did not matter to her. She continued to cast that superior stare down

upon him, and he found himself studying her. It had
been some time since he had seen her. She was an
extraordinary woman. He knew that if he were on a
level with her, she would still be tall for her gender.
Tall enough that she wouldn't have to look up very far
to meet his eyes. She was blessed with a glorious head
of ebony hair. As rich as a moonless night, as sleek
and burnished as the wing of a bird, it swept and
waved and cascaded down the length of her back. In
contrast, her face was as fair as fine ivory, tinged at
the cheeks with a beautiful, natural shade of rose. Her
lips, too, were wondrously shaded, beautifully defined, and tinted to a dusky beauty. Surely no goddess
or Christian angel had ever been more glorious.

A goddess, perhaps, for such creatures were known
to have tempers and whims. But she certainly could
not be an angel, not from his understanding of the
creatures. Despite her great beauty, there was nothing
forgiving about her, nothing that hinted of surrender.
No, this beauty was no angel, not with that look in her
eyes.

And not with the pride that stiffened her spine. But
then again, he knew well, humility was not among her
virtues.

She hadn't changed. She was not so very different
from the child he had met here so long ago. That day
she had been so victorious!

Because of him, he reminded himself with an inward
grin.

Ah, but that had been a different day. Then they
had joined forces, and she had gained her victory.

Today she had taken his help—and then closed the
gates on him!

But he had broken the wall, and *she had been
beaten.*

She would never escape him again, he thought

suddenly. Never use guile, strength, or anger against him, never twist or wriggle her way out of anything!

He smiled, determined to see the color of her eyes. He knew it well. As he knew her.

He lifted the visor of his helmet, wanting her to see his face and wondering if the defiance would at all leave her gaze. It did not.

He dismounted smoothly from his trusted stallion and took the first step. He had not realized that he still held his sword in his hand until he felt its weight. It didn't matter. She had shed the mail she'd worn on the battlefield, but she still held her elegant blade. He paid it no heed as he took one step and then the next, coming closer and closer to her.

She shifted her stance slightly so that she could watch him come. Her gown was a soft mauve, a shade that enhanced the luster of her hair.

She had shed the mail she had been wearing when she had been out with her troops he thought with some amusement. Had she imagined that he had not noticed her there?

It would not happen again.

But that she would be made to understand. There was quite a lot she was going to have to be made to understand this time.

He studied her gown again and the way it looked upon her. It seemed created of a liquid fabric, one that shimmered and swayed with her each subtle movement. She swirled just enough to keep him easily within her view as he approached her. He leapt from one step to another, then faced her across a few feet of broken stonework.

Her chin arched higher.

She was a creation of even greater glory than he had remembered. She had matured extremely well. Her bones were fine. Her face was a perfect oval, the cheekbones high, her chin delicately and exquisitely molded—even if it was set irritatingly firmly. Her lips, so beautiful a rose, were as cleanly drawn and defined as her bones, yet they were generous, even taut as they now were. Everything about her was beautiful. And yet more stunning still than her bones or her coloring or even the perfect proportions of her face was the startling loveliness of her eyes.

They were large, set apart within the fine lines of her face. Ah, he could see them so clearly now!

He'd never seen eyes quite like them. They surpassed blue. They were not the mauve of her gown, but something deeper. A violet that now seemed as wild as a night sky when the ancient gods would have their way, when storms threatened, when lightning flared and thunder crashed. Indeed, they were eyes to challenge even the mighty Wodin, eyes that knew no threat of mortality, eyes that defied and dared, and cried out their own victory.

But she was not victorious.

He was the victor.

And she . . . she was nothing but his prize. No matter the look upon her face.

He grit down so hard upon his teeth that he heard their grinding. Being this close was suddenly painful. She's always had the power to compel men—old Ragwald had been no fool, sending her out to lead troops that long ago day. Conar was convinced he had seen no woman more beautiful in all Christendom—or outside Christendom, for that matter. She had something greater than beauty. Something that had made him determined to send her to a nunnery when they had first met, something that had made him dream of her by darkness and by day, something that had bolted him from sleep too many times, leaving him bathed in sweat.

Something that had made him long to take a switch to her when he had learned that she had come here.

And something that now made raw desire burn in him like wildfire. Perhaps something that had always blazed deep and rich between them, something he had touched once and been damned for ever since in the aching nights that had stretched out since he had seen her.

Something that made anticipation very, very sweet now.

Perhaps it was the defiance in her eyes. Perhaps it was something she didn't see herself, that simmering sensuality that touched her every movement, her gaze, even the hatred within her eyes.

Perhaps it all had to do with the fact that he had touched her, that he knew every fascinating subtle nuance of the woman. And knowing was a fever, one that lived with him, leaving him hungry all of the time.

She would never forgive him for being what he was!

That didn't matter. Not tonight. Not ever again.

"Ah, Melisande!" he said softly. "What a warm way to greet me when we have been apart so very long!"

" 'Tis a pity I did not manage to greet you more warmly still, my lord Viking. There were so many burning arrows about! What a shame we lacked one to heat your cold Norse heart!"

"I am wounded, Melisande. Deeply wounded."

"I only wish it were so!" she whispered.

"Melisande, one would think you might consider pretending to be courteous! After all, think on it, lady! Think on all that you have done. Why, I should not be hesitating here, but rather I should have my fingers wound tight upon you—"

"There's been a battle here today!"

"—baring your sweet flesh to my ever blistering touch. Why, by all my laws, by *your* laws, I would certainly have the right to do so! Perhaps you'd like to rephrase your greeting?" he suggested.

She smiled sweetly, but a violet fire continued to

rage within her eyes. "I said, 'Your every wish shall
be our command.' "

He laughed loudly, leaning upon his sword. "Oh, I
don't think that is what you said, Melisande!" he
murmured. His eyes raked over her. "But I do promise you, milady, that it will be so!"

"Don't make promises you can't keep, Viking."

"Melisande, when I make a promise, I always keep
it. And I might remind you, I was born in Dubhlain."

"Your ships are Viking ships—"

"The very best," he agreed. His eyes narrowed.
His tone became hard. "I understand that you were
about to offer yourself to our old enemy Geoffrey."

She stiffened. She didn't realize how easily her men
were willing to speak with him, believing in his power.

"I—" she paused, seeing his fury. She shook her
head. "I didn't really mean to go. Damn you, can't
you see? I wished to save lives—"

"Even think of it again, milady, and—"

"And?"

"There will be no hesitance. I shall strip you naked
and flay you half dead."

"You would never dare."

"Would you dare tempt me?"

"And what if Geoffrey had me?" she inquired
coolly, her eyes raging still.

"Ah, well, then I should have to think deeply of
what rewards could be gained if I did or did not
retrieve you. But then, you are *my* prize, never his.
Perhaps I would have to come for you. I never let
anyone take what is mine."

"You needn't do me any favors," she told him,
violet eyes still burning brightly. "And if you had but
heeded my pleadings, they'd never have come so far!"

"Had you but heeded my warnings, you wouldn't
have been in the path of danger!"

"But this castle would—"

"This castle is wood and stone!"

"Wood and stone filled with people!" she cried.

"I arrived on time, milady," he swore savagely, looking away. Once again he had almost been too late. He fought to control his temper. He had owed her nothing!

"Then," she murmured, fighting to keep her voice level, "have you come to stay for a while?"

He smiled slowly. "Ah, Melisande! Not a 'Thank you, milord. After all, you arrive at such an opportune time.' Just 'How long are you staying? Please don't let it be long.' Of course, I'm sure it would have been more fortunate had a blazing Danish arrow made it to my heart, but alas, I fear I have not availed you so."

Her eyes narrowed. "Indeed, a pity," she whispered, then quickly formed the right words. "Thank you for arriving at such an opportune time," she murmured. Her eyes lowered for a moment, then rose to his. Truly they burned now! "Though, milord, I must ask, what difference does it make, one Viking or another?"

Damn her.

She would always ignore what she chose to, and she knew how to cut quickly to the heart.

He grit his teeth again, willing himself to control both his temper and any display of emotion. He forced a smile to his lips. "Well, then, milady," he said softly. "If I find that I do need to negotiate with Geoffrey or some Danish jarl at a later date, I will know that I don't offend you in any way if I offer up your glorious person in exchange for some other concession on their part."

Ah! Now that one had cut, too! He saw the violet fire leap to her eyes. Her anger struck so quickly that she had no time to control her emotions. She was still carrying her elegantly engraved sword. She lifted it quite suddenly—and lethally—and it was only the speed of his battle reflexes that allowed him to quickly parry her blow. It had been a strong one, and his response had been strong as well. Their swords reverberated on the air for a moment, and his eyes met hers—filled with fury and promise. She cried out suddenly, losing her footing upon the broken step. She dropped her sword, seeking some hold on the wall. But there was only stone for her to touch. He dropped his sword, bracing his legs, reaching out for her just as she would have plummeted to the rough earth below. His arms curled strongly around her waist, dragging her hard against him. She gasped in a ragged breath, then her head fell back, and all the tempest he had remembered burned within the gaze she gave him.

He smiled slowly. No matter how many times he saved her, she hated him so!

Yet even as he held her now, he remembered. Remembered the feel of her flesh, the supple perfection of her form. Longing, hot as lightning, hard, aching, ripped into him. Rigid with it, he spoke to her quickly, all too aware that he hadn't the time at this moment to deal with her as he so desired.

"You little fool! You'd kill yourself to get to me! Well, milady, I'm damned sorry, but today was just a skirmish in what is to come, and so help me God—"

"But you don't believe in God, do you?" she taunted.

His arms tightened. Her fingers curled around them desperately, but she knew she'd never free herself. She gritted her teeth, going still, her hatred still smoldering in her eyes when he shook her to silence her.

"We are going to present a united front, my love. You've half an hour to prepare yourself, Melisande, and then you will be down in the fortress yard to greet me so that we can both greet my men and your people. There's going to be enough death. You will not add to it."

"I have never sacrificed my people!" she retorted angrily. "Indeed, I have been the sacrifice!"

"Poor little martyr. Ah, well, that is the godly way, Melisande."

"Let go of me!" she commanded.

"Ah, tempting! Let you fall down all those steps to the ragged earth below. Destroy such beauty—and such sweetness! Alas, Melisande, know it well now. I will never let you go!"

"Aren't you afraid that I shall take my sword to you in the night?" she demanded coolly—still struggling against his rock hard hold.

Ah, but she was warm! Vibrant. The rise and fall of her breasts was extremely provocative. The huskiness of her voice so seductive as she struggled for breath.

He leaned nearer her, smiling still. "When I've finished with you tonight, milady, you'll not be able to move a muscle, I swear it!"

She paled at that, turned white as a ghost, but recovered quickly—kicking him hard on his unprotected shin. He almost cried out, caught himself just in time, and leapt up the next step with her. To his rather bitter amusement she clutched him desperately rather than plummet to her death.

With a few more strides he reached her tower room. He tossed her down upon her bed and was once more treated to the ironic pleasure of seeing her leap quickly up, her pulse pounding frantically against the lovely white column of her throat.

"Can it be? Melisande, afraid. Of a *Viking* touch? Perhaps you remember it all quite too clearly. Is it fear then, or longing? Anticipation—or dread? Fear not, my fair lady! I haven't time for your welcoming arms at the moment. But then again—don't fret. The night will be long."

"Fret!" she choked out. "You invite hell upon us both! You—"

She broke off with a gasp because he had come for her. Wrenched up into his arms, she was pulled hard against him. "Heaven or hell, lady. Maybe a bit of both. I don't believe I will offer you such hardship, but then again, I am lord here, and will have my Viking way!"

"Oh!" she cried in fury. "You sea snake! You bastard, you—"

"I cannot wait to hurry back to your arms!" he assured her. "Tonight, Melisande, there will be no escape." He released her. She fell back but quickly caught herself, leaping up and backing away from him.

"I didn't mean to escape you!" she whispered frantically. "I was needed here, and you wouldn't come. You claimed you were needed elsewhere—"

"In my father's house!" he reminded her angrily. "For all that your only term for me seems to be *Viking,* I am a prince of Dubhlain, and aye, I have many responsibilities!"

"Well, I have just these here!" she cried passionately.

"And we are seeing to them now!" he told her, turning. "When the ceremonies are over, I shall require a bath. So shall you. You might ask your people to see to it."

"I'll not—" she began, willing her lip not to tremble. But it did not matter. They were interrupted.

"Conar!"

They both started as he was called from the doorway. The man standing there was Swen of Windsor, always Conar's man, at his side, at his back when needed. He was tall with fiery red hair and a pleasant freckled face that belied his great strength in battle.

Seeing Melisande, he bowed to her quickly. "Milady."

"Swen," she murmured softly.

"Conar, you are needed. We do not know how you would deal with the prisoners."

"I'm coming now," Conar told him, still watching Melisande.

"Wait!" Melisande cried. She hesitated, strange for Melisande. "What—what do you intend to do with them?"

"The prisoners?"

She swallowed hard. "You can't just—kill them!"

He lowered his head for a moment. He didn't want to have to do so. But they were dangerous. They remained enemies.

"Conar—"

"Half an hour," he told her.

"Die a slow, lingering death!" she hissed to him.

"Half an hour—and if you've any love for your people, don't even think of defying me this time." He swung around, his mantle billowing out behind him. He clapped his hand upon Swen's shoulder, leading him out.

The door slammed in their wake.

"Before all the gods!" Conar swore savagely. "That woman is the worst witch I have encountered in all the known world!"

Swen's eyes slid his way. "Now, come, milord Wolf!" he said lightly. "You cannot feel quite so hostile—"

Conar shot him a deadly blue gaze.

Swen inhaled deeply. "Ah, well then, perhaps you shouldn't have *wed* the lass," he said idly. "But then again—"

"Then again what?" Conar demanded.

Swen grinned. "She's also the most beautiful witch in the known world. And she can be quite delightful."

"To anyone but me!" Conar muttered.

"Milord?"

"She came with a great deal of property," Conar

said angrily. He waved a hand in the air. "I accepted her when she was little more than a child because of that wretched Ragwald." He hesitated, then added slowly, "And because I came too late to save her father. My uncle had promised I would fight with him. We came too late. Still"—he gazed to Swen, eyes burning—"she was little more than a child then, and I never imagined that—"

"That she could twist a wolf by its tail?" Swen suggested, starting to smile, then quickly wiping the grin from his lips. Conar seemed in no mood for this.

He hadn't been since Melisande had managed to gain passage here on one of Conar's kin's own ships. It was her land, of course. Her birthright. But still . . .

She had lied to them all, of course, swearing she had Conar's consent.

And when he had returned . . .

"She was a child!" he roared suddenly.

But she'd been a damned beautiful child, too, Swen thought in silence. With Conar's present dark mood, he decided to keep the thought to himself. She had always brought about the deepest emotions within Conar—ever since he had discovered that his bartered bride was a wayward and independent creature, determined to manage herself and her inheritance.

Things had always been tempestuous between them.

They were doomed to more storminess now, but the time had come. Melisande was indeed grown up, but she didn't seem to have realized yet that Conar had come to stay. He had to. A true tempest was brewing here, with the Danes amassing in the thousands to ravage the countryside.

Because of his Melisande, and their property, Conar was called upon to thwart them.

"Well, milord," Swen murmured uneasily, trying to soothe his temper somewhat, "I must say you have always behaved with great restraint, sending her first to the nuns until she gained her years—''

"She considered that the worst of tortures!" Conar snorted.

Swen held silent for a moment. Conar's motives might well have been missed. She had been young when they had met. But already she'd been more than stunning. She'd been alluring. He might have been putting her out of temptations way from himself!

Swen lifted his hand absently. "You have, er—like I said, always shown restraint."

"No more!" Conar vowed suddenly, his blue eyes like daggers. "No more!"

For a moment Swen wondered which would be greater for Conar—his battle with the Danes, or his battle with his wife.

Whichever, it seemed that the days ahead would stretch very long. For there was one thing perfectly true that few men could see, and most assuredly, Melisande herself did not see it. For all that he was so constantly furious with her. Melisande definitely held a piece of the warlord's heart.

"Find Ragwald. See that he gets his people gathered on the slope to the sea. I will see to the prisoners, and meet Melisande here within the yard, then we'll go before them together."

"As you wish," Swen said, eyeing him speculatively.

Conar smiled suddenly. "She will be there, never fear. She would not risk her people. That is in her favor."

Swen hurried off to do as he was bidden. Conar watched him a moment, straightened his shoulders wearily, and whistled for Thor. The ebony stallion obeyed his summons instantly, trotting to him.

"If only women were so well behaved, eh, fellow?"

he whispered to the horse, then mounted it and rode quickly outside the wall.

His prisoners were an assorted lot, perhaps twenty-five in number, fifty percent Danes who stared at him with murderous hostility, the other fifty percent followers of the fool Geoffrey, who was so damned determined to take what did not belong to him.

He should have them beheaded, Conar thought. Not a one of them seemed worth keeping alive. But even as he stared at them, one of the Frankish men broke from the ranks and came rushing over, falling to his knees, grabbing Conar's foot. "Mercy, great Lord of the Wolves! Mercy, I beg you. We were tricked, we were—"

"Kill him, Conar of Dubhlain!" one of the Danes cried out in his father's language. "Or we shall do so ourselves!"

Conar looked down to Able, Brion, and Sigfrid, the three of his men guarding the group.

He felt tension seeping into him as he remembered his wife's pleas not to kill the men. She never did understand that he despised such things. But she should have understood by now just how dangerous Geoffrey's men—and definitely the Danes—could be. He sighed inwardly.

"Separate them for the time being. Have the smith make shackles for the lot of them, send the Danes to the east pit beneath the tower, and take the others to the long house east of the fields. Make sure they are well shackled, for we cannot afford trouble from them now. They must be guarded until we can decide what to do with them."

"Some are injured," Brion told him.

"Send some women to tend to them then, but keep a wary eye upon them."

Sigfrid shrugged. "We should behead them, have done with it!"

"For the moment, they will live. When these men are attended to, we will gather at the sea slope. There's much to celebrate. My lovely wife and I reunited and this fine land held firmly in our own hands. There will be much to fight for again, but for tonight I intend to enjoy the evening. I hope the same for all of you."

He rode back through the broken wall, making a mental note that it must be repaired immediately. He'd come as quickly as he'd been able to manage, and still he'd nearly been too late. But maybe he'd needed the sea voyage to rein in the anger he'd felt at first.

Yet every moment of delay had been torture, his anger knotted with passion, his hunger for her eating away at him, his fury with himself for having been so easily taken by her growing with his fear that some ill would befall her.

At long last there was tonight. Nothing in hell or Valhalla would stop him!

When he came on through the courtyard, she was there, awaiting him. She was mounted upon her magnificent horse, Warrior. The animal was huge, adding to her remarkable dignity.

He thought the same as old Ragwald once had— *men will follow her*!

"Come!" he told her.

Violet eyes lit on him. He smiled, nudging Thor forward. She followed, just at his heels.

They came to the strip of beach. As he had commanded, the people were gathered there. His seafaring warriors. Her guard, and the farmers, the smiths, the craftsmen, their wives, their children. The priest and his plump mistress, their little barefoot waifs. They were all there, a strange assortment, some speaking the Irish, Norse, and Frankish languages, and some understanding only one of the three.

He caught hold of Melisande's hand. She longed to

rip away from him—he could feel the tension in his arm. But she did not do so.

"We have joined together today as it was long ago destined to be!" he called out. "We have beaten back the foe, but greater battle is still to come, for our enemies would ravage this land straight to Paris! We must remain united here and fight them. As Melisande and I have come together, so shall you. Tonight we are triumphant! Celebrate with us."

A cheer went up. The people all cried out, whether they had understood or not.

He repeated the words in his mother's Irish, then began to speak to them in Melisande's Frankish.

But Melisande was speaking already, fluidly, melodiously.

And determined that she was going to rule.

Not me, my love! Not me! he promised in silence. She had already led him on many a merry chase. She had stolen his damned soul!

Tonight it would all change.

She was staring at him now with daggers in her eyes.

"Smile, my love. Lift your hand in a gallant wave, and smile."

There *was* a beautiful smile on her face. *Angelic!* he thought with some amusement. The people were shouting their adoration for her, as well they might. Her hair was about her like a cape, spread out over the cloth of gold that streamed down her back and over the horse's haunches. Her face remained the fairest he might have imagined, eyes ablaze.

She looked at him, her forced smile quite near plastered in place. Her hand moved to encompass the crowd. Though she smiled incredibly sweetly, her words were hissed, and for him alone. "You are an unholy bastard," she murmured, her expression never changing.

He smiled pleasantly in turn, his hand waving to

encompass the crowd. "Your flattery will go to my head, Melisande."

"I hardly think there should be room for it."

"Pity your arrows aren't as piercing as your words," he informed her coolly. "You'd have bested us all—Danish, Norse, Irish, Swedes—for sure. But alas! None here is as talented with a weapon of steel or wood as you are with your barbed tongue!"

"Indeed," she promised, smiling and waving to the crowd still. "You had best take care of those barbs. They might well undo your might and muscle and slice you to ribbons!"

He laughed. "I shall have to take my chances with your tongue, Countess."

"I warn you, it will be dangerous."

"I thrive on danger."

"You thrive on command!"

"Be that as it may. I am victorious, I will rule this land, and you. So come, kiss me, my beloved witch," he returned.

"I should sooner kiss a toad!"

"I don't believe you!" Still they smiled, facing the crowd, waving to prove to all that the houses were united.

"Melisande, my love! I demand a kiss before these good people!"

"A kiss?" she inquired. "You'd best be daring, Viking. My barbed kiss could too easily slice you to ribbons."

"But, Melisande, I am willing to be sliced, wherever you would set that tongue!"

Even over the roar of the crowd he could hear the grating of her teeth. She edged her horse closer. She offered up her ruby lips. "You truly belong in hell!" she assured him. He leaned over and touched her lips. Just barely. Breathing in the sweet scent of her. Assessing her anew.

The crowd went wild with cheers of approval.

"See how you please them?" he murmured.

"Charming," she said, smiling into his eyes as if she adored him. "I absolutely despise you."

"Careful, my beloved. I am evermore certain that my night would be far more pleasant were you gagged."

"Ah, but you thrive upon the dangers of my tongue!"

"I do intend to," he promised softly.

"You are a demon!"

"And you are a witch!"

Dark lashes fell over glorious eyes, then her violet orbs burned into his.

"Then perhaps, milord, having accomplished what you wanted here, you will be wise enough to leave me alone!"

"Accomplished what I wanted? Ah, beloved *wife*, I haven't begun to do so, but I shall. Surely you're not forgetting that we have wed. Vikings are supposed to rape and ravage all women, so surely I could not be a credible Norseman were I to do any less with my wife! Ah, look! There's the clergy! Give them a nice and happy wave, Melisande. Let all know just how pleased we are to be together!"

She waved her hand, her smile still not faltering. "Lord of the Wolves!" she taunted. "You are none other than the Norse Lord of Dragons and Dung!" she said softly to him.

He sighed. "My brother is English, kin through marriage to Alfred the Great," he said. He kept his voice very low, but he could feel the force of his temper rising. "And my maternal grandfather was one of the greatest Irish kings to ever live."

"Ah, yes! And you deny being one of the butchers of the seas!"

"Oh, no!" he assured her, and Thor edged so close

against her mare that he had to pull back on his reins to control his horse. "Butcher of the seas, milady? That is what you would call my other grandfather's people. Alas, rest assured. I do not deny being one of them. They are great seafarers."

"Great invaders, great butchers—"

"And conquerors, milady! Don't forget that! I would not dream of denying that they, too, are a part of me."

"You have conquered nothing!"

He felt his own smile deepening and nudged his ebony war-horse closer to her mount. "Oh, but I have, milady. I have. And you will find that out, my love. I swear it." His temper flared and he reached for her, suddenly, fiercely. This time his lips burned upon hers. Seized them, forced them apart. His tongue invaded her mouth with a searing hunger, and when she would have protested, he pulled her closer. Their horses crashed together. He dragged her from Warrior to hold her before him. Her fingers wound in a frenzy around his arms as she fought him.

He did not let go.

He tasted her. Tasted her lips, and remembered. Filled her mouth with the force of his tongue.

And remembered.

Felt the furious, vibrant heat of her, the rise of her breasts, the sweep of her breath. She tried to twist from him. He held her still, his mouth hard atop hers, demanding that she give, while the roar of the crowd rose in his ears like the rush of his own blood.

Her fingers loosened their wild grip. Her lips gave way, she fought him no longer. He raised his mouth from hers and saw the violent tempest in her eyes. Her lips were wet and parted still. Fire seemed to explode within his loins.

"You will have me, lady, Viking or no!" he promised her.

He waved his sword triumphantly to the crowd once again. Then she cried out, clasping him as Thor rose high on his hind legs, then turned and raced back toward the fortress walls and the high tower above the keep.

3

"What are you doing?" she cried to him, her hair an ebony stream that entangled around them both, whipping with the wind.

"I've waited too damn long to rape and ravage already," he assured her.

She stared at him, going very pale, then slowly turning crimson.

"It's early! Surely there must be more ceremonies—"

"Private ceremonies only, my love. Why, you never meant to leave me, right? And I have missed so sorely having you at my side!"

He slid from Thor, dragging her with him.

"No!" she whispered frantically.

But he ignored her and used the broken steps to bring them back to the parapet, and from there to the tower room.

The room with the broad bed and the clean linen sheets. With the low fire burning in the hearth. With the furs spread before it.

And with the wooden hip bath set before the fire, a fine steam rising above it.

He set her down, surprised that she had obeyed his command in such a thing.

He stared at it a moment, then tore his coat of mail over his chest, so accustomed to it that he did not notice its weight. He spun around to stare at her, arching a brow.

"Ah, Melisande." She was backing away from him. He smiled. "Shall I take the bath first? No doubt you would disappear should I do so. But then again, it was kind of you to see that it was brought here, as I requested."

"You may trust in the fact that I did not have it brought here," she informed him.

"Then your servants are far wiser than you are, milady. Shall you have the first or the second bath, my love?"

"Neither. I am convinced that there are a dozen things which must be done here—"

"Perhaps you should go first," he said softly. "I have the strange feeling you are longing to escape me. Maybe you would not be quite so quick to run along the parapets naked. But then again, as you've told me, one Viking is the same as another. If you were to provoke another attack by one hungry just to seize you, you might not care."

"Rot and die, Viking!" she told him, lifting her chin.

"The solution?" He stretched out his arms to her. "We bathe together!"

She cried out, but too late; his hands were upon her. They ripped the elegant cloth of gold she wore from her shoulders. He lifted her up and cast her down upon the bed, and while she struggled up, he grabbed her shoes and then her hose. She wriggled like a worm, making things very difficult.

But he was very determined. And the softness of her bare flesh against his fingertips definitely gave him incentive to strive more valiantly.

She went still suddenly, her eyes huge. "Please!" she whispered softly.

He felt his lip curl, and he moved his thumb tenderly over her lip and cheek. "Ah, I remember your saying that word just so once before . . ."

The pallor that hit her cheeks assured him that she, too, remembered the occasion. Her manner changed instantly.

"Get off me, you wretch!"

His grin deepened. "As you wish, milady."

He was up instantly, with her upon his knee. In seconds he had wrenched the beautiful mauve gown over her shoulders, ripping the soft linen undershift she wore beneath it in his haste.

He didn't give a damn. She was suddenly naked in his arms, naked and perfect with her tiny waist, flaring hips, long limbs, full, rouge-crested breasts, and seductive black triangle. The waves of her hair were entangled around them both in a web of softness. For a moment the feel of her was more than he could bear. He felt the thunder of her heart, the gasp of her breathing. The fire within her. He wanted to hold her forever.

Her fists slammed against his chest. He lifted her, remembering that he had no choice.

She could no longer do the things she had once done. She couldn't escape him, fight him, or keep her distance from him. It could mean death, or capture. He could not afford to have to bargain for her.

"I can't be wed to you!" she cried to him, her nails digging into his shoulders right through the thin leather vest he wore. "I can't!" she whispered. "I will not be so dominated in my own home! I was just a child, I didn't do it, I never meant—"

"Ah, Melisande! How innocent! You never meant any of the things you did to me, did you?" he taunted.

Oh, she had meant many of them! She'd had so

many emotions regarding this man, Melisande thought desperately. He was too powerful, too muscled, too quick; his mocking words came too quickly, his iron fist of command too ruthlessly.

And the way that he touched her was far too seductive, demanding, compelling.

And there were far too many others in his life. Too many women too eager to please him. And it would be far too easy to love him. Never, never, she vowed to herself.

He was a Viking. It didn't matter where he had been born, and it didn't matter what he called himself. He would always take what he wanted, and when he was done with it, he'd simply discard it.

She drew in a shattering breath, growing dizzy. Dear God, it had been like this before. Heaven and hell, all in one, just as he had told her.

The things he had done . . .

The things she had tried to forget . . .

"I swear, I shall scratch your eyes out!" she promised him. "Let me down!"

He did. Right into the steaming water. It enveloped her. She closed her eyes for a moment, praying for strength. She opened her eyes.

He had stripped. Quickly.

Her mouth went very dry and her breath seemed to catch in her throat. He was formidable in his mail.

He was more so stark naked.

He might be any of the things he claimed to be, but in appearance, he was all his father, all Viking. He stood well over six feet, nearly a head higher than most men, and every bit of tedious training for war he had ever undertaken showed in the muscle-hewn structure of his body. His shoulders were incredibly broad, his arms bronzed and hard, his chest rippled and corded, his stomach dead flat and lean, his legs long and shapely and heavily muscled, as well. His chest

was covered with red-gold hair that swirled to a thin
line that ran almost invisibly across his waist, only to
thicken richly again well below it. The hot and cold
shivers that so easily overcame her when he was near
came bursting upon her. He was only too ready to
fulfill all his promises. His sex seemed as muscled and
hardened and long as the rest of him, as arrogant as
the man himself.

And no matter how she despised it, she felt the swift
rise of a fire deep within herself. She tried again and
again to swear that she would never give in to him.

But she had.

*Because the fascination was just as great as the
anger. Because he had drawn her from the beginning.
Because she wanted him even more desperately than
she loathed him.*

Now he intended surrender. This night.

She dragged her eyes up to his and lifted her chin.
"You know that you can force me," she managed to
inform him coolly. "But you'll not seduce me."

His lip curled slowly. An amazingly sensual gesture
in a man of his stature. Blue eyes framed by the wealth
of his golden hair blazed upon her with amusement as
he stalked the tub, coming behind her, leaning over
her.

"That's all right. Vikings don't mind force. We're
very good at it."

The warmth of his breath touched her throat. She
gasped as he stepped into the tub, toes touching hers,
knees rising high as he sat. Water splashed over the
rim of the tub. His eyes fell hard upon hers.

"Ah! Wedded bliss."

She grit her teeth, splashing water into his eyes,
determined to rise. In a second he was up with her.
She stepped from the tub, but he caught her in his
arms. In seconds she found herself flung back upon
the bed, the wired strength of his body atop hers. His

fingers curled around hers, pinning her arms to the bed. The sleek muscled wetness of his body was a brace around her. Then his lips touched hers.

Much as they had before. She tried to twist her head, but his strength was overwhelming. His mouth was forceful upon hers, his tongue parting her lips. Entering her. She moaned deep within her mouth, protesting.

Praying for the fire to go away.

His tongue found hers. Drew upon it. Entered more and more deeply into her mouth, slick, hot wet. She felt his hand, cupped over her breast, the palm easing over and over her nipple. His hand was large, his fingers long, encompassing her body as he explored her torso, cupping her hip, her buttocks. She gasped, but he was kissing her still. She did not realize that her hand was free, winding into the linen sheets on the bed.

His lips lifted from hers. He caught her eyes. Then his mouth touched her throat, his tongue bathing the pulse there. The tip of it slid down the valley of her breasts. The pressure of his face eased over to her breast, his mouth captured the nipple, tugging upon it, the tip of his tongue laving it. She cried out, her hand flying from the sheet to his hair, her fingers entangling within it.

He slid down the length of her, hands sliding around and beneath her hips, stroking and encircling her buttocks, lifting them. She felt the lick of his tongue against her thighs and cried out, tossing, writhing to escape his grip. He had promised no mercy, and he granted none. She felt the intimate thrust of his tongue, stroking, demanding.

Arousing. Sliding deeper, withdrawing, teasing, evoking, hungry.

She cried out his name, so seldom uttered from her lips, the entreaty deep and rich. She felt the length of

him atop her again, caressing her arms, finding her lips
again, then held above her by the great power of his
arms.

The blue of his eyes seared into her.

"Force? Or seduction?" he whispered.

She closed her eyes against him, trembling, aching.
"Force!" she lied.

He laughed. The laughter so triumphant. Yet despite
it, his arms were infinitely tender as he swept her
within them, taking her then, denial or no.

She shuddered violently as the fullness of his sex
sank deeply within her. She wrapped her arms around
him, her teeth catching her lower lip. She felt she died
a little. Felt as if he touched and caressed her from her
womb to her heart. He moved very slowly at first,
taking her with him. And he did so easily. Within
seconds she was slowly writhing to meet him, aching
for him a heartbeat before he moved again. Suddenly
the slowness became a tempest, waves seemed to
crash and cascade around them, and hers was as
rampant as his own, her longing as fierce. He moved
that magical time within her, and a startling, shimmering climax burst upon her, like light against darkness,
stars falling from the skies. She nearly cried out,
caught the sound, and lay shivering against him, the
taut slick feel of his bronzed body exquisite against
hers. She felt the incredible constriction of his body,
then the easing of it, and in seconds he fell beside her.

She sprang up, furious, ashamed, hating him, and
hating herself. Before she could move far, his hand,
with its startling long fingers, curled around her wrist.

"And where do you think you're going, Countess?"

She tried to tug free. "I need to bathe *now,*" she
informed him, trying not to meet his eyes.

To her surprise he released her instantly, inching up
on the bed to the nest of goose down pillows by the
carved headboard. He laced his fingers behind his

head, watching her. He was angered by her words, she was certain of it. But Conar was always in control, so it seemed. He gave no sign of his anger. "Please, my love," he told her. "Go right ahead. Be my guest."

She turned away from him quickly, her hair a sleek cloak down her back. She sank into the water, eager now for the warmth, but it was fading. Shivering, she drew her knees to her breast.

"Can't you at least go away now!" she demanded.

She heard him rise, felt his soundless movement to the back of the tub. He knelt behind her, lifting a tress of her hair.

"You are cruel, Melisande. Cold and cruel. I thank all the gods—and your God, too, of course—that I do not love you. Even your great deity would pity me were I to fall in love with you, for you do so easily tread upon men's hearts! All of your men—all of my men, for that matter!—are so willing to die for you! They trip over one another to serve you. Even my foolish sister and brother fell to your wiles."

"They are more courteous—"

"For Vikings?"

"It is possible to detect that they have some Irish in their blood."

He laughed softly, yet there was a bitterness to the sound.

"I am not the cruel one!" she exclaimed. "I am not cruel at all! I am not the one who commands and demands and orders—"

."And conquers?" he suggested softly.

"I keep telling you!" she whispered. "You have conquered nothing."

"But I am determined that I will."

"All that you survey!" she whispered. "But not me!"

She felt his finger streaking down her neck. She seemed to feel that touch with the length of her body,

feel its heat against the cold of the water, feel it down
to those intimate places he knew so well, touched so
deeply.

She bit her lip. She would not desire him, she could
not, it was impossible to fight him.

"Please go away!"

"Alas, I do have to go away now. There are some
things I must deal with. But don't miss me too dearly.
I will be back. I don't think you're really weary
enough to be trusted through the night—yet."

"Cease your taunts! You'll not best me—*Viking*!"

He stepped away, reaching for his clothing, his
skintight chausses, his linen shirt, leather vest His
mail he left where it had fallen, but when he'd pulled
on his deerskin boots, he reached down for his sword.

She was startled when it fell upon her shoulder. The
point of it reached beneath her chin, forcing her eyes
to his.

"This is it, Melisande," he warned very softly, blue
eyes seeming to impale her. "I taunt you no longer.
Playtime is over. For all that you have seen in your
young life, my love, there is nothing like what is to
come. I will need all my strength, and I will not have
time to deal with you as I have in the past."

"Deal with me?" she snapped angrily. "You don't
understand! I had to come here because you could
not! This is my land, my fortress—"

"I beg to differ, milady. You and the fortress and
the land were given over to me on a battlefield long
ago. And since then—"

"You have been an odious tyrant! A—a Viking.
A—"

"Need you say more?" he taunted her. The sword
shifted suddenly, causing her to catch her breath. The
point lifted a long lock of her hair from her breast,
easing the damp mass down her back. "No more,
Melisande. No more disappearance, and above all, *no*

more appearances in golden mail! You might very well
have been taken by Geoffrey today.''

"And if I had—"

"We all would have had to die for your honor,
milady. All those fine men out there you claim to hold
so dear to your heart. Even if you feel that one Viking
is the same as the other, I regret to inform you that I
am the Viking you have wed. And for that matter,
Geoffrey is no Viking, but one of your own.''

"He might as well be a Viking!" she cried.

"Ah, yes, for that term covers all that is wretched
and evil, is that it, Melisande?''

The point of his sword hovered at her breasts. She
grit her teeth suddenly and shoved it aside. "I thought
you were leaving.''

He knelt beside her. "I want you to know that I will
be back.''

Was his elegant blond rune reader with him? The
jealousy she so hated in herself surged through her.
What did he want of *her* when he brought the other
girl with him everywhere he traveled? Oh, she hated
it! But he had already touched her again, and she felt,
despite herself, terrible pain in wondering if he would
touch another in like fashion, even here.

"Are you sure you wish to spend the night here?''

"What?" he demanded.

"What of—" she broke off, unwilling to say the
name.

"What of who?" he demanded.

"Never mind. Just leave—"

"Who?" he seemed to roar.

She hugged her knees more tightly to her. "Brenna!
Your Viking rune reader—"

"She is half Irish, too.''

"Damn you all!" Melisande cried furiously. But that
brought about his laughter.

"So you are still jealous, my love!"

"Never. Relieved when you are led in different directions," she lied smoothly.

"Ah, well. Have no fear. I am going in no other direction tonight, Melisande." The mocking tone suddenly left his voice. "Melisande, listen to me. Battle is just engaged. You cannot imagine how rough the future shall be."

He didn't seem to realize just how rough the past had been.

"Melisande!"

She tossed her head back and stared at him with cold fury. "So come back!" she hissed. "I haven't the strength to throw you out."

"No, you haven't," he informed her.

"So go!"

"Just be aware," he said softly, "that I sleep lightly. If I were to awaken to find a knife at my throat, I would definitely act the Viking."

Her lashes swept over her eyes. "You have already acted the Viking!"

"With the greatest pleasure. We face incredible odds, Melisande. So from this moment forth, I warn you. You are my wife. And so help me, Melisande—by your God, by all my father's people's gods—you will not risk yourself again! Geoffrey covets you as he does this fortress. I fear his efforts to have you as I fear nothing else about the man. Heed me, Melisande. You will do as I command. Listen to my words, obey my orders!"

Her eyes opened, glaring into his. "I cannot be your wife now! Too much stands between us! I—"

"You may start by getting out of the water!" he snapped. His sword fell, and his hands were upon her, pulling her up. She pummeled him viciously but only found herself on the bed again, Conar straddled above her. "You're pruning, my love. You wouldn't want that!" he assured her, eyes narrowed. "And," he added more softly, "you are shivering like a toad in a frost." He was silent for a moment, then the tip of his thumb moved down over her cheek and rubbed her lower lip. "Like it or not, Melisande, this is what will be. Loathe me as you like, Countess, but I am here to stay." He moved close to her, whispering softly. "And I will return, *your husband,* to sleep with you, lie with you, from this night onward."

"Don't count on my being here!" she cried passionately.

"Oh, but I will," he warned her.

She clenched her teeth, feeling the rise of desperate tears to her eyes. She would not shed them. She bit her lower lip, looking away, determined to keep silent so that he would leave.

At last he lifted himself from her. She curled quickly away from him and didn't glance his way as he caught hold of his sword once again and left the tower room.

She clasped one of the furs on her bed and sat shivering there, afraid to think of what had been, afraid to think of what was to come. He was coming back tonight. To sleep here, to make the marriage incredibly real again. To take what was his, to have it, hold it. She shuddered. *Thank God I do not love you!* he had said. *Dear God, dear God, dear God! Don't let me love him. Please, God, don't let me love him!*

She would not! she promised herself.

"I hate you!" she cried out loud. It was childish, but she suddenly felt very young and forlorn. "I hate you, hate you, hate you!"

She buried her face in her hands. It was true, it wasn't true. She hated him, wanted him, feared him . . .

Wanted him.

Loved him, too.

But so much lay between them.

The battle was about to ensue, he had said. He was here, to lie with her, sleep with her.

He would come back.

No!

She did hate him . . .

Love him.

No, no, no. She had promised herself she would not.

She started suddenly, hearing a sound within the room. He had come back, she thought, silently, as was his way.

She turned, aware that she must always be ready with him.

But it was not Conar who had crept so silently into the room. She gasped, a scream rising in her throat as she saw who had come.

Geoffrey Sur-le-Mont, her most loathed enemy. Tall, lean, with his cruel, handsome face, gold-tinged hazel eyes, lank dark hair. He stood there, staring down at her as she clasped the furs to her.

She inhaled, ready to shriek and scream like a wild woman. She had no chance. As she stared at Geoffrey, a hand clamped hard over her mouth. She struggled valiantly, kicking, wriggling, but there were three men in all, Geoffrey and two of his ablest henchmen, Gilles and Jon de Lac.

"Bastards!" she gasped, breaking free for a moment, but Geoffrey had ripped the sheet and it was instantly tied around her mouth.

She was trussed into the furs, her hands tied behind her back. They rolled her and picked her up. Gilles threw her over his heavy shoulders, and Geoffrey, chuckling softly, lifted her head by her hair, meeting her gaze.

"I have said that I will have you, Melisande! And see! I do have you! And I will have this fortress, too, before God! I swear it!"

She shook her head wildly. He moved the gag just a half an inch.

"He'll kill you!" she gasped.

"Ah, you think so? I heard some of your conversation. I don't think he'll realize at first that you were abducted, dear Melisande. You did threaten not to be here. And he is fully aware you are less than fond of his presence! Ah, Melisande, if and when he realizes that you did not leave here of your own volition, it will be much too late!"

"You will never get out of this castle with me!" she hissed.

"Ah, but I will. My Danish friends are remarkably like the Wolf's own Norse warriors! We shall just act drunk and wind our way among them. It is a celebration tonight, Melisande. I will celebrate, you will celebrate! It's as it should have been, all those years ago!"

"You will die, Geoffrey, he will slice you to little pieces—"

"That he will, Count Sur-le-Mont," Gilles said quickly, looking nervously about. "We must be gone!"

The gag was still off her, Melisande realized. She inhaled and quickly began to scream. Just as quickly the strangling gag was brought back over her mouth.

"What if she screams again?" Jon demanded.

"She won't," Geoffrey promised.

He had his assurance of her quiet well planned. Even as he spoke, he lifted a brass candle holder from the trunk at the foot of Melisande's bed.

And brought it down hard over her head.

There was little she could regret or bemoan at that moment.

Some time later she awoke. She was still tied, still wrapped in furs, tossed over a horse. They had managed to escape the castle with her. And God alone knew where they were now.

"Ah, you're awake, my lovely!" Geoffrey's husky tones touched her ear. "Soon, very soon, we'll be there. Where, you would ask—if only you could! Ah, the ruins of the old Roman fortress—yes, that same place where your father found so much of the stone for his excellent castle! The Viking will not find you there. And if he does . . . well, I've a very large Danish contingent there. They're going to Rouen, and on to Paris. All they really want is plunder. And all I really want, my love, is power. And you. So the Viking must die."

Flapping against the horse, bound as she was, Melisande could not reply.

Geoffrey suddenly stopped his horse, leapt from it, and wrenched her from the brown mount she'd been cast across. As he lifted the gag from her mouth, she stumbled over a piece of the wrap of fur that covered her. "A cloak!" Geoffrey commanded, catching her before she could fall, completely uncovered, to the ground.

He hadn't minded his henchmen's finding her naked to help him, but now it seemed he was finding the decency to see what he coveted clothed.

He wrenched her around, untied her hands, and swung her back to him. A cloak was produced and he put it around her shoulders just as the fur fell to the ground. Someone picked it up. Melisande kept staring at Geoffrey.

"He will kill you," she promised him. "You will be in so many pieces, you will not be recognized. Unless you let me go now—"

"Ah! And are you so very sure that he will come for you, Melisande? Can you believe he loves you enough to risk all?"

She kept her eyes coolly level with him. "He has risked his life for me many times."

"Maybe. And maybe he has risked his life for your very desirable property."

"He will come for me!"

"Because he loves you?" Geoffrey taunted.

"He will come for me because I am his!"

Geoffrey shook his head, furious with her calm. "Not this time. *Do you understand?* Not this time! He will sacrifice everything to do so!"

He wrenched her around again, throwing her up on the brown horse. She scrambled to stay seated, lest she break a limb and destroy any chance of escape.

Geoffrey stared into her eyes as he grabbed her mount's reins. "Gilles is to your left, Jon to your right, milady. Make a single move, and one of them will pierce your leg with an arrow, and you'll not walk again for a week. You see, you won't need to walk for anything I desire of you."

She stared right ahead. "How long do we ride?"

"You can see the ruins in the light from the moon," he told her. "There, ahead. Not far now."

Not far—it was much too close. They were too quickly there.

And indeed, there was a large Danish contingent there. So very many! Camped among the ancient stones, almost invisible in the shadows!

There was a place for her. Down a flight of ancient steps that led into the earth. Geoffrey had her brought there, allowing Gilles and Jon to drag her struggling form along. She bit Gilles and he cried out. She went flying into the center of the dank cellar at the bottom of the steps, and fell to the cool stone.

Looking up, she saw that Geoffrey was there, unruffled, smiling.

"I have to see to our defenses, Melisande. But I'll return as soon as I may."

She swallowed hard. How many times had she tried to fight Conar?

Each time wanting him, but so afraid! Fear at first, then the rising fascination. Then the pain of missing him, of jealousy, of fear again. Yet always the aching, always the hunger, the desire.

The love.

And now—this! She wanted to die.

"He will come for me!" she told Geoffrey. "He will come for me!"

Geoffrey started to laugh. "We shall see, won't we?"

He whirled around. A heavy door swung shut. She was left alone with only the darkness.

She wrapped the borrowed cloak tightly around herself, trying not to sob out.

"He will come!" she cried out loud again. He would, he was the Lord of the Wolves, no man bested him, *no man took what was his*!

Please, God, I do love him, don't let him die, don't let me be taken, let him come, let him come.

Yet why should he? She had fought him since the very beginning. Defied him, vowed to hate him.

But would he put it all together and come for her anyway, would he want her enough, despite everything?

She lowered her head to her knees, cold, frightened, and feeling the sudden warmth of memory flooding over her.

Aye, they had hated.

But aye, in their way, they had loved!

It seemed so long since the first time they had met, on a day so very much like today . . .

Before . . .

4

Summer, A.D. *879*
The Coast of France

"He's home!" Melisande cried. "Father is home!"

She had watched the old Roman road for hours each day for the past week, knowing that he had promised to return for her thirteenth birthday, and knowing that if he had promised to do so, he would.

Ragwald, who sat in his student's chair, head sunk wearily into his hands, immediately came to his feet, forgetting that his young ward was exasperating him no end. He was immensely glad to discover that his lord had returned, for these were the most treacherous of times for travelers. Not only were the Danes and other *Vikings* continually plaguing the shores and rivers, but in defense against those Viking, many barons, lords, counts, and wealthy landowners had begun a somewhat new way of life. Ragwald was old, and in his memory things were not so terribly different. Military strength had always been tremendously important. But it had been in this century—with the coming of the Vikings, or so it seemed—that their system of *feudalism* had arisen. Great lords now designed fortresses or castles, trained the right men to fight for them, and took in a number of vassals, men and women to work the land. These vassals provided the food and bounty, and received protection in return. With all these castles and fortresses risen across the land, the law had gone into the hands of those strong enough to hold it. A traveler could easily be waylaid—indeed, he could easily disappear completely.

Ragwald quickly joined Melisande on the parapet wall to watch with her as her father's party neared the castle. He smiled. He shouldn't have worried so. Count Manon de Beauville was one of the most powerful of the barons—and, Ragwald had determined, certainly one of the smartest. For one, he had taken Ragwald into his employ many years ago.

More than that, Count Manon was a noble with a keen mind, a man who looked to the past to learn from the mistakes and triumphs of others. In studying the Romans and their effect upon all the peoples they had conquered, he had discovered the many usages of stone. His fortress was one of the finest in the land. Motte and bailey, and as was customary, the main buildings were set upon a mound, a great trench was dug around them, and a wall was created before that trench. There were four towers to the castle, one to face the sea, one to face east, one west, and one south. Parapets in wood and stone lined the walls between the towers, giving the men a fantastic fighting ability from within. Few offenders had ever come too near the castle, for the retainers within the walls were expert with the firing of burning arrows, and they excelled with their caldrons of boiling oil. Strength brought respect in these days, and they were able to live within the castle walls in a realm of peace. They had never been attacked by any countryman seeking greater glory, and the almost inescapable raids here by the Danes had been quickly repulsed. Mostly the Danes came to plunder and take what they could.

Sometimes, though, they came seeking their own lands, younger sons with nothing for them in their distant homes. When they found themselves battling Count Manon, they quickly went on to easier pickings.

There was so much of the coast that was unprotected!

Ragwald set a hand over his eyes, shielding them from the sun, watching as Count Manon rode his massive stallion, Warrior, across the trail through the fields. He was followed by mounted men all with linden shields, two carrying the blue and red colors of the castle with the battling rams of Beauville upon them, an insignia chosen by this count's grandfather when he had served Charlemagne.

The count himself was a striking man, tall, dark, with just a few strands of gray in his head. His eyes were deeply blue against the sun-bronzed shade of his face. He sat on a horse very tall and very well. Seeing his daughter and Ragwald so eagerly awaiting him, he lifted a hand and smiled, then spurred his horse.

"Father!" Melisande cried delightedly, and ran from the parapet.

"Melisande!" Ragwald called after her. "By all the saints!" he cried in aggravation, lifting his hands to heaven. "Melisande, you are the heiress to a mighty stronghold, milady. Will you show the world some dignity, please!"

He spoke to empty space. He lifted his hands again in surrender, and followed her down the south stairs to the courtyard below.

The great gates had opened in anticipation of the count's arrival. Manon rode through, and his daughter came running to him, pitting herself against Warrior, so very anxious to reach her father.

"Melisande!"

Count Manon threw his leg over the animal's haunches and fell with an agile thump to the dirt, encompassing her into his arms. "Ah, sweeting, I have missed you sorely!" he assured her.

"You came back!" she said, overjoyed.

He nodded. Ragwald noted that the count studied his daughter with a slight frown. As well he might! In the few short months in which he had been gone, Melisande had changed. She would be thirteen years old in a few days' time. She had grown very tall, taller than many men. Her hair, as rich a black as man might imagine, fell down the length of her back in beautiful inky, soft waves. Her face was no longer a child's face, but finely sculpted, a face with exquisite bones and coloring, one to rival any beauty of the ancient Greek or Roman tales. She was quickly acquiring a woman's shape, as well, Ragwald determined, deciding then and there that the count must soon be reminded that he had avoided making marital arrangements for his daughter.

For the moment, though, the joy that father and daughter found in one another was so deep that Ragwald kept his distance while the count spoke of presents and the girl demanded to know if he had been well, and then, of course, that he tell her everything about where he had been.

As the count told his tale, he slipped one arm around his daughter, then one around Ragwald, escorting them to the main tower, the keep. The ground floor, dug into the earth, stored their food and weapons, the upper floor housed their bedchambers, and the middle floor afforded them a great hall with a huge fireplace and massive oak table, a hall where a number of men could meet, or where their small family could gather intimately.

Everyone was delighted the count had returned, from the meanest of his vassals to the most affluent of tenants. The servants flocked to see him, and their best efforts went into the meal that welcomed him

home. While he was greeted, he entertained them with
stories about Paris, about the pilgrimage he had begun
from there, about his visits with the Burgundian king.

The hour at last grew late. The servants had left
them, and the count sat in one of the huge oak chairs
before the fire, studying his daughter while she poked
at the fire. Her cheeks were still pink with pleasure at
his return, Ragwald noted.

"Gerald has called often in your absence," Ragwald
said, referring to the count of the neighboring land that
jettied out into the sea.

"Has he? To see to the welfare of this place? Why,
he must not know the mettle of my men, to think that
Philippe and Gaston would not have had the fortress
secure!" He smiled.

Ragwald was not so quick to smile. "I don't trust
him," he muttered.

"Well, what do you think he is after?" the count
demanded.

Ragwald shrugged, then felt his eyes stray to Melisande. "I don't know. Perhaps your daughter."

Melisande, still poking at the fire, started, and spun
around to look at him, her delicate nose wrinkling. A
wise young judge of character, milady! he thought, but
did not say so out loud.

The count himself was frowning. "Gerald is older
than I am!"

"Such things have never stopped a marriage before.
And perhaps he does not want her for himself, but for
his son, Geoffrey."

"I like Geoffrey even less," the count murmured.

There was a definite look of relief upon Melisande's
face. She looked to Ragwald with a certain triumph in
her violet eyes.

He ignored her, addressing the count. "The girl is
your only heir—"

"And there have been numerous laws stating that

there is no reason a daughter should not inherit when there is no legal male issue!'' Count Manon said firmly.

Ragwald inhaled and exhaled slowly. Noblemen could be so very difficult when they chose!

''My point, milord!'' Ragwald said at last. ''This is a powerful fortress—no man who knows it has dared attack it. The foreigners who have invaded here have quickly fled for more promising places. Someone might well covet your daughter *and her holdings,* Count Manon!''

The count watched Melisande. ''She is only twelve years old—''

''Nearly thirteen. And children are oft wed at birth!''

''Betrothed,'' Manon corrected.

''What difference is it?'' Ragwald replied impatiently. ''Many girls are brides at her age.''

''Well, she will not be,'' the count said stubbornly. ''Unless . . .'' he began thoughtfully.

Melisande quickly leapt in, coming behind her father's chair and staring at Ragwald. ''Did you know, my *dear* tutor,'' she said sweetly, rubbing her father's shoulders, ''that King Charlemagne never had his daughters wed, but kept them home and at his side, determined he would share them with no others.''

Ragwald waved a hand in the air. ''Aye, lady! And wretched lives those girls then lived, for they did not wed, but took lovers, and their children were illegitimate!''

She frowned at him. ''Ragwald, I have been taught as well as any son—''

''And you think that you will be as strong as a man?''

''Nay, sir! I shall be as strong as any woman!'' She smiled. ''You have taught me about the strength of my gender, Ragwald. Think of Fredegund, the wife of

King Chilperic! She schemed to have his first queen repudiated, and then to have her slain, and she managed all manner of political assassinations once she was in power!"

"Oh, indeed! Think of her!" Ragwald snapped. "She ended her days being tortured and executed!"

"You are missing my point. She caused as much mayhem as any *male* might!"

Ragwald shook his head wearily. Count Manon was watching his daughter with amusement and affection. She was an incredibly bright young woman, ever thirsting for knowledge—and despite her youth, very aware that her father's men assumed that she would marry and, when she did, give her power over to her husband.

She was very determined to hold tight to what she considered hers, and hers alone.

"What do the *stars* say, astrologer?" Count Manon demanded with a certain humor.

Astrology was an ancient science. Sometimes it seemed that the count properly respected it as such, but sometimes it seemed that he regarded it with as much humor as he did the old Roman legends that a god like Jupiter turned into all manner of animals to seduce human women.

Most often Ragwald would have defended the study of the stars instantly, but tonight he suddenly could not. Strange, but he felt as if he had been somewhat blinded recently. He watched the moon and knew when the tides would rise high. He watched it grow and wane, and knew when the people would be in good spirits and wild, knew when babes would be born, when some men would go mad. But he felt as if he could see nothing, nothing at all of the immediate future but an awful black void, and that frightened him terribly.

"The stars say your daughter must marry for her own safety," he said stubbornly.

"Perhaps." The count spoke softly, smiling up at Melisande. "But to me she is still a child. And I'd like her opinion on the few men I have in mind."

"A child's opinion?" Ragwald challenged.

"An *educated* child's opinion!" Melisande answered sweetly, her violet eyes amused and victorious.

He started to wag a finger at her, then gripped his hands tightly behind his back instead. This young ward of his was too precocious.

The count stared at the fire, watching the fantastic display of colors, listening for a moment as the logs snapped and crackled. "I would very much like to see her marry for love," he said thoughtfully.

"Love!" Ragwald exclaimed, so amazed that he flew around, his ragged cloak circling him as if he were a pagan dancer. "*Love!* Dear Lord above us! Who ever thought of such a foolish requirement for an advantageous marriage!"

Count Manon grinned, looking from his daughter to his old mentor, and back to the fire. "I was in love with her mother," he replied, his voice still soft, reflective. "So much so that I could never take another wife when I lost her. It is a marvelous thing, love, Ragwald. You must try it some time."

Ragwald sniffed. "You're jesting."

"Father is very serious," Melisande assured him.

Ragwald shook his head, lifting his hands in bewilderment. "Count Manon, you married Lady Mary at your father's command, you must recall. The *love* came later." He cleared his throat delicately. "I believe, milord, that it is the, er, *living* together which creates this wonder of *love*."

"Still, it is something I wish for my daughter."

"Milord—"

"We will talk of it no more tonight. I am very weary from my journey, and I've presents for you both!" He rose, striding quickly toward one of the many trunks that had been brought up to the keep. He drew his calf knife and slit the rope that bound it, then threw open the top. He took a leather satchel out first and presented it to Ragwald. "There, astrologer! This may well keep you busy for a while!"

Ragwald looked from the satchel to the count. "And my good count? This is?"

"Open it, open it, nothing that will bite!" promised the count. "It is filled with medicinal herbs, purchased from a Greek physician serving the Burgundian princess, a very clever man. They are acquired from all over the world."

Ragwald smiled, delighted with the gift. Chemistry was another science he adored, and he was fascinated with the healing qualities of herbs and how they might best be combined. For a moment, he forgot his determination to see to Melisande's future well-being.

"And this!" the count exclaimed. "This is for you, my dear daughter!"

And so saying, he produced a tunic of mail.

Ragwald set the herbs aside and stared at it. It was magnificent. The mesh was extremely fine. It would be incredibly difficult to penetrate. At the same time, the garment was beautiful, decidedly feminine. It was decorated in elegant patterns with a fine gilding. The golden coloring glittered magnificently in the firelight.

"Father!" Melisande exclaimed. "It's—exquisite!"

"Of course, it's for ceremony," he said.

"For ceremony," she repeated, taking the garment from him almost reverently.

"You'll need it soon enough, for you'll ride with me, and learn more and more of how the fortress must be managed."

"Oh, Father!" she threw her arms around him, her eyes alight.

He kissed her forehead. "You must go to bed now, Melisande. For I am very weary."

"Of course, Father, of course!" she said quickly, penitent that she might have tired him in any way. "Now that you're home, it doesn't matter. It doesn't matter! I'll have you in the morning and hours and hours after! And days! And weeks, and—"

"I believe your father mentioned going to bed, Melisande," Ragwald said, staring at her.

She smiled. She even kissed his cheek. "I love you, too, Ragwald. Sleep well!" She kissed and hugged her father again, then hurried up to her bedchamber, the mail still clasped in her hands.

Ragwald looked back to Count Manon, then sighed deeply. "Milord, there are many men who believe that the whole of the collapse of the Roman empire might have been because of the emergence of women's legal rights!"

Count Manon laughed loudly. "Those who think it must be very weak men!"

Ragwald leaned forward. "We live in a feudal society, Count Manon! This fortress is based upon your might, upon your skill! A woman's place is to bear her lord's children, to see to the management of the household—"

"She wields a sword well, I have watched her with her masters."

Ragwald inhaled and exhaled. The sun rose and set on Melisande, as far as the count could see.

But he didn't really understand. Ragwald loved her, as well. And that was why he worried so.

"She has an excellent mind, she is talented. But as good as she is, a stronger *man* would best her. Have you purchased that coat of mail so that she can go to war with your men? Would you see her wounded by a sword, her head split by a mace? An arrow might not pierce the armor well, but it might well catch her in the throat!''

"I do not intend her to go to war! It is ceremonial armor. It is armor for men's minds!'' the count insisted, tapping his head. He shrugged. "And my daughter is right. Women have ruled. Wives for their husbands, mothers for their sons. And most oft—''

"Most oft, as we mentioned, they came to evil ends!''

"Not always. We both know our history, astrologer!''

"What of Melisande herself?'' Ragwald argued. "Would you have her spend her life alone, defending her property?''

"No. I would have her be strong, and make her own choices. She is an excellent swordswoman—''

"Fine. As she is bested by a man twice her weight, we will all commend her strength!''

"Ah, but a weaker man would lose.''

"She detests warfare.''

"So should we all.''

Ragwald sank deeper into his chair, exhaling a groan. "Have you any of that excellent Burgundian wine left, milord? You have given me a great need for it!''

Count Manon laughed. "Indeed, Ragwald, indeed!'' And he rose, poked the dying fire, and procured the wine himself for his old friend and adviser. "I am not so careless as you might think, Ragwald. Perhaps I have given you a twitch in that head of yours on purpose! I have looked carefully to a few men who might prove worthy of my daughter.''

"And they are?''

Count Manon stroked his chin. "One is the nephew of an old friend, an Irish prince—''

Ragwald made a strangling sound. "The son of the Wolf of Norway?"

"The son of the man who seized and built Dubhlain and claimed himself the Ard-Ri's, the High King's, daughter in the making of it!" Manon continued softly. Then he leaned down on the chair, staring tensely at Ragwald. "I do have enemies, and they can be crafty and powerful. We are prey to constant invasion. Who better to best an invader than one who is bred from such warrior stock himself?"

Ragwald shook his head, staring at the count. "I think you're ma—" He cut himself off. He and the count were the very best of friends, but it was still better wisdom *not* to suggest that one's master might be bordering on insanity. He shook his head. "You spoke of love! Melisande has watched countless invasions, heard all the tales. And you think that she will fall in love with a *Viking*?"

Count Manon shrugged. "An Irishman. A prince of Eire. It all depends on how you look upon a jug of wine, eh, Ragwald? It might well be half full—and then again, it may well be half empty. It's better to savor the jug for the exceptional quality of the wine that is in it, rather than rue the fact that there cannot be more. This is an exceptionally fine wine!"

"The logic eludes me!"

Count Manon grinned. "Well, we shall see. That is all. We shall see. I've thought long and hard on it. I've visited with noble families here, I've looked to their sons. I am not completely a fool. Gerald swears his friendship, and I know that he is interested in Melisande—whether for himself or his son, I am not sure. You tell me constantly that what I need is power. That is why I have looked to a half-Viking prince. Why I have issued an invitation for him to come here. I will have them meet. If they become enemies, then we will need to think no more of it."

"What is a child going to think of a man!" Ragwald sniffed.

"Conar of Dubhlain is not so old, nearly twenty-one. He has already waged war with his father, brothers, and uncles on numerous campaigns. He is reputed to be one of the finest sword arms in all the world."

"That shall surely win Melisande over immediately!"

"Actually, he was here once, long ago. His uncle often rode his ships along these shores, more oft the trader than the invader. We swore peace between us, and so Conar will feel obliged on behalf of his own relations to honor us and aid my daughter in any difficulty."

Ragwald sniffed again. "The honor of a Viking!"

"This is an unusual Viking, as I have said. Through marriage his brother is kin to Alfred of Wessex. Many of the maidens in the households I have visited would dearly love to be ravished by a Viking—were the Viking he! You have not seen his like, my friend."

Ragwald shivered, oddly cold. He sighed. "When will this Irish Viking come?"

"Soon. But of course, it will still be years before I even think of allowing Melisande to become any man's wife!"

Ragwald shivered again, startled as a fiercer chill suddenly seized him. He tried to shake it off.

"Years, aye, years. You are right, she is just a child." he agreed. "A very beautiful child growing a sumptuous form, but a child nevertheless . . ."

The count laughed. "Ragwald, you will not sway me! I am right in this."

"I pray it is so," Ragwald agreed.

They both looked to the flames. No matter how warm the fire, the chill seemed to stay with Ragwald.

What was it?

The stars had told him nothing. It had to be nothing.

He looked at the count, grateful that he had returned, and the count smiled in turn.

" 'Tis nice to have a peaceful night, eh, Ragwald?"

"Indeed."

Neither of them had the least idea that it would be the last they would ever share.

For the count was not right at all.

Tragedy and circumstance were destined to alter all their plans of that evening.

And Melisande would wed before her birthday.

Indeed, she would wed before another twenty-four hours had passed them by.

5

"Father!"

Melisande had slept little that night and had arisen early. Shivering with the cool air of morning, she had hurried out to the parapets to watch the fortress awaken. The guards, on duty through the night, dozed with their heads bent down upon their own shoulders. Far below, the bakers and their wives were well into their day's work, and the sweet smell of freshly baking bread was beginning to permeate the morn, thankfully taking away some odors that were not quite so pleasant. She could hear the blacksmith's hammer, the song of a dairy maid. It seemed a very average day.

Then, suddenly, she became aware of a rider coming over the ridge from the eastern side. Coming from Gerald's territory. She arched a brow curiously at first. Gerald himself had come often enough in her father's absence. There seemed nothing odd about his coming. She didn't like the man and despised his eldest son. Geoffrey was twenty, yet Melisande, at twelve, felt years his senior. From what she had always seen, he spent his days endlessly torturing the hounds or trying to wrest any little trinket of any value from his younger sisters and brothers. He was tall and well built, a handsome enough youth, but with a certain light to his eyes and twist to his lips that made her acutely uncomfortable. His mother had been dead as long as Melisande could remember, and their household seemed a wild one. Everyone wondered and speculated on when Gerald would take another wife, and it had occurred to Melisande that he might intend for it to be her. The servants had whispered about it often enough.

She shuddered at the thought. Marie de Tresse, the young maid who was her personal servant, had thoughtfully begun to teach her all the things she must know, though in truth, she had gleaned much of it by simply studying animal husbandry! The thought of being with Gerald in any such way made her feel violently ill. Yet the feeling did not persist, for she was assured in her father's strength of will and determination. Maybe Gerald thought it natural that they should join their households together. She did not!

Nor would she ever entertain the thought of being a wife to his son! She could imagine sitting at night with him, watching him try to throw his dinner bones at the hounds' noses!

"Father will never let it be!" she assured herself.

But the rider was coming closer, and she felt uneasy. Was this some message from Gerald regarding her? Would her father's very definite refusal give cause to trouble—or battle—between them?

She hurried away from the parapet, racing for her father's tower bedchamber. It was a huge place with a great canopied bed in the center, a fireplace far before it, tables and chairs and trunks strewn about so that he might be visited within his personal rooms. Count Manon had already risen and was sliding his sword into the sheath at his waist.

"Father!" she cried, bursting in on him, but he was quick to comfort her.

"I have seen the rider coming. I'm going out to meet him."

Melisande hesitated. "Father, truly, you wouldn't begin to consider making an arrangement—"

He laughed, pausing to kiss the top of her head. "Truly, Melisande, never! Now let me see what is going on out there. He claims that I consider my land and my daughter superior—aye, girl, and that I do!" he said, smiling. But his smile faded, and he looked seriously into her eyes and stroked her cheek. "Truly you are superior! I have watched you grow into a young woman with a wisdom that far exceeds your years. You have a tender touch for all beasts, a kindness in your heart for our people. They are dependent on us! All dependent on us, that is the world we live in. And you do not look to your own value, but give great concern to theirs. You have done me very proud, Melisande. Any man must prove himself worthy of you."

Melisande stood up on her tiptoes, throwing her arms around her father's neck, kissing his cheek. "If I have grown well at all, sir, it is because I have the wisest and kindest of all fathers!"

She realized then that someone stood behind them. She swung around. Philippe, captain of the fortress guard, was there, staring hard at the count. "It is Gerald himself at the gate, begging an audience with you. He warns of danger, and asks that you come beyond the gates so that his words may be for your ears alone."

Ragwald hurried up behind Philippe. "I do not like this, not one bit, Count Manon."

Manon sighed deeply. "Ah, well, he warns of danger. I must ride forward and see what that danger might be!"

He started forward, then turned again, kissing his daughter's head tenderly once again. "Remember my words, Melisande. Always." He hurried to the stone steps leading from the tower parapet to the ground below. Someone had already brought his great horse, and the count swiftly leapt upon the animal.

He called out the order for the gates to be opened and rode out.

Melisande remained on the parapet, uneasily watching what took place below. All eyes in the castle were trained on that meeting just beyond the gates.

That must have been why, Melisande realized when she saw the danger at last, they had been so very oblivious to it at first.

Other riders were coming over the ridge now.

She saw it all too late and all too quickly. Gerald had led her father out some distance from the gates. He had come alone as a lure.

And her father, in good faith, had followed him. Now riders were bearing down on him with deadly intent. So very many of them. Melisande stared at them and realized that many of them were different, they were not all Gerald's men. They were Vikings. Clad in conical helmets, skin boots trimmed in fur, wooden shields carved just a little differently. They were Vikings. Just like those who had come to ravage the coast, like those they had beaten back upon occasion from the fortress walls. Vikings *riding with Gerald.*

Because alone, Melisande thought, *neither they nor Gerald could best her father. They had strength, Gerald did not. Gerald could reach her father, deceive him . . .*

And the Vikings could not!

Melisande began to scream. For a moment she saw her father's eyes. Below her, in the courtyard, the guards, too, realized the danger. There were screams and shouts, men mounted their horses and went racing out on foot.

And all too late, as Melisande saw clearly. Gerald drew his sword against her father, and her father,

excellent swordsman that he was, parried the first
blow, and the second, and the third.

But by then the horsemen racing down from the
ridge were upon him. It seemed a dozen gleaming
swords shimmered in the daylight, silver growing red.

She began to scream again, sinking to her knees. All
of Manon's men were industriously engaged in the
battle now, and all too late. She had seen her father
fall from Warrior. She had seen the gates fly open
again as the men from the fortress poured out, confused, fighting wildly, screaming, shouting.

Their leader downed.

She had seen Warrior come trotting back in through
the gates, lost, as the others went racing through them,
and she knew. With certainty.

Her father was dead.

Upon the parapet she leaned back against the wall,
trying to breathe, trying to fight the staggering power
of the pain and loss that seized her. Nothing on earth
could cut so deeply, tear at her with such deadly
agony. He was gone; she could not live without him.
The tears came pouring down her cheeks and she cried
out in a shrieking sob.

But there was no one there to hear her. Ragwald
was gone, having raced down the parapet, in shock
himself from the sheer brutal treachery of the assault.

The pain that gripped her was so great at first that
she could think no further. Yet it was thinking of her
father that at last gave her strength to rise again.
Gerald had come to slay her father and then do battle.
He had known that *if he killed Manon,* he would have
destroyed the heart of the fortress, taken away the
crucial guiding point for all the men within the castle
walls. There was no one left for them to follow now.
Philippe was their captain, of course, but the fighting
would be different in the hearts of all the men.

Ragwald had taught her military issues as well as

legal ones. The enemy always sought to kill the leader, and thus cause confusion within the force of men.

Gerald had done so. He had caused the gates to be opened. And even if they were closed again, he had done his damage. With his Viking warriors, he had created a powerful horde.

With Manon gone, the castle guards were fighting without heart.

Gerald would win. He had slain her father, and now he would take all that he wanted. There would be no one to stop him, especially once he had sworn homage to the king in Paris, because no one could ride out to settle petty disputes in a lawless land, where the strongest castle was always the one that decreed its own law . . .

She came determinedly to her feet. Gerald thought that he would kill her father, condemn her to whatever gruesome fate he desired, and seize all that her father had created.

She could not allow him to do so. She would rather die.

She gripped the wall of the parapet, staring down to the courtyard. Warrior stood there, alone, forlorn.

She pushed away from the wall, and she thought of the beautiful gilded coat of mail her father had brought her. For ceremonial occasions.

There would be a ceremony tonight. Her father must somehow lie in the chapel vault below, and they must all stand vigil.

They must live to do so. And somehow, somehow, best Gerald.

She looked to the heavens. "Dear God, let us slay him somehow! Please, God, any way on earth. Let me see him die today, or let me die myself in the effort!"

She pushed away from the wall and hurried for her tower room. She dressed in the mail, started out, but fell to her knees. "God, however you seek to help me,

I will be grateful! By any means, fair or foul, let Gerald be beaten! I will accept any penalty you send my way, *I will rot in hell,* if that is your desire, but I beg of you, let this man be beaten!''

She stood and grasped the sword that fitted into the finely decorated scabbard that came with the mail. She shivered suddenly, violently. She didn't want to die.

But her father was already dead. And she wasn't so terribly sure that she wanted life without him. She was afraid.

Suddenly she heard his words echoing in her ears. *"You have . . . a kindness in your heart for our people. They are dependent on us. They are dependent on us . . ."*

What reward for seizing this castle had Gerald promised the men he fought with? The women and girls who resided within it? The clothing they wore, the plates they ate from, the precious little pieces of jewelry they might have obtained? The silver chalices in the chapel, the golden crosses there? The dairy maids, the seamstresses, the maids, the cooks . . .

The men murdered, the rest of them slaves. She dared not think of the fate Gerald would have for her.

Death might well be preferable.

With that thought in mind, she rose. She would spend her life hating Gerald and his kin and Vikings!

However long or short that life should be.

Far down upon the parapet Ragwald was seeing a new dimension give a different shape to the fray taking place before him.

Great waves of *sea beasts* were coming. With each white crest that broke across the water, the rise of the ships could be seen again. They lined the horizon, those ships with their serpent heads. Prow heads snarling, teeth gnashing. Dragon ships, *Viking* ships.

They rose, again and again, seeming to leap across

the water, their dragon prows rising anew, no matter how roughly the sea raged. The day, so bright with morning, had turned ominous. Gray clouds roiled on the horizon. Jagged streaks of lightning came down from the skies as if the great Norse gods Wodin and his son, Thor, had banded together with a vengeance and now, in a fury, rode the billowing, windy gray day, tossing down golden and rippled spear after spear of fire.

Dragon prows . . .

Ragwald stared upon the coming ships. Heedless of all that was going on, he raced down the stone steps to the courtyard and shouted for a horse. A mount was brought to him, and he leapt atop it quickly. He ordered the gate opened, and rode through the mass of men engaged in hand-to-hand combat, not fearing them at all, he was so incredulous. He rode hard to the shore and leapt down from his horse. With the melee still going on behind him, he stood there unbothered, as if he were immortal, the sea wind picking up clouds of his graying hair to blow it across his ancient wizened face, his gray eyes suddenly ageless.

A man who counted astrology—along with other curious wonders—among his talents, he was amazed that he had not seen this great catastrophe that now seemed destined to befall them.

First Gerald, and now this!

The ships, those magnificent, horrible ships with their great raging dragon prows and red and white striped sails!

He looked from the ships to the land.

How could any prophet of any kind claim credibility when he had not foreseen *today!* Oh, he'd felt those shivers last night, but he hadn't begun to *see* any of this! He might have warned Manon against it all!

And now! This fury from the sea!

With Count Manon already dead. Butchered by so

many men, beaten by their swords and maces, a battle-ax nearly cleaving his fine head from his warrior's body. They were already in such very grave trouble. Ragwald could see from where Gerald had drawn his strength, bartering for it with some of the marauding Danes who were forever pestering the coastal byways and rivers of France.

The people here would know it, they'd all know it! Gerald was a distant cousin, and he had long coveted this piece of land, where high rock surrounded a safe harbor, where the sand of the beaches quickly turned to rich soil. Manon had worked too well here when he had taken the wooden fortress and slowly, surely, turned it to stone. Stone that shone white against the blue of the sea and sky and the rich tones of the earth.

But what was this new element? Viking prows leaping and flying across the sea? Coming like a hundred pounding horses, bearing down upon them!

Ragwald turned quickly again. All was nearly lost. With Manon slain, his men were beginning to run in panic. They were good men, loyal men, but with the thoughts and hearts of men.

What was left to fight for if Manon was gone? Better to run to the safety of the forest, rescue their wives and children, run with them!

Men needed a leader, someone to stand behind, someone to fight for, to die for.

And all that was left to them was Manon's young heir.

His daughter.

Ragwald inhaled and exhaled. He stared to the sea, trying to think. What would these ships matter, if Manon's men could not regain their strength after Gerald's attack? First things must come first, the enemy must be taken in order!

He leapt upon his horse and quickly turned his mount around, riding through the clumps of still fighting men, riding hard for the gates to the stone fortress, closed tightly at the moment.

Few fighting men were left inside the great gates. There would be no choice but surrender. Gerald's men would seize them, or the dragons who came from the north would.

"I need Melisande!" he cried to the sentry. "I must have Melisande!"

There was a hesitance. Melisande should be in her room, awaiting the news of the battle. Perhaps with Marie de Tresse, perhaps with some other woman. Someone should be comforting her, hiding with her.

Ragwald sat grimly on his mount. Nay, not Melisande. Aye, she would be in pain, agony. But he knew her better than anyone else. If he called her, she would come.

One of the kitchen women, pale with her fright, looked over the parapet. "You cannot send a child to fight a battle for men, Ragwald!" she cried in dismay.

When the men are dead, I have nothing but a child, he thought.

Yet neither could he really think of her as a child anymore.

He heard her voice, soft, melodic, very feminine, and for all its youth, very strong.

"Open the gates. I will pass."

Someone slid the great bolt, the gates parted outward, and she appeared.

Melisande.

She was trembling, Ragwald could see. She had loved her father dearly. But no tears ran down her fine ivory cheeks. Nor had she chosen to ride out on her small mare, Mara; rather, she had mounted on her fallen father's great stallion, Warrior. Seeing her now, Ragwald realized quite suddenly that she had indeed grown up. She was tall for her years, extremely dignified now.

And she was clad in the armor they had all admired so greatly last night. The incredibly beautiful chain mail armor, decorated lavishly with gold and silver.

Her hair, rich, thick, and bounding well beneath her knees, flowed about her.

She was a figure to lead, a figure for men to fight for, for men to die for.

"You have heard?" Ragwald said softly. "Your father is dead. You are the countess."

Her lower lip trembled, and he could see the wealth of tears about to spill from her beautiful violet eyes. She nodded. She would not spill those tears. Not now.

"There is a great deal of horror before us," he continued gently. "But you are our only chance. Can you ride before men?"

She was afraid, yes, certainly. But the emotion showed in her eyes just briefly. She lifted her chin. "I am the countess. I . . ." She hesitated a moment, for they both heard—suddenly, clearly—the hard sound of an ax connecting with flesh and bone, and the agonized cry of a man. She paled, her pain for the man evident, but then she continued quickly, "I am the countess, and I will lead our men."

Ragwald suddenly wanted to cry. Shivers ripped along his spine as he realized again the very great beauty of this child, the girl he had taught and now must serve. If they were to lose the day, if she were to be taken, what would befall her? She was somewhere in that strange age between childhood and womanhood, so innocent, so tender, so achingly lovely.

He had given this great thought. So, apparently, had she. There was no choice but for her to ride.

For a moment the petty little wars that they seemed to wage so constantly with one another meant nothing at all. His heart ached, and he reached out to her. "Come, Countess," he said, bowing low to her. "Come, and we will rally our troops!"

They rode forward, he and Melisande. Men were slipping from the crest of the battle, heading for the deep forests.

"You must call them, speak to them—" Ragwald began. But it seemed he didn't need to teach her any longer.

Melisande cried out to them. "My friends! We must fight on! We cannot give over this land to the men who betrayed my father! We cannot let them steal our livelihoods, rule us, slay us!"

Those who had been disappearing paused. Swords crashed and thundered, and one of the enemy fell before the huge captain, Philippe. On foot he hurried to fall before Melisande. "Countess! What can we gain? We fight this bastard—and look to the sea! More dragons come, more and more!"

Melisande saw the ships at last. Ragwald had thought it best not to mention them to her, but now he watched her violet eyes widen as they took in the multitude upon the sea.

"Maybe they have not come to wage war!" he said suddenly. Someone had to meet them. Beg for help, promise some reward. "They are a strange lot, and if they are Norse rather than Swedish or Danish, they might well fight *with* us rather than *against* us."

Anguish seized him. He needed to meet the Vikings. He had been Count Manon's aide for years, he had brought messages, he had negotiated peace again and again. He had to go.

And Melisande had to stay here, golden and shimmering, inspiring their troops to victory. To fight until help could come. Yes, yes! The Vikings had to fight with them, had to.

"Strange Vikings!" Philippe cried suddenly. "Look! Look beyond the dragon on that helm!"

It was the first time that Melisande was ever to see Conar MacAuliffe, and oddly enough, it was then she began her hostility toward him. For whether Ragwald managed to encourage the man to fight with them or not, she could not bear his look behind that dragon's visage at the prow of his ship.

She had never seen a man quite like him.

The day had grown increasingly stormy. The sky was gray, the wind was vicious. Yet no matter what the violence or rage of the whitecapped sea, he stood without wavering. One foot, booted in skin and fur, rode the helm while he looked to the shore, his great arms crossed over his chest. Golden blond hair caught what slim light filtered through the gray of the day, and over a breast coat of chain mail, he wore a mantle most similar to that Melisande had seen upon the Irishmen who had come to her father's house. It was caught at his shoulder by a great broach in a Celtic design. He was strangely dressed—like a Viking, yet not like a Viking. His ship cut the water like hot steel, there was something very wild and raw about the way that he stood, and the way that his ship moved.

There was also something of absolute confidence and arrogance about him. There was a dignity in the way he stood without flinching or faltering.

Suddenly Melisande was certain he was looking at her. Straight at her. He couldn't possibly see her eyes, for she could not see his. But she was certain that he was staring at her, and that he saw her as a child, and nothing more.

"Strange Viking . . ." Ragwald said. Then he gasped, "Why, 'tis him! Jesu, what a daft fool I have been here! It is *him*!"

Melisande stared at him. Indeed, he had become a very daft fool!

But Ragwald stared at her, aggravated. "Conar MacAuliffe, son of the Wolf—and grandson of the Ard-Ri of Eire. Kin through marriage to Alfred of Wessex!"

Melisande followed his words quickly. Alfred was the greatest king they had ever known across the channel. He had fought for his people, and held his ground, in countless battles. He had forced the Danes to treaties.

And this man was kinsman to him?

Philippe cried out suddenly, warning them all of a greater danger. He pointed to the crest southeast from them, Gerald's land. "There rides Gerald himself! The bastard! With more men. The coward! He tricks your father out, sees that he is slain, and then retreats again until the battle is nearly taken. Now he rides out himself! And our forces are so greatly weakened!"

"Melisande," Ragwald warned firmly, "you must cry out again, gather the men around you. I will go for help!"

"From those heathens from the sea?" she cried.

"Girl, you can't understand as yet. I'll explain it all to you, but aye, *there will be help from those heathens from the sea*!"

"Ragwald!"

There was no time. "Cry out again, Countess!" he warned her. "We must fight hard *now*!"

She was suddenly alone, it seemed, though not alone at all, for hundreds of men, dead and alive, littered the battlefield. But indeed, *she was alone*. Her father was gone. Blessed father, he was gone. The incredible tall, kind man who had been her life, who had taught her dignity, who had stood behind her, and loved her more deeply than any man could love a son. Who had always given her an incredible worth. He was gone.

It could not be.

He could not be dead. He had been too tall to die, too strong, her protector. He had seemed as invincible as the gods, and now she dared not look down to where he lay still.

The people were dependent on her.

She was the countess now. And no matter how she shivered inside to sit atop Warrior and look out over these men, she must do so.

Gerald had pretended to be her father's friend. He had betrayed him. And he meant to take their fortress and have it for his own. And God alone knew what would happen to them all if they did not beat back Gerald's forces!

She opened her mouth, determined to create some new rallying cry. For a moment, though, she was torn by what she saw around her. Her mouth went dry. The words would not come. Men lay about so haphazardly! Men like her father, strong men, men who had so recently lived and breathed, smiled and laughed! Now they lay about, mangled, torn, swept up in pools of their own blood.

She could not do it! She could not ride forward!

She could not let her father lie unavenged!

She drew the small sword from the scabbard about her waist. She raised it very high on the air. "For God and Our Right, my friends! For my father, slain, for our lives! Mon Dieu! Onward!"

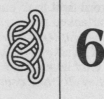

6

She hadn't known that she intended it herself—perhaps she never had—but Warrior, so accustomed to battle, suddenly leapt forward.

And there she was, a few days short of her thirteenth birthday, leading her forces directly into the fray. Panic seized her along with the whipping of the wind. She clung low, suddenly, to Warrior's neck. She had no desire to wield the sword she had held so high against another man. She didn't want to feel the cracking of bone, the splitting of flesh. She didn't want to feel the hot wet slickness of blood splashing over her.

And more than that, she didn't want to feel the cold steel of a sword herself, or the merciless weight of a battle-ax.

Too late! She could hear the terrible clash of steel all around her, she could hear men's battle cries, and she could hear the pitiful walls that escaped even the most powerful man, for flesh was flesh, and all men had been created to bleed.

Warrior, the great horse, stood his ground, awaiting her command. She sat upon him, her fingers curled tautly around her handsome sword. Then she realized that one of Gerald's people, a stocky man with reddish hair and wild eyes, was moving her way. She cried out. In defense she held her sword tight.

From the rear someone else attacked the man.

He fell back.

Against her sword.

His eyes widened, staring into hers. They never closed. He died with his eyes wide open in amazement.

A scream rose in her throat. She dared not let it escape, dared not let her people see her absolute horror and terror. She swallowed it. Warrior pranced hard, forward, backward.

She heard Philippe at her side. "Retreat! Call a retreat, Countess. We are outnumbered! We must get you safe somewhere, let Gerald have the fortress—"

"No!" she cried, and realized that she was fighting tears once again. Gerald had betrayed them all *and slain her father, who had given her everything*!

Gerald wanted it all. Even the life and the blood.

Gaston of Orleans came riding up hard beside Philippe. "We must take the countess from here! She is all we have now. See how the men rally to her. *We must keep her alive!*"

Philippe argued with him quickly. "I am beginning to think that we must surrender. We have tried. We are outnumbered."

"Sweet heaven above us!" Gaston, more wizened, older, maybe wiser than Philippe, moved his horse closer to Philippe's, trying to keep his words from reaching Melisande.

He failed.

"Mother of God, don't you see? Gerald wants any excuse to slay the child. Then this will all be his! There can be no surrender. We must escape!"

"Slay her!" Philippe repeated, then shook his head. "He wants Melisande, he has always wanted the girl, just like the land. Maybe it makes no difference, maybe we must surrender, and then he would not dare slay her!''

"But if she fights him, and Melisande will—" Gaston flashed her a quick glance and broke off.

She bit into her lower lip to hide her fear. Even as he said the words, Melisande realized the peril of their predicament.

Her people had come through for her, rallying to her cry. But they were badly outnumbered. And now, even as Gaston spoke with Philippe, she saw new danger. The three of them were being cut off from the others.

She saw Gerald again. She thought bitterly that they were distant kin. Her father had been his second cousin. And he had done this anyway. After all those years when he had benefited from her father's largesse.

She stared at him with the utmost hatred.

He was a large man like her father. Tall and well built. Just a bit older, with a leaner face, and a curl to his lip she had never really trusted. Something about his thin-lipped smile had always made her uneasy—she had hated to kiss his cheek and had always done so as quickly as possible.

Now she knew why.

And she wanted to shriek and scream at the triumph she saw in his face as he watched her now.

She started, realizing that she was hearing something different. Then she knew what she heard that was so strange. The clang of swords had stopped. The cries had ceased.

What she heard was the sudden sound of silence, for everyone was watching her and Gerald. Watching and waiting.

Gerald sat atop his white spotted stallion and smiled. "I will take my little cousin off your hands now, Philippe. Give me the child, and you and Gaston and the others may lay down your arms and live."

"You've slain her father through the most vile treachery!" Gaston cried out bravely. "And you ask us to entrust you with her?"

Gerald pointed to Melisande. "This delicate child, has taken arms against grown men. And slain them, so it seems. And I might point out, my good fellows, something that you have missed. *You have no choice!*"

"You will not hurt them!" Melisande cried suddenly and fiercely. She fought tears again. She had tried so hard not to look, but she could still see her father's body on the ground. She didn't care if she died or not anymore. All she wanted was to scratch Gerald's eyes out.

She set her heels against Warrior's flanks.

It was a brave and foolish gesture, and had she been just a little bit older, she might have realized just how foolish. She could ride well, even as well as her battle-experienced distant kin. She reached his side easily enough, with everyone still standing incredibly still and watching her. But as she reached his side, her courage—and her foolhardiness—remained with her, along with the awful rage and anguish that were tearing at her heart. She threw herself from Warrior to land atop him and take him to the ground. Gerald swore angrily, condemning his men-at-arms. A gasp of astonishment went up from the men surrounding them, Gerald's and her own, for such a slender young woman to have unseated such a hardened warrior.

Melisande managed to rip her nails into his throat, tearing at his flesh.

"Hell's fire, someone get this she-devil off me!" Gerald raged, trying to protect himself. He stared at her with fury and amazement, and Melisande tried to strike him again, but this time his men were there. She was caught mercilessly by each arm and dragged back.

But as he stared at her, Gerald didn't smile his thin-lipped amused and cunning smile. There was blood upon his cheek, and down his throat. He wiped at it furiously. "You'll pay, sweet cousin!" he promised her. "Wretched little bitch!" He staggered back to his feet, having been weighed down by his chain mail. "Run them all down!" he shouted to his men. "Kill each and every one of her infernal protectors!"

"You swore they'd go free if you had me!" Melisande cried.

Gerald's squinting hazel eyes touched upon her briefly and he smiled. "Ah, but I didn't have to trade, vixen. You threw yourself so gently upon my mercy!" He raised his voice again. "Slay them! Slay them all! And you!" He directed a finger at her. "You shall learn to obey me in everything, or else you shall die an exceptionally slow death!"

"You wouldn't dare! The king would have you disemboweled!"

"We'll see, won't we?" He reached out, catching a swatch of her ebony hair, jerking her toward him. He was a powerful man. Before she knew it, she was being thrown upon his horse, with him leaping behind her. "Pretty child!" he mused. "Maybe I can sustain my hatred enough to see you enslaved by some of my Danish friends! Maybe they'll be willing to wait for you to grow up. Maybe they won't give a damn if you grow up or not. There's not much difference between a pretty boy and a little girl. Then again"—he laughed—"maybe I don't care much myself! Your father thought you too pure for a union with me or mine. Maybe I don't give a damn if you're completely formed or not!" He raised his voice suddenly. "The girl is mine!" he cried in triumph. "Witness all, the girl is mine, the fortress is mine!"

There was silence for a moment. A silence like death, that seemed to stretch out forever.

But then that silence was strangely broken. The earth seemed to be trembling. Even with Gerald's restricting arms around her nearly suffocating her, Melisande could feel the wild shaking of the ground.

Riders. Riders coming hard.

And then they appeared over the ridge.

He appeared.

He rode a pitch-black mount, a huge one, and horse and rider both seemed bigger than life for several long moments as they rode forward in the lead. He sat on his horse with an incredible ease, tall in the saddle, one with the beast. He was very broad shouldered, and that size was emphasized by the mantle that flowed over his shoulders and the coat of chain mail he wore beneath it over his torso. The mail glinted in what little sunlight peeked through the clouds.

He wore a conical Viking helmet, silver in color, with a nose plate, leaving only his chin and eyes visible. His chin was strong, squared, set in a cold anger.

His eyes, as he approached, blazing out from the silver of his helmet, were the most extraordinary she had ever seen. Framed by his helmet, they were true blue, the brilliant blue of the sky on a summer's day, the blue of the ocean, a blue that pierced and sliced and assessed. They seemed to see everything at once, seemed to see through everything.

She found herself shivering violently as he stopped perhaps fifty feet before her. She realized that she was far more afraid of him than she would ever be of Gerald, which made little sense, for Gerald wouldn't bat an eye before slicing her throat.

But Gerald didn't wield the same kind of incredible power that this man seemed to exude. The power that touched the soul, that demanded all and brooked no resistance.

Fool! What did he think? she wondered. That they

had not fought Vikings here before? That a Frankish count did not have the men to slice his meager forces to shreds?

Perhaps not. She bit her lower lip. She hated all Vikings. The Danes had invaded these shores as long as she could remember. They had killed, raided, captured, raped, and pillaged. They had now joined forces with Gerald, for whatever reward he had promised, to kill her father. They were—all of them!—a race of *creatures*!

But this Viking was definitely one to be reckoned with.

One to be feared even more than others!

She had never seen one quite so finely muscled, so well displayed in both armor and clothing. One so golden, or one who seemed to sit upon his horse quite so easily, quite so tall. Should she ever need to describe the Norse god Thor, the great, raging god of battle and thunder, she would need only recall this man!

"Who in the Devil's own hell are you?" Gerald demanded of him in a snarl.

The startling eyes within the frame of the silver helmet seemed to burn with a wild blue fire. "Conar MacAuliffe of Dubhlain. Friend to one Manon de Beauville, slain upon yonder field, and therefore now, *foe to you*, or so it does appear."

Melisande felt the pressure of Gerald's hand as he pushed her forward and drew his sword swiftly from its scabbard at his side.

"Another enemy?" he inquired. "That is your choice. You may die with these Frankish swine with whom you have cast your lot."

"Let the girl go," Conar commanded him, and for the briefest moment she felt the blue ice of his eyes as they swept over her.

Then she felt Gerald's rise of tension, his arms tightening around her.

"Over my dead or dying body, Viking."

There was a short silence. The air itself seemed alive. The Viking smiled slowly, no warmth touching his piercing eyes. He spoke softly, yet his tone was deep, and seemed like death upon the air.

"You need to use this girl as your shield?" the Viking said mockingly.

"If I die, she dies."

"Oh, I think not, you treacherous fool! I think not!"

Suddenly the Viking was riding toward them with startling speed, with ice-cold fury and raw determination.

Gerald didn't have time to slit her throat. He was indeed busy clasping her against him as a shield. His arm around her, he drew her back hard against his chest. Melisande could see his hands locked around her rib cage. They were mottled a deep red with his fury. He seemed to be choking.

She decided to take her advantage. Suddenly straining against his hold and shifting, she sank her teeth deeply into the flesh of his right hand. His concentration had been on the Viking. He screamed out, easing his grip for one moment, and Melisande seized upon that moment. She pushed free from his other hand and slipped from Gerald's horse and started running.

Someone shouted. She spun around. One of Gerald's men had been about to hurl a dagger at her.

He had been stopped. The Viking was amazingly quick. The man was screaming in agony, his hand pierced through by the Viking's blade.

And still, the man on the great black horse charged down upon Gerald, his sword high, barely having blinked to save her life when she had fled!

Gerald let out a cry of absolute fury. He spurred his horse, charging the Viking.

The Viking, with his deadly blue eyes, smiled his wickedly cold smile as he raced onward to meet his foe.

For a moment it looked like a scene out of Valhalla. The two fantastic warriors, all alone on the plain. The day had darkened so that it seemed they both raced through gray mist. Their horses' hooves did not need to touch the ground.

Swords swung, the horses thundered ever closer to one another, and then they met.

Melisande turned away at the awful impact. She heard the rise of a cry, a cheer. She started to turn back, but Philippe had come to her, sweeping her up and running with her back toward their own lines.

"What is it? Let me see!" she cried.

"You don't want to see."

"Who—"

"The Viking is victor here," Philippe said. He paused a moment. "And Gerald's lying head no longer sits atop his body."

"Oh!" Melisande gasped. She clasped her hand over her mouth. After all that she had seen she was not going to be sick. She had to maintain her dignity and courage. Somehow her home had been saved for her. She had to prove that with help, Philippe's help, Gaston's help, *Ragwald's* help, she could hold on to it.

"Up, Countess, to Warrior!" Philippe said, helping her atop the great stallion.

A chill seized her. She looked out across the field. Gerald's men had fallen back. They waited uneasily upon the ridge. Now they dared not flee.

The Viking had not come alone. His men, with their miraculous abilities, were lined up behind their leader. Waiting, and with her father's men. Her men, now. Gerald's people were far across from them, equally still. Not even the shuffling of horses' hooves upon the ground could be heard. *It was as if they were afraid to move!*

Her men had nearly lost the fray when her father had been killed. Now Gerald lay dead, and his forces were the ones in confusion!

Between them and around them was the gray mist of the day, making it all seem like something out of a dream world.

If they so chose, Melisande thought, her forces could mow down the offenders like harvest-ripe wheat if they made one single movement.

The temptation was great.

The gray sea mist remained upon them. Bodies littered the ground. Her father's body among them, her heart cried out. Broken, fallen, bits and pieces of carnage here and there.

What did she do?

Then, out of the mist he rode, his massive sword slicing the air above his head, his hoarse, guttural cry one of victory and warning.

He needed go no farther. The offenders, Danes and native men—instantly and as one—whirled their mounts about, and began to race into the oblivion of retreat.

The Viking paused, his sword reaching to the sky, as if he took his power from a thunder god. His black horse reared high, the sword touched the very heavens. Then the horse fell to its four legs, swirled about, and once again the Viking was facing Melisande.

The chill that had gripped her deepened. There was little to see of his face, as his helmet covered so much of his features, but even that Viking helmet he wore made him different from other men. Through distance and haze, his eyes still seemed to burn.

What was this that she and Ragwald and her father's men had done to acquire victory? Sold themselves to devils and demons? Made pacts with heathens?

What price would they pay?

He came toward her, his searing eyes touched upon her, and she could not look away.

She straightened her shoulders. She reminded herself that her father was dead. That he had always sworn this land would be hers. She swallowed hard, swearing that she would not tremble before this arrogant man. She reminded herself that she was of the finest Frankish blood.

She was her father's daughter.

"We thank you, friend, for all that you have done here today," she said regally. "We welcome you and offer all of our hospitality."

He was silent for a moment, and she wondered quickly if he spoke their language, if he understood her. Then something flickered across those extraordinary eyes. A trace of amusement, she was suddenly certain.

"Indeed? You welcome me? And who might you be?" he inquired.

"Countess Melisande," she informed him. "And as I've said, we are grateful, and we welcome you!"

"Ah, well, you will do much more than welcome me, Countess!"

"And that is?"

Those blue eyes flickered over her. "Obey me, little girl."

Anger ripped through her. "Obey you! What arrogance! I don't even know who you are, and I do not *obey* heathen Vikings!"

"Melisande!" Philippe whispered. "Remember, please, what he has done—"

"He's a Viking!" she hissed back.

"Milord! Milord!" came a cry, and it didn't matter what she had said or thought, because Ragwald was coming forward now. He hated to ride, Melisande knew, and he looked very strange upon the war-horse, his cloak flapping about him, his hair and beard wild.

"Ragwald," the Viking acknowledged.

Melisande realized the two knew each other. Of course, Ragwald had ridden out to meet him, to entreat him to save her from Gerald's forces, from Gerald himself.

There was more. Maybe Ragwald hadn't actually known the man before, but somehow, she was certain, *he had known of him*!

"Melisande!" He frowned at her severely in warning. "This man is Prince Conar MacAuliffe, of Dubhlain. We are entirely in his debt!"

"Then our debt must be paid," she said in return.

But the Viking with the very Christian name was looking past her to Ragwald.

"*This,* then, truly, is Countess Melisande?" He seemed dismayed.

"Indeed, milord, every bit as beautiful as promised—"

"She's a mere child!" the Viking exclaimed.

That did it. A child, indeed! One who had just seen her father slain. One who had gone to war.

She had not done so very badly!

"As I've said, milord *Viking,*" she spat out coolly, "we shall do everything in our power to repay our debt."

He still wasn't looking at her. He was staring, baffled, at Ragwald.

"A *child*!" he repeated.

Ragwald began to speak very quickly. "But it was her father's intention that you should form an alliance. In intended time, of course. He hoped you would form an affection for one another. Of course, now we haven't the luxury of time. There must be a lord here, else we shall face this daily—"

"*What?*" Melisande gasped, but they were all ignor-

ing her. How extraordinary, when she had been so
very important just moments ago!

"Milord!" Ragwald entreated. "Aye, certainly, it
will take some time to consummate the marriage, but
it must take place! I implore you! Perhaps you shall
wait for a bride, but you will gain these lands, rich
lands! You have yet to really see the fortress, and it is
a treasure, I assure you—"

"The fortress is *mine!*" Melisande gasped out. She
felt as if she were strangling. She stared at Ragwald as
if he had lost his mind. He *had* lost his mind, surely.
They had won! They had won, and now Ragwald was
trying to get this Viking to stay here!

Ragwald and the Viking both paused to stare at her.

"*Mine!*" she repeated. "Ragwald, *I am countess
here!*"

The Viking looked back to Ragwald. "A very *ill-
mannered* child!" he exclaimed.

"What!" Melisande gasped again.

"A beautiful one!" Ragwald countered.

Those blue eyes lit upon her again. Raked her. She
felt stripped and assessed.

"Aye, and I imagine there's a great deal of trouble
to come," he said wearily.

"Milord, I entreat you—"

"Let's see the fortress then," the Viking said
coolly.

Melisande, stiff upon Warrior, felt a streak of fury
whip along her spine. Ragwald was trying to entice
this pagan into marriage with her! He offered her—
and the fortress. She had been found lacking, and so
the Viking was determined to see if the fortress was a
better bargain.

"Oh!" she cried out. "This is incredible, this is
inexcusable! Of all the arrogance—"

"Indeed!" the Viking interrupted very softly. "It is
quite inexcusable, your behavior, girl." He turned to

Ragwald. "I would determine her upbringing. I know where she can be more gently tamed."

"Ragwald!" Melisande cried out softly. She realized then that many people were around them. All of her father's men. The men who had fought for him.

All of the Viking's men.

She would not sit here and argue before them!

"I will not do this, do you hear me? I will not do it! Be damned with you!" she told Ragwald softly, and spun Warrior around toward the castle walls, determined to escape them all.

But despite Warrior's great strength and power, she had barely raced across half the plain before she felt the thunder of hooves behind her. She turned, just in time to see a muscled arm reaching out for her. She cried out, nudging Warrior hard in the flanks, but her efforts were too late. She was swept from her horse and over to the Viking's. Color and heat flooded her as he raced on, his arms tight around her, the cold metal of his mail clashing against her own, his chest seeming like an inferno of heat behind it.

They tore for the castle gates that way. And the gates opened to their approach.

The Viking did not slow his pace until they were within the courtyard.

"You oaf!" she cried, shaking, trying to elude his hold. "You've no right!" She tore at the hands holding her. Large hands, startlingly fine, with incredibly long fingers. "I'll bite you!" she promised. "I had Gerald bested on my own, and I will best you, too—"

She broke off. He had leapt down and now reached up for her. He held her above the ground, her feet dangling. "Bite me, little girl, and I will spank you until your nether regions are raw, it is a promise!"

"How dare you—"

His eyes narrowed, he smiled, and then started to

laugh. "I have been duped here to wed a child!" he exclaimed.

"I will never wed you!" she swore. "And if you even think about laying a hand against me—"

"Ah, little countess, I will think about it, indeed!" he whispered softly. "As to the wedding, well, we shall see." He set her down. She could hear the other riders now, coming in their wake.

She remembered her father. Lying dead, beyond the gates.

"Let me go!" she entreated softly. "You may see to the fortress. I must—"

"You must what?"

"See to my father," she said quietly, fighting tears.

He released her. "Go then," he told her. She started to walk away. "Melisande!" he called her back, and she turned.

"Be advised, whatever your feeling, I will have no more outcries such as that before the men, do you understand?"

"I am the countess here," she said.

He took a step toward her. "Let me try again, milady *Countess*! If you cannot behave as your situation in life demands that you must, then I will see what I can do to improve your manners."

Her eyes narrowed and she grated hard on her teeth. "I will not be taught manners by a *Viking,* I assure you!"

"Oh, lady! Don't delude yourself. You will be taught, I swear it!" he promised.

"You haven't the right!"

Golden lashes quickly flicked over his eyes. He surveyed the walls of the fortress.

"Then it seems I will have to wed a child to obtain it!" he informed her very softly.

She swirled around. He caught her hand, drawing her back for a moment. "Run now!" he told her quickly. "For I think that this wedding will take place. And once it does, well then, little girl . . ."

"Then what?" she demanded, head thrown back, eyes narrowed, passion and fury gleaming deep within them.

"Then you will be in my power. Completely in my power. And I will see that you learn manners, Viking or other!"

She ripped away and fled from him, vowing that no one could possibly put her beneath his power. She would not allow it.

But even as she ran, she could hear the echo of his laughter, so close behind her . . .

7

When she came beyond the gates, Melisande discovered that, mercifully, others had come to her father first. He no longer lay on the field. When she turned, looking for him, she felt Ragwald's bony but surprisingly strong hands upon her.

"They've taken him to the chapel," Ragwald told her. "I'll bring you to him there."

She wrenched free from his touch, staring at him as if he were the greatest traitor in all the world. "I know where the chapel is. You stay away from me."

Ragwald sighed deeply, trying to come near her again. She backed away from him.

"Melisande, stop it! You've got to listen—"

"We had won! We had won, and you sat there bargaining with that *Viking*. We don't need him, I hate him, I will not marry him, Ragwald. My father is dead, I am countess here, and you cannot make me!"

"By your father's soul, girl, have some sense!"

"I have sense! Gerald is dead, the Viking killed him—"

"And you are a very weak and very young *girl*! You cannot hold this land, you can't provide the strength needed to support these men who were so willing to fight and die for you today. This *Viking,* as you insist on calling him, was your father's choice.''

"My father's choice!" she exclaimed, astounded.

"He can call upon help from across the seas, he can fight the Danes because he knows how to fight as they do. Melisande, you are not of an age to take power. Your welfare is left in my hands.''

"Then stop this!" she demanded.

Ragwald looked at her sadly. "I was against it when I first heard of it, Melisande, but I think now that it is the only way you will be allowed to live long enough to care for this great fortress.''

"Well, I won't do it!" she insisted, coming closer to him. "I won't do it! I'll not be here when you and he come around to finishing with your *bargains*!" She was alarmed by the sense of panic growing within her every time she thought of what her fate might be at the Viking's hands. He didn't want her—other than to crush her. He wanted her fortress. It was humiliating. "I will run—" she began, but she paused, hearing a soft footfall behind her. She turned around and quickly became aware that she and Ragwald were surrounded by the Viking's men, a very strange lot of them, for some were so fair they were near white-haired, some were freckle-faced with fire-red hair, and some were very dark. Some were very Norse in their dress, while others wore the Celtic jewels and mantles so particular to Eire. She counted quickly. Ten of them surrounded her and bowed gravely as she stared at them.

One stepped forward. He was nearly as tall as his leader, broad-shouldered, and with a full head of deep auburn hair. "Your father, Countess, is tended to now. If you'll come with us, you might pray for his soul. Astrologer," he continued, "my lord Conar seeks your council now.''

Hot tears stung Melisande's eyes. She wasn't going to let them fall. She lifted her chin. "You all will

accompany me to a Christian chapel to pray?'' she
inquired with an edge of sarcasm to her voice.

But the man who had addressed her was careful to
take no offense. ''Milady, our island has long been a
place where the greatest of Christian beliefs flourish.
You must come there sometime. You will be amazed.''

''Your island,'' she said with a sniff. ''And tell me,
do they make those dragon-prowed ships of yours in
those same places where your Christian beliefs flourish?''

''Melisande!'' Ragwald hissed.

''Do they?''

''Indeed, lady, they do. We have taken from King
Olaf's world all that is good and combined it with all
that is fine from our homeland, and there we have
found an incredible strength and beauty between the
two.''

He smiled and would not be disturbed. Melisande
suddenly found her arm grasped by Ragwald again,
and he was leading her through the crowd of men back
toward the walls. His fingers were tense around her
arm. ''I have taught you all these years. I have
frowned upon your father's giving you lofty ideas, for
it is a brutal and wearisome world beyond, and you
must be made to see that! You have a fine mind, you
are wise well beyond your years. You were willing to
ride to your death this afternoon, but now you do not
see how necessary this is for you and all who reside
here. Do you care nothing for the people? Will you
see them attacked again and again, laid low, beaten,
massacred, because you are afraid of one man when
you were not afraid of hundreds?''

''I'm not afraid of him,'' she whispered back furiously.

''Then—''

''I simply loathe the man.''

"That is no reason not to wed him!" Ragwald exclaimed angrily.

"I'm too young to marry—"

"Girls have been wed from their cradles. Think on this, you may wed him now and most probably not *see him again for years*! But you will be safe and strong, don't you see?" His voice dropped still lower. "Have you no respect for your father's memory? Have you no dignity on his behalf? Of all times, Melisande, you cannot act like a child now!"

"But I am a child. You keep telling me how young I am! As he says, I am a little girl!"

"You cannot act like a *spoiled* one! You will mock your father, even in death!"

If he wished to hurt her—but in so doing reach her—he had done so. Her heart and head still reeled with the simple fact that her father was dead. It was unbearable.

She walked through the gates with Ragwald. They came to the center of the courtyard, and she spun around, staring at him. "Do what you wish then, *astrologer*! Cause this *thing* to happen. But don't offer your advice to me again!"

She whirled around and left him, aware of all the men behind her, but oblivious to them. The chapel was in the far north tower and she hurried there. The milling mass of her people, some white-faced, some with tears staining their cheeks from their own losses and hers, quickly made way for her.

She burst through the doorway. She stood there a moment, accustoming her eyes to the dim and smoky candlelight within. The chapel was a simple place with rough wooden benches leading to the altar, an aisle in the center. A runner of crimson cloth had been cast down the aisle.

Her father had been laid out on a like cloth on a wooden litter before the altar. Someone had tended to him carefully, the blood had been washed from his face and features, a cloth had been set around his throat where it had been so deeply severed. His eyes were closed, his fingers were folded around the hilt of his sword, so calm in death. He was a handsome man, a *young* man, Melisande realized.

And when she looked at him now, she felt the tears she had fought so long burn like arrows in her eyes. She cried out, heedless that anyone might be near her, and she tore down the aisle to kneel at his side, to touch him, to let her tears flow.

He looked so very much the same as when he had lived! But he was so stiff to her touch and growing cold so quickly. "No, no, no, no, no!" she cried over and over again. The tears fell from her face to land on his hands, and she felt against his coldness and his stiffness, *his death*, when she tried to wipe the wetness away. He could not be dead, she had to hear his voice again, his laughter again. She had not realized how very fragile life was, any life. The loneliness assailed her even as she sobbed, touching him still, hugging him, as if she could warm him back to life with her own body. She threw herself upon him, sobbing, praying that she might wrench him up and somehow breathe life into him once again.

She suddenly felt a strong, warm touch upon her, one that was very much alive. She tried to fight, but the power behind it was too much for her. Seeing her father, feeling his body grow cold, had been more than she could bear. She hadn't the strength to stand.

Blindly she struck out at the arms that held her. She was not released, but pulled firmly away. She started to fall and was lifted up. She found herself staring into the endlessly blue eyes of the Viking who had avenged her father's death but now stood to take his place.

"Leave me be!" she begged him.

"You cannot be with him, you cannot die with him. No living soul can do that for another," he told her.

A new well of tears sprang forward.

"Hush," he told her, and gently held her head against the breadth of his chest. "Shh, the pain is great, but it will lessen."

"Never!" she whispered. He was carrying her somewhere, she didn't know where. She was dimly aware that they left the chapel behind them, that people broke apart to make way now for the Viking who held her.

Darkness was falling. It had been just hours since her father had died.

And already he was so cold.

So stiff.

Gone. . .

She started to shudder and sob again. His fingers came to her face, smoothing dampened hair from her cheeks. A few minutes later he set her down in one of the mammoth carved chairs before the fire in the great hall.

The hall was very quiet, yet there were men there. She could see them all as he set her down. Ragwald was there, very tall and lean, watching her with a strange, sorrowful light in his eyes. The great red-headed friend of the Viking was there, along with Philippe, Gaston, and a few others.

The redheaded man came forward with a chalice. The Viking, down upon one knee before Melisande, took it quickly from him, pressing it into her fingers. "It's warmed wine. Drink it. It will help."

"Nothing will help."

"Aye, time will help."

She drank the wine. The room remained very quiet. She felt the great heat and power of the man before her, watching her as she drank the wine. She had had it oft enough before. Even very young children sometimes had sips of wine with their meals, it was all that was set upon the table to drink at times.

This wine was potent. A rich wine her father had just brought back from his visit to Burgundy. That thought nearly brought the tears back to her eyes. She didn't sip the wine, but drank from it deeply. It warmed her insides and nearly made her gag. In the aftermath of the warmth, though, she felt the first numbing of the pain.

She drained the wine from the chalice and stared into the cool, demanding blue eyes of the stranger who suddenly seemed to be dictating her life.

He watched her in turn, judging her, she knew. For the moment she kept her silence, though she bristled. Her lashes lowered at last, and she thrust her chalice back at him. He rose from his knees before her and strode back to the center of the men, then turned and faced her from a distance.

"We have found your father's documents," he said. He waited for her reaction, but she allowed him none. "He had already had a marriage contract written with his agreements clearly set forth. Would you like to read it?"

Her breath caught. She couldn't believe it. Her father had meant to marry her to this man! He had always promised that she would have some say, that she would choose.

She felt so numb that she couldn't quite form an answer. In a way she was betrayed. Her father, like everyone else, had doubted her ability and her power.

There was no way out of this, she realized, and anger seemed to flow through her body as hotly as the wine. She would not let them ridicule her in the future. And she wasn't going to run again and be dragged down by this Viking.

She stood, startled to discover that she was a little wavery on her feet, but she carefully hid that fact. She was glad that, even at her age, she was taller than some of the smaller men present.

Not taller than *him,* though. She was certain that not many men were.

I will not be afraid of him! she vowed to herself. "I don't need to see the papers," she said coolly. "In my father's honor, I will follow my father's wishes." She stared at Ragwald.

Long strides brought *him* back before her, blue eyes strong upon her. "Can you manage the chapel?"

"The chapel?"

"Aye, Melisande. It is best to do this properly. In the chapel, before God and all the people."

"Even while my father's body lies there?"

"Especially because your father's body lies there. Do you need more time?"

"I think not," Ragwald murmured uneasily. The Viking looked his way, and Ragwald shrugged unhappily, gazing over to Melisande. "I don't think Melisande needs time to think now, nor to be alone—"

"Because she might run away?" the Viking asked.

Ragwald didn't reply. The Viking smiled, shaking his head. "No one runs from me, Ragwald. I run faster, you see. She must have it her way in this. I ask you again, Melisande. Do you need time?"

Those eyes! *No one ran from him!* Because if she ran, he would catch her. And life would be far worse. He hadn't wanted any part of this, but he had made his decision now. And that was it, the law, as great as God's own, so it seemed.

One day I *will* run from you! she thought. Far, far away!

But her breath caught then, as she realized what he was trying to tell her. Her father lay dead in the chapel, and they must go there now and marry, with his cold body alongside them.

Count Manon would, after all, be present for his daughter's wedding.

She curled her fingers into her hands, her nails biting her flesh. The people. She had to do this because of all the people. The farmers, the smiths, the craftsmen, the milkmaids. They were weak now, so vulnerable. And this would make them strong.

"I'm ready now." She stared at Ragwald. "I am not running anywhere." She stared from one man to the next in the room, and a distant smile curled her lips. "It wouldn't matter anyway, would it? You would do this all by proxy, and nothing I said would matter."

"The church demands your agreement," the red-haired Viking assured her.

She lifted her hands, shaking her head. "So it's said, but I've yet to see a woman's choice in any matter mean a thing. Indeed, I remember a cousin's wedding, in which she did not agree, yet wound up in her would-be husband's arms, with his forceful grip upon her head causing her to nod at the appropriate time. Messires, I ask you, wouldn't the same fate befall me?"

"Alas, milady, surely no—" the redhead began.

"Indeed, it is quite possible!" Conar MacAuliffe strode before her again, his blue eyes searing into hers. "Shall it come to that?"

"Why are *you* doing this?" she asked him. "You were so opposed to a *child*!"

"Children grow," he said with a shrug. "And I have assessed this land. It's worth the wait."

"You could die in battle while you're waiting," she told him quickly. "And therefore die with no heir or issue."

"You're a very clever child," he told her. "And perhaps my wait will not be so long." He grew impatient then, turning from her and striding across to the great table, where documents had been strewn about.

"I hereby swear to honor Count Manon's demands as regards his daughter and his property, and set my hand and seal to it now, thus vowing my life to this new course."

He plucked a quill from the table and signed a document. A candle was quickly brought, and wax dripped upon it. The Viking pressed the ring from his little finger into the wax upon it, and thus the contract was signed.

He turned back to her. "Shall we go?"

"Isn't my signature needed upon it?" she inquired.

He shook his golden head slowly, eyes upon her. "This is just the contract. Your father signed it."

Melisande seethed. He couldn't have meant *this,* she thought. Not Count Manon. He couldn't have meant to so cruelly cast her into this world where her thoughts and wishes meant nothing.

She clenched her teeth. It was a world in which a woman's desires meant little or nothing. A woman was her father's ward until her marriage.

And then her husband was full guardian.

Perhaps there would be no real marriage tonight. But this Viking would not be her guardian.

She almost sank back to the chair. Then she vowed she would not. He would learn that she had been raised to be independent, to think, to rule her own destiny. And if he did not, well then, both their lives would be hell.

"We shall go," she said, and turning, started from the great hall. She bit into her lower lip, determined that no more tears would fall from her eyes before them, before *him.* Despite her best efforts, they blurred her vision as he hurried down the stairs to the entrance of the tower, then burst back out into the courtyard.

It had grown dark at last. The sounds of moaning and confusion had faded. The dead had been collected, the injured attended to. Torches lit the courtyard in an eerie glow, because there seemed to be no light from the moon that night.

She felt his hand upon her elbow suddenly. "Melisande," he told her softly, "it is far more proper if you walk with your intended lord."

"You are not my intended, you are my father's."

"I will not parry words with you tonight."

"Then perhaps you had best not speak with me."

His fingers curled around hers tightly. He didn't really hurt her. He wielded just enough force to let her know that he could cause her head to nod if he so desired.

"I am weary, too," he told her.

"Your father does not lie on a slab in yonder chapel," she reminded him.

"I am sorry for that, deeply sorry. And so, milady, I have forgiven much. Tonight."

"Ah. Tomorrow you will forgive no more?"

"Tomorrow you had best take care. The more I speak with you, the more I find you to be overly wise for your years, too determined, brash, and reckless."

She spun on him quickly. "It is how I was raised. How my father intended my life should be."

They had come before the chapel at last. Behind her, Ragwald was reading from the marriage contract, announcing the union of two noble houses, informing all the people that because of circumstances, the wedding would take place immediately.

"I intend, milady, that you should live long enough to provide heirs for this fine estate," the Viking said flatly. "And as that might well take some time, you can no longer be so determined, brash, and reckless!"

"Where's the bloody priest?" Ragwald muttered.

"I am here!"

Melisande was dimly aware that their priest, Father Matthew, had arrived at last. She hadn't seen him all day. Father Matthew was not the bravest of men. He had surely been hiding in the storage rooms beneath the chapel throughout the day.

If the Viking had come to him before, Melisande was certain, Father Matthew had certainly promised that he would wed the two of them—and put the fortress in *his* hands—no matter what Melisande should or shouldn't say.

Father Matthew, snow white hair wild upon his head, let his small dark eyes fall briefly upon her, then he quickly looked away. In his way the priest was a gentle and caring man. She was certain that he was *sorry,* but that he intended to act anyway.

The night air was cool. It made the chain mail armor she still wore icy to the touch. Melisande closed her eyes and felt the air brush her cheeks. Father Matthew stood upon the first step to the chapel and announced her name and title and family to the people who had begun to gather after Ragwald's announcement. Then he announced the Viking's. Impressive. He was the son of the king of Dubhlain, grandson of the high king of all Eire, and son of a very great Norwegian jarl.

Viking! Melisande thought.

Yes, it took one to fight them!

"Melisande!"

It was Ragwald hissing at her. She realized that she hadn't been listening, hadn't heeded the proceedings.

"Do you enter this union of your own free will?" Father Matthew repeated.

No!

The priest cleared his throat, but the Viking spoke for him impatiently.

"Do you enter into this union of your own free will?" he demanded, his words strong, his voice very sure.

Any second now he would pluck her up, nod her head for her, she was certain.

It was her father's will. She had said that she would do it. For all the people who depended on the lord and lady of the fortress.

"Yes!" she snapped. "I do this of my own free will."

Those Nordic eyes were upon her again. Icy blue. Yet tinged with just the smallest light of respect.

"A ring," Ragwald whispered, to the Viking this time. "It's very important here that you give her the ring at the doorway to the chapel. Then we may enter in."

The Viking drew the ring from his finger, the ring with which he had set his seal to the wedding contract. He set it on her third finger, then tried her thumb. She wrapped her fingers around it so that it wouldn't fall to the ground.

Were that to happen, the entire crowd would moan as one, and everyone would be convinced that the Danes would wipe them all out by morning, that their children would burn to cinders, and that a plague of locusts would descend immediately.

The ring didn't fall. Father Matthew announced that they would enter the church for the wedding mass.

"Do you really go to mass?" she inquired of the man at her side, her tone cynical.

"When it is opportune, most certainly," he assured her. Melisande opened her mouth to speak again but fell silent.

Her father lay before them. She nearly tripped, nearly fell. Strong arms were there to prevent her from doing so.

"I cannot do this!" she whispered.

"You must. Lean on me."

It was the last she really remembered of the ceremony. Father Matthew spoke of her father, of his goodness, of how he had been slain. He spoke of the strength needed to hold steady against their enemies, and thus this unseemly haste in a marriage. He spoke of the fact that Conar MacAuliffe had slain Gerald, who had slain Manon, and thus it was fitting that the avenger should sit in the lord's house. And when all this had been said, he at last moved on to the wedding.

In the end she had to be nudged to speak again. By then it didn't matter what she said at all. She would have sworn to marry twenty dwarfs from the forest. Upon her knees before the altar at his side, she heard Father Matthew pronounce them duly wed, before God and men.

She couldn't quite seem to stand on her own, but Conar helped her to her feet. His lips touched each of her cheeks.

There was no cheering, no revelry. He led her from the chapel and back to the south tower.

And there Marie de Tresse was waiting. She slipped an arm around Melisande and brought her up the stairs to the bedchambers.

They passed by the room where her father had slept. They stopped. Melisande went stiff, staring into the room. She wanted to go there, to touch his things.

"No!" Marie whispered gently. "Not now." Melisande felt numb at that moment, so cold and so weary. Marie pushed her beyond that door and down the small hallway to her own room. Once there, Marie helped her to slip off the suit of mail, and then Melisande collapsed upon her bed. Once again she thought of her father. Tears began to fall down her cheeks.

Marie came to her, brushing the tears away. But Ragwald came, too, and Melisande turned on her side, away from them both.

"Melisande!" Marie said softly. Ragwald caught Marie's arm and led her away. "Let the girl be," he said softly. "She needs the tears."

The door closed. And Melisande was alone. A bride—and an orphan.

In all of her life, she had never felt so surrounded.

And never, never so alone.

8

Not until the next morning did Conar give much serious thought to his precocious young bride. It was Brenna who made him look at her through new eyes.

Brenna was the child of one of his father's dearest friends and greatest warriors—and one of his mother's favorite women. They shared a wild heritage, that of the fierce defenders of Eire and the determined seafarers of Norway. The closest of friends since they were very young children, born within the same week, they had never been anything deeper, and loved one another like sister and brother.

Not that he didn't have enough siblings of his own. There was Leith, of course, the oldest, his father's heir. Then Eric, who he seemed to resemble most. There were his brothers Bryan, Bryce, and Conan, and then his sisters, Elizabeth, Megan, and Daria. It had been a full household with vibrant personalities, but because of all that had been shared within it, Brenna had found a place there, too.

Brenna always traveled with him. She had no interest in warfare and always stayed far behind the fighting, but she was often his right hand in many ways. When she had been very young, Mergwin, his grandfather's ancient adviser, very akin to a mystic, versed in Nordic runes and the ancient Druid ways, had touched her hand one day and declared her his pupil.

In recent years Conar had come to realize just what Mergwin had seen in Brenna. She had an ability to read men, she knew when they lied and when they told the truth. She could see into the hearts of people and know their motives. She could read runes, of course, but many had the ability to cast the Norse runes and read their message. As a *Catholic* prince—his father had embraced Christianity for his mother's sake—Conar didn't put great faith in the reading of runes other than as a greatly entertaining and sometimes intriguing form of amusement.

Maybe that wasn't quite the truth. He had set great faith in Mergwin throughout his life, as had all of his family. Mergwin could *see* things, and they all knew it. He guided them all, steered them from danger when he could. He oft foretold the future, but warned them always that their own actions would forever influence destiny, and that they must remember that life itself called upon strength not only of the body, but of the spirit. In his heart Conar believed that there must be a heaven and a hell, and that it didn't matter much whether it was peopled by one god or by Wodin and his hordes, whether men reached for the clouds or the halls of Valhalla. And just the same, it did not matter to him if Brenna read runes or looked to the stars and prayed to God for guidance—or even if she practiced the ancient Druidic rituals Mergwin had most assuredly taught her. He very often sought her counsel, no matter how she arrived at her wisdom.

On his first morning in the fortress he awoke still exhausted, which might have had some bearing on his future relationship with his child bride. His head throbbed, his muscles were sore from battle, his flesh ached from minor wounds sustained in the fighting. He awoke in Count Manon's bed, which caused him

some sorrow, for although he had met the man only
once before, while learning sailing—and therefore
fighting—with his uncle, he had earnestly liked and
admired Manon. The count had been intelligent,
strong, and fair, and with a pleasant sense of humor.
In turn, he had seemed to admire Conar very much,
and when Conar had received the invitation to come
here, he had thought that Manon might sense some
danger. Yet he had never imagined that he might arrive
in time to fight it—but not to prevent the treachery
that had seized his host's life.

He saw Melisande instantly upon waking. Perhaps it
was even her presence that had awakened him, for he
had learned to be a very light sleeper. She stood in the
doorway, staring at him, her face pale, violet eyes
stricken. He found himself staring into those eyes.
They touched him now, as they had touched him the
first time he had seen them. Their color was unique,
so very deep a hue, and they were large and fringed
with rich and exquisitely long, dark lashes.

She had come to go through her father's posses-
sions, he thought.

She had not expected to find him here.

He pushed himself up, sitting on the bed, and she
went a shade paler, then turned and fled. "Melisande!" he called, but she was gone. He realized that
he had been sleeping naked, that the battle scars upon
his shoulders might well be alarming, and then again,
quite frankly, that she didn't like him one bit—even
though he had saved her from having her throat slit or
from being raped and enslaved by the very man who
had slain her father.

She didn't give a damn about the battle scars, he
determined. She didn't like his sleeping in her father's
bed, and she had no intention of obeying a single word
he had to say.

Well, she would learn. And soon.

He rose, sliding into tightly knit trousers that served as leggings as well, pulled on his boots, and donned a linen shirt and heartier tunic. There was no need for battle dress today, but he was never without the knife he sheathed to his ankle and seldom went without his sword, sheathed in the scabbard he wore about his hips. Just as he buckled his scabbard, a boy brought water for washing, and he drenched his face, trying to awaken more fully.

He left the bedchamber behind him, admiring the fortress once again. He liked the way the bedchambers rose just above the hall, and the way the hall was set above the ground and the storage. Air passed more freely here, so it seemed, allowing the scent of the castle to be a sweeter one. Thanks to Mergwin's determination, he had studied the old Roman ways of building their fortresses, and he could see all the advantages in this one. There was no moat surrounding the works now, but there was a trench before it to set the fortress itself upon the motte or mound, and it would certainly be an easy enough matter to deepen it and fill it from the sea, if that ever seemed necessary.

When he came down the steps to the hall, he found Swen—Norse-named but extremely Irish with his red hair and fine flurry of freckles—sitting at the table, and beside him, Brenna. They were alone, but it seemed that the workings of the castle moved smoothly along despite the recent demise of the count. Handsomely carved wooden plates had been set out along with chalices and ale and trenchers of food, smoked eel, fresh bread, fish, fowl, and slabs of venison. He hadn't realized the extent of his hunger until now. The long hours of yesterday had been so filled with events that none of them had thought about eating.

He sat down and Brenna quickly stood, reaching for one of the chalices, pouring him ale.

"So, milord, how did you sleep?" she asked him.

He shot her a curious gaze, accepted the ale, and looked to Swen, who shrugged.

"Well, you must admit, Conar, that we did not think we'd come here to stay."

Conar shook his head. "We've not come to stay. I cannot stay now. There is too much at risk at home."

"There's grave risk here!" Brenna said. She continued to serve, piling a plate high with food, setting it before him. "And this is now *your* home. Look around you, Conar. You've managed quite well. Your father would tell you that you have acquired an excellent estate."

"And my father would tell you that upon occasion, estates must manage themselves. I've not spoken long with this man of Manon's, Ragwald, but I'm quite certain that he can keep things running smoothly in my absence. I'll not be gone for very long."

"No one will be able to manage things and protect this place—not with the girl here," Brenna said.

Frowning, Conar set down the crust of bread he had chewed. Sitting back, he crossed his arms over his chest, eyeing Brenna. "All right, then, Brenna, just what is on your mind. What difference does it make where I leave the girl?"

"Have you gone blind?" Swen demanded, incredulous. He saw the glittering in Conar's eyes and quickly amended himself, "I beg your pardon, Conar, but . . ." His voice trailed away.

"What are you talking about? Both of you?" Conar demanded, throwing his arms up in exasperation.

"Have you taken a look at the girl?" Brenna asked him softly.

"A good look?" Swen added.

Conar stared at them both. Brenna sat on one of the carved chairs at his side. "Manon sent for you because he felt danger increasing here, because of his daughter.

She would be a prize if she were haggard and hairless because of this fortress. But word is going out about her, many men have see her, and she is growing older.''

"Manon's daughter is not yet thirteen!" he exclaimed.

"*Your bride* is an exceptionally stunning girl," Brenna told him.

Irritated, Conar slammed down his chalice. "To me, Brenna, she is a child. I agreed to this wedding because Ragwald was so insistent, because it seemed the best way to protect these people—and yes, because I have been handed an incredible inheritance. But the girl is to grow, we have all agreed on that."

"Yes," Brenna agreed. "She is young, but women do become wives at thirteen. You might wish to recall the time when you first discovered an interest in my gentle gender!" Brenna said.

"Now, Brenna, how would you know—" He broke off. Brenna was smiling. Brenna had known. How old had he been when he had first found himself in the fascinating arms of the young dairy maid?

Older than his new bride, surely . . .

Maybe not so terribly much older. But somehow that seemed very different. He had no patience for this situation.

"I've no intention of taking her with me as my wife at this time," he said firmly. He gazed hard at Brenna. "Since you know me so well, you must be very aware that I've no interest in ravishing a child when—"

"When diversion and entertainment so easily come your way," Brenna interjected softly. "But though you've no interest, milord, you must bear it in mind—others might. It is dangerous for her here, and her presence adds danger to the fortress if you are not within it."

"I've wed her—wasn't that the point of the ceremony, that she should have a husband and thus keep those who would prey upon her at a distance?''

"If a marriage is not consummated, it is too easy to dissolve. Even legally. Popes can be convinced—if one is eager to have Christian sanction!" Swen warned him.

"And what do you suggest?" Conar asked angrily. "That I ravish this hostile young orphan?"

"Of course not," Brenna replied, tossing a lock of golden hair over her shoulder. "But I do suggest that you take a good long look at the girl. And that you bring her with you. Somewhere safe!"

Somewhere safe . . .

It was then that Melisande walked into the room, and it was then that he did study his bride at long last, really study her.

They were right. There was much to be seen about Melisande today that he had not realized yesterday. The chain mail she had worn had hidden certain things. Her body was long, lithe, slim . . . and beginning to grow curves. She was elegantly tall, with her stream of ebony hair cascading down the length of her back. Her face was young, but exquisite, and then there were . . .

Those eyes. Large, violet, passionate, and very, very beautiful. Brenna was right. The girl was going to grow to be exceptional, and he couldn't take risks with her. She was a walking temptation as she was now. And there were many men not adverse to wedding— or bedding—young women.

The strangest tremor shot through him. Hot, hard. He had not come yesterday expecting to take property or a bride; he had come as a guest, to explore the future perhaps. It had all happened suddenly, but now this place was his.

As was the girl.

And though he did not want a child bride, neither

could he bear the image of her being seized by any other. Her beauty was trouble. An immense headache with all that he already had in his life.

Brenna leaned toward him, whispering softly. "You can leave this place fortified with half our men. But you cannot leave her *here* without you. Warfare is constant. Raids come daily. Yet if the place were seized in your absence, it could be taken again. Unless *she*, Melisande, is seized with it, for though the wedding contracts make this fortress yours, she is the heiress, and the blood will speak. You must keep her safe, away from those who would covet her."

The little minx was walking toward him now, and he was suddenly aware of the sway in her movement. She moved with grace, soundlessly, regally. She stopped before him, heedless of both Swen and Brenna, though Conar was certain that her eyes had touched upon Brenna with a sizzling hostility as well.

"You've no right to my father's bed," she told him, and though the words were sure and spoken with a chill dignity, there was a rasp within them.

"Indeed, milady," he murmured, and his gaze fell over her again. She wore a soft mauve shift with a tunic in a deeper purple, and that color seemed to match her eyes.

"He is not even cold!" she hissed.

He stood, infuriated that she would so speak to him at all, much less in front of others.

"I slept with no disregard for your father, but with sheer exhaustion. May I remind you, milady, I did not seize and plunder this place, but rather set my own men to die in the defense of it—at your father's request. And may I also inform you that when you have such matters to discuss with me, it had best be in private in the future."

"May I suggest then, *milord Viking*, that you do not do things which might cause you public humiliation?"

That was it, the final straw. He set a hand upon her upper arm and swung her around.

"Conar!" Brenna said with alarm, starting to rise also.

"Sit, Brenna, please!" There was a moment's startled silence, and Brenna slid back into her chair.

Melisande silently tried to tug free from his grasp. He ignored her, speaking to Brenna and Swen. "You will be so kind to excuse me, as the countess and I need to have a private discussion."

"There's nothing more I have to say to you—" Melisande began, but he cut her off quickly.

"Milady, there's a great deal I have to say to you."

"I'll not—"

"You will!"

He heard the tremendous intake of her breath and was prepared when her nails tore into his hand. He was still smiling to Brenna as he tossed Melisande over his shoulder, ignoring her shriek of rage.

Best to have this over with now.

He took the stairs back up to the living quarters, down the few feet of hallway to the count's bedchamber, and there sat upon the bed, bringing her face down over his lap.

He wasn't sure what he intended. No real violence, for he had seen her in the chapel and knew that her heart was ruled by the anguish of her father's passing. But no matter how she had been raised, how independent she had been taught to be, *he* could not be expected to tolerate this behavior!

He had to talk to her, and truly, that was all that he intended. She had to be threatened so that she understood. He opened his mouth to speak, but the words turned into a growl of pain as she sank her teeth into his thigh.

"Little witch!" he cried, and what he considered his very patient and tolerant determination just to talk with the girl fled his mind with the haste of a winter wind. It was not what he had intended, but it was her own damned fault. His hand fell hard upon her posterior, once, twice, and again, and then he caught hold of his temper, throwing her up before him. Her eyes were wide and wet as she backed away from him, but there was no remorse in them, only pure fury and hatred.

"How dare you, how dare you!" she cried.

"I dare again, milady, if you do not hush and do so quickly!"

"Milord!"

The call from the bedroom doorway came from Ragwald. He rushed into the room, hurrying to the girl, sweeping an arm around her shoulders and pulling her protectively close.

"She means you no insult—" he began.

"I mean him every insult!" she cried in protest.

Conar crossed his arms over his chest, disbelieving all that was occurring. This should have been such a simple thing! He had wed a child. One with a strange air of both sensuality and innocence about her. One too beautiful—and far too wild—for her own good. It really was a wretched situation. He shouldn't be dealing with it now, he should be supervising the rebuilding of the wall, determining just how many men were needed to protect the property, and how long he dared leave it. Instead he was staring at violet eyes so alive with tempest that he'd be afraid to turn his back on her, no matter what her tender age.

She was his wife, he thought, and the irony of it suddenly seemed quite ridiculous. He was not going to argue with her. He was going to give the orders, and quite simply, they were going to be obeyed.

"She's dangerous, Ragwald. Dangerous in her passion. Perhaps the kindest thing would be if you were to leave her with me now," Conar said coolly, "and she will know how to behave in the world when I have finished.''

"Milord, I beg you, think on all that has happened here! Have tolerance, pity.''

"I don't want his pity, I want him out of my home! Out—of my father's bed, out of my inheritance!'' she snapped.

He threw up his arms. Despite the way Ragwald tried to protect her, Conar found himself ignoring the man as he strode toward the girl, his temper worn ragged. He clutched her by the arms and lifted her off her toes, bringing her eyes up to meet his. ''*Mine* now, Countess, do you understand that? *Mine*. Now, astrologer, take your *delicate* and innocent little beauty here, and get her out of my sight before I see fit to confine her, bound and gagged, to her own room!''

Even held so, she did not bow to his command. "This will be my room! It was my father's room, and it will be mine.''

She had driven him to the brink. He was ready to toss her over his shoulder again and carry out his promise of binding her hand and foot and leaving her to think and fume within her own chamber. But something within her touched him then. Something in the glistening eyes, the knowledge that she was fighting her own pain as thoroughly as she was fighting him. She had dearly loved her father. She had just lost him, had not yet seen him interred in his final resting place. No matter how angry she made Conar, he had to admire her brash courage, too. But that, of course, might well be a part of youth. And stupidity. She'd no right to rush against Gerald in the way that she had. Had she been his concern then, he might well have raised a hand against her with far greater vigor than today.

He swore. Heedless of her *innocent* ears. He set her down, forcefully thrusting her back to Ragwald's care.

"For now, my man, you may deal with her. I warn you, talk some sense into your young pupil, astrologer, for I am weary of the effort!" He turned impatiently and strode out of the room, still seething as he returned to the great hall. Brenna and Swen had been joined by various members of the fortress household, the most important being Philippe, captain of the guard, and Gaston, his elder, righthand adviser. The plans for the fortress castle had been laid out on the table, and Conar quickly turned his attention to them, marveling anew at the care and detail given to the workings of the structure It could withstand quite a siege, Conar thought. The towers were placed so that approaching danger could be seen from all angles. The only weaknesses might be in the walls themselves.

Or in a treachery such as that which had been practiced yesterday.

"This is an exceptional prize!" Swen said softly at his side. Conar looked up. Philippe was looking at him with pride, nodding in agreement. Conar took in the look of the man and determined that he was a fine commander within the fortress, that he knew it better than any man. Perhaps he needed someone else here with the power of his name and homeland behind him, but he would do his best to leave the bulk of the power in Philippe's capable hands. Gaston, too, seemed a sage fellow, and both knew the fortress inside and out.

"Swen," Conar said, "I would like to study these plans at greater length. Perhaps you would look over all the workings with Gaston and Philippe, and report back to me. What has been damaged must be repaired. Quickly. I promised my father that I would not be gone long."

Swen nodded. Brenna naturally rose to accompany him, and Conar was left alone with the plans on the table before him.

A few seconds later he felt a slight chill and looked

up. Melisande was back, keeping her distance from him, remaining at the stairway landing that led into the great hall. He grit down hard on his teeth, startled that he hadn't heard her the moment she had come.

"I do hate to disturb you from savoring your gain," she said, those violet eyes so fierce and condemning, belying the soft and taunting tone of her words. "But—" She hesitated just a moment. "But—Father Matthew has come and has asked when he might say the funeral mass for my father. I assured him that now seemed an excellent time. I am leaving for the chapel."

On the table his fingers flexed and unflexed. What was it? He longed to wrap his hands around her elegant little throat.

"You will leave, milady, when I say."

"It is my father we bury."

"It is your place now to obey my commands."

"You've no right to deny my father a Christian burial."

"I've no intention of denying—" He broke off. She was doing it again, pulling him into an argument as if they were *both* children.

He stood up. She wasn't going to manage it. He bowed suddenly and deeply to her, sweeping out his arm. "You wish to bury your father now, milady? We will do so. Now." He strode across the room to her. Before he could reach her, she turned quickly to flee. He stretched out an arm, managing to get hold of a handful of her hair. He tugged her back to him with that soft ebony mass, met her violet eyes again. "I will escort you, Melisande. In your haste, milady, have you allowed it to be mentioned to your father's closest companions that the time has come for his mass?"

She clamped down hard on her jaw, tugging her hair free from his grasp. "Ragwald has gone to inform all within the fortress walls. He will call down from the parapet."

"Fine. Then we will go."

He took hold of her elbow. She detested his touch, but refrained from jerking away again, and from speaking. They strode in silence from the south tower to the north one, and the chapel on the second level there. The space was already filling. Conar saw that, indeed, the men had been informed, and Philippe and Gaston stood closest to the carved wood stone where Count Manon lay, now shrouded in soft white gauze. Ragwald knelt at the count's feet, and Melisande broke free from Conar to join him there.

Conar let her go.

Father Matthew entered the chapel and began to speak. Obviously he had been as fond of his lord as Manon's daughter, servants, and friends, and as he spoke of the count's youth and goodness, the chapel began to fill with the soft sounds of tears. The stoutest, hardest of men stood within the chapel that afternoon, their eyes liquid with tears. Conar felt again the deepest sorrow for the man who had built this fine fortress, who had invited him here. It had not been so long since his own grandfather, Ard-Ri of Eire, had lain so before his funeral procession to Tara. He could remember the pain of losing Aed, and despite himself, he felt his heart go out to his child bride once again.

If only she would cease to fight him so, perhaps something could be worked out.

As the service ended, Manon's closest friends came forward to lift him for his last journey, the one to the family crypt. It was below the storage level, deep within the foundation of the place. Double doors led to the blackness of the crypt, where, though it was day, only the torches gave light to lead the way to the stone bed where Count Manon might rest now for eternity, shrouded in his white mist.

Through it all, his young daughter had not broken. If she had cried, she had done so silently. But as Father Matthew spoke the last words and they turned to leave the crypt behind, Melisande stopped. "Give me a torch, Philippe. I would not leave him here alone so quickly now."

Conar did not like it. The firelight barely touched the shadows here. The crypt was not heavily peopled with the dead, but he could see the shrouded figure that lay so close to Manon. The count's wife, Conar was certain, and there were several other white-clad forms within the cold stone confines of the chamber. It did not seem a healthy place for the girl.

"Melisande," he said. Those who remained within the chamber stopped at the sound of his voice. She turned to him, as if suddenly made aware of him. "It is not wise," he told her.

Philippe quickly stepped before him. "I implore you, milord, let me abide with her for a while. I will see that she does not stay long."

Conar hesitated, then sighed. "Nay, my good fellow. You go on with the others. I will abide here with her."

Philippe nodded after a moment, setting a torch into the wall. He followed Father Matthew out, and Conar was left alone with Melisande in the crypt.

She did not kneel, but stood at her father's feet. Watching her, he was struck again by her slim height and easy grace, the simple dignity in the way she stood. Her head was bowed, and he could not see her eyes, only the inky length of her hair, touched by the firelight.

He waited and time passed. The torch burned low, the hour slowly and surely grew late. Conar shifted his weight at last and strode toward her. "It is time to leave."

"He will be alone in darkness forever."

"He will ascend to heaven, if he was but half the man his reputation claimed."

She was silent for a moment. Her eyes touched his. "Heaven? Or Valhalla?"

She goaded him. Even here. He would not be pushed, not at this moment. "Perhaps they are one and the same," he replied coolly.

She was silent again. "Come," he insisted. "It's time to leave now."

"Just one more prayer," she whispered, and he realized then that tears were streaming down her cheeks, tears she had not wanted him to see her shed.

He found himself slipping his arms around her once again. And for once she did not fight him but sobbed into his chest, soaking his tunic. He carried her determinedly from the crypt, closing the heavy door behind him and looking to the light that filtered down to them from the stairway.

He was startled then by the way it felt to hold her in his arms. It was amazing after everything else, but she awakened something of tenderness within him then, and he suddenly wanted to hold and protect and soothe her. He sat upon a low step, stroking her hair, marveling at its richness and mass, at the softness of it, the sweet fragrance of it. He rocked with her, feeling her shoulders shake and tremble with the violence of her sobs. He whispered the same words over and over, that the pain would ease, while the memories would last forever.

"How could you possibly know?" she gasped.

"I lost someone I held very dear. Someone very like your father, loved by everyone."

"A Viking?" she whispered.

"No," he replied with some amusement. "The Ard-Ri, my grandfather. The High King, my mother's father. He was one of the greatest kings ever to gather the lesser kings of Eire together. What peace we have had has come from his strength and wisdom."

She fell silent, seeming to have no argument for that. Then she whispered, "But you see death every day."

"Not every day. I do not seek it. In fact . . ." His voice trailed away for a moment, and she was surprised when she prompted him.

"In fact what, Viking?"

He sighed. "My mother used to hate it when we all practiced for war. She wanted her sons to find their destinies on Irish soil—peacefully. But my father warned her that peace could be won only through strength, and that her sons, all of her sons, had to learn the arts of peace—and those of warfare. And as it happened, when my grandfather died, and my uncle Niall was to take his place as the Ard-Ri, warfare broke out. We were all called upon to fight for peace in our own land. That, I think, was my grandfather's greatest strength. He knew when to fight and when to negotiate. But he always knew that he could never sit back and have peace come to him."

"My father knew that," she whispered. "For all of his life, you see, the Danes invaded here. And the Norwegians and the Swedes!" she added quickly. "So he made this fortress very strong, and they would come and look at it, see its strength, and ride away. But then he was tricked!" she whispered. She suddenly seemed to realize that she was on his lap, that her hand lay against his chest, that her head had rested there, too, that her tears had wet his tunic.

She lifted herself away from him, struggling from his touch. "I'm quite all right now. I'll not—I'll not cry again!"

She escaped him, coming to her feet. She backed away from him, swallowing hard. Even in the dim light, her eyes were bright and beautiful. "Thank you for honoring my father," she said, "but I feel that I must tell you this. I don't agree with his choice, and I believe that Ragwald has behaved detestably. So have you, of course, but you are a Viking, while he is a Christian and—"

"Melisande," he said, grating hard on his teeth, "Ireland is among the most Christian of places—"

"And my father's man, his friend. And mine. He should have known better. I will let you know now that though I am grateful you slew Gerald, I am furious that this marital arrangement has been forced. I do consider you to be a Viking, one with the hordes who have descended upon us all for so long—after all, bear in mind, your father did invade your mother's land!— and I do not forgive you for anything. If I've made myself clear, I shall excuse myself, and keep my distance until you at last feel that you are free to leave."

He was so amazed by the arrogance of her speech that he only stared at her, eyes narrowing, for a long moment. She hurried past him and up the stairs. He could have stopped her, but for the moment he chose not to do so. He let her go.

"Damn me for a fool again!" he said softly to the cold walls around him.

Ah, but she would not rub his temper so raw again, he swore it!

Moments later he rose and followed her out to the light of day.

The count had been interred, his people had wept. They still wept, but they also went about the struggle to live, to survive. Children chased their geese, the blacksmith was back at work in his forge, and the rich scent of roasting meat wafted through the air.

Life went on, always, for the survivors.

He started back for the south tower, determined to go through the plans once again.

But he paused, for he saw Melisande standing by a well with one of the guards.

Not much of a guard, he thought, watching the pair. Rather a boy, certainly no more than sixteen.

Yet as he watched the two of them, he felt a heat flare within him. The boy was consoling her, he realized. Touching her hair, speaking to her softly. Melisande was staring at him with her beautiful wide eyes, bright still with tears, but her lips were curled into a rueful smile, and she was nodding. There was something intimate in the way that they stood. They were both so young.

And maybe both so innocent, and maybe not. He had seen the beauty within the girl, but perhaps not the fire that Brenna seemed to be warning him about. When she spoke with the boy, her voice was softly, sweetly melodic. Her every movement was lithe and sensual.

He clenched his hands into fists at his sides and strode back to the south tower. When he reached it, when he saw that food had been laid out once again, he sat down to eat, then found himself slowly joined by Philippe, Swen, and Gaston, who sat with him. He asked questions about the fortress, and they answered him.

Ragwald came in, hesitated, then took a seat. He stared at his plate, then looked at Conar, interrupting the conversation. "Milord, if I may ask, where is Melisande? She has not eaten, I'm afraid."

"When she is hungry, she will eat," Conar said.

"But—"

"I believe that she is not particularly eager to join me at the table. In fact, Ragwald, she is not eager to join me in anything. I do not foresee any mutual understanding between us in the near future." The others could not see her yet, but he was aware that she had returned at last, and that she was upon the stairway, determined to escape them all and slip back upstairs to her room.

Or to her father's room—his room.

It would be good for this conversation to continue now, and quickly.

"But, milord," Ragwald was saying worriedly, "it is my understanding that you are returning to Ireland. Strengthening our position here and sailing away for some time. I will see to her, I have always done so—"

"Melisande sails for Ireland immediately. I have the perfect place for her."

He had the distinct pleasure of seeing her go dead still as she tried to tiptoe past them.

"And that is?" Ragwald asked anxiously.

"I've an aunt who is a nun. Melisande will reside with her for the time being."

Her gasp was audible to them all. She no longer had any intention of slipping by them. She hurried into the great hall, having the good sense to stop far out of arm's reach.

That did not stop her tongue.

"You're going to send me to a nunnery!" she cried.

"Indeed, I think it best. We've all agreed that the marriage shall not, as yet, be consummated. Yet I find myself somewhat afraid to leave you to your own devices."

"I belong here!" she insisted.

"Alas. Didn't you hear? The place I had in mind is in my homeland."

She was still stunned, not grasping it all. "A nunnery!" she exclaimed, whirling around to stare at Ragwald. "You said if I married him, I wouldn't have to see him again for years! And this is how I am to avoid him? I am to be sent away to a nunnery!"

Ragwald looked guiltily from her to Conar. "Milord, if you would only reconsider—"

"He need not reconsider," Melisande declared

firmly. "Oh, no, he need not reconsider!" Wild and exquisite, her eyes were on his. "I simply shall not go!" And with that she spun around and left them all.

Conar stared down at the table. Damn her! He inhaled and exhaled, then rose.

He could not lose battles with his own wife, and that wife a child!

A beautiful one with violet eyes and a quick easy smile for handsome young men nearer her own age.

"She goes tomorrow, Ragwald," he said. "I need you to remain here."

"But—"

"You, good friend, are far too easily influenced by her." Both Philippe and Gaston stared at him. He needed them to serve him, not the young countess. "There is no one gentler, kindlier—or wiser—than my aunt, I promise you. Melisande will be tenderly cared for, but I must keep her safe, as Ragwald has so forcefully taught me. Else all might be lost. She sails tomorrow."

He turned and left them, and they all knew that he was going to inform Melisande of that fact. He climbed the stairs and found that she had entered her father's room and bolted the door.

He hesitated, then swore. He threw his shoulder against the door. It shivered but did not give.

He was aware that all within the great hall must be hearing his effort.

Well, there was little that he could do. He threw his shoulder against the door again and again. He knew the bolt was about to break when he heard her cry out.

The door shuddered violently, then flew inward. She was behind the great bed, and he realized that she had been preparing to run. She was dressed in a heavy cloak with a satchel clutched in her hands.

Standing in the doorway, he shook his head. She

was truly a thorn in his side, a temptation straight from the gods.

"Where do you think you're going?"

"Away!" she whispered. "Until you're gone. Until I can return. I am the countess here."

"You are going to Ireland, tomorrow."

"I'm not—"

"You are." He slammed the broken door shut behind him, then sank down before it, resting his hands behind his head quite comfortably.

"What are you doing?"

"Watching over you—until tomorrow. At first light I will either walk or carry you down to one of my ships. You may sail either sitting—or stretched out on a plank, I really don't care which. You will cease to be a wretched pain in the nether regions to me!"

"You will not do it! I'll scream and shout every step of the way. My men will rise up in arms against you!"

"We will see, won't we?"

She would give in now, he thought. Surrender.

But she did not. He did not budge; neither did she. It was hours before she at last dropped her satchel, hours more before she sat herself against a wall.

Sometime in the night he slept. He heard her first movement, though, as she tried to find a way past his body—that obstruction blocking her way.

"I think not!" he said.

She backed away, her cloak swirling. She took her seat against the wall once again.

"I pray that you die a slow, lingering death somewhere and that the gods throw you right out of Valhalla—right on your nether regions!"

"Perhaps it will happen—but it's doubtable. I'm an excellent warrior."

"Any man can be killed."

"Aye, that is true! If only any lass could be silenced!"

"Truly, you will be made to pay for this!"

"Countess, I pay dearly as it is."

"Don't do it!"

"My mind is set."

"Unset it."

"Never. I cannot wait until the dawn breaks!"

"I will not go."

"One way or the other, you will."

Much, much later, with the sun breaking high in the heavens, Conar stood and watched as four of his ships set sail and seemed to reach out for the pink-streaked horizon.

He smiled and shook his head.

Dear God, but she had a will of steel!

Indeed, Melisande had sailed.

But he imagined they were just now loosening the linen sheet he had wrapped her in so that he might get her to the ship!

She had so loved to taunt him for being a Viking! It seemed ironic justice, indeed, that he could use his very Christian *Irish* heritage to bend her to his will!

He laughed loudly and then paused, remembering how he had felt, watching her with the young man by the wall. A tremor shot through him, and he wondered suddenly, fiercely, what she would be like when he saw her next.

What would those fiery violet eyes hold when he met their gaze once again?

9

Summer, A.D. *884*
Approaching Wessex

"We near the coast!" Bryan called to his brother.

Conar, who had been facing the wind that had sped their journey eastward, turned at Bryan's words, smiled at his dark, green-eyed brother, and saw the land before them.

English soil, land held by Alfred of Wessex, the now legendary king of England. It was also land that belonged to his brother Eric, won by casting his hand to the aid of the English king against the Danish he and his Norwegian and Irish family had battled so well.

Watching the shore, he felt the rise of his temper once again. After all these years *she* could still draw his wrath like no one he knew.

Conar had definitely meant to part ways with his young wife that morning at the fortress, but he had never imagined that following that morning, Melisande would manage to part ways *with him* quite so frequently.

Nor had he begun to imagine that she would manage to twist *his own family* so totally to her will!

He had returned to Eire soon after he had sent her

there, fully expecting to find she had been an absolute terror, but that Bede, resolute, with her deep beliefs and tremendous energy, had found a way to deal with the girl.

But when he reached Dubhlain, he discovered that Melisande had taken a deep about-turn, charming everyone in the household, and so impressing Bede with the hunger in her young mind that Bede had taken her on a pilgrimage through the countryside, ably protected, he had been assured, by his brother and sister-in-law Conan and Marina, and a select guard of their best men. There was nothing to fear. Bede was delighted with the girl, Conar's mother assured him. "She's such an incredible mind!" Erin said.

Incredibly devious mind, Conar thought. But he kept his silence, his mother seemed so pleased. He sat at their elegant table in the warm great hall of Dubhlain, and Erin slipped her arms around his neck. "I'm so delighted, and so saddened, too, of course. Tell me of these lands you've acquired. She misses home so! It must be a wonderful place."

Perhaps he should be relieved Melisande was in good hands—and not in his own. Although his family had heard everything that had happened on the coast, he had sat with his father through the night describing the place, the battle he had fought there, and the aftermath.

"I saw to the strengthening and repair of the tower and the walls, added the strength of my men to an able force there. It is a commendable fortress, Father. Manon knew how to build, how to borrow from history. He learned a great deal from the Roman ruins near him, and used it wisely."

"And fell only to treachery," Olaf mused, filling his son's chalice with some of the rich wine he had brought back.

"The man who betrayed him is dead."

"So I understand. But the man you slew had a son. You'll have to take care in the future. You've made an enemy you'll keep a long, long time."

"Perhaps." He paused. "That's why I sent the girl here. Since I had never planned to stay and had sworn to aid Niall in his efforts to hold Eire together, I dared not leave her behind."

His father leaned forward. "Don't *ever* leave her behind," he warned.

"She's given you that great an amount of trouble?"

"Trouble?" His father sat back, smiling. "She has been the very example of an angel."

"Melisande?"

"She's won hearts all around her."

"Father, lest she win *your* heart too completely, I should warn you that she despises Vikings of any make or breed, and it matters not in the least to her that I am only half Viking!"

A small smile tugged at Olaf's lips. "Conar, your mother despises Vikings, yet we've been together these very many years and the ships that sail from our ports—with her full knowledge and blessing—are ships with the design of *my* country." Olaf was silent a moment, then continued, "You were wise to send her here, for she is indeed a great prize. Though it is my understanding that this man Gerald was distant kin of your wife's, and I imagine the laws of consanguinity should prevent a legal Christian marriage between Melisande and any of his heirs, it is true in this world that *holding* is the greater part of *having*. So if you would protect her and your new inheritance, you would be wise to have her with you at all times."

"Or in safe keeping."

"Aye, or in safe keeping." Again Olaf was silent for a moment. "I'm not sure you are aware of all that you have acquired."

"I am aware," Conar said, "that she is an extremely

clever creature, Father. She has certainly managed well enough here.''

"However she may exasperate you at the moment, Conar, she is a stunning young woman. A greater prize than any plot of earth." Olaf rose suddenly, situating cups and bowls of fruits to create a map. "Your land, Eire, Alfred's Wessex. And here, Ghent, Bruge, the Danish bases. Now look to the past and the lawlessness that has taken a firm foothold on the coast. Keep an eye upon history, Conar. Not since Charlemagne has there been a leader to give real strength to your Frankish kingdoms. When Louis the Pious died and all the land was divided between his sons, the way was let open for the Danes. For it must be said, I admit, of Vikings, son, that most are mercenaries and will fight for any army that will pay. Oft enough men of all nationalities hire the very invaders who plague them at other times to battle their own people when there is war within the realm. Now, with Alfred having stemmed the tide in England, great armies of invaders are left with nothing but conquest on their minds. That will leave us all looking to our defenses in the years to come. And you, Conar, will definitely need to see to it that your wife is kept from the hands of those who might too easily see her marriage annulled and find a way to force another upon the church. I warn you, with or without such fine property—and hers is extensive, offering a fine, deep harbor!—your young wife is a prize for others to covet. Look to her well-being.''

"Well, I would do so now, Father, but she has managed to receive your permission to travel about the countryside.''

"I had not imagined that you would object.''

He lifted a hand. "I don't object." He didn't, of course. He had wanted her out of his hands.

Yet he was somehow disturbed. He didn't want to be bothered by her, but still . . .

His father didn't need to give him warnings about her. He wanted her beneath his own watchful eyes, though he thought that she had to be quite safe with Bede.

It was good to be home, yet it made him nervous to know that she traveled away from him, even in his brother's custody, for peace had been tenuous here since his grandfather's death. Indeed, he had not been home a fortnight before they were called north to help his Uncle Niall repel invaders who had come to stay in Ulster.

The invaders fell before the show of force sent from all the Irish kings. The campaign seemed a long one, but the losses were not heavy—they were learning how to fight their enemies, and many of the Irish who had once been his father's enemies were now his strongest supporters, fully aware that Olaf the White knew how to plan strategy against their mutual enemies, the Danes. Olaf stood with his brother-in-law, Niall of Ulster, acknowledged as the Ard-Ri since Erin's father's death, and their loyalty to one another helped hold the ties created among the Irish. It was a good campaign, a successful one, but it seemed to stretch forever, and though his father had returned home at intervals, Conar had felt compelled to stay with Niall until the bitter end. The time he had spent on the Frankish coast seemed to have slipped away from him. He was deeply possessive of his property, but his actual holding of it was going to have to wait. It was all right, he was certain. Messages came from Swen to Dubhlain, and from Dubhlain to Conar in the north. He had nothing to worry about. The fortress on the coast of France was in good hands.

So was Melisande.

He gave her little thought.

By the time he returned to Dubhlain it had been a good two years since he had seen his bride. To say the least, he'd been quite startled by her. She'd been with his mother in the great hall when he'd returned, so quiet and dignified that he hadn't even seen her at first. But when his eyes fell upon her, he wondered that he could have missed her.

She had changed greatly within the time that had passed. Her slenderness had taken on stunning new twists and turns, her eyes seemed to have deepened in color. Knots seemed to twist in him at the sight of her. She might still be young, but she had taken on the form of a vixen. Everything that he had been told was so true. She was incredibly beautiful. Her coloring was so startling, her bone structure perfect.

And her eyes, of course, were a tempest, no matter how silently she stood, staring at him. She hadn't forgiven him, not a whit.

He was somewhat amused by her calm and easy demeanor when they met. She accepted his kiss of greeting on each of her cheeks and asked politely after his welfare. Still, it seemed, she escaped his presence as quickly as she might. He was surprised, therefore, when he ordered a bath, to find her entering his chamber, keeping her distance, but managing to make her demands.

"I have been here over two years," she told him.

Weary, he wondered why she was plaguing him at such a time. He set his linen bath cloth over his eyes and leaned back against the rim of the wooden tub he'd had brought to his own room in his father's manor. "Indeed," he murmured.

"I came here as you commanded—"

"You came here because you had no choice."

"But I have been an excellent student and a very good guest, as you'll discover if you ask your mother or father."

"My father the Viking?" he mocked.

He heard her coming closer to the tub and was

somewhat surprised. She didn't make him feel terribly secure, and he pulled the cloth from his eyes, watching her carefully.

"Just what is it that you want?"

"I want to go home."

He closed his eyes, leaning back again. So that was it. He heard the whisper of motion as she came closer. He was startled when he felt her hands upon his back, fingers curled around the bath cloth and soap, and working a surprising magic upon the tenseness in his shoulders. "I'm aware, of course, that you may have loyalties that bind you here, but I think it *necessary* that I return home soon."

"My neck," he said.

"What?"

"Go a little higher. Rub here."

He felt her fingers move surely against his neck. Knots seemed to ease out of it. She was very good. He imagined she must have rubbed her father's shoulders often enough, and since she had loved him so dearly, she had learned to give comfort.

No matter where she had learned it, it was quite a touch!

He was suddenly very aware of the changes that had already taken place in her. Her scent was sweet.

Her touch was damned sensual.

He grit his teeth, staring down at the water, aware that all the tension she had eased had crept back into him. Lots of it. New tension. One particular tension that seemed to be standing near painful alert at this moment.

He almost groaned aloud, yet remained in disbelief. It seemed to pound into his head that many men would think her well *over* the age to be a true wife.

Not yet, not yet! As long as he did not make the marriage real, he need change nothing in his own life. And not far from his father's house, just outside the walls of Dubhlain, was a small farmhouse, and within it, a slim golden blond widow named Bridget who had offered him comfort often enough. She demanded nothing of him. He wasn't ready to change things.

But those delicate fingers working against his flesh still made him feel the birth of fire. And a new thought, one he had not imagined coming so quickly.

Soon . . .

He could take her now, he'd have every right. She had certainly grown to an impressive level of maturity.

"So?"

"So?"

"May I go home? I'm sure that someone within your father's household would be willing—"

"No," he said flatly. He'd just realized what a tempting and tender morsel she might be. The last thing he intended was to send her home without him.

"What?" Her fingers stopped moving. She came around the side of the tub, violet eyes brilliant in her fury.

"I said no, Melisande."

"But I have stayed here quite *obediently*. I—"

"You've not stayed here, you were gone when I first arrived. And if you've been at all obedient, it's because my *Viking* father does have a stern eye, you've surely realized that."

Her lashes flickered, her eyes narrowing upon him.

"I need to go home!"

"No."

"You don't seem to understand, you stupid *Viking*! I have done everything, I have learned your history, I have—"

"No! And if you're not going to rub my shoulders anymore, you might want to get out of here."

She remained there, staring at him furiously.

He arched a brow. "Unless you wish to join me in here? I have actually done my very best to practice restraint—against your *sweet* innocence, of course. But if you feel so determined to linger, I might begin to believe that you are anxious to begin marital duties in full."

Color rushed to her face, washed over it like a tide. For a moment he was certain she had controlled her temper. She turned away from him. There was a kettle of hot water heating over the fire, ready to be added to his bath.

"Ah, marital duties!" she whispered. "Do, please, let me see to your bath!"

Too late he realized her intention. She had the kettle up, and the scalding water cascading in upon him.

He let out a cry of rage, leaping up and out of the bath just in time to avoid any real injury.

She stared at him, all of him, her eyes widening in a sudden panic. The kettle clattered to the floor. She turned to run, but his fingers wound into her hair, and she flew back into his arms. Perhaps it was a revelation to them both. He had never imagined the way her breasts would feel, pressed through the linen fabric of her gown against his naked chest.

And he was quite certain that she hadn't been prepared at all for the raw and aroused feel of his full body flush against her own. He heard her gasp, felt the wild pounding of her heart. Indeed, she was equally aware of him!

"You are no longer newly orphaned!" he warned her tensely. "You know that I will not hesitate to deal with you. But it has been some time since I have seen you, so I will offer you this warning—don't ever seek vengeance against me! I will tend to you, my love, in turn. I assure you!"

"Please!" she gasped, violet eyes wide, ebony hair curling around them both. "Let me go."

He did. Then he cursed in fury because she managed to kick him in the shin before departing. He counted to ten, and then a hundred, to control his temper. He managed to do so, and let her go.

That had been the first of it.

In the weeks that followed, Melisande kept her distance from him. It was not so difficult, for his mother had given Melisande rooms above the floor of his own chamber, assuming Melisande would find the view of the river close to that which she would have had from her own chambers across the sea.

She appeared dutifully at mealtimes and sat quite politely at the table, even responding to him when she was spoken to. That, of course, might be a part of her great performance for his family, because she continued to seem nothing less than perfection when she was with them. No matter what his anger with her then, he found himself watching her, and once again, granting her a grudging admiration. She did have an incredible mind, and she learned with astonishing speed. She'd had some smattering of the Irish language when he'd sent her here, he'd known that, for she'd used it upon occasion with him, though she had more frequently slipped into the Norse words she had apparently known very well when she was angry with him, which was often.

He and his brothers—and his sisters, for that matter—had always been taught the languages of their neighbors across the seas, since his father had known that with a brood his size, many would leave home and have to make their way upon distant shores. In the same way, he was certain, Melisande had learned the Norse language—in self-defense, perhaps. The more astute households with power were often careful to speak the language of the sea invaders themselves—making it easier to negotiate whenever possible. Besides which, many of the Norse who had already sailed had acquired new homelands, like his father, and now traded liberally throughout many ports.

But in this household Melisande had quickly learned to speak with the others as if she were a native. Upon occasion he even saw her smile, but that was not so strange, for his father's was a lively household. Leith, Elizabeth, Conan, and Megan had married, and were sometimes in the king's residence with a supply of toddling babes to keep them all careful of their movements. Eric was most often across the sea on Alfred's coast, and their youngest sister, Daria, most often remained there. Bryan and Bryce were two and four years, respectively, behind Conar, and usually kept up a lively discourse through any meal when they were home. All of them donned battle gear and fought when they were called to service by their uncle. It was the way of things. It still made his mother grow pale after all these years, but she had watched her brothers fight for peace, and now she had to watch her sons do so, too.

Bede still dined with them sometimes, though she seemed to think she had carried out whatever Conar had wished of her when he had sent Melisande. Perhaps she had done so, for Melisande gave all appearances of being perfect. She spoke beautifully, and he was certain, had gained an honest affection for his mother and perhaps even his father.

She had also formed easy enough friendships with Bryce and Bryan. Conar noticed that upon occasion she even laughed with the two, and then her eyes would light up. Once he watched her and then found his father's gaze upon him, and he was forced to admit that there was a magic about her, that she definitely had his brothers entwined within her web of charm, and that she was, quite simply, every bit as beautiful as he had been warned.

A prize.

Yet he had not been back so very long when one of the ships that now moved constantly between his home in Dubhlain and his new acquisition across the channel brought a message from Swen urging him to return immediately. They had been watching Conar's neighbors, and there had been a great deal of activity on the ridge to the west.

Gerald's son was growing bolder, watching them constantly.

Conar had thought it best not to tell Melisande, but he hadn't realized that she received constantly long letters from Ragwald and that she returned them, keeping her people well abreast of all that happened within Dubhlain. She was determined that she was coming with him, and he was equally determined that she was not.

She ceased to argue, and he realized that he was in all the greater trouble. If it hadn't been for Bridget, he might well have been tricked by her once again, for on the night before he was due to leave, he visited his mistress and stayed with her very late. It was easy enough to move about in Dubhlain, for though there were nominal guards around the house itself, Dubhlain was a fortified city. He slipped into his father's house very silently, determined that he would not disturb anyone sleeping within.

And that was when he saw her.

She was moving down the stairway with an equally careful and silent tread, a great hooded cloak over her shoulders, a leather satchel in her hands. He stared at her, frowning for a moment, then realized that she meant to reach his ships and hide away within one.

He allowed her to come down to the great hall. He watched her in the firelight and felt his temper rise, and still he found himself staring at her. The beauty and perfection of her features caught him, the wild violet of her eyes seemed to steal upon the senses.

And yet with all the facilities of her able mind, she could not seem to grasp the danger to herself—or the fact that he did not intend to lose anything that he had taken as his own. Had Swen not warned him of danger, he might well have brought her. He had tried to tell her that, but she had refused to listen.

She had pretended to accept his bidding.

He watched her spin around, the cloak billowing out around her in a shimmering beauty. She saw no one, for he was in the shadows against the door. She walked toward it, reached for it, and came in contact with his chest. A gasp left her lips, nearly a scream. He clasped his hand around her mouth, determined to silence her tonight in his own way.

"Where do you think you're going, Countess?" he asked softly, his whisper against her fragrant hair, her body caught tight to his. He eased his hand from her mouth.

"For a walk in the moonlight!" she returned. "If you'll just let me go—"

She started to scream again as he swept her up. His hand locked determinedly over her mouth, and no matter how she struggled, he managed to carry her up the stairs. He brought her not to her chamber but to his own, throwing her down upon the bed then quietly closing the door and sliding the bolt. By the time he turned around, she was up, staring at him. But her defiance seemed tempered by fear, and she was watching him very carefully.

He leaned against the door, arms crossed over his chest. "I repeat, where were you going?"

"For a walk," she said stubbornly.

"To the ships perhaps?"

Her eyes narrowed hard upon him. "Perhaps I missed you, milord, and was anxious to see if you had returned from your visit with your whore!"

He arched a brow. Silence fell. She stepped back, as if horrified herself by the words she had spoken.

Conar walked into the room, angry, intrigued. "I rather doubt that," he said softly, and stood across the bed from her. "But then, of course, I hadn't realized that you were quite so concerned with my movements. Indeed, it seems to me that you are always happiest when I am absent."

Her gaze lowered, the richness of her lashes sweeping over her downcast eyes.

"I am!" she whispered.

"Yet you are suddenly so anxious for my presence that you are willing to stow away on one of my ships. And I hadn't the least idea that my activities distressed you. If I'd realized just how much you longed for me yourself, I'd have taken great care not to sleep elsewhere."

"You may sleep with the whole of your father's flocks of sheep for all I care!" she hissed back. Once again she seemed to become aware that though his tone was light, he was both weary and angry. She took another step away from him. "Truly, I just want to go home!"

Tension gripped him, he sighed, stripped off his mantle, and threw it across the trunk at the foot of his bed. She jumped a mile high. "You cannot come now, Melisande, and that is that."

"We shall see."

She started to stride by him. He caught her arm and flung her back. She landed upon the side of his bed.

"We won't see, Melisande. You cannot come now."

She stared up at him, her jaw locked. Her gaze lowered itself again, and she was silent. He realized that she would leave him and run to the ships just as she had intended—once she had pretended to return to her own chamber, of course.

He knelt beside her, reaching for the brooch that clasped her mantle about her shoulders. Her eyes fell upon his, wide and brilliant—and, he realized, alarmed. A smile curved his lips. She managed to cause him enough sleepless nights.

Her long, delicate fingers fell upon his frantically, but he had the mantle and cast it away. "What are you doing?" she demanded breathlessly.

He rose, ignoring her startled cry as he picked her up and cast her farther upon the bed, straddling her. "I just hadn't realized until tonight that you were so concerned with my nocturnal activities. Perhaps I have been sorely remiss. Perhaps the time has come . . ."

"No!" she gasped. There was a tremor to her voice, and he was certain that it was no act for anyone's sake now. "I won't go," she whispered. "I'll stay here—"

"Indeed, you will." He fell from her, lying by her side. He laced an arm around her slim waist, pulling her tightly against him. "I have told you that you will." He whispered.

For eons, it seemed, she was silent, afraid to move. Then he felt her breath expel. "If you'll just let me return to my own quarters . . ."

"I think you'll sleep here, Melisande. And I think that you will do so without further words or movements, lest I realize that you are old enough now to perform all the sweet duties of a wife!"

For once she was entirely obedient.

He didn't think that she moved a muscle for the rest of the night.

Oddly enough he did not sleep himself. All through the hours of darkness the scent of her hair teased him. Beneath her clothing he could feel her still. Slim, warm, vibrant.

And, he realized, when she turned in her sleep, a woman now indeed. The pressure of her breasts against his back was a cruel taunt. He bit into his lip, amazed at the desire that suddenly ripped through him.

She probably prayed for his death daily, he reminded himself. She loathed him, fought him. He would not desire her in his life, he would keep her tamed within it! He tried to remember his hours with Bridget, but somehow they suddenly seemed to pale.

He didn't wait for the dawn, but was ready to sail by darkness, his only relief the sure knowledge that he had left her safely in his room, his brother Bryce there to guard against her determination to follow. His father, too, knew the extent of danger in having Melisande with him. He would never allow her to leave the house.

When he reached the coast of France and what he recognized as his own fortress, he was greeted soundly by Swen, Brenna, Philippe, Gaston, and Ragwald. The old man was glum and quiet, but seemed to respect and understand his determination not to bring Melisande home as yet. As they sat in the great hall, Swen told him of a count, Odo, who was quickly becoming a power in the region and who had recently visited the fortress. "We had him stay, of course, and entertained him richly in your name. What frightened me is that he is seeking peace and wants a treaty signed between you and young Geoffrey, heir to Gerald. I explained that it would be difficult to come to any peace with the man since his father had slain Count Manon. But Odo is anxious to see you, and a man keenly aware of the threat of the Danes facing us."

"Well, we must send a message to him, then, that I am in residence here."

"I have taken the liberty of doing so, having estimated that you would arrive this week."

He nodded, then told them that he was weary from the journey and would see them in the morning. He was glad to see how smoothly all was moving within the fortress. The trade between the two places had stood them well. Ships sailed from here with rich wines, salt, and finished clothing from the looms. They returned with metal workings, the finest weapons fashioned in his father's works, with raw wool, with the beautiful, delicate jewelry the Irish had become known for.

He discovered that Manon's chambers had been changed. The lord's things had been packed away. His own filled the trunks, his turtleshell comb sat upon the washstand. Someone, it seemed, assumed that he and his wife no longer kept separate quarters, for he discovered that Melisande's things were also there—a beautiful brush, her coat of mail, carefully laid away.

He lay awake again that night, wondering why. He seemed to ache from head to toe and constantly tossed and turned. He had to get her out of his mind because there was so much business at hand. But thoughts of Odo and Geoffrey seemed to haunt him through the night. He clenched and unclenched his fists, rolled to and fro. When he awoke, exhausted, he realized that he had never felt as possessive about anything in his life as he felt about this fortress.

Or Melisande.

He was not sure which was more important to him.

In the days that passed, his mind eased somewhat. He had dearly missed Brenna and Swen and was glad to discover that both Philippe and Gaston now gave him a fierce loyalty.

Gaston and Ragwald were his messengers during the months in which he exchanged communications with Count Odo. When they at last agreed to meet, Conar realized that he had actually formed unity within his own house—these men might have come from different places with varied backgrounds, but they had all decided that this was their home. They would work well together.

When Odo arrived to visit with him, the two Franks rode immediately behind him, showing their staunch support for the man who had wed Manon's heiress.

Conar discovered quickly that he admired Odo. The man was a decade his senior, far more action than words, and a wise, far-seeing warrior. He was not as tall as Conar, but Conar had gained his height from his father's people, and few men were so tall. Odo was broad-shouldered, husky, a well-trained man, dark-haired, hazel-eyed, impressive.

They spoke of the fact that Alfred had so successfully held his piece of England that the Danes were turning elsewhere. Then Odo broached the subject of peace

within their own realms, and Conar answered him as
honestly as he could.

"At this time there is no peace I am willing to sign with
Geoffrey. Perhaps he is innocent and eager to sue for
peace. But trust must be earned anew, Count Odo. His
father tricked and slew my wife's father. Perhaps in
time . . ."

Odo nodded, then leaned forward in the great hall of
the fortress. "Perhaps some arrangements could be made
to make you feel more at ease with Geoffrey being so
near a neighbor."

Conar arched a brow, willing to listen.

"Perhaps you and Melisande might renew your vows
before a bishop in Rouen, and you would receive greater
recognition from the Pope and the people."

"Perhaps such a thing can be arranged," he had
agreed. "I will pursue it, as you suggest."

"You and Melisande must be my guests. We will not
let this matter go too long."

Conar agreed. When Odo had left, Conar discovered
that his household had been at the various doors, listening. He quickly found himself joined at his table by
Brenna, Philippe, Swen, Gaston, and Ragwald.

"You are the Frankish astrologer," he told Ragwald.
"What is your opinion of this man?"

Ragwald looked at Brenna. It seemed that the two of
them had come to some deep understanding and could
speak through their eyes and mind. But Ragwald quickly
turned to Conar, ready to answer what he had been
asked. "It is my belief that Odo will prove to be the most
powerful of all Frankish barons."

Conar looked to Brenna. "There is no treachery in the
man?"

She shook her head slowly. "No, not within the man
himself. He—" She paused, seeming troubled.

"He what?" Conar demanded.

"I believe that in his quest for a united front, he may

upon occasion put his faith in those who are not deserving of it. But I agree with Ragwald. Perhaps the fate of the people will rest in his strength. He is a good ally.''

"I believe, then, that I will send for Melisande as he has suggested." He winced inwardly. He had finally ceased to think of her and had gone about the business of living here and strengthening his hold upon the land. He had discovered the fascinating widow of a Flemish baron residing in the town just west of the fortress, and though he had been dismayed to discover himself wondering about his wife upon occasion while he visited his mistress, he had begun to sleep again. He did not want his life haunted again by his wayward young wife.

But it was necessary that she come here. He intended to write to his father's house, asking that she be sent, but he decided that he did not want her sailing without him. He would go for her himself. He did, however, send her the message that he was coming. He did not tell her that he would be bringing her home, only that he was coming for her.

Let her stew with worry a little while. He was quite certain that though she managed to learn a great deal in his absence, humility and obedience would not be among the virtues she might have acquired. Melisande was ever proud, and far too independent.

But when he arrived at his father's house, he discovered to his great fury that his omission of *where* he was taking her had apparently not set well with her.

His father was not there to greet him when he arrived, and that in itself was curious. Nothing was prepared, and Erin was the greatest believer in the importance of Irish hospitality. A stranger was offered the finest display, therefore a returning son was offered all but the moon itself.

Distressed, Erin sat in the great hall, ordering a meal, and looking at him with her emerald eyes in a tempest. "We'd no idea you were coming!" she said.

"I very specifically told Melisande when I would arrive."

Erin frowned. "There must be some mistake. Melisande sailed with Daria and Bryce for Wessex just a week ago. Conar, your message must not have reached her."

Conar stood, feeling as if Jupiter himself were casting lightning bolts against his temple.

"No, Mother," he managed to say evenly. "I'm quite certain that Melisande received my message."

"Conar, I allowed her permission to sail, your father and I, for that matter. She was with your sister Daria and Bryce, and well under Eric's roof. They would go nowhere near the coast of France—"

"It's all right, Mother. She will be entirely safe under Eric's roof, I agree."

"I'm sorry, Conar! It's just that I have had her for so long that she is nearly a daughter. When she begged us to see Alfred's England, we saw no harm in it."

"There is surely no harm in her seeing Alfred's England, especially since my brother will guard my interests well," Conar assured her. He managed a smile.

"We shall send a message to Eric and have him return her immediately."

Conar shook his head. "Never mind. I will go for the girl myself. Perhaps Bryan will want to sail with me since it seems things are well in hand here for the moment. I will sail again in the morning."

"We can easily have her returned—"

"I think it important that I go for the girl myself," Conar said softly. He kissed his mother's forehead and started to leave her. Erin called him back softly.

"Conar!"

He turned to her. "Perhaps you deceive yourself, my son, to refer to Melisande as a *girl*. She's a woman now, and you must bear that in mind."

Conar nodded. "Aye," he agreed. "Aye, mother."

And so, years after he had been so determined to send

her away, he was coming for her. Now she was gone when he was ready to retrieve her.

Girl . . . *woman,* his mother had said.

He did not think that things between them had changed so very much.

A shudder suddenly rippled through him.

Perhaps, he thought, now they would.

The coast of Wessex lay before him, Alfred's land, his brother's land.

His hands were suddenly itching. He simply couldn't wait to set them upon her.

So she hadn't received his message, eh . . .

Oh, she had received it. And returned it in her very special fashion . . .

"Lower the sails!" he cried to his men. He could hear the ripple as his command was obeyed. From where he stood he could see his brother's fortress, even closer to the sea than his own.

Eric had come down to greet him. He saw his golden-haired brother, towering over Rhiannon, his wife, his hands lightly upon her shoulders. Bryce was there, too, waving an enthusiastic greeting. Even Daria had come to welcome them to shore. They were all there, the children, as well, his brother's young son at his knees, his infant daughter in his wife's arms.

Others were about. His brother's men, old friends. In fact, there was a goodly crowd awaiting them.

The only one missing was Melisande.

Deep within him he felt his blood begin to burn. Where, in the name of all the gods, was his wretched little minx?

He would find her. By God, he would find her!

And when he did, she would greet him.

10

"He's come, you know."

Melisande jumped up. She had been sitting by the side of the stream, her shoes off, her feet in the cool water, just letting the beautiful summer afternoon pass her by.

She hadn't come here alone. Gregory of Mercia was distant kin to Alfred of England, a guest in Eric's house, as was she. He was one year her senior, a handsome young man with reddish brown hair and a very quick smile.

He was constantly charming to her. They'd hunted together, ridden together, and talked endlessly together since she had come. They were even able to spend long moments of very comfortable silence together, as they had done here now, by the stream. Silence was a wonderful way in which to allow fantasies to grow. She'd actually been enjoying a few rather pleasant daydreams until Mergwin, the very strange old man who had once been the Irish Ard-Ri's close friend, interrupted the beauty of her lazy thoughts.

She had thought for a while that Conar might not come, that he might reach his parents' home at Dubhlain and decide that while he had managed to spare himself her presence this long, a little bit longer would certainly be advantageous to his peaceful state of mind.

She wished that he had stayed away. She was actually enjoying herself very much for the first time in years.

Even the simple matter of coming here. She had so enjoyed the stream since the first afternoon she had arrived. It was just beyond the castle walls, and no one seemed to think there was anything wrong with her riding here with Gregory since he was the very example of what a young nobleman should be. Not even Conar's brother Eric, the lord of the place, who bore an uncanny resemblance to his sibling. Melisande had nearly jumped away the first time she had seen him, she had been so startled by the resemblance. Except that this cub of the Norwegian Wolf seemed of a far more even temper than his brother. He had politely welcomed her to his home and inspected her with a certain amusement, arching a brow to his wife and wondering aloud why on earth Conar would be in France while sending his wife here. Melisande quickly reminded him that Conar hadn't sent her, that she had come because Daria suggested that she sail back with her, and because Bryce had assured her that she would be welcome, and that he would be glad to escort his sister and sister-in-law. She was very pleasant to Eric, of course, and refrained from mentioning that it was Conar's letter warning—very coldly, she reminded herself—that he was on his way home that had inspired her trip.

Eric seemed to accept her desire to travel, and they all appeared to consider it exceptionally proper for her to do so when she chose to travel where her brother-in-law could act as her guardian and protector. Olaf and Erin had given her their permission to come here, and so to Eric her being here must seem quite natural.

If that was the way that he saw it, then Melisande

was glad. Upon closer inspection of Eric, she realized that Conar was a little bit different. He was several years younger, and perhaps his eyes were a slightly lighter, cooler shade of blue. The brothers were very much alike, though, built alike, even moving alike, and in that, Melisande decided, they both must be very like their father.

She certainly had no intention of ever telling Conar, but she hadn't been able to spend the months—years!—living in his father's household and not come to care greatly for the man. He was stern, she had learned, but fair. She had constantly been amazed by his easy shift in languages, his attentiveness to others when they were speaking, and the sense of fairness that seemed to hold his strange kingdom of Norse and Irishmen together. Since the night she had failed in her attempt to reach home as a stowaway, she had known that her father-in-law had been keeping a watchful eye on her. He had even taken her out one day to try to explain just how dangerous it could be for her to fall into the wrong hands. That warning, however, had brought a curious smile to her lips, and she had asked him softly, "Dangerous for whom? The land is my inheritance, the people are mine to care for and guard, and yet for me to keep it, Conar imprisons me across a sea!"

"You are not imprisoned," the king of Dubhlain had assured her, yet he had seemed to assess her anew. "It is simply the way of things. You'll return home soon enough," he promised her. "You see, you've grown up now," he said very softly. "In time you'll have sons to inherit after you and Conar have gone, and that will give you both the strength to hold what you love so dearly."

She paled slightly at that, unwilling to tell the man who had come close to being a father to her that the last thing in the world she wanted to imagine—and certainly the last thing that would make her feel secure about her future—was that she and Conar should have children together. All she could think of was the cool blue fire in his eyes when he had caught her that night, and how she had lain awake for hours, shivering, feeling the heat of the man beside her.

He had come home late because he had been spending his hours with his mistress.

And he had most probably been determined to return to France without her so that he might spend his life with his slim blond rune reader, unencumbered by any necessity to look after her.

Conar was such a stranger. And yet, in ways, she knew him very well. He had managed so deftly to rule her life with an iron fist that she spent half her waking hours despising him, and half of her very best dreams meeting him in battle with a sword, and seeing him down on his knees at its end, begging for mercy.

Recently, since she had met Gregory of Mercia, she had decided that she would allow him the chance to live if he would help her acquire an annulment from their marriage. She had some beautiful dreams about returning to France with Gregory and living there with him, carefully tending to their land and their people, as her father had taught her. Upon occasion she did feel a qualm of guilt for her dreams, since Conar's family—though watching her with eagle eyes—had offered her every kindness, making her imprisonment—for yes, no matter what Olaf said, she was a prisoner—a gentle one. She could not possibly have sailed for France from the king of Dubhlain's house, she had been certain. Yet it had occurred to her, since she had received Conar's message and determined to come here, that once she was convinced Conar had sailed from France himself, she might well manage to do so from here. It had been an exciting thought.

Rhiannon, Eric's wife, was a golden blond beauty

who was extremely kind and charming and a great
deal of fun. Melisande had been very careful not to
say a single word about Conar that was unkind, or give
away her emotions regarding him. Rhiannon therefore
offered her every freedom in the world. It would be
difficult to curtail her activities anyway, since she
spent so much of her time with Daria, who had a
streak in her just as wild as that in any of her brothers.
Daria, despite her exuberance, usually had her brother's trust, and Melisande felt as if she had found her
best friend in her sister-in-law.

Everyone else had been lost to her, she thought
upon occasion. Marie de Tresse remained in France,
as did Ragwald—she had never imagined she would
miss that old tyrant—Philippe and Gaston. She wrote
constantly, and heard from them in return. None of
their letters had reached her here, though, since she
had been careful to leave as quickly as possible once
Daria had invited her.

She had tried to keep her distance from Eric since
she had come here, and that had been easy enough
because Rhiannon was so charming, and Daria so
constantly on the go, and the fortress on the sea such
a hive of activity. She had enjoyed her host's precocious and toddling young son, Garth, and his infant
daughter, Aleana. She kept herself busy and out of the
lord's way, which was easy—there was so much to see
in the countryside. Daria had been the one to origi-
nally suggest that she come to Wessex, and when she
had received the letter from Conar, informing her after
all this time that he was returning and she should be
prepared—well, it had certainly seemed the right time
to her to vacate Dubhlain!

She had enjoyed Mergwin, too. She was certain that
she had never met a man quite so old in all of her life,
but Mergwin's great age made him all the more fascinating. He was fantastic to look at, very tall and

skinny, with flapping robes, a wild mane of silver hair, and a beard that rippled past his knees. His eyes were ancient, almost the color of his hair, and all-seeing.

Too all-seeing. He watched her often with disapproval, but she found that she still liked him very much, for though he taunted and warned her upon occasion, he also spent long hours with her talking about Eire and England and history and her own country's past—and future. He reminded her very much of Ragwald and seemed a link to home for her—even if he was the one person who seemed to read something that was not quite innocent into her relationship with Gregory.

"I repeat, milady," Mergwin said firmly. "*He's* here."

Gregory frowned, looking from a suddenly pale Melisande to Mergwin. He plucked his feet from the water and smiled pleasantly. "*Who's* here?"

"Conar MacAuliffe," Melisande said briefly.

Mergwin bowed deeply to Gregory. "The lady's husband," he added carefully.

Melisande waved a dismissing hand in the air. "In truth, Mergwin, this lady has no husband, only a dictating tyrant."

"Milord Eric's brother?" Gregory murmured.

Melisande inhaled and exhaled slowly, wanting to shake him. "There is nothing to be afraid of," she said, staring at Mergwin.

"Oh, indeed not!" Mergwin exclaimed, smiling at Gregory. "After all, milady Melisande is not afraid in the least, is she?"

Melisande grated her teeth together, not letting her eyes fall from Mergwin's. "Not in the least," she assured him. And she wasn't afraid, she told herself, she was just deeply disappointed—and angry. Conar had been so damned determined to be rid of her, to send her away from home. And now, when she had finally begun to enjoy the sweet taste of freedom, he was appearing. Well, she wasn't a child anymore. And he wasn't going to dictate to her forever, and after all this time she'd see him when she damned well chose to do so.

"Perhaps you might wish to come to the house," Mergwin suggested, his tone annoyed. "I'm sure that the ships have docked by now, but if your lord husband finds that you have, at the least, hurried to meet him there . . ."

"I'm not hurrying anywhere."

Gregory stood, his eyes upon her, still caring, but deeply concerned. "Perhaps—"

"Perhaps nothing!" she cried. "Mergwin, if you wish it, you go back to the house and greet him. You may send my regards, and I will come along shortly. I—" She broke off for a moment, a chill running down her spine as she remembered that she had come here under false pretenses and that he had sailed specifically to retrieve her.

Well, if he had let her stay home where she longed to be, then he wouldn't have had to retrieve her.

"I'll give Conar your apologies, and assure him that you will be with him soon," Mergwin said. "Very soon."

"But that's not what I wish—" Melisande began. It didn't matter. Mergwin was gone. He had been her friend, her companion. She realized bitterly that that didn't matter at all. Mergwin had served the Ard-Ri, and then his daughter, and thus his son-in-law. And now there was no ill that could be done by the offspring of Olaf and Erin. Once Conar entered upon the scene, Mergwin served him. She should stand well advised.

She sighed, watching the old man go, unease sweeping through her. Maybe she should follow him, be with him. No! She wasn't going to return to Eric's coastal fortress. She didn't want to see Conar any sooner than she had to, and she wasn't going to hide behind the old Druid's robes.

She suddenly wished with all her heart that she had somehow managed to run away from Conar years ago.

But she couldn't have done that. She intended to return to her own land—*her* inheritance.

Gregory was still standing, barefoot and awkward, looking at her, his eyes warm, his young face handsome and sincere. "Melisande, you said you barely knew him, that he wouldn't come for you. I truly think that perhaps you should go. You can only make matters worse. You'll have to go to him eventually. You did marry him."

She walked toward him, shaking her head, placing her hands upon his shoulder. She came to him for strength, for support. They were of a height. She felt such a warmth for him, such a gentle affection! "Maybe I don't really have to go back!" she said softly but desperately.

"But—"

"I married him, yes. There had been a battle, my father had just been killed. He was strong, and my people seemed to think we needed that strength. But we parted right after. I was very young. It has never been a real marriage," she said earnestly. "Truly, he has been like a guardian, nothing more. I'm of age now. Old enough to choose, old enough to know my own mind. And I've beautiful lands of my own, Gregory. They are mine, you know, not his. Perhaps . . ."

He inhaled swiftly, staring at her. A hunger went into his eyes for her, or for the promise of a rich future, she wasn't sure. But the moment was suddenly very sweet. The scent of the earth was rich and inviting, the sound of the bubbling brook seemed to lull her senses. His mouth was so very close to hers.

She leaned forward, not really knowing what she

intended, or what beckoned her. Her lips touched his.
They were soft, pliable. She felt no great desire, just
the most tender warmth, and still it was very nice. His
hand pressed suddenly upon her shoulders. He
touched her cheek, lifted his face from hers, met her
eyes, and kissed her once again.

And it was then that she heard her name, and a wall
of ice seemed to form around her.

"Melisande!"

She had never heard it spoken so coldly, with such
a fierce bite of anger. She didn't need to turn to feel
the ice continue to form. A great wave of dismay
washed over her, cascading fiercely down her back,
causing icy rivulets to sweep through her.

It was one thing to come to him when she so desired,
or leave him waiting as he had so often left her. It was
another to be caught like this when she really hadn't
been guilty of anything.

Conar remained behind her. She did not want to
turn to see him.

But Gregory was watching him.

He stepped swiftly away from her. So swiftly, she
might have fallen had she not made a valiant effort to
balance herself. She saw Gregory's eyes first, and they
were wide with sinking fear and vast dismay. She
stared at him, stunned as he fell to his knees in the few
inches of water, head bowed low.

"Milord! Your pardon."

He stood quickly, and Melisande turned at last.

Conar had indeed come.

It was amazing. Apparently, he hadn't been willing
to wait for her to come to him—startling after all this
time. He had Thor with him and sat atop the huge
black horse in a rich crimson mantle, ermine-edged.
His brooch held the shield of the wolves, his father's
insignia from the house of Vestfold, while his sword
hilt was decorated with one of the Celtic crosses of

Eire. He sat upon Thor as easily as always, silent, still, staring at them both with the blue eyes that cut like fire and ice.

She was not afraid of him, she assured herself, she was the injured party in this. She had been sent away from him—from her home—by force. Equally, she had been kept away from home by force. He lived his life as he chose, with no thought for her. She owed him nothing. She was suddenly quite determined to get an annulment.

She moistened her lips, dismayed that Gregory was so quickly and ardently intimidated by Conar. Perhaps Conar was intimidating, he seemed so tall upon the horse, so broad and as if molded of steel, hard and striking with his sweep of golden hair and rugged features. She swallowed hard again for strength, swearing that he would no longer hold her beneath his will.

"So you've come, Viking!" she said lightly, determined that she had done nothing wrong.

He nudged Thor, and the huge war-horse carefully picked his way down to the water. Gregory struggled for the sword he wore in the scabbard at his side. Before he could begin to draw the weapon, Conar's steel was touching his hand where it lay upon his sword hilt.

"Leave it, boy," Conar warned.

"You'll not hurt him—!" Melisande began, but those glacial Viking eyes were on her quickly, and to her dismay, she found herself falling silent.

"No, I'll not hurt him. I do not do battle with boys."

Gregory was down on his knees again, kissing Conar's boot. "I thank you for your mercy, milord. I—"

"Gregory!" Melisande cried, deploring his subjugation.

"Ah, Gregory. I believe she thinks you should be quite willing to die for her. But, alas, I am not willing

to slay my brother's young kin for my lady's foolishness. Go home, boy. Now.''

"Milord!" Gregory agreed. He was instantly on his
feet.

Melisande discovered that he could run very fast.
He raced from the stream to his horse, mounting him
in a frenzy, and quickly disappearing.

And she was, quite suddenly, alone with Conar, her
husband, the stranger she knew only too well.

He stared at her, very long and very hard. The
rivulets of ice that had come dancing down her spine
now seemed to be full rivers. She forced herself not to
move, returning his cool stare. The silence between
them seemed incredible. She could hear the soft gurgle
of the water, the swaying whisper of the trees. It was
so beautiful here, so peaceful, with little rocks in the
way for the water to dance upon. She heard the
chirping of a bird, and still no sound at all from him.

"Well?" he murmured at last.

Melisande hiked a finely arched brow, determined
that he'd never know how she stood there shivering.
"Well, what, milord?"

He dismounted. She found herself backing away a
step, and then forced to halt as he stood before her
since she had backed her way against a tree.

"It didn't occur to you that I might have been ever
so slightly displeased with the fact that you fled across
the sea to England when I sent a message specifically
to inform you that I was coming for you? Ah, and
then, when you knew I was coming here, you didn't
think it might be wise to greet me with the others, and
somewhat soothe an ever so slightly heated temper?"

Ever so slightly heated . . .

She could see the fury of his pulse, ticking against
the corded strength of his throat. Maybe she was a
fool. She'd fought him before and lost every time.

But she'd been a child then. She refused to be one any longer.

"Well, milord, you will forgive me," she replied smoothly, her chin high, "if I refuse to take any message of yours to heart. You sent me away bound up in a sheet once. Therefore it is difficult to believe that you are eager to find me once again."

"Trust me," he warned, his voice with an edge of danger, "I would like to see you bound in a sheet at this moment." He stared at her still, shaking his head with disbelief. "By the gods! I cannot begin to believe your behavior now! Have you no sense?"

"Sense?"

She gasped as the tip of his sword swung like mercury in the air, coming to rest just at her throat. "Some men would take great offense at your actions, lady. Not only do you defy me, but I find you in the act of seducing some poor boy in the woods."

She froze for a moment, her breath gone, wondering if she hadn't gone too far, if he would, in fact, skewer her through. She inhaled raggedly, seeking some emotion in his eyes, but there was nothing there except for Nordic blue frost. So she had offended him. All that he had done to her meant nothing.

Let him skewer her.

She touched the sword with her fingers and thrust it from herself, challenging him. "Really? Some men would take offense! Well, milord, I have taken grave offense, many a time. So you are angry that I did not run to beg your pardon when I heard that you were near! And you are disturbed that I have acquired friends within the households of your family. Pray forgive if I do not quiver with fear! Just what is it that you intend to do, milord, in retribution? Steal my land, perhaps? Seize my property? Why, I do believe that's already been done!"

"Take care, Melisande, I can surely find something."

"Ah, well! I don't think that slitting my throat the Viking way would serve you well. If I die, my property will revert to my father's nearest male heir, I believe."

He sheathed his sword, staring at her. "You are quite incredible, Melisande. Time has not improved your manners in the least."

He seemed so calm. She had done well to stand up to him, she thought. She still wished that the tree was not so tight to her back, that he did not seem to tower over her so. He created a certain breathlessness within her. She had felt it all that miserable night when they had last met. She felt it now. That and a heat that spread throughout while she continued to shiver at the same time.

She arched a brow again. "I have been left in the care of your family, milord. Surely, then, I have matured as you might have wished."

"Umm. Perhaps. And then again, perhaps it is a pity that I have not had much time to see to your *maturing* myself!"

Her hands pressed against the tree at her back. She realized that she was using it for strength. "Shouldn't you be with your family now?" she demanded.

"I don't think so," he told her. He took a step closer. One of his hands landed against the tree, as well, just above her head and to her right. No matter what her sense of victory had been, she discovered then that she was tempted to spin to her left and run. She forced herself to stand still, meeting his gaze.

"I think I'm exactly where I need to be. With my wife. Remember, Melisande? That is what you are. My wife."

She moistened her lips, her eyes falling from his as a new wave of shivers swept over her.

"By a contract only. It means nothing."

"It means everything. And you will learn that, mi-lady!"

"It has meant everything to you—"

"You are a little fool—my love. I tried to consider your feelings. Your dislike for me—"

"Ah, milord! Dislike? How gentle a word! I *despise* you!" she assured him swiftly.

"Forgive me for so sorely understating your gentle heart, Melisande. But then you must bear this in mind. It's a good thing the boy wasn't a shade older," he snapped out, his voice so raw that she could feel its fever. "I'd not have stayed my hand."

The passion and fury in his words suddenly frightened her, not so much for herself as for Gregory. Perhaps she had wanted Gregory to stand up to Conar, but now she was afraid. Conar was older and harder and far more experienced. He had learned everything he knew from his father and the fiercest fighters on earth. He was built like brick and steel and remained as quick and agile as a buck.

"Nothing happened here!" she whispered, furious herself. She didn't want to whisper, she wanted to cry out. But then suddenly she saw her opening. "Yet if you are in the least concerned, I beg you, have this marriage annulled. I'm sure—"

"Nothing happened?" he demanded, arching a golden brow.

"Nothing. You may ask Gregory to swear so before God. Gregory is a Christian noble—"

"How applaudable. I'm quite sure that he is many things I am not!"

She didn't like the cool tone in his voice. He was still absolutely furious, and she was painfully aware of it. "Speak with him if you so desire."

"Ah, but I've no intention of asking that poor besot-ted boy a thing."

"Then if you've doubts—"

"If I've doubts, I will still them myself, milady."

Jesu, if he came any closer, he would be on top of her! She wished fervently that she had realized he was coming, that she had been in Eric's house, that she had stood with his family to greet him. Anything to take him away from her now. She was too keenly aware of his heat and vitality, his height and breadth.

The fury in his eyes . . .

And that simmering of tension within him. He stayed very still. He didn't touch her, didn't reach for her throat, and didn't begin to threaten to strike her. But still, just looking in his eyes and feeling the great warmth that seemed to spill from him, she realized ever more fully just how angry he was. His temper was under control, but just barely. His shirt sleeve had fallen back when he leaned against the tree over her, and she could see the taut bulge of muscle within his arms, the sinew, the steel of it.

She stiffened her spine, wishing that she were not finding it so hard to speak.

"No true marriage, eh?" he said suddenly and very softly. She realized that he had come upon them when she had been telling Gregory that she didn't consider herself obliged to Conar in the least. If the tree hadn't been behind her then, she might have fallen. But she wouldn't be able to bear having him so very near her much longer. She wanted to scream as it was, strike out against him.

"You're extremely rude to listen to other people's conversations."

"No true marriage, and I am merely a guardian?"

A rush of color made its way to her cheeks. "You shouldn't have listened."

"You shouldn't have spoken."

She inhaled, wishing she could run from him now, and it didn't matter where. If she took a step, he would drag her back, and once he had moved, once he had touched her . . .

"I didn't say anything that I didn't mean," she informed him in a brash rush. "The land is mine. You've no interest in me, that has certainly been evidenced over the years. An annulment could surely be had easily enough, if we were both agreed upon it. You could move onward wherever you liked, you'd be free—"

"Ah, yes. The property is yours. I'm the one who risked my life for it, but the property is yours."

"The inheritance—"

"No."

"Damn you—"

"No."

He was a tyrant. Standing here condemning her for a silly tryst in the woods with Gregory when he kept mistresses by the scores, not to mention his precious Brenna. He was too close, he was suddenly denying her all her dreams. It was perhaps the most foolish thing she had ever done, but she lashed out at him with fury, her fingertips catching his cheeks before he had a chance to lash his fingers around her wrist.

"No!" she cried, trying with all her strength to wrench free. She tore away from the tree, whirling before him. Her nails clawed at his hands but he didn't seem to feel them, his eyes were so hard upon hers.

"I gave you playtime, Melisande," he said, his voice still raw, his tone husky. "Time to grow. Time to live. I was told so very often that you were old enough to be a wife, but I still gave you time. Well, my love, that playtime is over now. You've wanted to enter the real world, milady, you shall do so now."

She managed to wrench her wrist from his hold. "I want my world!" she cried to him. "My home, my land. I do not want you!"

"Your home and your land come with your husband, Melisande."

"With or without your help, I will get an annulment!" she swore to him.

He was silent for a moment, his jaw locked, his eyes like ice.

He stood with his foot resting upon a rock. She didn't know what stupid demon possessed her then, but he always managed to make her behave wildly, rashly. She suddenly rushed toward him, hurling her weight at him. He was falling, she realized triumphantly. The great Prince Conar had fallen into the cool bubbling brook, and his very handsome mantle was sodden. She spun around, ready to run at long last, but she gasped instead, for his fingers were wound tightly around the hem of the blue linen tunic she wore over the deeper blue full-sleeved bliaut beneath. "Let go!" she cried, grasping at her hem.

"I'll never let go," he promised her.

The next second she was down in the water with him, her clothing drenched, her hair soaking down her back. She gasped for breath, then realized that he lay at her side. In a split second she was up, and running once again.

She tore downstream in the shallow water, inhaling deeply, wishing just to escape him for a while. She needed some shadowed sanctuary now, somewhere to still her racing heart, to calm her spirit.

She paused, jumping upon one foot as she rubbed the other, for she had hit hard upon a rock in the stream. She thought she heard someone in pursuit and spun back. He wasn't there. The trees, dense here, surrounded her with their green darkness. Rays of light shone between the swaying branches in delicate flashes of brilliance. She narrowed her eyes, searching for him, then turned to run again.

And there he was. He had mounted Thor and ridden

the crest of the stream to come before her. She grit her teeth and turned to run back. The war-horse slammed through the water, spinning to cut her off. She turned, and he was there again. Once more she ran, once more the horse followed her, cutting off her route of escape each time.

"What!" she cried. "The great Lord of the Wolves cannot catch his own wife on foot?"

She panted, playing for time. He leaned down to her, blue eyes acute. "I use whatever is at my disposal, milady, to gain what I am after. And I repeat, milady, I will never let you go."

He dismounted from his horse, water spraying from his boots as his feet hit the water. She was nearly out of breath, but she backed away from him. In doing so, she tripped upon a stone. She cried out, falling backward into the water. He reached out for her, catching her before she could strike the ground. In a second she was swept up into his arms, and long strides quickly brought them from the water to the pine-laden floor beneath the towering trees. She was shivering wildly from the cold of the stream, from the feel of his arms.

He set her down and straddled her.

"Let me go!" Melisande whispered.

"I told you, milady, I will never let you go."

She brought her hands up to slam them against his chest. They were captured within his grasp. She stared into his eyes, seeking something in their blue depths. She bit her lip, still staring at him as he leaned low against her, pinning her hands to the ground just above her head.

She had felt such ice when she had first seen him. Now she felt as if all the fires of hell had invaded her. Her breath came too quickly, mercury seemed to leap through her. Despite her great heat, she shivered suddenly, looking at him, at the hard lines of his face, at the startling color of his eyes. At the breadth of his chest, at the ripple of muscle within his arms as he held her.

She had hated him forever, so it seemed. Yet to her great dismay, she realized now that she didn't actually hate him, she hated what he had done to her. Not only was there her anger against him, there was something else, too. She didn't know exactly what it was. He was a challenge, she had always enjoyed defying him.

Even though she had meant to win.

Now, having him atop her, she was frightened of him in a way she had never been before. Because she wasn't really frightened of him, she was frightened of herself, of the way that he was making her feel, of the sudden longing within her for something that she really didn't understand. She moistened her lips, shaking her head. "An annulment would make so much sense. Your heart always seems to remain in your father's country, you would always fight there first. There is so much else that you want!" she told him breathlessly.

"There is nothing else that I want," he corrected her. "At this moment there is nothing else in the world that I want."

"We've got to go back," she said desperately. "They'll miss you, your family will miss you."

"*Now* you're worried about returning to the fortress!" he exclaimed softly.

"Please, milord, if—"

"Ah, lady!" he murmured, and it seemed his cool blue eyes raked her face, her heart, and soul. "It's far too late for 'Please'! Alas, I'm afraid that I must convince you that an annulment is entirely out of the question."

She stared at him, his meaning slowly dawning upon her.

"No!" she protested.

But her protest was quickly swallowed by his lips.

 **11**

He hadn't known what he intended when he came to the stream to find Melisande.

He might have been so angry at first that his inclination might have been to drag her back by the hair.

But then he had seen her, and everything had seemed to stop.

She had been changing, subtly, as time passed them by. He had known when he had left her that she was swiftly leaving youth behind and becoming a woman.

Still, he had not imagined the creature he met today.

She had grown very tall, lithe, supple, graceful. She moved effortlessly and with a gentle sway. She had grown into exquisite curves that added a mesmerizing sensuality to her slightest movement. And her face, her beautiful, exotic face . . .

Her cheeks had become slimmer, adding a fascinating maturity to her. Her lashes had grown richer, her wealth of silken ebony hair even longer. And her eyes, when they touched upon his at long last . . .

Their violet was open, compelling. In his life, he knew, he had never seen more beautiful eyes. Indeed, in all his life he had never seen a more beautiful woman. And this one was his wife. The pretty, precocious child had grown into a stunning adult.

It hadn't surprised him that she didn't come to greet him. Or that she hadn't been within the fortress walls. She would always do whatever was within her power to defy him.

It had stunned him to see her with the youth, Gregory. Watching her, seeing her earnest conversation, he thought back to the day when he had watched her with one of the young guards in the courtyard of her father's fortress. The feelings of anger and jealousy that stole over him shocked him. He could scarcely catch his breath. His heart slammed within his chest, and it was all that he could do to control his temper.

She was incredible, Melisande. More than willing to defy him, she was determined to go much further. When he walked to her, he saw that she was willing to fight him forever, her chin high, her eyes blazing, meeting his, determined that she had done nothing wrong.

And determined that she would have an annulment.

He had to have her now, he thought. He had to have her now quite simply because she had to forget that thought. He had taken her as his wife, he had taken Count Manon's place, the land was his, the fortress was his, and she was his. He had discovered, looking at her today, touching her, even waging war with her, she was his. Their destinies had been locked together for a long time now. Now she was his.

He wanted her, with a fever such as he had never known before, with a desire that blinded him to all else. She lay beneath him, cool and wet from the stream, her flesh like marble, her lips like a rose.

Warm when he touched them, full, sensual. He touched them with the fullness of his mouth, pressed inward with his tongue, seeking the play of hers. She lay still a moment, and he seemed to taste all the haunting sweetness within her, touched a wealth of fire and heat. She tried to twist from him, gasping, and he raised his head from hers, meeting her eyes.

"Please!" she said. "We've all this time between us. I don't know you anymore, I'm not accustomed to—"

"Kissing?" he asked softly against her lips. "Ah, but it appeared you were adept at it when you were kissing the young Saxon boy!"

She tried to shove against him. She couldn't budge his chest, nor twist away from beneath him.

She stared into his eyes again, angry. "You've absolutely no right—"

"Indeed?"

Blazing violet eyes met his. "You spend years neglecting me, milord, and becoming quite adept at all manner of things yourself."

"I'm ever so sorry I've neglected you. I intend to rectify that now."

His mouth descended hard upon hers, his hand easing from her wrist to hold her cheek. He stroked its exquisite lines, feeling the softness of her flesh. Her hand pushed his shoulder. She writhed and twisted, but he granted no quarter, not moving in the least. She tasted of sweet wine and mint, and he kissed her ever more deeply, fascinated, exploring, hungry, his tongue pressing hers. A pulse came alive within him, hammering, demanding. A whimper left her throat, and he lifted his lips from hers at last, fascinated then by the sleek wetness upon them, the way they parted slightly as she gasped for breath, those violet eyes now condemning and seething.

"You can't mean to do—this—here. In the woods."

"I'm quite partial to streams, milady. And woods. The sway of the branches, the kiss of the breeze. And, I might remind you, you were quite willing to be here with another man."

She shook her head wildly. "You came upon a moment's warmth—"

"I am partial to warmth, too, milady," he assured her, his voice hard.

"It was a gesture of friendship—"

"Indeed, I am waiting for such friendship."

"It was a tender kiss—"

"It was scarce a kiss at all," he replied with a disdainful snort.

"And you are so much better!" she cried.

"Indeed, I am," he murmured, "and I'm damned sure that you know the difference!"

"Your Viking sword is going to rust!" she warned him.

"My Viking sword will soon be sheathed."

She went so pale that he was suddenly convinced that nothing had ever gone further than the kiss she had shared here today, but even that had to be rectified. As long as she continued as she was, she lived with the hope that she would acquire an annulment from him.

His temper soared suddenly. What had she wanted out of life? He had come at the right time, he had slain the man who had murdered her father. Marriages were arranged, and hers should have been no great hardship.

But that didn't matter. Wanting her did.

Yet, despite himself, despite the great anguish of his desire, he suddenly felt a welling of pity within him. He didn't want to rape his own bride.

And maybe there was just a little bit of guilt mingled with that emotion. How had he ever managed to neglect her so?

Easily, he reminded himself. She had been hostile and superior from the very moment they had met. And perhaps he had even known from that moment that one day he would be paying this price, wanting her with a haunting desperation, falling prey to the violet in her eyes, her exquisite beauty.

"After all this time!" she whispered, sensing his hesitation. "Not here, not now, like this!"

For once her eyes seemed to be nothing other than pleading. They captured some small piece of his heart, and he finally felt the chill of the water that soaked their clothing.

"If not now . . . ?"

"Please . . ."

He shook his head slowly, wondering what would be gained from this delay. "What do I gain?" he asked her softly. "You are too eager to escape me, Melisande."

"I will make it up to you. Tonight," she promised swiftly, "as it should be."

"Ah," he said softly. "So you would barter for time."

There was a sizzle in her eyes once again when she reminded him, "I have had years of it, milord, I cannot see what a few more hours can matter."

"Melisande, with you, it might well matter greatly. I wonder if it will be worth my while to take the chance! Surely there is some other hapless lad you might find along the way . . ."

"How dare you—" she began furiously, but a quick look in his eyes seemed to remind her of just what she had been doing when he had come upon her this evening. "There is no one else to come upon," she said frigidly.

"Hmm. I do have brothers here."

"Your flesh and blood," she murmured bitterly.

"I think," he said, a taunt to his words, yet the taunt against himself, "I think I shall die a thousand deaths if I leave you now."

"You've never had difficulty leaving me before."

"Ah, but things have changed. You have changed."

"I'll see that you are not disappointed," she promised rashly, pushing against him then. She'd had her victory, she sensed it.

But it wasn't going to be that easy for her. He leaned low against her. "I want a willing wife, my love," he told her. "Bathed and perfumed, waiting and willing."

She was silent, staring at him, waiting for him to move away from her, he was certain.

"Your promise, Melisande."

"Yes!"

He *would* die just a little bit if he let her go now, he thought, fiercely gritting his teeth against the longing that still assailed him.

But the promise she had made him . . .

It was too intriguing. He had to see if she would willingly keep it.

He leapt up and reached a hand down to her. When she stood before him, her lashes quickly fell over her eyes. She started to turn away, but he caught her arm.

"I'm just going for my horse—"

"I think that you can ride with me. Your horse can follow."

She wanted to argue the point, he knew. Melisande wanted to argue anything that he suggested. But she kept silent, and he realized that she was shivering as he lifted her onto Thor and leapt up behind her. She was stiff as she sat before him, and they dripped together as he guided Thor from the stream. He found her horse tethered at the water's edge, and grabbed the white mare's reins to lead her back to the fortress.

She was silent, trying impossibly to keep a distance between them. Yet when they reached his brother's handsome fortress by the sea, entered the gates, and came before the keep, she had a question for him, violet eyes suspicious and narrowed. "Why have you suddenly come for me?"

He didn't answer, and she twisted around to look into his eyes. "I'll tell you tonight—my love," he promised.

She swore softly, trying to dismount from the stallion, but discovering that she was caught because he would not let her down. He dismounted himself and reached up for her.

"I can get down on my own!"

"Give in, Melisande. Let us have some peace!"

She stared at him, shaking her head, her eyes blazing. "You seek peace, milord? Not with me. I have been too long neglected and abused."

A smile suddenly pulled at the corner of his lip. Without her consent he set his hands firmly upon her, and her sodden body pressed close to his as he lifted her down without allowing her toes to quite touch the ground. Unwilling, her hands fell upon his equally sodden shoulders.

"The neglect I will cease," he promised. "But you had best take care, else the abuse will have just begun!"

"Conar!"

His brother Eric was calling him. He set Melisande upon her feet.

She spun around to leave him. The long wet strands of her hair flew in the air with the vehemence of her movement, slapping him in the face.

He caught her shoulder, wiping his damp cheeks, pulling her back hard against him. Eric was coming to them, a frown knitting his brow.

"I see that you have found your wife, but are you two all right?"

It was certainly a fair enough question. They both still dripped.

Conar smiled, lifting a length of Melisande's ebony hair, stroking it gently with his fingers. "Indeed, Eric, we are just fine. Melisande was so eager to greet me

when she saw me that she cast us both into the
stream."

She shivered suddenly beneath his touch, rigid as
steel, but she didn't deny his words. She was very
cold, he realized, and so pressed her forward. "Go in,
milady, bathe. I will join you soon enough."

She sped past them, and Eric clapped a hand upon
Conar's shoulders. "Come. Let's indulge in some of
that very fine wine you have brought me."

"I'm afraid that I am dripping—"

"I'll have the wine brought to your quarters."

Together they entered the hall. Rhiannon was ordering the table seating, and they paused there for a
moment, Eric explaining that his brother and sister-in-
law had fallen in the brook.

"Aye," Rhiannon said. "I sent your wife to her
room with a tub and water." She hesitated a moment,
watching Conar curiously. "She is in the far room at
the left of the stairs. I have had your things sent to the
chamber beside it. There is a door beneath the tapestry connecting the two. Is that what you wish?"

He caught his sister-in-law's shoulders and kissed
her cheek, careful not to drip upon her beautiful blue
gown. "It is perfect," he assured her.

"A tub and hot water will arrive soon," she advised.

"And—" Eric began.

"And wine, milord husband," Rhiannon added with
some amusement.

"Thank you, my love," Eric said. He had no difficulty sweeping her into his arms, and did so, placing a
tender kiss upon her lips. Watching them together,
Conar felt as if something seared his heart, and for the
first time he realized that he was jealous of this
brother. Not because he had come here and so firmly
established himself on the land, but because he had
done so in such . . . happiness. He served a great king,
he ruled a strong household, and he was loved by this

elegant golden blond beauty. He had a fine strong son
and an infant daughter. There was warmth here that
seemed to radiate from the hearth, and the laughter
spread to the coldest nook and cranny of the place.

He hadn't really been looking for warmth, he realized. He hadn't even known that he desired it, until
this moment. He had been too busy to do so, fighting
in Eire as he was obliged, then spending his time upon
his land, determined only to keep his grasp upon it.

Melisande's land.

He thanked Eric himself and started for the stairway
ahead of his brother, gritting his teeth. She accused
him now of neglect! What other choices had he had?
She'd been so young, he'd had to let her grow.

When he reached the room high above the hall with
his brother behind him, Conar discovered that Eric's
servants were pouring the last of a steaming caldron
into a wooden hip tub for him. He cast aside his
drenched clothing and stepped gratefully into the tub,
sighing. Eric handed him a chalice of wine, and Conar
grinned at his brother.

"You'd make someone a fine wife, Eric, cub of the
Wolf!"

Eric frowned at him severely and then laughed.
"Alas, brother, I think something is lacking in your
life if you're so easily pleased." He took a seat upon
a carved chair before the hearth, resting his feet upon
a deerskin-covered stool, still grinning at Conar as he
lifted his own chalice. "To your health, Conar!"

"And to yours," Conar quickly responded, then fell
silent for a moment. He shrugged. "There's a lot
lacking in my life," he murmured. "But then, when I
look back, there's little I might have changed."

Eric lifted a hand, comfortably leaned back, shrugging his shoulders. "I don't see the cause of your
displeasure. They are already calling you the Frankish
Wolf, the great savior from the house of Vestfold. You

earned your reputation fighting with Father and for Uncle Niall. You apparently bested the Danes so well on the coast of France with your first encounter that they are still speaking about it.''

Conar leaned back in the water, soaking his face and hair, letting the steam sweep around him. He surfaced, and blinked the warm water from his eyes. ''Having is one thing. Keeping is another,'' he said wearily. He drummed his fingers on the tub and looked at Eric. ''Ever since the day I first sailed to the coast of France at Manon's invitation, when I fought the Danes there and won the land, I have been hearing reports of a massive Danish army that is gathering together to invade the Frankish kingdoms, straight to the heart of Paris.''

''I've heard these rumors, too,'' Eric told him. ''Alfred has done well here in the southern kingdom. Many Danes have grown weary of going against him, and so they are looking to greener fields. There is little that binds your country together, Conar. The Frankish nobles are too divided, as the land has been since it was all split between Lothar and his brothers, Charlemagne's heirs. The power lies in estates, such as yours, and in powerful barons—such as yourself.''

Conar arched a brow, sighing. ''Perhaps. I have formed an alliance with a man, Count Odo, and I believe that we will both defend the land until the end. But I've also acquired enemies.''

''Geoffrey, son of Gerald, neighboring count,'' Eric said lightly.

Conar arched a brow. ''What have you heard?''

Eric shrugged. ''Jugglers, singers, lute players, all travel, brother. Not to mention that we have a large and talkative family. Still, there has been a very long poem written about you saving your wife from the arms of a fiend.''

''Umm. Is that how the poem goes?''

"Well," Eric replied, rising to refill Conar's chalice, "that's how it goes, aye. But I saw Melisande watch a rendition of the poem, and it strikes me that she may think she has traded one fiend for another."

Conar stared swiftly at Eric, only to realize that his brother was amused. His fingers gripped the edges of the tub as he willed himself to fight his temper. His first urge was to leap out of the tub and wrestle Eric to the floor—the whole lot of them had tussled enough as children. But they weren't children anymore.

Besides which, his brother was goading him.

He leaned comfortably back in the tub, laying his white linen bath cloth over his eyes.

"If I should recall," he murmured thoughtfully, "your wife was less than enamored of you when first you met. In fact—if I remember correctly from that very talkative family of ours, didn't she once impale your thigh with an arrow?"

He felt a hand upon his head, ready to push him beneath the surface, and he laughed, ducking under, coming back up. He threw the linen cloth at Eric, managing to soak his handsome shirt and tunic.

"Alas! The trials of a large family!" Eric murmured.

Conar grinned but then sobered. "I know she thinks that I have been cruel to her."

"It is difficult to know what she thinks. She is gracious and polite, but keeps her distance from me. She enjoys both Rhiannon and Daria—and Bryce, for that matter. She is quick to laugh with the children, and her eyes are very gentle and warm when she takes them. But despite her closeness with Daria and Rhiannon, I don't believe she shares her true thoughts with them." He shrugged. "Daria is, after all, your sister, your blood. A fool could see how close this family is, and your wife is hardly a fool. Indeed, she's an extremely clever young woman—and a talented one, in many ways. I've seen her in the courtyard with Bryce, learning swordplay from him, and teaching him a few moves now and then, I'd warrant."

Conar shook his head irritably. "The day I met her she was clad in gilded mail, having led her troops— and having fallen directly into the hands of the enemy! Can you wonder that I have tried to keep her safe?" He scowled suddenly, flashing Eric a quick glance. "She teaches more than swordplay, by the way, brother. When I came upon her by the stream, she had Rhiannon's young kinsman well within her spell."

"Gregory."

"She was instructing him in love play."

"Gregory?" Eric repeated, startled.

"You needn't be alarmed. I am convinced she was making a last effort to seduce the lad into somehow saving her from me. I believe it was an innocent encounter on his behalf—he was quick enough to beg my pardon."

"He's just a boy—"

"Aye!" Eric sighed. "Yet at his age, you and I had already ridden with our father many times."

"Father knew what we all must face. Alfred is now hungry for learning. He has fought and worked hard. He is due his time with musicians and mathematicians and learned men. I believe it is his wish that Gregory join the clergy, though he will leave the decision to the boy. However, I must beg your humble apology as well, Conar, for your countess has been residing beneath my roof—"

"At her own volition, Eric. She came here to thwart me, and truly, I know her far better than you can imagine. You have faulted me in no way, brother." He hesitated a moment. "Again, I realize that she considers me a monster. A Viking monster. Yet, Eric, I never intended cruelty, though she has tempted me to much. There is so much at stake! Gerald was distant kin to her father, yet ready to kill him! I'm aware that his son covets both the land and Melisande.''

"Surely the church would never sanction a marriage between Melisande and this man, even if she were free to be wed!''

Conar shook his head. "I don't know if you truly see the picture. In Ireland there are many kings, yet most of them recognize the authority of the Ard-Ri. Here Alfred has fought long and hard not only to rule, but to create laws for men to live by. You were right when you first spoke—the Frankish lands are divided. The kings are weak. The barons have created their own bastions against invasion, and it becomes a case where the strongest survive.''

"That brother, is the world,'' Eric warned him.

"But if this man were to abduct my wife, he might well manage to find a way to keep her! And, well, if he thought he could prosper more by her death than her company, I don't think that he would hesitate to cut her throat.''

"Surely he would not go so far!''

"I don't know. I do know that he would seize her the very first opportunity he had.''

"But would the other barons allow it?''

Conar shook his head slowly. "That's one of the reasons I've come for her now. I am taking her to Rouen as guest of Count Odo, and we are going to renew our marriage vows before some select guests. Odo believes that will strengthen my hold upon both Melisande—and the land. She *is* the heiress,'' he admitted wryly.

"The heiress,'' Eric agreed, "but perhaps you have paid more than you realize for your right to claim her fortress. And there is something you're forgetting.''

Conar arched a brow.

"You are a power in yourself, grandson of a very great Ard-Ri of Ireland, son of the mighty king of

Dubhlain, and also a prince of the Norse house of Vestfold.''

''And that means?'' Conar inquired.

''That if the Danes do come upon you in hordes, brother, you might be surprised to discover the mass of fighting men you will have at your call.''

Conar smiled, leaning back very comfortably again. He looked at his brother. ''Thank you.''

''Not at all. I take it, then, that you are not staying long here?''

Conar shook his head. ''I think the time has come to lay claim to the fortress together. The sooner our union is sanctified, as Odo seems to think necessary, the easier I will be. I know that the real test is coming, that Geoffrey will align himself with the Danes. I mean to give him no added fuel for his fire of longing and revenge. Melisande must be indisputably mine.''

''I see,'' Eric murmured. ''Then you must sail as soon as possible, with the tides. Might I suggest something?''

''Aye?''

''An heir would be a fine touch to secure the land!''

''I'm well aware of that, brother.''

''You've tarried quite a while.''

''Trust me. I will tarry no longer.''

''Well, then,'' Eric said, striding to the door. ''If the night is filled with screams, I will try to assure my wife that you are not slicing the throat of yours.''

Conar groaned. ''If you've nothing better to do here than torment me—''

''I am going, Conar. I'll see you shortly in the hall below. We dine soon, so you might wish to make haste. I think it might prove to be an entertaining meal!''

Eric slipped from the room, grinning. Conar stared across the width of it to a tapestry against the wall. It blocked the doorway that connected the rooms, he knew.

He wondered if Melisande was aware of the doorway's existence. He smiled slowly, certain that she was not.

He was tempted to rise dripping from his tub and test his theory here and now, but he had waited this long. And he had extracted a promise from her. If he bided his time but another hour, he could demand she keep her promise.

He rose soon, as his water was growing cold and his flesh was beginning to wrinkle. He dressed simply in a shirt and tunic and chausses, and by habit, even in his brother's home, he buckled his scabbard about his waist.

He kept his sword with him always. Even in his own house. His sword and the knife sheathed at his ankle. Peace, even here, was not guaranteed. He had been trained well. He was ever wary.

Still, when he came downstairs soon after, he was comfortably dressed, as were his brothers, Bryce, Bryan, and Eric. His sister Daria, not quite so tall as Melisande, but elegant and dignified in her height nevertheless, was wearing a tunic and gown of buttercup yellow and deepest gold. Her eyes were brilliantly blue against the yellow. She chatted easily with Bryan and Bryce, and Conar noted that they were a handsome group, all of them, Bryan and Bryce dark like their mother, Eric and Daria and he as golden as their father. They were a close-knit family, perhaps because they had been like an island themselves at times, one against those who decried either their Norse or their Irish heritage.

Brenna and Mergwin were deep in conversation by the fire. It had been some time since the two had been together, and perhaps it was natural that they should have a great deal to discuss.

Planning all our futures, Conar thought dryly.

Swen was with him and joked with Bryce and Bryan. Rhiannon came to greet him, kissing his cheek, welcoming him again. She slipped a delicate hand beneath his arm. "I've arranged that you be at my side, my long-wandering brother-in-blood. Melisande can be at your other side, Bryce at hers."

He lowered his lips to whisper against her ear. "Where is my dearly beloved?"

Rhiannon arched a brow to him. "I'm sure she'll be down any moment now."

But Melisande did not come down. Rhiannon delayed serving the meal, then nervously murmured that she would send a servant to see to her health. A young girl with plaited hair was sent up the stairs, then quickly returned. "Lady Melisande has suggested that you begin the meal without her," the girl said, bowing briefly before Rhiannon. "She has quite suddenly been taken ill and asks if you will all please forgive her this evening, she is going to try to sleep."

There was a vast silence within the hall. Conar felt all eyes rivet uneasily upon him.

"I cannot believe that she really wishes to miss this meal," he said, forcing a polite smile to his lips. He bowed to Rhiannon at his side. "Forgive me, lady. I will attend to her myself, and see if she cannot be persuaded to join us."

His simmering anger allowed him to take the stairs very quickly. He followed the hallway down to the heavy wooden door to her room, thought about throwing his shoulder upon it and bursting in on her, then took a deep breath. He knocked loudly and awaited her reply.

He heard a soft moan.

"It is me, Melisande. Open the door."

"I cannot. I cannot rise to do so."

He hesitated a moment, teeth clenched so tight, he

wondered if they would snap. He didn't want to break doors in his brother's house.

If it had been his own, he would not have hesitated.

He was not going downstairs without her. He strode down the hallway to his own room, entered, and strode to the tapestry. He thrust it aside and found the small doorway there. Bending low, for the doorway did not permit his height, he slipped into the adjoining room, thrusting another tapestry out of the way to fully enter.

She did not see him, had not heard him enter. She sat at the foot of her bed, freshly, beautifully gowned in a silver tunic over blue, her brush moving through the waterfall length of her hair. She was staring at the door, as if she expected further action from him, prayed it would not come, and dreaded the next few minutes.

He stood still, arms crossed over his chest, watching her. After a moment she rose and crossed the room. She came to one of the windows and looked out to the courtyard below. The last rays of sunlight drifted in to set blue fire highlights to her hair and elegant shadows upon her face. He felt the same rise of hunger within him that had seized him earlier by the water. There was something within her that compelled the eye, something that haunted a man, something that seethed with a graceful compelling sensuality.

She was his wife.

And as hostile as ever, he reminded himself. Her promise to him regarding this evening didn't seem to mean much to her. Her cheeks were pale, he admitted. But that was because she waited for his next move.

She turned and saw him standing there. A small, startled cry left her lips, and her eyes drifted quickly to the door and back. She bit her lower lip.

"I'm terribly distressed to see you so ill," he told her.

The pallor in her cheeks was replaced by a crimson

flush. "Perhaps it was the water. I'm so sorry. If you'll just forgive me this evening . . ."

"Certainly." He strode across the room to her, placing his hand against her cheek. "Aye, my love, I'm ever so grateful that you don't seem to have a fever. Still, let me get you undressed. I shall send down and tell them that I intend to stay with you."

"No! You mustn't! Join your family, enjoy their company—"

"And leave you—*neglect* you now—when you are ill?"

"You've neglected me for years!" she snapped, momentarily forgetting her ploy.

He smiled. "Ah, and there she is, my lovely wife, doing well enough, so it seems. Well, you've two choices, milady. You may take my arm and walk down to join the others, or you may disrobe right now and join me in my bed. Actually the latter is far more my preference."

"You are despicable! You doubt my word—"

"Indeed, I do!"

"I tell you, I do not feel well—"

"I'm sure that you don't. My appearance here has most probably caused you quite a headache. But I promise, I will tend to that later. Which will it be, Melisande?"

She swept by him, reaching the door, pausing when she saw the bolt she had slid across it. She stared at him.

"Naturally, my love, there is an entrance from my room. This is my brother's house, remember?"

She slid the bolt and threw the door open.

"One moment, my love!" he called.

She paused, turning back to him.

He strode to the door, lifting her chin with his forefinger. She wanted to knock his touch away, he knew, but she held still, seething.

"What—milord?"

"You gave me your word, wife, that you would play the part this evening. Your word, Melisande."

"I am not feeling at all well," she insisted regally.

"Lady, unless you are stone cold dead, you will keep your word to me."

She lifted her chin higher than his finger, eyes blazing. "You're being extremely crude," she whispered furiously. "You're behaving just like a—"

"Viking?"

She held silent, staring at him.

"Perhaps. Yet it seems to me that I am acting like a husband—nothing more, nothing less."

"Blood shows!" she hissed.

He laughed, a hollow sound, and pressed the door open for her, sweeping her a low bow. "Be that as it may. One way or the other, lady, I will see that you keep your promise."

 **12**

Conar managed to catch up with Melisande before she reached the stairway. He caught her elbow, slowing her gait.

"Milady, we will arrive together."

She bowed her head slightly, and her rich dark lashes swept low over her eyes. She kept silent for a moment—which he was sure took her a great deal of willpower. Before they had come halfway down the stairway, her lashes had risen, and her eyes, a violet blaze, were upon his.

"Because we are so close and tender a couple?" she challenged him, her voice both soft and mocking. "How curious. Those here know that we are all but strangers."

"Some of those here know that we shall not remain strangers much longer," he told her lightly. "My brother is even aware that he needn't be alarmed by screams in the night."

She colored at that, her lashes falling again. "You are compelled to discuss everything with your family?"

"You were the one assuring me they were all aware that we were strangers," he told her, and smiled. Her eyes clashed with his again. "Behave," he warned her, for they had reached the foot of the stairs, and straight ahead lay the great hall, where the others had gathered at their places, waiting.

"Melisande!" Rhiannon, concerned, quickly rose and came to her side. "Are you quite sure you're feeling better now?" She touched Melisande's cheek. "You've not acquired a fever?"

"Something by the stream seems to have affected her," Conar said smoothly, "but she now seems determined to dine with us."

Melisande cast him a quick, sizzling glance, then smiled for Rhiannon. "I am most eager for your company, Rhiannon."

Conar's fingers locked around her arm. "Well, then, they have been waiting on yours for quite some time now. Shall we sit, my love?"

It wasn't much of a question. He guided her to their seats at the long U-shaped table. She sat, and he noticed that she was quick enough to smile for Bryce. It occurred to him with a startling pang of envy that she was close with this younger brother of his. He might even have felt a tug of jealousy, except that he trusted each of his brothers and sisters; he would do so with his own life and that of his wife.

She was quick to turn her back on him, discussing horses with Bryce, and history, and arguing certain points with him. Conar gave some attention to their conversation, but then turned to Rhiannon at his side.

"You must be patient," she said softly, her silver eyes sparkling upon him. "From what I understand, dear brother, you have been quite a tyrant."

He arched a brow to her, and her smile deepened. "You remind me so much of Eric, of your father. Outraged when you are determined you have done your best. Give yourself a chance, you might discover that you like your wife."

He smiled slowly in turn and spoke softly. "I never

said that I did not like my wife. Indeed, I am quite
entranced with her.''

"Ah, entranced!" Rhiannon said, but she had been
wed to Eric for a long time now and didn't mind in the
least being bold with her husband's wild family. "I
said nothing about desiring her, milord. A dead man
might awaken to desire her. I suggested that you might
like your wife. Don't take offense, Conar. I speak with
love for you both."

He curled his fingers over her hand. "Fair sister, I
would take no offense from you. But I don't dislike
my wife. She simply—" he paused, then shrugged.
"Infuriates me at almost every turn. I'm a Viking to
her, nothing more."

Rhiannon reached for her chalice, sipping wine and
studying him. "You have to imagine what it is like not
to come from a household such as yours. Since Lin-
desfarne was raided in 797, we have all feared the fury
of the Norseman! It is often hard to accept that one
can become an ally." He stared at her, and she continued. "Conar, you must admit, Vikings do raid, brutal-
ize their dead enemies, plunder vast cities, rape, rob,
and murder."

Eric suddenly leaned past her, meeting his brother's
eyes. "Is she talking about me again?"

Conar shook his head. "No, I think it is me this
time," he said lightly. Rhiannon smiled quickly. Eric
touched her lips with a gentle kiss, and Conar turned
away, granting them their moment's tenderness. He
reached for the chalice set between him and Melisande, the one they were to share, as was the custom,
and his fingers brushed his wife's. Her eyes met his
swiftly, but he realized that she had not been talking
to Bryce, nor had she been paying any heed to his
words with Rhiannon.

She had been staring down the table, watching
Mergwin and Brenna.

But now, with her eyes on his, her fingers flew from the chalice as if it had burned her.

"Please, you must go first," he told her.

"Nay, milord," she said. "Always you."

He lifted the chalice, handing it to her. "Drink the wine, Melisande. You may well need it."

She took the chalice and drank deeply, so deeply in fact that she returned it to him empty. "I've decided I may well need a great deal of it," she informed him.

"That you may," he agreed. "I shall summon the servant to bring more."

The young girl with the plaited hair was there quickly to replenish their cup.

Melisande turned away from him, but Bryce asked him what his intentions were. "Are you staying here for a while, Conar?"

He started to reply, then remembered how curious Melisande was on that very subject, and he answered evasively. "I'm not quite sure how long. You know, it always depends on the wind."

Bryce knit his brow, aware that though, yes, the wind and the tides certainly controlled sea passage, Conar had learned to sail under any condition. He didn't press the point, but told Conar it was good to see him.

"Aye, it's good to have come. I know that Melisande is delighted, as well. She has been so—neglected."

She looked from him to Bryce. "It's an incredible pleasure," she said, and Conar was instantly aware, of course, that it was anything but. He smiled, spearing a piece of meat with the small blade left at his side. The table was covered with boar, venison, rabbit, and several fowl. All perfectly seasoned and roasted slowly over a searing fire. This was how a household should be run, he thought, and felt an edge to his temper. Indeed, it would be something to see Melisande interested in the domesticity of her home. He was certain, though, that her main interest was in seizing the power to run the place, in dressing up in her gilded mail, in usurping him in any way that she could.

Perhaps that wasn't fair. She had been away from home a long time. Away from him a long time.

He might like her, Rhiannon had said.

But he did like his wife, he realized. She infuriated him, but her hostility was open and honest. She defied him as few men dared. She had courage, and it was that courage that frightened him so badly in regard to her welfare.

She suddenly seemed aware of his eyes on her and turned to face him. She flushed, reaching for the chalice again. He swept it from her fingers. "I would like you pleasantly at ease," he said softly, "not passing out before you are able to carry out your promise."

"I will never be pleasantly at ease with you!" she promised him vehemently.

"Then you will learn the pretense of being so," he returned, again willing his temper to subside.

There was a sudden hush as a young man arrived in the midst of the U of the tables. He bowed low to Eric and Rhiannon. He spoke in the Saxon language of his hostess's people, yet there was an accent to his words that indicated his native language was that of Eire. He introduced himself as William, son of Padraic, and seneschal, storyteller, now, in the household of Eric MacAuliffe.

Tonight he would honor another MacAuliffe, Count Conar, who had come to them so recently from the sea.

Far behind him a lute player began to create a background of soft music for his words. He spoke of Conar's stand for his father and family, of the wealth and richness of Eire. Then, as any good storyteller, he began to recount Conar's deeds, his excellent swords-manship—and his excellent timing in coming upon a maiden in dire need upon the coast of France. He spoke of how Conar had avenged his host's death and rescued the man's daughter, and now held her dear to his breast. When he was done, he turned his eyes on Melisande and said softly that a brave warrior had found great beauty. He bowed deeply once again and was rewarded with applause from all those around the table.

Except for Melisande. She didn't do anything. Her hands remained in her lap, fingers laced together. Her eyes remained on the young seneschal.

Suddenly she rose and came around the table, softly asking the man if she might borrow his lute player's instrument.

"She must be welcoming you in her own special way," Bryce said softly. Conar frowned and Bryce quickly smiled. "She entertains us often. She has the voice of an angel, you will see. Truly, Conar, you have been away too long."

Indeed, he had. That quickly became apparent. Melisande did have the voice of an angel. Strong and sweet, she sang as naturally as she spoke, and her fingers moved with ease upon the lute. Her song was so beautiful that it took some time for him to begin to listen to the words.

She sang of a hapless warrior, one born to sail the seas—and die upon them. The raider found himself raided upon the windswept waters.

The song, he realized in time, was about Alfred's seizing of Danish ships, and so for all outward appear-ances, there was nothing wrong with it. But she didn't refer to the invader as a Dane each time, merely a Viking, and the song was therefore about a Viking who received his just due.

Himself, he knew well.

The hall burst into applause once again when she finished her song. Naturally, Conar thought. She'd sung like a lark, and she was the picture of beauty, her hair caught by the firelight and shimmering with blue-black lights, her violet eyes wide, surrounded by ebony lashes. She smiled, and the curve of her lip was haunting, compelling.

She returned the lute to its owner and paused at the end of the table to speak with Daria. Conar saw that Mergwin was watching his wife, his old brows knit in perplexity.

And then Melisande went into her true performance for the evening. As she spoke, she suddenly cast the back of one hand to her forehead, clutching her stomach with the other. She groaned softly. Conar leaned forward, studying her.

Bryce was already on his feet, running to her side. Daria was up, making her sit, calling for cool water to press against her forehead. Rhiannon was quick to reach her side, too.

"It's nothing, really!" Melisande assured them all, her wonderful smile in place.

Indeed, it was nothing. He was damned well convinced of it. But they were all around her now, so concerned as to her welfare.

Conar stood, eyes narrowed, and watched her from a distance. She suddenly stood. "If you'll just please forgive me, I think a night's sleep is all that I need. I'm so sorry, this being Conar's first night here . . ."

"Conar?" Rhiannon spun on him, her eyes wide, concerned—condemning him if he thought to bother his wife in any way.

"Oh, I think she must go to bed. Immediately," he said politely. He walked around the table, not coming close to Melisande but pausing behind Mergwin's chair instead.

"I'll take you up, Melisande, and Conar can remain

here,'' Daria assured her. Jesu! How could his own sister believe that Melisande was seriously concerned with his whereabouts. All she cared for was that they were distant from her.

He set his hands upon Mergwin's shoulders. ''Is she sick?'' he demanded softly for the old Druid's ears only.

''Perhaps she is weak from excitement—'' Mergwin began.

Conar's fingers tightened upon the fantastic old man who had helped raise them all. ''Is she ill?'' he repeated.

''No,'' Mergwin admitted.

''Thank you,'' Conar murmured.

He strode through the others and saw the alarm in Melisande's eyes as he swiftly swept her into his arms. ''If you are ill, my love, I wouldn't begin to allow you upon those stairs alone! You could fall and injure yourself, Melisande, and I would be desolate should such a thing happen!''

''But you've just arrived!'' she cried. ''You scarcely see your brothers now, or your sister. You need time with them.''

''They'll understand, I'm certain.''

''Of course, Conar!'' Rhiannon said quickly. ''Is there anything that I can send up, anything that we can do?''

''I think that Melisande is right,'' Conar said firmly, his eyes locking with his wife's. ''I intend to see that a good night in bed cures this fever of hers! Our deepest thanks, and good night!'' he said swiftly, carrying her from the hall with long, quick strides. She was silent on the stairway, but her fingers held tightly the fabric of his shirt upon his arm, her eyes radiating fury as they met his. He didn't give a damn. She'd made him a promise. She would keep it.

He reached the heavy door she had blocked against

him before and cast it open with his shoulder, his eyes never leaving hers. She cried out when he dumped her none too gently upon the bed, then turned back to bolt the door himself. When he turned again, she was on her feet—and obviously seeking the way he had managed to enter before so that she might exit quickly now.

He strode across the room to her. "You gave your word," he reminded her.

She backed away, moistening her lips, allowing her lashes to fall over her eyes.

"I am ill!" she protested. "Too frail—"

He snorted his disbelief. "You're as frail as a healthy ox, my love."

"How dare you!" she spat out. "How can you begin to think that you know me, anything about me. You've no right to me. If you so much as come near me again, Conar, I swear that I will scream—"

She did scream, a scream that was choked off with speed when his hands suddenly wrenched her against him. She was lifted up and off the floor and thrown hard upon the bed, where he braced himself over her. "Scream, Melisande. Scream long and hard. Let the entire household hear you. No one will interfere with the union of a legally wed husband and wife. Let them all hear. They will know then that you are mine, and that I will never let you go."

She was pale, stricken. She lay against the bed gasping, but not moving. She lashed out at him in an anguished whisper. "That's all that you want! The consummation, the guarantee that you are count, that the *property* is yours."

Damn her! He was irritated with his family, that they should so easily fall prey to her! But there was something in her voice, something that drew tenderness if not pity from him, despite his anger, despite his desire, and despite, even, his resolve.

He brought his knuckles down over her cheek, noting its marble beauty against the rough texture of his huge, battle-worn hands. Her eyes were so very wide, so liquid in their violet shimmer.

"I tell you, Melisande, you are mistaken. There is nothing I want so much as you."

Her lashes swept over her eyes. "I don't believe you."

"When I am done this eve, you will."

Her eyes rose to his again.

"You gave your word, Melisande. When you give it to me, you will keep it."

"I cannot!" she cried out softly, her lashes falling again. He could feel the fierce pounding of her heart. Could she be afraid? Melisande?

"How strange!" he said softly. "I would have thought that Manon's daughter would keep a vow."

Once again her gaze was upon him. He had struck upon the perfect words to reach into her soul, he saw, and realized then that she trembled violently beneath him. How odd. She had drawn such a fury from him today, and even in the hall tonight. He would have taken her swiftly, and with a certain violence, if he had been forced.

But now he wanted to draw her to him. Gently. "Bathed and perfumed, waiting and willing," he reminded her softly.

She didn't reply, and he rose from her, keeping his eyes locked with hers. "I'll give you a few minutes, Melisande. When I return, I expect you to keep your promise."

He turned, departing her room by shoving the tapestry aside, opening the small connecting door, and entering his chamber.

He closed the door thoughtfully behind him. "You fool!" he charged himself aloud. He walked to the hearth and spread his hands out before the low flame.

What would happen now? Was she already tearing through the door, ready to disappear downstairs and give Rhiannon a tale of some terrible illness that required the soothing hand of a servant through the long hours of the night?

"Ah, lady! It must be done, it will be tonight!" he whispered to the flames. And still he waited, weary and aching, wishing that this particular battle could be over.

His face grew warm with the heat from the flames. He pushed away from the fire at last and headed for the connecting door. She would be gone. And he would be forced to retrieve her. He didn't know what he would do then, only that he couldn't allow her to escape him.

But his heart seemed to shudder and then stop when he quietly reentered her room.

Melisande was there.

She had changed into a soft, sheer gown that was very nearly the color of her eyes. Her back was to him, for she, too, faced the fire. Her hair was loose, just brushed, and like the finest silk he might find for trade anywhere along the Mediterranean. It curled and waved in a glorious black tumult down her back while the sheer gown gave away everything and nothing at all. The elegant curve of her back could be seen, the curve of her hips.

He found himself striding swiftly to her, his hands falling upon her shoulders. He lifted the length of her hair, and felt the fierceness of her trembling. He placed his lips against her throat and felt the speed of the pulse beating there.

A soft mauve cord was tied just below her neck. He pulled it and stepped back as the flimsy garment fell with a soft whisper to the floor. A small sound escaped her, yet she remained with her back to him. He pressed his lips to her shoulders, his fingers easing down her back, tracing the shape of it.

"I thought you'd be gone," he said huskily, spinning her into his arms.

She gasped again as the tips of her breasts were crushed to his chest, as she felt him with the naked length of her beauty.

"I always keep my word," she murmured.

"Do you? Or did you think, perhaps, that I would find you, wherever you were to go?"

Her eyes rose to his, deeply, richly violet with wild emotion. "Could we please . . . get this over with?"

"As you wish, my love. As you wish."

He lifted her again, feeling the fierceness of the hunger she so swiftly awakened within him. He stretched her out on the bed and lay beside her, still aware of the way she shook. She longed to leap up and flee and fought the wild desire to do so, he knew. She did not close her eyes, but stared at the ceiling, avoiding his. He smiled slightly, seeing her start as he touched her, the tips of his fingers running softly down the valley of her breasts to her waist, then circling the flesh of her belly below. By all the gods, she was glorious. Her flesh was as pure as cream, silk to the touch. Her breasts were large and firm and beautifully shaped, the nipples a deep dusky rose. Her waist was slim, her hips delicately curved. Down the soft expanse of her abdomen, a soft display of ebony temptingly triangled about her sex. He let his fingers wander there and heard the sound she tried to choke back too late.

He smiled again and leaned over her, capturing her lips with his own. She tightened against him for a moment, but he forced her lips apart, his tongue plunging deeply into her mouth, demanding a response. He lifted his lips from hers and her breath came in great ragged gasps.

"I cannot breathe."

"You don't need to breathe."

His mouth descended upon hers once again, raw now with its hunger and need, giving excitement as well as demanding it. Her hands lay at her sides, fingers curling. They fell upon his shoulders at last. He didn't know if she had intended to push him away, but it didn't matter. Her fingers went still. He kissed her until he had his fill of the sweetness of her lips, then parted from her mouth at last and met the dazed look in her eyes. He kept his eyes upon hers, then lowered himself against her body, capturing her breast within the palm of his hand, cradling it, stroking it, running his thumb erotically over her nipple. Her breath caught, she froze, swallowing hard as she stared at him.

And still he kept his eyes locked with hers even as he closed his mouth over her nipple, teasing it with the tip of his tongue, surrounding it with the fullness of his mouth, sucking upon it until the bud hardened like a pebble beneath his liquid touch.

Again a sound escaped her. She closed her eyes, her face pale once again. She still trembled, ceaselessly, but she was no longer rigid against him. He brought his lips to her left breast, teased and tarried there, and while he did so, he began to move his hands upon her again, cupping and stroking her hip, her thigh, her belly, and once again her thigh. At first he touched her everywhere but that sweet, tempting triangle. And then he began to stroke it lightly with the tips of his fingers, with his palms. He rose above her again, capturing her wild gaze as he wet the length of his fingers with his tongue, then brought them back to that silk and ebony triangle, delving within it to find the pink petals of her sex.

She gasped, her knees rising, her head twisting. He lay the pinioning weight of his body half atop her again, leaving him free from her protest to have his way. He parted her, stroked her, sought out the most sensitive of places, then delved more deeply within her with his sure, demanding stroke. She was incredibly tight. Sweetly damp, but tight.

Touching her, feeling her warmth, her movement, seemed to create all of the fires of hell within him. She had instinctively tried to close herself, yet had whispered no protest. Still he found himself fighting the strength of his hunger for her, the ache in his loins. He had demanded her bathed and perfumed, waiting and willing. Perhaps that had not been quite what he had received, but she was definitely bathed and perfumed, her own sweet scent mingled with that of lilacs, enticing, tempting. "Look at me," he demanded, and when she did, her eyes huge, shimmering and challenging still, he smiled slowly, still touching her, and lowered his lips to hers, tasting wine and mint. She did not twist from him. Indeed, her lips parted slightly. He felt the rush of her breath before his mouth devoured hers.

He began his descent down her body once again, stroking her breasts, her thighs, rubbing his palm over the ebony triangle, slipping his fingers within it, dipping deeply into her. His mouth touched her breasts, her belly. He watched her face as he descended. Her eyes had closed again. She did not touch him. Her fingers were wound into the sheets. He stroked her thigh, lifted, then slowly slid his tongue upon the tender flesh his touch had so recently awakened. She did cry out then, trying to turn. His hand was firm on her leg, his weight strong against hers. A "no" formed upon her lips, but the desperate whisper didn't quite reach the air. He slid his tongue very slowly over her once again, felt the wild pull of her body, the trembling, the arching. Then his touch was not so light. He stroked and delved, tasted, plunged.

Her fingers moved, tearing into his flesh, his hair, the sheet again. A searing heat shot through him as he felt the response of her body, tasted its sweetness. Mercilessly he continued his seductive assault upon her, ignoring the thundering in his skull, the agony of tension and desire that gripped him.

A cry suddenly burst from her. She writhed and went as taut as stone. A wave of victorious pleasure swept over him, and in seconds he felt the hot burst of her body's sweet release. He had longed to arouse her, seduce her, and he had done so. She was incredibly wet and warm now, and that very fact seemed to goad him to a greater, white-hot desire.

He rose, kicking off his boots, stripping down his chausses. Even as he did so, she tried to curl within herself, turning from him, drawing her knees to his chest.

"Nay, lady!"

He drew her back, heedless that his shirt remained upon him. He straddled her, fanning her hair out in an ebony arc. Her eyes closed, she sought not to see him, not to meet his gaze.

Not to face the truth of just how swiftly and surely he had touched her.

But he brought his lips to hers again, forced them apart, forced his tongue within.

"Taste our love," he whispered, then wedged his weight determinedly between her thighs. His sex throbbed with a fury, and she swallowed hard, feeling it against her. He touched her, carefully thrust the smooth tip of himself just against her. She was as pale as the sheets. She bit into her lower lip. He pressed farther. She gasped, and bit her lip again, determined not to cry out. He moved as slowly as he could, but his next movement at last drew a ragged cry from her. He wrapped his arms tenderly around her, aware that she reeled with the pain. "It's over," he assured her, and held her against him. He felt the pulse of himself inside her, the desperate need to be assuaged. He held her close, caressed her buttocks. She buried her face against his shoulder, fingers gripping like steel into his arms. He could no longer bear it. He began to move.

She was slick, warm, yielding. Her body closed around his like a fitted sheath, each stroke driving him to new heights of searing desire. He held her achingly tight against him, thrusting himself more and more deeply, his rhythm growing with his need, with his thirst for release. He filled her again and again, impaled her, held her, began his storm anew. He kept his hand firmly upon the smooth beauty of her rounded buttocks, molding her to him, forcing her to meet his thrust, to come, to arch against it.

To writhe.

To seek something herself once again, the sweet surcease she barely knew.

Hot, slick, wet, their bodies met and melded. Then Conar felt the heat of a thousand flames burst forth within him. He climaxed wildly, thrusting, thrusting again, filling her with the burning rush of his seed from his body, once, again, again. His climax was volatile, exquisite, a storm. It swept over him, shook him, riddled him. He nearly fell atop her with the full bulk of his weight, yet caught himself in time.

And in time to feel the arch and trembling of her supple form against him, the proof that he had reached her, touched her.

He eased himself swiftly to her side, gasping raggedly for breath. Long moments passed before he gazed her way and saw that her eyes were open, dazed, and fixed upon the ceiling once again. She must have felt his gaze, because she lowered her lashes swiftly and turned away from him.

He clamped down hard on his jaw, amazed at the

pleasure she had brought him, bitterly disappointed by the hostility she still seemed to bear him.

"Was that too barbaric, my love?" he mocked softly.

"You told me I must be willing!" she hissed in return.

Her back was to him. Incredibly tempting. He stroked his fingers up and down its length. "I'm ever so delighted that you were."

"I had no choice."

"No, of course not, you gave your word. Yet I truly thought you might run again, denying me."

She swung on him suddenly, her eyes a tempest in violet. "And if I had? What then? Would you have let me be?"

He smiled, leaning upon an elbow, fascinated anew by the view he was now receiving of her full, dusky crested breasts.

"Perhaps."

She let out a strangled oath of fury and tried to turn away again. He caught her, encircling her in his arms even as she struggled. He laughed. "But probably not. I am Viking. I would have found you and ravished you one way or the other. Is that what you want to hear?"

She clenched her teeth hard in fury. "Is it what would have happened?" she demanded.

"We'll never know, will we? Because you were here, bathed and perfumed. Waiting . . . and at least pretending to be . . . willing."

Her lashes fell again. "Well, then, milord, you are well served. All is yours. The marriage is legal—and consummated. Perhaps now you will be good enough to let me be. You've everything that you wanted."

He stroked one of the magnificent tresses of ebony hair that fell over her shoulder and lay tangled between them. The touch against his flesh was as soft as silk, sensual, enticing.

He smiled. "I told you, Melisande, that I wanted you."

"And all that goes with me."

"You," he said firmly.

He sat up, ripping his shirt from his shoulders at last. Her gaze fell upon the breadth of his chest, the ripple of muscle within his arms.

Then it fell lower upon his body, down the length and strength of the shaft bulging there once again, growing even as she stared.

"No!" she murmured, starting to draw away.

"Yes," he returned, and slipped her beneath him once again.

Her hands strained against his chest.

But her lips . . .

Her lips parted sweetly to his kiss.

 **13**

At some point she at last slept, and in sleep the night seemed to take on the soft, hazy unreality of a dream. Yet there were solid elements within that dream. The feel of his arms around her, that of his shoulder beneath her head, the soft stroke of his fingers, even when they lay at rest. The dreaming was sometimes sweet. She felt that she had fought so bitterly, surrendered so completely. But in her dreams she dared marvel at the intimacy between them, at the tenderness he offered when he chose, of the magic in his rough touch. While dreaming, she could forget that she should have fought herself as well as him, should have stayed strong, should have kept her pride, her dignity, her soul, all away from him. She could remember the outrage of each first intimate touch he so arrogantly took and demanded, but then the memory of the excitement it created would sweep upon her, even in her dreams. She couldn't have fought him and won. But surely she could have waged a better battle with herself.

She would deny him forever, she promised herself.

But the promise was no good.

Several times it seemed that he reawakened her when she had just fallen asleep at last. Yet he did so in such a slow and sensual manner that she was doing his bidding before she awakened once again.

It seemed she had slept deeply for a long while when she opened her eyes and discovered his searing gaze burning into her, studying her face. She was startled by the intensity of his stare, and for one unwary moment she was also startled by the striking, rugged handsomeness of his face. She didn't want to see it, didn't want to admit in any way that he was arresting, yet how could she deny it now? Even as he stared at her, she felt a trembling begin deep within her. He always managed to cause some passionate stirring of emotion inside her. Now things had changed, and she could never change them back again.

Now she could never escape him.

Most of all she didn't want to care about Conar, didn't want to wonder or care whether he slept through the night. He took what he desired and would then do what he chose, and she had yet to learn why he had come.

Except for this.

But why now, when he had let her be for so very long?

His hand cupped her cheek, and he murmured harshly, "No annulment, Melisande. There will be no annulment."

Had she ever mentioned the possibility of trying to get an annulment to anyone before she had so swiftly and rashly whispered the words to Gregory yesterday? It seemed like eons ago. She might have been a different person, living in a different place. She closed her eyes, still exhausted, shivering. He would have found her last night, she thought. If she had not stayed, if she had not kept her word to him, he would have found her anywhere she might have gone. He had been absolutely determined to consummate their wedding vows. His voice stroked her ear now. "You know that now, milady, don't you?"

She rolled to her side, curving her back to him. It was no deterrent. His hand moved lightly but possessively over her naked hip. There was even a feel of tenderness to the touch. Oddly, after everything else, that brought a glistening of tears to her eyes.

"There will be no annulment," he repeated. The words were soft yet fierce. She had to respond to him, lest he take his touch further once again.

And she respond once again.

She clenched her teeth tightly together, then spoke. "Aye, milord Viking, I am aware that there can be no annulment now."

She hoped that he was satisfied with that. Perhaps he was. But his fingers remained splayed upon her hip, and though her back was to him, she was keenly aware of the incredible muscle structure of his shoulders and chest, and the soft feel of the golden hair where his sex nestled. She was also very aware of *that* now. It seemed to live a life of its own, imposing even at rest, so quick to grow and bulge and pulse and demand.

Just the touch at her spine made her remember, made her burn, made her feel again. She'd never been prepared for this, never. Never these feelings, never this longing, this aching. This needing.

And hating every minute that he saw all he so easily achieved.

He was silent, though she was certain he didn't sleep. She felt his touch, the slick length of him. She closed her eyes again. She could not sleep with him so.

She could not dislodge him.

In time her exhaustion overrode all else, and she did close her eyes and sleep deeply.

When she awoke again, late in the morning, she was alone. Her eyes opened very slowly, and she didn't think that she'd ever awakened before to feel so exhausted. Nor so torn by such a tempest of emotions. His scent lingered with her, his down pillow retained an indentation from his head.

Ah, yes, his mark lay all upon her, she could feel it still, from head to toe. She was incredibly sore, yet it was exquisite. She still trembled to remember how he had made her feel. He was good, he compelled, he seduced, he demanded. She had thought to endure the night with fortitude, she had never imagined just what the darkness might bring.

Ah, but now daylight was with them! She had never been so sore, so torn, and so alarmed, she thought, tugging the sheets up around her breasts. It was a very strange tangle of emotions. Over time she had struggled with two possibilities, one being that she would come of age, manage to get an annulment, return home, and perhaps acquire a husband of her own choosing.

Then, of course, there had always been the possibility that Conar would actually come for her and take her as his wife. She had always been wary of him, impressed by him, and infuriated by him. Perhaps the attraction had always been there, perhaps that had bred some of her hostility. She had even realized at times that her fury was compounded by his lifestyle—Conar did know what he wanted and with whom. She was supposed to be chaste and pristine, while he went about his life. There was the woman in Dubhlain and probably one in France. And there was Brenna, with him so frequently, quick to dip her blond head and laugh at his words, quicker still to touch his arm, softly advise him. Bede, of course, had been amused with her fury against the injustices of life and had reminded her that a woman's lot was different since she was meant to bear her husband's heir. Naturally it was necessary that she therefore cling to a husband, even if the husband was unaware that she did.

Yet Conar had received his great inheritance through her. Therefore, nothing seemed fair at all.

Of course, Bede had also warned her that she could not expect the world to be fair.

But she had long deplored her situation with Conar, and yet it had been bearable. He hadn't been with her enough to wield his power.

Until now.

He had managed to wield a new power over her. One she had never expected.

She groaned softly and buried her head back into her pillow. She wanted desperately to forget it all, to pretend that none of it had ever happened. To pretend that she remained untouched, with no idea of what could be.

"No!" she whispered softly into her pillow. She slammed a fist against it. Her covers fell, and she reached to retrieve them. Her eyes fell upon the little specks of blood that dappled them, and her temper suddenly left. She sat up, throwing the down pillow upon the lower section of the bed and inching away from those spots. "I hate you!" she whispered fiercely, and both her palms landed on the pillow again. "I hate you!"

She was stunned when she suddenly heard his voice.

"I'm truly sorry, my love," he said. She turned to see that he had come into the room, having entered through the door behind the tapestry once again. His words had a true Norse chill to them, and even hearing them, Melisande felt a shiver streak along her spine. With no effort at all she had offended him. Had there been any warmth within his Norse heart, she might have even hurt him.

No, she hadn't the power to hurt him. She had

managed to inadvertently anger him again and that was all.

She felt ever more keenly her great disadvantage with him, for he was fully dressed in chausses, as was his custom, linen shirt and over-tunic, his mantle broached at his shoulder. His men wore many types of pants, loose-fitting with hose beneath, some long, some short. She had noticed his preference for these hugging garments each time she had seen him, for they made his movements effortless, unencumbered.

He wore his scabbard about his waist, and his unusual sword with the Celtic design and Viking style within it. His knife was sheathed at his ankle. He seemed indomitable, yet she suddenly felt another chill about her heart, and she didn't know why. Any man could be caught with an arrow in his heart. Every man was flesh and blood. She knew that. She had seen her father die.

She suddenly knew, with a startling, frightening clarity, that she didn't want Conar to die. She had thought him a thorn in her side, someone to escape, indeed, someone to hate. Yet she didn't ever want him to fall.

He would never believe that now, she thought wearily, and it mattered little, for she had no intention of ever telling him. His eyes were a pure blue ice-fire upon her, and she felt their cold seeping through her. She realized that she sat up, the sheets barely covering her lap, her hair a wild tangle curling over her back—and her breasts bare. She closed her eyes briefly, her fingers curling into the sheets, wrenching them upward and clutching them to her breast. She was careful to survey him then with the same cool regard and scramble about for what shreds of dignity she might muster. "Does it ever enter your mind, milord, to knock upon a door and enter a room the customary way?"

His eyes swept over her. She couldn't begin to fathom their emotion.

"When I left you, milady, you were sleeping as soundly as the dead. If you still slept, I didn't intend to waken you. I assure you," he murmured, and a mocking tone was back in his voice, "I didn't intrude upon your display of temper with any malicious intention!"

"So why did you intrude?"

"It's too late to sail with the tides today," he told her. "I want you to be prepared to go at dawn tomorrow. I'm quite certain you pack quickly and efficiently—you managed to come here swiftly enough."

"I pack quickly and efficiently when I seek to go somewhere. But as you haven't seen it necessary to tell me any of your plans . . ." She broke off, shrugging. "Then I see no benefit to packing quickly at your slightest whim."

He was silent a moment, his gaze upon her. He strode across the room and stood by her side, seeming to tower over her with his height and presence. "Then don't pack, milady. Come without your belongings. Come naked as you lie now. But you will come!"

"I am the countess, the heiress," she reminded him, eyes rising hotly to clash with his. "You are mistaken if you think that you can still command me as if I were one of your household servants."

"I would never command you as I do my household servants, lady, for I have never had a servant so willful or stubborn. You should know me by now. I have said that you will come with me. You will."

How did she fight him? How did she change this?

How long would he be with her before he disappeared, seeking the company of his golden Brenna or one of the others?

She lowered her lashes quickly, determined that he would never know her true thoughts.

"You never ask, Viking!" she hissed softly. "You cast out your commands as if you cracked a whip. Perhaps you would find yourself more readily obeyed if you learned to listen to others."

She inched back upon the bed, her sheet against her breasts, as he sat beside her suddenly, leaning toward her. "I've listened to you, Melisande. I've listened to you command and demand, and I even wrote and carefully sent a message, warning you that I was coming for you. My mistake. I should have written to my father. You received my letter, smiled to my unwary little brother, and escaped here as quickly as you could. Then you immediately began to plot with that poor young fool, Gregory. Thank God, lady, that we discovered the proof of your innocence that so angered you this morning, else I might have been tempted to slit his young throat despite his tender age!"

She flushed furiously, drawing her knees up beneath the sheets, trying to hug them to her. She lifted her chin. "Next time, milord, I will be careful to see that my travels take me far from your family's domain! What did I do that was so terrible? My mistake! I came here!"

"And what did you gain?" he demanded in a roar that caused her to stiffen quickly so that she would not flinch.

"I thought," she said softly, coolly, "that you might just go away."

"And leave you here. To young Gregory."

Her lashes lowered despite herself. "As I said, milord," she whispered, her eyes rising to meet his again, "next time I will take care to sail far away."

"There will be no next time, Melisande." He rose, and started for the door. "I sail for the coast of France at dawn tomorrow."

"Home?" she gasped. He was still walking. She was

so stunned that she forgot her lack of apparel and leapt to her feet, racing naked after him. She caught his arm, pulling upon it, causing him to turn. "You're taking me home?" she demanded again.

She paused, swallowing hard, for he did not answer her right away. She felt the blue fire of his gaze burn over the length of her, and where it touched her she was warmed. She dropped his arm, backing away from him. She awkwardly attempted to cross her arms over her breasts, then realized just what that effort didn't cover.

"Home," she repeated again. "You're taking me home?"

He walked back toward her. She kept moving away from him, seeking out his eyes, but losing them, for they had fallen upon some other spot on her body.

"Conar!" she exclaimed. She stood by the bed, then leapt back into it, swiftly drawing the covers over the length of her body to her chin.

They were just as swiftly ripped away. She cried out softly as she realized she couldn't possibly have positioned herself any better for his advantage. She started to leap back up, but gasped as his weight pinned her to the bed. There was a glitter of amusement in his eyes now, but it was a fevered one, a determined one, and she was coming to know it all too well. Her hands fell against his chest, and he leaned upon an elbow, his long limbs cast over hers with the easy strength of fallen oaks. His right hand was free to torment her.

"Are you eager to go home, Melisande?" he asked her softly. "Does that make the difference? Will you live happily with a hated Viking if you are just able to go home?"

His gaze was on her now, holding her with a strength as great as that of his limbs. She tried to form her lips so that an answer could fall from them. But his hand was upon her, his palm moving slowly along the curve of her side, rounding her hip, rising to her breast, and stroking its fullness.

Her fingers wound upon his, halting them.

"You ordered me to pack."

He arched a brow, eyes still alive with laughter. "You're suddenly going to obey me?"

She flushed, trying to pluck his hand from her flesh. "Surely it's late. And it's broad daylight—"

"Perhaps it's the daylight that fascinates me so."

She could not halt his touch. His hand moved again, the roughened palm rubbing erotically over the tip of her nipple. Despite herself she felt a fierce jolt of fire raging through her, awaking that sweet center of need deep within her. She grit her teeth, fighting it, fighting the sting of tears that threatened. She didn't hate so much that he had the strength to hold her here, to do this to her. She hated that he touched her and that she wanted him.

She grabbed hold of his straying palm once again, pushing it firmly aside. She managed to wriggle out from beneath the weight of his legs and leap to her feet, crying out furiously, "You cannot think to neglect someone for years and then demand—"

"Alas!" he mocked. "I am trying so very hard not to neglect you now!"

"Milord, you are dressed!"

"Ah, lady, but it is not a permanent state! If it distresses you, I will remedy it."

And he, too, was on his feet. She turned to flee. He caught her arm, spinning her fiercely into his arms. His mouth descended upon hers, hot, hard, demanding, sweeping her breath away. More of his sizzling warmth seemed to sear and sweep into her. She couldn't breathe. Her heart pounded fiercely.

His lips rose from hers, his gaze meeting hers with a reckless challenge.

She brought a fist up, slamming it against his chest.

He laughed, and lifted her, tossing her down upon the expanse of the bed.

Gasping for breath, she stared at him. His scabbard was unbuckled and on the floor. His tunic and shirt were over his head. She started to rise again, but before she could move far he was with her again. His lips found hers. Suddenly gentle, teasing, licking, seductive . . .

She ceased to fight him, the wealth of fire within her rising as if touched by the same wild wind.

"Home," he whispered softly to her. "Remember, milady, I am the price of your homeward passage!"

It didn't matter, not in the least, but she would not have told him so. His hands were upon her, his mouth upon her throat, her breast. The world began to spiral and spin, and she began to fly.

Later he lay at her side, his fingers gentle as they idly stroked her arm while the fever that had seized them slowly, sweetly eased away. He sighed, as if he were truly unhappy to leave her, and rose to his side of the bed.

"It's very late." He was silent for a moment, then she felt his hand on her hip. "Do I understand this correctly, my love? Since I am taking you home, you are willing to be ready to sail with me?"

He was amused again, she thought, and that irritated her unbelievably. She didn't reply at first.

"Melisande, I am speaking to you."

"Yes!"

"You're willing to spend your nights with me, sleep with a Viking?"

She spun around, suddenly furious. "I would sleep with the Devil himself," she hissed, meeting his eyes.

"Isn't a Viking one and the same?"

"Yes!" she cried in agreement.

"Ah, poor Melisande!" he murmured, his fingers curling around one of her ebony tresses. "I cannot

seem to make you happy. I stay away, and I neglect
you. I come to retrieve you, and I force you to sleep
with a demon. Yet you do not seem to suffer too
greatly.''

She clenched her teeth, tugging upon her hair to try
to wrench it from his grasp. He held tight, smiling. He
leaned close, his eyes amused and challenging once
again. "Melisande, I have told you, I will never let
you go. But at least you will not be neglected further.''

She emitted an oath of frustration, closing her eyes
against him. She felt him untangle her hair from his
hold, and she quickly turned her back on him. "Pack
what you wish,'' he commanded her. "I will be down
with my brother, that other wretched Viking devil.''
He was silent a moment, then added softly, "And yet
you seem to get on so very well with Bryce and Bryan!
Don't be deceived by my mother's dark hair and green
eyes upon them! They, too, are surely Viking demons
at heart!''

"Go away!'' she told him, groaning. He laughed and
rose. She heard him dress. She was outraged to feel
the sting and hear the sharp slap as his hand landed
upon the smooth flesh of her buttocks.

"You're sleeping the entire day away, Melisande.
It's time to rise.''

He left by the hidden doorway, laughing again as
she threw a pillow after him.

When he had left her at last, she leapt up. Shaking,
she poured water from her pitcher into her wash bowl
and grabbed a cloth, determined to scrub herself from
head to toe. She wanted a bath, but did not want to
wait for tub or water. When she finished, she started
over. And when she was done this time, she paused,
eyes closed, teeth biting lightly into her lower lip.

She could still feel him. Feel his touch.

She realized then that she always would.

She dropped the wet cloth and strode across the

room for her clothing. There was little that she had to
do, as she had come with her things packed in the
trunk at the foot of the bed, and had taken out only a
few pieces of her clothing, her perfumes, oils, and the
mint she chewed for her teeth.

She dressed quickly, then started down the stairs.
She might have been angry with Mergwin for so
quickly seeming to turn from her on Conar's behalf,
but he had been a good friend. Perhaps he had reminded her a great deal of Ragwald, though the two
men were so different in their pursuit of their "sci-
ences."

Mergwin didn't begin to deny that there was magic
in the world, that there might be spirits, that the
ancient Druid ways might be evoked when needed,
that the Norse stones were equally telling when they
were read.

Ragwald studied the stars in the heavens, and his
readings on life were therefore not superstition, but
complete science.

Still the men were very alike, for when challenged
and cornered, they were both quick to remind her
indignantly that they were Christian men, serving
Christian rulers—even if she did have her doubts about
Olaf, the king of Dubhlain—and that in the end, it was
all God's will.

She started out of the room and then realized that
her heart was beating swiftly, painfully. Home. Perhaps Conar had never realized how cruel he had been
to make her leave. Maybe he had never intended that
cruelty, for no matter what she might say to him, she
had been treated like one of their own by Olaf and
Erin, and she had never wanted for anything among
any of Conar's family.

All that she had missed was her home. Ragwald,
Philippe, Gaston, even Father Matthew. They had
been all that had been left of her family.

She paused for a moment, breathing slowly, then started down the stairs again, hoping she could just slip out and find some of the others, Mergwin or Daria, Rhiannon, the children, Bryce or Bryan. But as she came down the stairs, she heard voices in the hall. Two of them. Eric's and Conar's.

"I wish I could stay longer. You know that if you needed me, I would. But you seem to be at peace here now."

"Ever ready, but at peace. At the moment," Eric agreed.

Melisande came silently down a few more steps. She paused when she could see the brothers. They were alone, each with a cup of ale, seated at the great chairs before the fire, almost identical sons of the Wolf of Norway, great, broad and golden, confident, arrogant—and amazingly arresting and compelling.

"There's a great deal more trouble at home these days," Eric said to his brother.

For a moment Melisande thought he meant her home. Then she realized he was talking about Eire.

"Father can always hold his own, his great walled city," Eric continued. "Since grandfather died, though, Niall has not been able to keep the petty kings so well under control. It seems there is frequently fighting again. But," he warned Conar firmly, "word has traveled for quite some time now. The Danes are amassing. Think of the Viking heritage! If there were trouble here now, I would call across the corners of the earth to gather my family to fight at my side. The Danes will extend this great quest farther. They will come in the thousands, it is said, and delve into the very heart of the Frankish kingdoms."

"The fortress is very much the same as Father's Dubhlain," Conar said. "Incredibly strong. The walls are strong and solid. A massive army can be held off from within."

"But the greater scene will be the land around you," Eric warned. He waved a hand in the air. "Think of where we have gone, brother, just in the house of Vestfold. Into the Russias, down to the Mediterranean. Even into the land of the Islams. If these invaders are fierce enough, they will fight to the heart of the land, and someone will have to make a stand against them."

"What I fear," Conar told his brother, "is that the Frankish barons will underestimate their foes." He leaned forward, seeming to see into the past. "When Father came to Eire, he quickly made use of the horses he had seized. Most men think that Vikings are sea raiders, that we strike quickly, seize things quickly. Those who have not seen it do not realize that many raiders are quick to learn. Father settled in Eire, and now we have Viking ships that carry horses with us, well-trained mounts. It's true that most Vikings will make use of their ships and the water. But there are those now who will make use of all that they take, who will fight on horseback and turn all that their invaded lands have taught them against the people."

"At least you are aware, and those you ally yourself with will surely have their eyes open."

"I think that one of the reasons I bested Gerald that day was that he never expected Manon's help to come in the form of any army—half composed of Vikings—who would come across the sea with their own mounts."

"There's where you will have to watch your back, brother. Enemies have long arms, and they stretch out across the years. You will have to take great care, to sleep with an eye open always."

"Alliances among the powerful barons are all that can save us, for the king in Paris is weak and is quick to pay danegeld, yet the price rises higher and higher."

Eric shrugged. "Remember, Conar, that we are here, if you need us. I pray that taking Melisande home and renewing your marital vows ceremonially will give you the edge that you seek. If Count Odo thinks that it is so, then it must be. And he will be a strong ally, I am certain.''

"So am I," Conar agreed. He continued, she could hear the deep tenor and passion in his voice, but Melisande didn't hear the rest of his words. She felt as if her face were flushed with fever, as if her knees had suddenly grown very weak.

So that was it! Anger gripped her with a sudden, painful ferocity.

He had met Count Odo! And that great baron had warned him that he might lose his property if the other barons did not recognize his union with his wife.

He'd had to come for her! It was no great kindness for him to take her home. He meant to have her repeat her vows to him. And with the marriage fully consummated now, there would be little she could say in protest.

But she could protest. She could cause him a great deal of trouble if she so chose.

Breathing deeply, she gripped the carved wood rail upon the stairs and raced back up the length of them.

She entered her room and leaned against the door, her heart still beating wildly.

So now she knew what he really wanted.

But it didn't change one thing. She wanted to go home. With every fiber of her being she wanted to go home.

She was going home. And with something in her favor now. She had discovered something he wielded so well. Something that she could reach out and grasp now, at long last. Something of her own.

Power.

And she intended to use it!

14

In the afternoon she found the hall empty and managed to escape the house quickly. She hurried to the stables, where the grooms had become accustomed to her, but when she asked for her mare that day, the boy seemed uncomfortable and said that he must summon someone.

She began to seethe, certain that Conar had gone about commanding she be given no freedom about the place—assuring himself that she wouldn't disappear by morning. He had mocked her so about sleeping with devils just to be able to come home! When he had to have her with him!

"Perhaps you should summon my husband, then, and quickly," she told the boy. "For I am going riding. I will manage on my own, and I cannot imagine that you've been ordered to drag me off my horse . . . ?"

If this was to be her last day here, she was going to go to the stream and say certain good-byes.

Perhaps to her past way of life, she didn't know. Something had already been lost. Innocence, maybe. And something had been gained. Knowledge, maybe. She needed to see the stream, to have some time there with the gently bubbling water. In one night she had realized that any dreams she had spun there were childish fantasies.

But even before the lad could turn, Mergwin made a sudden appearance. "Get Melisande the mare she rides, and bring me my gentle old nag, lad. She will be in my care."

For a moment Melisande thought that the poor stable lad would protest again, but he looked into Mergwin's eyes and quickly nodded his agreement. He disappeared to bring the horses, and Melisande stared at the old man and smiled slowly. "You knew he was coming and knew that he would take me home, didn't you?"

"I knew," Mergwin admitted. "I fear my timing was rather poor, but then, had I had greater warning, I doubt if you would have paid me much heed anyway."

She smiled, biting lightly into her lower lip. "Maybe not." She hesitated. "I haven't seen Gregory—"

"He was very anxious to return to Alfred in Wexham. The climate seems to have grown too warm for him by the coast."

The boy brought their horses. He offered Melisande a hand, which she accepted, though she was quite able to leap up unaided. "Get over here, my young lad!" Mergwin commanded him. "The lady is as agile as a mountain nymph, and I am as old as the mountain."

Melisande smiled, watching the disgruntled old man catapult his skinny body atop his equally old gelding with the lad's help.

He turned in his saddle, staring at her. "Well? Shall we ride?"

She nodded and led the way. She leaned low against her mare's neck when she reached the field, allowing the horse to canter slowly across the long grass. She saw the ridge and the trees and began to slow her gait, and in a moment she heard Mergwin wheezing as he cantered up behind her.

"I said ride, not race!" he warned her sternly.

She turned around and saw the warm light in his old eyes and apologized quickly.

"I forgot—"

"It's all right. You think that if you run hard enough, ride fast enough, you can escape."

"You're wrong. I don't want to escape. I'm going home."

He was silent. Melisande reached out, touching his old gnarled hand where it rested on his saddle. "I am going home!" she repeated, a note of pleading in her voice.

He watched her a minute and then sighed. "Aye, lady, you're going home. It has all begun."

"What has begun?"

"Great wheels will be in motion."

"The Danes," she murmured disdainfully. "They are always coming. There is no great foresight in that!"

"Your difficulties lie with more of the Danes."

She spun on him. "My difficulties lie with Conar. If you have missed that, Mergwin, you are one blind seer!"

"I'm not a seer," he denied indignantly.

They had reached one of the little trails that led to the water. Melisande slipped down from her mare and started walking down the trail, pausing at the cool water, bathing her face with it. Mergwin followed.

"There lies the danger!" he warned her softly.

She sat back on a log by the stream, feeling the sun waft down through the trees to touch her face. She looked at Mergwin, aware that his old eyes were on her.

"The danger?" she asked softly.

He came to her side, and she was startled when he

knelt there, holding her hand tightly between his own two. "You must take great care not to be divided."

She shook her head, hearing how earnestly he spoke, and ever aware that he had acquired a very strong affection for her. She freed her hand and touched his cheek. "I shall miss you!" she assured him. "I shall miss you with all of my heart. Unless—do you sail with us?"

He shook his head. "Brenna will come home with you."

"Aye. Brenna," she said coldly, and looked to the water.

"Melisande, pay me heed—" Mergwin began.

She turned on him, feeling an absurd tug on her heart because he had mentioned Brenna. "I must not be divided from Conar?" she said. "Mergwin, I didn't want to leave my father's land. He wrapped me in sheets and had his berserkers drag me out to his ships—"

"He did not trust you to berserkers, ever, lady. Berserkers are those who fight so fiercely that their mouths foam. They bite their shields, fight in bear-skins. In their wild furies, they may at times slay their own. Some say they are possessed of the spirits, children of the gods. He gave you to no berserkers, just good Dubhlainers."

"Mergwin, it was my land!"

"And you were in danger on it."

"Ah, but now he wants me back on it!"

"Because it has come time for you to claim it together."

"Yes," she murmured. "It has come time for him to realize that I am of age, and he cannot claim it without me."

Mergwin shook his head sadly. "Melisande! You were so young when you were wed! What would you have had of Conar? He but waited until . . ."

She arched a brow.

Mergwin shrugged. "Last night."

She flushed. "Do you know everything?" she demanded irritably, and he shrugged again, a small smile curving his lip. "A blind seer might have known that, Melisande!"

She colored, drawing her knees to her, looking to the water again.

"Lady, you are stubborn!" he warned her. "But for both of your souls, for your future, your happiness, I pray you, remember my words!"

He was so earnest that she touched his cheek again, then hugged him, holding tight a minute, slowly letting him go. She looked past his shoulder and started. Conar stood there, Daria, Bryce, and Bryan lined up behind him. She felt his eyes upon her, and she rose quickly, helping Mergwin off his old knees as she did so.

He didn't say anything. Daria was moving quickly toward her with her beautiful eyes bright and her lips curled into a wry smile. She stepped past Mergwin, hugging Daria fiercely. And then Bryan, and then Bryce, with whom she'd come to feel closest.

"We shall miss you!" Daria told her. "I shall miss you! All the reckless rides, the books, the poems, the bawdy songs."

"Daria!" Bryce sighed.

Daria grinned and then shook her head. "Rhiannon will miss you, the children love you so."

Melisande suddenly blinked, aware that tears were brimming just behind her eyelids. The three of them surrounded her, and she felt their warmth and affection. "I'll miss you all," she said huskily. "Very much."

She looked up and discovered Conar was still staring at her. His eyes met hers for a long moment, and then he turned and walked away.

Daria began to speak excitedly again, "You're not so far away, you know. Conar says that you will be traveling to various cities near you in the near future, but never fear, we are all great sailors, you know, and we'll be there to visit you soon enough."

"I'll be looking forward to that!" Melisande promised her. She sank onto the log again, suddenly having little strength. Daria sat with her, Bryan hunkered down to his haunches, and Bryce came down upon a knee.

"It's not far back here, either," Daria said.

"And Dubhlain is not much farther," Bryce said.

"Thank you," Melisande murmured. "Thank you all. I hope that you do come. This is beautiful, and Dubhlain is incredible! But the fortress is fascinating, too. I hope desperately that you will come."

Bryan assured her, "There are occasions that draw us one and all, Melisande. Never fear. We are away, but never apart."

They talked a while longer, and as they did, Melisande realized that Mergwin had left them. She had not even seen him go. He had followed Conar, she thought, and she wondered if the old man had given her husband the same cryptic warning.

Darkness fell and they were still at the stream. They started back to the house. Melisande paused when she reached her mare, for Mergwin's old gelding was still tethered beside it. She noticed that there was another horse there, as well.

Mergwin was still in the forest somewhere.

With someone else.

Daria seemed to sense her concern. She mounted her own horse and said softly, "Brenna will sail with you. He is giving her his last good-byes."

Melisande arched a brow, confused. Surely the elegant blond woman so at her husband's beck and call could not be . . . intimately . . . linked with the old Druid?

Daria waved a hand in the air, smiling. "They discuss the world and the stars and the heavens—and try to foresee all our futures!" she said. "Come, let's hurry back. Rhiannon will have ordered everything edible in the vicinity for a feast tonight, her way of saying good-bye."

It was true. When they returned, Rhiannon and Eric were waiting in the great hall.

Eric's arms were around his beautiful wife. The snapping blaze picked up the fiery red highlights in her hair as she leaned back against her husband's broad chest.

Melisande found herself looking away, but Rhiannon had seen her enter the hall, and she quickly disentangled herself from her husband to wrap her arms around her sister-in-law in an affectionate hug. "It's been so good to have you. You are always welcome here, Melisande."

"Thank you. I know I'll be back. And I pray that you'll come to me—to us—too."

"Of course! We will. We have a way of getting together, so it seems," she said, smiling. "The children are upstairs, but they have come to love you dearly, if you wouldn't mind taking a few minutes now to say good-bye."

"Of course, I will see them immediately!"

She turned and ran up the stairs. Garth, like a little man, was waiting for her at the door.

"Mother said that you would come. She said you would never leave without saying good-bye to me!"

"And I never would."

Melisande plucked him up from the floor and sat at the edge of the bed with him on her lap, rocking him, even though he was a very big boy.

"I will begin to dine in the hall very soon," he told

her. "I'm nearly old enough. And soon I will ride out with my father and my uncles."

"You musn't be in such a hurry," she warned him, glancing up at the pretty young servant who tended to the children.

"You're a woman. You don't understand."

"I'm a woman, but I've ridden into battle. And you shouldn't be in too busy a hurry to do so!" she insisted.

"Do you have to go?" he asked her.

"Aye, that I do. It's my home we're going to now, just as this is your home. You understand that, don't you, Garth?"

His gaze touched hers. So like his father's.

Like his uncle's, too.

She trembled suddenly, and Garth felt the movement. "Are you shivering, are you afraid?"

She shook her head. "No, no I'm not. I'm anxious!" He shimmied from her lap to stand. "I suppose you want to hold my baby sister."

"I do want to hold her." Melisande stood and hurried over to the baby's finely carved cradle. She picked up the cooing infant and held her tenderly. "She've very precious, Garth. You must look after her."

"I do," he promised. His hand fit into the crook of her elbow. "If you have babies, I shall look after my little cousins, I promise!"

Babies . . .

She discovered herself shivering again, then looked up, past the young serving girl, to the doorway.

Conar stood there. Blue eyes hard upon her, as always.

Tremors streaked down her spine.

Garth turned and saw Conar, too. With a little cry he ran to his uncle. He was swept up, thrown into the air. Then Conar hugged him hard and set him down upon his sturdy young feet. He gripped the boy's hand. "We'll see you soon enough on the coast, eh, my boy?"

"Aye, Uncle!" Garth agreed. "Whenever I am needed!"

Melisande set the baby back into her cradle and stroked her wonderfully soft cheek. She hurried across the room, suddenly wanting to escape. Conar was here with the boy. She had said her good-byes. She just needed to slip by them.

"Melisande!"

She stopped as Garth called to her. She turned slowly back to him.

He ran quickly to her, throwing his arms around her legs. She was nearly unbalanced, but caught herself just in time, slipping her arms around him. She bent down to him, lifted his chin, and kissed his cheek. "Good-bye, Garth," she said, then stood quickly and slipped out of the room, leaving him alone with his uncle.

She fled down the stairs.

The soft sounds of a lute filled the hall when she returned to it. Servants carried huge platters of food to the tables, atop which sat whole wild pigs, and pheasant still adorned with colorful feathers, wild berries beautifully decorating the edges.

Rhiannon saw her return and lifted a brow, then offered someone a slow smile. Melisande spun around. Conar was coming right behind her.

She heard a whine and looked down. One of the big wolfhounds bounded into the hall. Dag was his name. He nuzzled his nose beneath her hand, and she stroked him. "I even have to say good-bye to you, eh?" she whispered softly.

The dog whined again and thumped his tail. He, too, seemed to look past her, wagging his tail with greater ardor.

Conar. He had reached her.

"Shall we sit? Rhiannon and Eric are taking their places."

He set his hands upon her shoulders, guiding her toward the table. She longed to shake off his touch.

She would bide her time.

They were all arrayed there once again, Eric and Rhiannon, Conar and Melisande, Daria, Bryan, Bryce, Mergwin, Brenna, a few of Eric's men, English and Norse. Again she shared a chalice with Conar. Again when her fingers laced around it, she smiled at him coolly and drained the whole of it.

He allowed her to do so several times. She spoke enthusiastically with Bryce about horses and told him how eager she was to see Warrior, her father's great bay stallion. "He's aged, too, I imagine, but Philippe and Gaston see to it that he is ridden and tended, and I believe he will remember me."

"It's hard to tell," Bryce warned her. "You were a young girl when last you saw him. Bear that in mind and take care."

"You'll hardly be needing use of such a horse," Conar said suddenly, and she swung around to stare at him in amazement.

Now he meant to tell her that she could not ride her own father's horse on her own property?

"Warrior is trained for battle. You'll not be riding into any more battles."

"But you have ridden into battle!" Bryce exclaimed. There was admiration in his handsome face. Melisande shrugged. "My father was dead, our people were losing a center of command. I had to go out—"

"How courageous!" Daria cried.

"Wonderfully so," Conar said dryly, entering into the conversation. "Why, haven't I ever fully explained? That's exactly how I acquired my lovely wife,

Daria. She was in the arms of the kinsman who had slain her father.''

"But, Conar, sometimes there is no choice," Rhiannon explained.

There was a sudden silence, and she blushed, feeling a number of eyes upon her.

"My wife is quite remarkable with arrows." Eric explained lightly. "She managed to send one flying into me once.''

"Could you refrain from giving Melisande any new ideas on the proper behavior of a wife?" Conar demanded.

He spoke lightly. Everyone laughed. But then Bryce said enthusiastically, "Melisande's weapon is the sword. She is really quite extraordinary with a blade. Have you seen her work with one, Conar?''

"Not as yet, but if you comment that she is talented, brother, I believe you.''

"She practices almost daily," Bryce continued.

"Does she now?''

Melisande had her fingers curled around their shared chalice, and she kept her gaze upon it. But she felt his look, felt his movement as he came closer to her.

"Are you hoping to ride into battle, my love?''

"I am always hoping for peace," she said smoothly.

"Then why the determination with the sword?" he asked.

She smiled pleasantly his way. The wine helped her do so. "Perhaps I am hoping to skewer you in your sleep, milord," she suggested, her voice as pleasant as her smile.

There was easy laughter around the table, but she was keenly aware that her husband's smile was very cold, and that his eyes held an ice-fire sizzle. She drank more wine.

He clasped the chalice from her, demanding softly, "For fortitude?''

She shook her head, her chin hiked in challenge. "I think not, milord. Not tonight. I have a few demands of my own to make tonight!"

"Do you now?" he said very softly.

"Indeed."

"And how is that?"

"It has come to my understanding that you are seeking things from me. If you would seek them, milord, then you must be willing to give in return."

"So far, I am going to be skewered through by your excellent swordsmanship. I must find some wondrous concession to make in turn!"

She tried to take the chalice. His grip on it was firm. "If you plan on bargaining, love, you had best keep your wits about you and slow down."

"Ah, so now you are interested in bargaining!"

"We shall see!" he told her softly. "Tell me about the demands you think you will make of me."

"Alas, not here, not now! We're in the midst of a banquet set before us by your gentle sister-in-law. The one who is so excellent with arrows."

"Aye, and who has since become such a tender wife!"

"Perhaps he has learned his lesson and become a far kinder husband."

"Perhaps . . ." Conar mused, his eyes narrowing upon her. "But then again . . . perhaps not!"

He suddenly pushed back his chair and stood, reaching for her arm. She stared up at him in astonishment as he pulled her away from the table.

"Conar—" she began, but he was already speaking with his sister-in-law at his other side. "Rhiannon, as always, you express the greatest warmth through the most spectacular meals. We thank you deeply for this wonderful banquet you have spread before us, yet forgive us—as we hope to sail very early, we need to retire early, as well."

Rhiannon leapt to her feet, Eric at her side. "Of course," Rhiannon said quickly. "You will want to retire early!"

"Indeed," Eric agreed, looking at them both somberly, but with a grin pulling upon his lip. Rhiannon leaned against his side, which caused him to grunt. His hands fell upon her shoulders, his fingers curling tightly upon them. "I was thinking of retiring early myself."

"We'll be up in the morning with you, of course," Rhiannon assured Melisande. "We'll wish you Godspeed."

"Thank you," Melisande murmured to her, so surprised by his sudden determination to leave the great hall that she could not think swiftly enough of a reason to stay.

Conar propelled her about the room. He called a quick good night, his fingers firmly set upon her arm, and led her from the hall to the stairway. He had to practically run her to the top of it before she managed to speak.

"What is the matter with you! I had barely eaten! Rhiannon prepared all that in your honor!"

"I'm very sorry, my love!" he said, his tone anything but. "Yet you are the one who brought about our premature departure."

"I—"

"You tempted me, goaded me. And I but took the bait."

"I don't know what—"

"But you do."

"I don't know what you're talking about! I do know that you're being incredibly rude and as crude and ill-mannered as any—" she broke off.

"Viking?" he finished. They had reached the door to her room. Her room! The one she had slept in before he had followed her here.

She started into it ahead of him, throwing the door closed behind her with all her might.

But it didn't close.

He caught it, shoved it open, and closed it deliberately behind him, and Melisande jumped as she heard the energy with which the bolt was slid.

"Let's have it, Melisande. What is it you think you have as bargaining power against me?" he demanded. His tone was cold. His arms were crossed over his chest. He leaned against the closed door, watching her.

She told herself that she had to be determined where this man was concerned, as determined as he was. She stood very still, lacing her fingers before her and speaking very softly. "You would never have come for me, Conar, unless you needed me."

He frowned at her. "What are you talking about?"

"You were given a bride you never wanted."

He waved a hand impatiently in the air. "I cannot win! I was a wretched Viking for taking you, and now I am a wretched Viking for leaving you alone."

She ignored that. "You need me now. You saw Count Odo, and he warned you that you needed the barons to see the strength of your marriage in order to solidify your position among them. So you have come for me—because you need me to repeat my vows in public."

"Ah . . ." he murmured. "And you think that this is your bargaining point?"

"I'm not a child any longer, Conar. You cannot force my words now, and neither can Ragwald. It would hardly stand you well if we were to enter the church and I were to denounce you!"

"Is that what you're planning on doing?"

"It is my bargaining point," she said flatly.

He entered the room, pacing before the fireplace. The night was damp and cool, and a low blaze burned.

He watched the flames for a moment, then his pacing brought him behind her. He lifted the fall of hair from her shoulder, allowing the length of it to sweep over his arm. He studied it. She started to twist. The warmth of his breath touched her shoulder and throat and earlobe. His lips didn't quite touch her flesh. She felt a spiraling of liquid heat seep slowly into her.

"Indeed. Just what is it that you would bargain?"

She turned, unable to bear him so close to her back, that near touch that sent hot tremors racing within her. She faced him, yet he held the rich length of her hair in his hands, and he remained uncomfortably close.

"Freedom," she said softly.

He arched a brow. "Restating your marriage vows before a sizable crowd is no way to find freedom— since I'm assuming the freedom is from me."

She spoke quickly, nervously, despite all her resolve, moistening her lips and starting over again. "Freedom in that I wish to be let alone. I'll sail back with you tomorrow. My eagerness to return home is certainly evident enough."

"As it's evident enough that you have found friends here!" he reminded her.

"I have longed to go home forever," she said softly, "and everyone knows it."

"Go on."

Her mouth was dry again. He remained too close, almost on top of her, one thigh brushing hers as he continued to run his fingers through the long fall of her hair.

She tried to draw the ebony length back. His fingers wound more tightly around it. "Go on," he urged her, and the tone of his voice was harsh.

She moistened her lips quickly again to speak, then felt the rise of her temper when she least needed it. "Are you daft!" she cried. "I'll go back with you, I'll state any vows you wish, but I want to be left alone. Sleep alone. I take my father's room. You keep out of it!''

He was dead silent for the longest time. Eons. She held her breath through all that time. Her heart began to pound too fiercely, but she did not draw breath, for she felt the searing ice-fire of his eyes pinning and impaling her.

He lifted the length of her hair between them, his fingers entwined within it. His voice was husky, nearly silken, not at all the explosion she had expected.

"I have told you—I will never let you go.''

"I didn't ask that you do so!'' Once again she tried to tear her hair from his grasp, tugging upon it. His fingers closed into a fist. "You're hurting me!'' she charged him.

He shook his head slowly. "Nay, lady, you are hurting yourself. Stand still, and your hair will not pull.''

She ceased for a moment, standing very still, staring into his eyes and realizing this had nothing to do with her hair.

They were discussing her life.

Obey him, and she would not be hurt.

Try to break his rein upon her, and the tendrils would be pulled back, one by one . . .

"Obviously I cannot best you in this room!'' she cried. "I cannot tear out your hair, throw you about! But I can create great havoc for you in Rouen, and I swear that it will be so unless—''

"Ah, threatening me now!''

"You are forever threatening me.''

"But I thought you were bargaining with me.''

She let out an oath of frustration. "Call it what you will, in any language! I can be the most charming of heiresses, the most giving. I can—''

"There's nothing for you to give me, Melisande. I

earned my title to that land, not by marrying you, but by coming when your father summoned me, slaying his murderer, and besting his enemies."

"Be that as it may!" she cried. "You are here now because Odo warned you that you need me."

He suddenly released her hair and strode back to the fire, stretching his hands with their long fingers before it. She watched him, praying that she had found some small victory.

He turned back to her, a rueful smile curved into the corners of his lip, his eyes sizzling. "Let me repeat this one more time, to be sure that I have it right."

"You know exactly what I've said—"

"Daft Vikings sometimes need to hear things twice," he said.

He began to walk toward her again, his hands clasped behind his back, his stride easy, lazy. "You promise to vow eternal love and obedience and all manner of wonderful things in Rouen as long as I leave you be. Quit this chamber now, I assume, sail to the coast, remove my things from the master's chamber, and let you live there alone in chasteness and purity."

She didn't reply. She didn't like the tone of his voice.

"Is that it, Melisande?"

Again her temper flared, perhaps because he had made her so very uneasy. "Aye, that is it. Are you so daft a Viking that it must be repeated one more time?"

As soon as the words had left her lips, she was heartily sorry.

Once again he stood dead still. Until he reached out, caught her arm, and drew her to him. Hard against the length of his chest. Her head fell back, her eyes met his.

"No," he grated out harshly.

"I can make your life hell in Rouen!" she cried, straining against his hold.

"You do whatever you damned well please in Rouen, Melisande."

"Damn you! Damn you!" she cried, trying to kick him. "You just sit there and let me go on and on—"

"You were determined to do so," he interrupted, swearing as her foot managed to connect with his knee. He swept her off her feet suddenly, and she was startled to find herself clinging to his neck, lest she fall.

"Set me down!" she cried desperately.

He did so, dropping her down upon the expanse of the bed. She was ready to leap away from him, but he turned away himself, striding back to the fire, stretching out his long fingers again, as if he could not get his hands warm. He turned at last with a weary sigh, striding back to her. She started to rise, but he sat by her side, and she remained there, leaning upon her elbows, her gaze upon his.

"You cannot bargain away what is, Melisande," he said at last. "Rouen is intended as a pretty show, but you are my wife now, lady, and have been, and I will not turn back again."

"But you want—"

His finger fell upon her lips, hushing her along with the force of his eyes. "I have told you before, Melisande, I want you."

His finger fell from her lips.

"How dare you take such a chance!" she whispered.

"Recklessness, perhaps," he suggested.

"Ruthlessness!" she returned.

He smiled, his finger stroking her cheek. Her lashes fell, she looked away, and his touch ceased. Her gaze fell upon the door. More than anything in the world, she wanted to run to it, escape. She had been so certain of her victory!

"Ah, the door! Freedom!" he murmured.

Her gaze met his. Clashed with it.

"And if I were to run?" she demanded.

"Ah, well, if you were to run, I'd have to come after you, of course. Drag you back by the hair, throw you down, and ravish you." His voice was light. The words were mocking.

Nay, he'd not pull her hair out.

But she would never leave the room.

"And if I were not to run?" she asked him, alarmed that she should be so breathless.

"Ah, well, then . . ." His fingers were suddenly upon the lacing of the soft linen tunic she wore. She clutched at his hand, but the binding gave. The shift she wore beneath it was as thin as gauze, and her breasts were all but bared. He stared upon them, then met her eyes again. "I would beg you to lie still. I would strive my hardest to seduce you," he informed her.

"That is far worse!" she protested.

"Nay, lady, nay. Far better!" he assured her.

His lips found hers, his weight pressing her back to the pillows. His tongue found entry, delving deep, stroking, bringing its touch of liquid fire.

His lips broke from hers. His gaze touched upon her mouth, then rose to her own.

"Lie still," he urged.

"It's better to run."

"Better to stay."

He lowered his head. His mouth closed over her breast, tongue stroking it through the thin veil of her shift. He circled her nipple, laving until the crest hardened into a pebbled peak, then sucked upon it until she began to writhe beneath him, the fires wild and rampant within her, her protest at the alarm that rose so swiftly in her heart.

"No!"

Her fingers tugged upon his hair. His lips rose from

her breast at last, but his answer was firm and unyielding.

"Lie still . . ."

His hand had slipped beneath her tunic and shift, drawing each up against the length of her limbs. Fingers stroked her upper thigh gently above her hose. Circular motions brought them higher and higher. The fabric bunched to her waist. His eyes were upon hers.

The palm of his hand caressed the ebony curls between her thighs.

She closed her eyes, swallowing hard. "No . . ."

Again, "Lie still" was his only response.

She started to speak, the inhaled sharply, for his touch was suddenly searingly intimate, parting tender, intimate places, delving within them, discovering the most sensitive and erotic feminine spots of her sex, playing upon them.

She stiffened wildly, straining against him, a gasp escaping her.

He silenced that gasp with his kiss, stroking her with his touch and with his tongue. Harder, deeper, more and more demandingly. He knew how to stroke, how to tease, caress, arouse.

She trembled massively and was so filled with the burning sensation of need he had aroused within her that she was startled when he rose. She realized two things then.

That each time he touched her now, she was more attuned to his touch, her body more eager for it, her flesh more traitorously willing to be kissed, caressed, and aroused.

And that her husband could strip more quickly than she thought humanly possible.

Strip and return to her, impatiently pulling upon the clothing that was all knotted around her now.

"You want to help!" he whispered.

She shook her head, violet eyes dazed as they touched him.

"I am not expected to help in a ravishment," she informed him.

"In a seduction," he corrected.

"You commanded me to lie still."

"So I did," he agreed. He no longer attempted to maneuver her clothing from her body, but tore upon it with his powerful hands. The fabric ripped and shredded to his will, and the vital, muscled heat of his naked body lay flush with hers, the hard pulsing thrust of his sex against her as intimate and arousing as all else had been. His weight thrust her thighs apart. Within seconds he was sinking deeply into her, and her fingers were curling into his shoulders.

And her lips were parting to accept his kiss.

Once again she was filled with that searing liquid heat as the steel of him thrust into her body. He stroked her tongue and lips as he began to move. He rose from her, his breath having grown ragged. A groan escaped his lips even as they closed around her breast, suckling hard, moving still, harder, faster, with an ever more erotic rhythm, more and more demanding, more and more a tempest. The wind swept her, lightning filled her.

Hours later she lay exhausted, frustrated, and dismayed that she could have given in to him so completely.

How could she be so weak?

And yet as she lay there, she became aware of the way he lay beside her, body curled to her back in a protective shell, leg draped over hers, an arm about her. His great golden head was above hers, chin resting upon it. His hand moved suddenly, fingers moving tenderly, curling around hers, and he shifted behind her. His scent was rich, his breathing deep, the masculine feel of him still warm and pleasant. Perhaps in all of her life she had never felt quite so well . . . used. Yet neither had she ever felt so strangely protected or secure or . . . comfortable.

Perhaps surrender had not been so awful a thing after all.

Not in the darkness, perhaps.

But daylight would come again. Daylight, with Brenna and his other mistresses and his autocratic tone of command.

He didn't sleep, either, she realized, for his lips were suddenly upon her back. Fingers brushed away her hair, damp seduction stroked along the length of her spine from her nape to her buttocks. His hand traveled at that same slow, sensual, mesmerizing speed, sliding under her arm, cupping the curve of her breast, caressing the rise of her hip. She caught her breath as she was turned in his arms, as her flesh knew his caress again, her lips the ardent, hungry fever of his kiss, so intimate, liquid fire against her, determined, no matter what protest left her lips.

No matter what soft moan, what sensual cry, no matter how she writhed, arched.

Exploded, like the burst of a log within a fire, beneath his expert manipulations.

Again he rose over her, demand written in the hard lines of his features, in the blue blaze of his eyes.

Daylight could wait.

Yet daylight came quickly, and with it, the change Melisande had expected.

She had just begun to sleep deeply, comfortably, in her warm cocoon when she was startled by the stinging strike that fell upon her posterior flesh and the sharp command that issued firmly from his lips, right against her ear.

"Up, milady, now! We sail within the hour!"

What was the matter with him? She was exhausted.

And all because of his doing. He might, at the least, let her have some sleep when he had had everything his way.

She groaned, rolling away from him. "Leave me be!"

But he dragged her back, and she cried out in a wild and earnest protest.

"If you strike me again, I swear I shall see the day that you are drawn and quartered!"

"Swear it, milady, but get up! It is time that we are about! We are sailing for the coast of France, and I will not lose the tide!"

He was gone quickly, already up and moving. She heard the sound of wash water sluicing over him.

She bounded up, suddenly very awake herself. His words didn't matter, nothing mattered.

She was going home.

At long last, home.

She was so eager, even if it did mean she had sold herself to a devil to return to France.

15

Leaving people she had come to care about had been difficult, but the sheer joy of coming home definitely made up for the pain of parting.

Conar's ships remained a distance from the beach, but she could wait no longer. She started to leap out, then felt his grip upon her arm.

"Lady, we are nearly there! Don't ruin your gown!"

She lifted her chin. "You can tear one, but I must not wet one?"

He let out an angry oath, but suddenly swept her into his arms, leaping from the vessel himself and carrying her through the seawater to the shore of her home at last.

They had been seen arriving from the fortress, and a group met them upon the shore. The second Conar set her down upon the sandy beach, she was flying in a hard run to reach Marie de Tresse, who stood waiting, her arms outstretched.

"Melisande, Melisande, milady, all grown up, now!"

"Ah, Marie, how I have missed you!"

But she couldn't linger with Marie long, for Philippe was there, and Gaston, and all her father's fine men. Swen was there, too, and she greeted him cordially, but with a reserve, wondering just what he had been doing with her property in her absence. She didn't dwell on that long, even as she refused to dwell on the fact that even now, Brenna was stepping upon the sand, having sailed with them, as well.

"Where is Ragwald?" she demanded of Philippe anxiously. Philippe grinned and stepped aside, and there was her old mentor, tears in his eyes as he crushed her to him.

"The fortress has been empty without you, child," he assured her, crushing her to him again.

She smiled. "And I have been empty without you all!" she assured him.

"Come, let's return there," Ragwald urged, shivering, for despite the season, there was dampness in the air, and the beach was cold. "We have brought another old friend for you to bridge the distance," Ragwald told her happily. He turned back, and one of the servant boys, clad in rough wool, came forward eagerly, leading Warrior.

She cried out softly, hurrying forward to stroke the stallion's nose. He whinnied once, backing away, then seemed to recognize her. He pranced closer to her then, nearly knocking her over. She cried out again with delight. "Ah, Warrior, you have not forgotten me!"

"Indeed, it seems that he has not," she heard.

Conar. He was at her back again. Always. She grit her teeth, remembering his words at Rhiannon's banquet table that night, that she would have no need of a war-horse.

Tears stung her eyes suddenly. She was not up to a mighty battle with him at the moment. She had just come home. She wanted peace. After everything, he had no right to deny her a horse!

Her lashes lowered themselves over her eyes. But

she was startled to hear his words again. "Come, milady, I'll give you a boost."

She gazed at him, grateful. "Thank you," she murmured awkwardly.

A moment later she was upon Warrior. She waited impatiently for the last of Conar's ships to arrive behind them, the ships he had had especially built to carry his trained mounts, for as he didn't travel without Brenna, it seemed, he did not travel without Thor. Perhaps that was one of the differences that had come with his father's landing upon Irish shores, for the offspring of Olaf, the Wolf of Norway, plucked their sailing, fighting, and living customs from whatever society they chose. And Conar had chosen to fight his battles upon Thor; it did not matter how difficult the transport from shore to shore.

But his crews, composed of so many peoples, were well trained and efficient, and the ships were quickly beached and unloaded. In a very short time they were riding hard for the fortress.

So little had changed!

The stone walls, her father's stone walls, still guarded the castle and keep. The fields outside the walls were growing richly, and all manner of inhabitants from within the walls themselves, the laundresses, the smiths, the artisans, were eagerly waiting at the open gates, waving their welcome. She greeted those she could, dismounting from Warrior with the help of Father Matthew as they rode into the courtyard. There was such a bustle of activity! Dear God! It seemed forever since she had been home. Almost six long years.

Then at last she was climbing the stairs to reach the great hall of her own castle, and she was soon seated before the fire, Ragwald insisting she must warm her feet, though he seemed more determined to warm his own! It didn't matter, it was so good to see his old,

worn face! Marie quickly brought her a chalice of
sweet warm wine, yet there was little conversation
between them because the men were soon entering the
hall and more servants were called, and everyone was
speaking while the wine and ale flowed freely.

She stared about and noted the absence of the little
touches that had so graced Rhiannon's hall. The
rushes strewn upon the floor were not so fresh as they
should be, several windows were left without tapestries to keep out the chill of the nights. She was home
now and determined that she would bring her father's
creation to full glory.

But then, she mused, the inner workings of the
fortress were not as important as the outer defenses.
First things first. She wanted to circle the walls, speak
to the carls, or guards, assure herself that they were
strongly defended from within.

She looked up. Conar was staring at her. It was
almost as if he read her mind, and his gaze upon her
warned her that there might be harsh battles ahead.

She looked away from him. "You must tell me
everything that has happened in my absence," she
told Marie and Ragwald, extending her gaze to Philippe and Gaston beyond them. "Do the tenants fare
well? Who have we lost? What have we gained?"

"William from the south fields passed on to greater
glory just last planting," Gaston said, crossing himself. "He was a good farmer, and a fine man, but his
son, another William, swore his fealty to you and
Count Conar through yonder Swen, for you were in
Eire, and Count Conar about with Count Odo."

She nodded, lowering her eyes. Swen! Her husband's man. Yet she bore Swen no great hostility,
other than that he was her husband's man.

There was still so much to say and so much to be
done. The day passed swiftly. Soon after their arrival
the tenants and serfs began to arrive, to greet her, to

renew their homage. It occurred to her again that the very Viking menace the Christian world feared had created their feudal society—these people served her, or Conar, for the strength of the fortress. They owed her homage, their work for three days a week, their loyalty and service. They lived upon her land. She granted them their livelihood, they gave her themselves. In turn they were owed protection.

By nightfall the tenant farmers, artisans, smiths, and other servants had all paid their homage. The hall was filled only with those who lived within it, and the banquet table in the great hall was laid out with a feast to rival any she had enjoyed elsewhere. She was pleased to view the fortress with new eyes—Dubhlain was a great city, huge, walled, wondrous. Perhaps her fortress did not quite compare with it. But, though it lacked some of the finer points of Rhiannon's hall, she thought its structure to be stronger and saw the wonderful strength of its defenses with great pride.

The fire had burned low and the hour grown very late when Melisande realized that she was very weary. "Perhaps, Marie, you will assist your lady to bed now," Conar said suddenly, and she looked to him quickly, startled again that he had been watching her without her knowledge.

"I am not so tired—" she began, aware that he was seated amid Swen, Gaston, and Philippe, and that the men intended to talk far longer on the affairs of the fortress. But she broke off. He had not argued with her over Warrior. She would begin to assert her own authority tomorrow, when she was not so weary, when she would have greater strength to do so.

"Perhaps I am," she said, her lashes sweeping low, and Marie was quickly up with her. She was so glad to be home. She once again bid good night to the men who had served her father and her so faithfully, hugged Ragwald, and started to leave the hall for the stairway.

"Melisande!"

She heard his soft call and turned back, biting her lower lip. She had purposely ignored him. Stiffening her spine, she came back into the room and managed to set a light kiss upon the top of his golden head. His eyes rose to meet hers. "I will not be long, my love."

"Please, milord, take all the time you wish! Take the night, if need be!"

"Ah, lady! I could not bear it. I shall be along shortly."

She clenched her teeth, smiled, and fled.

She came to her father's room. It remained as huge as she had remembered it, as warm, too. A warm bath awaited her by the fire, and a soft gown lay ready on the bed. She sank into the water with Marie's assistance and found that she was telling her all about the distant places and foreign lands where she had lived, avoiding any mention of Conar.

But she could not avoid thinking about him herself. Her things had all been brought here.

As had his.

She rose from the tub at last. Marie offered her a soft linen towel and she wrapped herself in it, then donned the exquisitely soft gown that had been left for her. She'd never seen it before. "Where did it come from?" she asked Marie.

"Count Conar acquired it in his travels, Melisande," Marie said.

"Ah," Melisande murmured and stood still as Marie helped her don the garment.

Marie kissed her cheeks and hugged her, Melisande promised that they would be together from then on, and then Marie left her. Alone in her father's room, she stared at the fire and wondered when Conar had acquired the gown, and if he had really intended it for her.

Or for Brenna, or some other woman. She almost wrenched it over her head, but then she heard his footsteps outside the door and dived beneath the covers of the bed instead, closing her eyes to feign sleep.

But he soon stood over her. He was silent and still for long minutes. Then she heard him moving about, discarding his clothing.

The sheets were pulled back. Naked, he was at her side. "Look at me, Melisande."

She didn't move.

"I know that you are awake."

He crawled atop her and she felt his warmth suffuse her. Her eyes rose to his, flashing. She tried not to view his hard, muscled body.

Or the other hardness that seemed to rise all too easily the moment they were alone.

His eyes tonight were not mocking but dark and brooding as he stared into hers.

"Why do you do this? Turn away from me? Fight me in your wearying way so endlessly?"

"I don't fight you—"

"You do. And I don't understand it, for I know I don't hurt you. I have been pleased, aye, astounded by the beauty with which you respond."

The ease with which she responded, she thought.

She swallowed hard, returning his stare. "I fight you," she said softly, "because you have taken everything that is mine."

He shook his head. "I have taken what you cannot hold!"

"You are a Viking!" she taunted. "Accustomed to taking!"

"Alas, then I must take you again, willing or no!"

She did struggle against him that night, twist and

fight him and yet to no avail. He never really forced her. He just held her.

And touched her and stroked her.

Kissed her.

Until her fingers ceased to knot against him, until her arms wrapped around him.

Until he won, once again.

Being home was wonderful. Hearing her own language spoken daily, watching the fields grow, spending time with Ragwald and Marie, Philippe and Gaston and the others, all delighted her. It was easy enough to avoid Conar by day—he seemed to be occupied continually with the fortress, worrying about weakened positions, one in particular that, he assured her curtly one evening, was about to crumble.

She staunchly defended her father's wall. He informed her impatiently that her father had never been at fault, time itself had done the damage, and that they would need to begin work shoring it up as soon as they returned from Rouen.

He hadn't informed her as yet when they were going. In fact, he never informed her about anything.

If he ever felt the need to simply speak with a woman, it was Brenna with whom he chose to speak.

On their fourth night home Melisande left the hall early. Hours passed, and he did not retire.

She came halfway down the stairs, curious as to what was going on below that would keep him awake so late.

Then she knew. Brenna. He sat before the fire with her, talking. The firelight played on both golden heads. She thought about striding in on them and sweetly stating the need for a cup of wine or ale, but withdrew instead, hating them both.

She feigned sleep when he came up at last. It did her little good. He disrobed with his customary speed and climbed beneath the sheets. Several moments later he spoke coolly. "If you feel the need to listen in on my conversations, you should make yourself known. You would learn so much more."

She didn't reply, and he continued, "You needn't eavesdrop upon us, Melisande."

"I had no desire to eavesdrop," she replied at last. "I had hoped that the hall might be empty, and that I might sit before the fire alone."

"And where else but the hall might I have been, milady, since I was not here?"

"God alone knows where you might choose," she said.

To her amazement he sniffed and turned to his side.

And did not touch her that night.

The following morning she found herself strangely restless and decided that she was going to take a long ride alone. She had discovered that she greatly enjoyed the stream that ran near Eric's castle, and she knew of a similar run not far from the castle walls.

Conar was nowhere about, and in truth it did not occur to her that he might object when she left. She rode out alone, neglecting to tell Ragwald or Marie or anyone where she was going.

Only the young stable boy knew she had taken Warrior.

She never meant to be careless. She had simply awakened with a rare tempest in her heart, and had determined that she must find a way to understand it, to still it. She reached the water she had sought, leapt from Warrior, and walked with a swift agility over the stones that crossed it, leaving Warrior to nibble at sweet grasses. When she came to the far side, she slipped off her shoes and wiggled her toes in the water and wondered why she felt so restless.

She had come here with her father years ago, when she had been just a child.

There had always been a danger of Viking raiders. But they came from the sea then, and the ships could be seen from the fortress. They had never known that danger could come from within—until Gerald.

She had loved this place once. Maybe that was why she had so quickly found the stream in Wessex.

Her cheeks grew hot and she placed her hands, cooled by the water, against them as she remembered how Conar had come upon her by that English stream. She could almost feel the heat of his eyes as they had touched her where she stood with Gregory.

She dipped her head, soaking her face again, as she realized the source of her restlessness.

Conar, of course.

She had wanted to beg, barter, or steal a safe distance from him. Maybe she had always known that it might be possible to care too much for him, find herself dangerously beneath his domination . . .

Wanting him. Feeling fierce jealousy because of him.

Wanting other women to sink to the bottom of the ocean and be consumed by fishes because of him!

Falling in love with him.

She sat up straight, hugging her arms about herself, swearing inwardly that she was not falling in love with him, only a foolish milkmaid would be stupid enough to fall in love with such a man.

And yet she had hated last night. Hated the coldness. What could she do? She didn't want him coming from Brenna to her, or from any of his more casual mistresses. Yet what help had she? What power? She would never give him her soul, never allow her heart to fall. Life would become unbearable then.

It seemed to stretch out very bleakly now, even here, even where she loved so many people so dearly and was loved in return. There was an emptiness in their lives. One that had not existed in either the walled city of Dubhlain or the Wessex fortress across the sea. Because there had been laughter there, and a different kind of love, that very rare and special love that could exist only between a man and a woman.

She didn't dare love him, she must fight against it, fight bitterly and without quarter to retain her heart and soul—and self.

"Melisande!"

She heard her name spoken by a voice oddly familiar. She looked up and across the stream, and her heart seemed to freeze.

Geoffrey Sur-le-Mont. Gerald's son, grown older, heavier, so much like his father now, dark-haired, hazel-eyed. Those same eyes, eyes that glittered with speculation and greed.

She straightened warily.

He stood across the stream from her, just watching her, making no move to come closer.

"Don't be afraid," he told her quickly.

"I'm not afraid," she lied with equal speed. She stood in the cool water, suddenly wishing that her shoes were on, and that Warrior, too, was not on the other side of the stream.

"I heard that you had returned," he told her. He didn't make a move toward her. He was a tall man, like his father, well built, his face long and lean, handsome enough.

Except for that strange flaw within his eyes, within the curve of his lip. Something that made her feel very uncomfortable now, as if he undressed her completely with his steady gaze.

"Aye. As you can see, I have returned," she murmured simply.

"You've changed greatly, Melisande."

"Have I?"

"You are the most extraordinary woman I have ever seen."

"Surely not, Geoffrey."

"But it's true."

"Perhaps your acquaintance with women is limited," she murmured.

He took a step toward her, balancing upon one of the stones, as she had done herself. "No," he told her. "My acquaintance with women is vast."

She reached for her shoes, heedless now as to whether she wet them or not. If it became necessary, she wanted to be ready to run.

"Wait!" he told her swiftly. "I've not come to hurt you. Just to speak with you." She stood still, and he was silent for a minute. "You know, once upon a time it was to be you and me."

She shook her head. "I'm sorry, Geoffrey, but I can't believe a word of that. Your father tricked mine, betrayed him ruthlessly, murdered him. Everyone knows the truth of that."

"And he was murdered in return by your Viking."

"He's not a Viking," she heard herself saying.

Geoffrey arched a brow to her, a small smile curving his lip. He came another step closer. "You cannot be happy with such a union, Melisande. Your husband's father is from the house of Vestfold, and even if they pretend at times to have become Christianized and civilized, they are Vikings at heart, mercenaries to the highest bidder. Conar fought my father—to gain you. His people might turn at any time. You never know them, they can be like mad dogs."

"Geoffrey, I'm sorry—"

"I have coveted you forever, Melisande. Once, your father did intend you for me."

"The church would never allow it anyway, Geoffrey—"

"The church allows what the powerful demand!"

"Geoffrey," she said flatly, "your father wasn't sure if he wanted to keep me for himself, give me to you—or murder me outright and have done with it."

"I've always wanted you, Melisande. And mark my words, I will seize you from that bastard Viking yet! Seize you—or rescue you. Which will it be, Melisande?"

"Your father murdered mine!" she cried. "I will never have anything to do with you!"

He took another step as if he would come across the stream. But suddenly they both became aware of the sound of horses. He stood still. In a second Melisande was relieved to see Conar burst through the trees on the opposite side, mounted upon Thor, accompanied by Swen and Gaston.

No armor adorned him. He sat atop Thor, his head glinting gold from the sun, his eyes a searing cobalt blue as he stared down at Geoffrey.

"Ah, the great Lord of the Wolves has returned!" Geoffrey murmured, undaunted. He offered Conar a deep bow, then his gaze rose once again, and he looked Melisande's way. "I had heard that you had returned with my kin, Conar, and when I saw Warrior disappear by the stream, I was afraid for her safety. But—as you can plainly see—she is perfectly well, unharmed, untouched."

"Aye, we've come in time!" Gaston said angrily.

"If I am guilty for my father's deeds, Conar, then you must be guilty for your sire's as well. King of Dubhlain he might be now, but it is my understanding he raided that land long before he ruled it! Ah, but then he gained recognition through marriage to the Ard-Ri's daughter, did he not?"

"I should slice you through here and now," Conar said softly.

Melisande was glad to see Geoffrey whiten beneath Conar's cool scrutiny. Still he held his ground, smiling as if with some secret knowledge.

"Slaying an unarmed, innocent man?" Geoffrey demanded, lifting his hands to prove that he carried no weapons. "That, Milord of the Wolves Viking, would not endear you to the other barons of France, would it?" he asked softly.

"Go, then," Conar warned him. "But if I catch you with my wife again—"

"Me with your wife, or your wife with me?" Geoffrey taunted him.

Conar suddenly nudged Thor. The great black warhorse pranced forward, and Gaston cried out with alarm. "Mon Dieu! Stay your hand, Count! He is not worth it!"

Conar reined in just as he reached the edge of the stream, not a foot away from the man. "Go!" he warned hoarsely.

Geoffrey leapt from the stone to the shore, turning back to bow deeply to Melisande only when he had put several feet between himself and Conar. Then he leapt atop his own mount and called out, "Good day, Countess!"

He spurred his horse and quickly galloped away. Melisande watched him, then felt Conar's furious eyes upon her. She turned to him, stunned that he could be so angry with her.

"You've called this upon yourself, Melisande!" he charged her.

"Caused this?"

"Get on your horse."

"But—"

"I'll not discuss it here, now!" he snapped.

She looked at Swen and Gaston. Both the young redhead and the older graybeard looked keenly uncomfortable.

She determined that she was not going to have him issuing any commands to her in front of the two. She leapt across the stones and strode swiftly toward Warrior.

Warrior was a match for any horse. She nudged his

sides, and he took off like a winged creature. She raced hard across the fields, back to the walls. Though Conar was close behind her, he could not catch her.

She leapt off Warrior at the entrance to the south tower, tossing the reins to a young groom. Hurrying up the stairs to the hall, she then rushed up the second flight to her room. She closed the door behind her and leaned against it, but a thunderous weight suddenly shoved against it, and she jumped away as he opened the door. His gaze met hers, then fell to her breasts. They rose and fell with her effort to find breath, with the fierce pounding of her heart.

"What a place to come to escape me!" he mocked.

"If you wish me not to escape you, milord, then you must cease to speak to me the way that you did before others. I shall not be yelled at and ordered about and constantly condemned as if I were a child!"

He started to stride across the room, and she jumped back, frightened that he meant her some violence. But he strode past her, coming into the room. To her surprise he suddenly started tearing through one of her trunks, not one that she had brought from Wessex, but an old one, one that had been transferred here from her old room.

Garments went flying as he sought something. His effort didn't stop him from speaking. "It is difficult not to speak to you as if you were a child when you behave as foolishly as one."

"What are you talking about?"

"Riding out alone like that, unescorted, without anyone even knowing where you were going!"

"But—" she gasped, stunned. "I am not a prisoner here!"

"You cannot ride out of the walls!"

She shook her head wildly, coming over to stand beside the trunk and stare down at him. "You've no right to tell me that, none at all! You made a prisoner

of me for years in distant lands. I will not be told that
I cannot ride in my own home—''

He stood suddenly, and she was so mesmerized by
his eyes that at first she did not see what he held in his
hands. "Melisande, you will not ride out alone again.
I can and will tell you that.''

"But—'' she began, but then her eyes were caught
by a glinting from his hands, and she gazed downward
to see that he held her coat of mail, the extraordinary
gilded tunic that had long ago been the gift from her
father.

"What are you doing with that?'' she cried.

"Seeing to its disposal. I'm afraid I shall ride out
and find you clad within it next.''

"No! No!'' she cried. She suddenly pit herself
against him with a wild vengeance, her fists flying
against his chest, her vehemence such that he was
actually forced back a step to keep his balance. "No!''

He dropped the suit of mail and caught her wrists,
dragging her against him. She stared wildly into his
eyes. "You can't! It was his last gift to me, my father's
last gift. You cannot take it, I will hate you forever if
you do, I swear it!''

"Ah, but you hate me already!'' he taunted.

"You will never know such loathing!'' she promised
him.

His hold eased somewhat. He seemed to be thinking. "Then I shall leave the mail in exchange for a
promise.''

She stiffened instantly, cursing herself for a fool. He
hadn't thought that she was about to ride out in the
suit of mail. It was a bargaining point.

He didn't make a bargain when she wished to, but
he was very adept at forcing his own.

"What promise?''

"That you'll not leave this fortress again without

my permission. That you'll do so only in my company, or that of someone I approve."

"Some other Viking," she said icily.

"Your promise, Melisande."

"I break promises," she reminded him.

"But not to me. I see that they are kept."

Her lashes fell over her eyes. She wrenched her wrists free from his hold and knelt to cradle the mail in her arms. She walked slowly back to the trunk and laid it out within it.

"I'm waiting," he told her.

She kept her back to him, her spine very stiff. "You have my promise, milord Viking," she said softly.

He would leave now, she thought. He had had his way. But when she spun around, he still stood by the door. "In the next few days it will not much matter," he told her. "We leave for Rouen in the morning."

Her heart slammed against her chest. A small smile curved her lips.

"Ah, Rouen!" she said softly. "Yes, milord, now isn't that the place where you're expecting me to meekly repeat my vows once more for God and countrymen?"

"Indeed, that's exactly what I'm expecting."

"Well, we shall see then," she murmured mockingly.

"Aye, we shall see," he agreed, then bowed low and left her.

Again that night he stayed late in the hall. She lay awake waiting, wondering, her heart and soul in a tempest of misery.

She stared at the fire that burned low in the hearth. Her eyes began to close, and she dozed.

She dreamed, she thought. She felt the most tender of touches against her lips. Felt a soft, seductive stroke upon her shoulder, her arm. Her breast was cupped, caressed, a slow sure trail was drawn down the valley between them, drawn lower and lower until her legs shifted against each other. Then there was a forceful touch upon her, rolling her to her back. Her eyes opened, for it was no dream.

He was golden in the firelight. Golden, muscled, gleaming in the night, his eyes a cobalt blaze.

"I slept!" she murmured in feeble protest, determined to hide the wild delight that had filled her body, the excitement that seized her limbs.

The longing for him that had entered every part of her, heart, soul, being.

"I swear to you!" she whispered again, "I slept! I beg you, be a gentle lord, a civilized lord, and let me be!"

"Aye, tonight you slept. And indeed, lady, most often I would hesitate before rousing you from such easy rest. But then again, you recall, I am not a gentle lord, rather a Viking, and tonight I think it especially important that I remind you of something," he told her.

"And that is?" she demanded imperiously.

"That you are my wife, lady. You are my wife."

"Nay . . ."

"Aye!"

His lips touched hers. His hands molded her against the fire of his body.

And in moments she had no doubt at all.

16

The journey to Rouen had been arranged as an elaborate affair.

Odo himself arrived at the fortress to accompany them with his own contingent of men. Father Matthew was to ride with them, as was much of their household. Melisande was amazed by the extent of preparation that had gone on without her knowing, and she was deeply angered by it. But even as she discovered it, there was little chance to do anything, or tell Conar what she felt, for she didn't find out about any of it until Odo's men waited beyond the walls. The horses and supplies had all been gathered in the courtyard, and the great count himself awaited her in the great hall, ready to scoop her up into his arms and give her a mighty hug, as if she remained a child.

"Melisande! Ah, child! We all warned your father you would grow to be the most exquisite woman the world over. How you've fulfilled that promise!"

At the mention of her father she felt a stinging of tears at the back of her eyes.

"He'd be proud today. Delighted!" Odo continued. "You'll have a magnificent ceremony to remember now, child, even if you were legally wed, though under much pain and duress. And today will give us the additional strength we seek!''

She lowered her lashes quickly as dismay filled her. Here was one of her father's best friends, the handsome, powerful Odo, assuming she would be happy to further pass on her power to her husband!

To bind herself to him anew before the eyes of all men.

"I'm not so certain, Count Odo, that my wife will be so pleased with these arrangements," she heard, and when she spun around, Conar was there.

He had seldom seemed so magnificent. The shoulders of his crimson mantle were adorned with a thick edge of wolf's fur, as were the high pelt edges of his boots, rising to his knees. Beneath it his form-hugging chausses were fawn, his tunic a royal blue that brought out the searing color of his eyes. Over the tunic he wore his glittering mail. His conical helmet rested in his hand against his chest.

"Not pleased?" Odo said, distressed. "Why, any maid would be delighted with such spectacular pageantry."

"Countess Melisande? Why, milord, 'tis quite possible that we will walk the aisle and my fair wife will decry me.''

There was a startling silence, then Odo burst into laughter. "Melisande has always known how battles must be won and fought, how life must be lived, property preserved. You young people jest at my expense. Now come, this will be a long and tiresome journey with so many in attendance."

Melisande stared at Conar and felt an odd shivering within her. Count Odo's hands were upon her shoulders, turning her. He led her from the hall, his arm lightly about her.

But Conar was right behind them. Helping her atop Warrior in the courtyard, Conar gazed at her intently.

But then he turned from her, mounted Thor, and rode to the head of their large armed party.

The gates were opened. They rode out, several hundred armed men with them—fortress men, Conar's men, Odo's men—Marie de Tresse and countless other maids and servants, and a large number of churchmen.

Odo rode at Melisande's side for quite some time. Later he rode forward with her to introduce her to his cousin, Lady Genevieve, come to serve as a feminine companion, and she talked politely with the woman, but found herself irritated to discover that Lady Genevieve was a deep believer in a woman's subservience first to God's will, and then to her husband's. Melisande managed to rein in a bit and allow the woman to ride on. Ragwald was with them, too, and she was suddenly determined to ride with him, or Gaston. Only Philippe had been left behind with the fortress guard.

She made her way carefully around Genevieve and rode hard through the long train of travelers to find Ragwald, then suddenly reined in.

He was very near the front of their procession, riding with Odo.

Behind him was Conar. And Brenna.

Their horses rode so close, they brushed one another. Conar's head was bent, listening to her words. He laughed softly and flashed her a warm smile.

Melisande felt dizzy. She reined back.

Odo wanted her to do this.

But then Odo assumed that she was pleased with her marriage. No, perhaps Odo would not care if she was or wasn't. Conar had been her father's choice, Conar had avenged her father. Odo might just assume that this was her duty, and that she would be too well bred to do anything other than strengthen her home and country.

"Lady Melisande!"

She reined in to see that Bishop LeClerc, the greatly admired churchman selected to perform the ceremony in the beautiful church at Rouen, was calling to her.

Alas! All she needed was a churchman at this time, when her heart lay in such tempest! She was not terribly sure that she was as Christian as she should be, if she really believed in God anymore. God had deserted her the day her father had died. He had not seemed present often since.

But she smiled, reined in, and awaited the man.

He had a full head of snowy white hair and a kindly wrinkled face, and reminded her somewhat of Ragwald. There was a deep wisdom within his eyes, yet there seemed humor there, too, intriguing in a man of such a pious reputation.

"Lady, do you feel up to all this?"

"My health is excellent," she assured him.

"We must thank God for that!" he told her, but his merry green eyes seemed to be sparkling with amusement. "But I asked, my dear, if you were up to this."

She lowered her head, lashes covering her eyes.

"Do you love your husband?"

She looked to him quickly, startled. His gentle smile deepened. "If you do, child, you are most fortunate. If he loves you, it is a greater blessing still."

"I believe this was all Count Odo's planning," she murmured.

"Aye, for Odo is a man deeply concerned with the welfare of our land and people. As was your father. Still . . ." He shrugged. "This is a solemn occasion, and the ceremony will be one under our Lord God in his heaven. Perhaps you should think on your vows again, milady. Stay with my household, lady, chaste in prayer these evenings while we travel onward."

She stared at him and realized what he was offering her. An escape for the several nights it would take their huge party to reach Rouen.

Conar would be powerless against the church he had been so willing to involve himself with.

She nearly smiled but managed to bow her head instead and answer gravely. "Perhaps deep meditation on God's will would serve me well these few days," she murmured.

"As you wish it, Melisande. You may think upon it, and then let me know."

They stopped at a monastery that evening, it being the only place along the way large enough to accommodate their party, with wide open fields for the fighting men and their horses, separate quarters for the nobles and their ladies. Melisande had scarce seen Conar throughout the day—he had spent it riding with Brenna and Ragwald.

Mainly Brenna.

Even as the monks scrambled about to serve their party, he was with Brenna, approaching Melisande only when she had set her plate down. He reached for her hand. "Come. We've been offered the nicest room in this sparse establishment."

She bit into her lip, ignoring his hand, then looked into his eyes.

"I cannot join you tonight," she told him.

"What?"

"Bishop LeClerc has suggested that I seek God again in prayer, that what we do is a grave matter."

"You've been my wife for years—" Conar began angrily, but then he broke off. He drew her suddenly to her feet, drawing her close, and his rough words were for her ears alone. "This is your choice, Melisande?"

"Mine. And you must abide by it—"

"Nay, lady! There is nothing I must abide by! You know that. Were it my choice, I would drag you away here and now, and none would dare stop me."

His hold upon her eased. His whisper remained

harsh. "But perhaps we both need an evening to reflect upon our situation. You will have the peace you desire. And perhaps my dreams will be filled with a gentle female who does not choose to fight and deny me night after night!"

He suddenly released her, and to her surprise her knees were so weak that she sank back to the rough plank where she had been sitting.

She retired soon to the minuscule, barren monk's chamber she had been so courteously offered.

She even tried to pray.

But the words would not come. She lay awake, tears stinging her eyes, and she wondered where Conar slept.

Melisande would be quick to deny that she was either stubborn or proud, yet her pride and her determination not to give to Conar more than he had already taken were all that kept her away.

It took them three more nights to reach Rouen. She ached through each of them, tormented herself, suffering cruelly. In her waking hours she tried very hard to be solemn with Bishop LeClerc and assure him that she thought carefully each night on God's will. She rode often with Marie and tried to spend time with Lady Genevieve, yet often found some polite means of escape.

She watched Conar, still riding often with Brenna, who knew him much better than she did, shared much more with him.

They came to Rouen at last, and there would be one night there before the solemn ceremony in the morning. Odo kept a huge house here with an abundance of servants, which was well, for the house was a crowded place and the meals required for all the guests were extensive.

That night she found herself swept along with Odo

and Swen before the fire where Brenna was casting runes from a skin satchel.

Her runes were fine, highly polished stone, the symbols beautifully carved into them. Melisande sipped wine beside her host, watching with a fascination that startled her—she was usually so careful to keep her distance from Brenna.

First the stones fell for a young woman. Brenna assured her that she would wed and have a house full of children. Genevieve, flushing, murmuring that she didn't believe in such pagan fortune-telling, found herself the next one for whom the stones were cast. Brenna looked into her eyes.

"Have I a husband there, seeress?"

Brenna ignored the words and paused just a moment. "I see the life that you desire. You, in your goodness and piety, lady, will become one of Christ's brides."

"I will enter religious orders?"

"Aye," Brenna said softly, and Genevieve was oddly appeased.

"I should have mine cast now!" Odo said, bowing low to Brenna. "If you will, my good woman."

A fire crackled high behind Brenna. She sat on a bearskin rug, her blond hair a cape around her shoulders, her eyes a fascinating shade between blue and green as she studied people, and then stone.

"Aye, Count Odo!" she murmured, and cast the stones out upon the ground.

Everyone was silent. The fire hissed and crackled.

"Well?" Odo demanded.

"You, milord, will march into the history of your nation. You will often be all that stands between life and death for what will one day be one of the greatest cities in the world. The warning, milord—hold strong, cling to those allies whose wisdom and strength will complement your own, who will hold fast to their loyalties at all times."

"Fair enough!" Odo said, pleased. His hands set upon Melisande's shoulders. "And now for milady . . ."

"No!" Melisande said quickly.

"I will not cast them, if you should choose that I do not," Brenna assured her.

"Come, come!" Odo said. " 'Tis all in the best of fun. The churchmen all sit there like muted birds. They will have their day tomorrow. Come, cast Melisande's runes."

Brenna collected her stones into her satchel and met Melisande's eyes. "Milady?"

Melisande shrugged. "Cast them."

The stones fell upon the ground. Once again the fire snapped and crackled, and then it seemed to roar with a sudden rush of heat. Brenna looked up at Melisande. She pointed to a stone with a symbol like an X upon it. "It is called Gebo, and it indicates partnership, a gift. A fitting rune for this evening, milady. There is no reverse for this rune, for the symbol indicates freedom, and all gifts flow from freedom. In a union of a man and woman, there is great giving."

She hesitated, but then pointed to another stone. "There might be danger in your way. This is Hagalaz; it indicates great disruptive forces, elemental power, upheaval, perhaps something of the gods, perhaps something of man. You must take care . . ." she murmured.

"Danger seems to surround my wife."

Melisande jumped, turning to see that Conar had joined them and stood just behind her. Brenna looked up, startled to see him, too. She had just begun to set her finger upon another stone, but abruptly decided to gather them all up into the satchel again. She stared at Melisande and said only, "We all form our own destinies, in truth. The runes just warn us of stones that may lie in our paths. If you will excuse me, I will retire now, as I am weary.''

She slid past them. Melisande noticed that Conar stopped Brenna, pulling her back. She was certain that he was quizzing her about Melisande's runes.

But Brenna shook her head, and Conar released her. His gaze was upon Melisande.

''It is late indeed. I will see you up to your chaste, private quarters, milady,'' he told her.

''I—''

''It is late,'' he repeated, his fingers lacing around her arm.

He thanked Odo for his great hospitality, then escorted Melisande to the hallway. Odo's house was vast, with several stories, but with many of the guest rooms right on a level with the hall. It was a wooden house, comfortable and warm.

Yet without the strength of stone.

Conar led her to the finely appointed room Odo had granted them for their stay, Melisande's alone this evening—theirs to share again tomorrow night.

Except that he dragged her within it, tonight, closing the door hard behind him, leaning against it, watching her. ''So what is it going to be, Melisande? Have you so truly enjoyed your distance from me?''

''Perhaps,'' she said. Her lashes were falling too swiftly over her eyes. She forced them to rise again, forced herself to meet his steel gaze.

''Aren't you going to try to bargain again?'' he asked her.

She smiled. ''I rather thought it would be more enjoyable to stand by the altar and denounce you for a Viking.''

He smiled and came toward her, finding her wrists, dragging her against him. ''You'd never dare!'' he challenged her.

"How can you be so sure?"

"Geoffrey will be among the guests tomorrow. He could seize upon you immediately."

"Perhaps that makes no difference."

"Nay, lady, I may be all manner of creatures, but I did not slay your father!"

"There are other men in the world!" she reminded him.

"But not many with my resources. Not many who have already laid claim to the fortress—and to you."

She narrowed her eyes. "If this is to be my last night of privacy—"

He laughed softly, interrupting her. "So it is your last night!"

She bit into her lower lip, struggling against his hold. "Not if you wish me to speak—"

He shook his head firmly. "Nay, Melisande, not that bargain! I will leave you tonight, for perhaps I have a few vigils of my own to stand! But I've told you time and time again, I will never let you go. And I will have you when I choose."

"If you would just unwind your fingers from my wrist—"

"But you're wasting such an excellent opportunity! Isn't there something else you might crave, something you might desire in exchange for your ardent vow?"

She went still, staring warily into his eyes. "You would grant me something?"

"Indeed."

She was startled, then her lashes fell again. A sweeping heat seared through her body, and her mouth was dry.

"What? You've come up with something, I feel it."

She couldn't quite bring her eyes to his. She tugged upon her wrists and he released her this time. She walked to the foot of her bed, paused, turned back to him.

"I want—"

"Yes!"

"I want you to cease sleeping with Brenna."

"What?" he demanded, a curious tone to his voice. It felt as if her heart were sinking within her. He would rather give her up, *and* all her property, she thought.

But she met his eyes and spoke again. "I want your vow that you will not spend your nights with Brenna."

"Sleep with her?"

"You've never spent the night with her?"

"Oh, yes, many nights."

"Your word!"

"So you are jealous."

"I am uncomfortable with my husband's mistress beneath my roof and ever so near."

"You're jealous."

"You started this. Do I have your promise or not?"

He smiled, a slow, lazy smile, and crossed his arms over his chest. He walked to her, cupped her chin in his hands, then pinned her to him when she would have escaped. His lips were very tender when they touched hers. "You have my vow. Except that you will grant me one concession in return."

"I walk into the church tomorrow and claim you as my rightful lord and husband," she said bitterly. "That is what you get!"

"Not enough."

"What do you want?"

"What I have always wanted. You."

Again her eyes fell. "You've assured me that you will have me when you want me—"

"Aye, and that I will. But for one night, if one night only, I want no fight, no restraint, no argument. My gift from you for our new vows. Wait, I want much more than that. I want you to come to me. Touch me. Awaken and arouse me."

"You are jesting!"

"I am demanding! And I demand, too, that you be exceptional."

Once again she tried to wrench away from him. He dragged her back. "Bathed and perfumed," he said softly. "Willing and waiting . . . and eager! Ready to tease and arouse and seduce."

Her cheeks flamed with color.

"Your vow, Melisande."

"But I don't keep promises—"

"Except to me," he reminded her again, his lip curving into a smile. He bowed to her then, quite suddenly, and before she could speak again, he was gone.

She quickly slid the bolt on her door. She hurried to the foot of her bed and sat upon it, shivering.

Jesu, what promise had he wrung from her?

Yet as she lay awake, she wanted the hours to pass, the day to come.

The night to fall again.

The church was spectacular in the morning, adorned with candles and flowers.

People had flocked from all around the countryside to attend the ceremony.

Indeed, even Geoffrey was there. Melisande saw him from the corner of her eye when Odo led her through the spectators to meet with Conar before the altar.

Her heart seemed to shiver as she stepped forward. He seemed like a god himself, his chausses dark, boots black, shirt and tunic pure white and trimmed with white fox, his mantle a sky blue, and rimmed with the same white fox.

She felt weak as she was handed to him, as they knelt together, as Bishop LeClerc announced slowly and carefully that they had come here today, man and wife already, to renew their love for God, and for one another, before the fine assembly gathered there, and before their heavenly maker. The union between man and wife was a sacred thing, and not to be entered into lightly.

And not to be broken by any man on earth.

He entered then into the mass, and it seemed to Melisande that it was a long one, endless, droning on and on.

Yet suddenly it was as if they had gone back in time. Back all those years, for Bishop LeClerc was asking Conar to state his vows, and he did so in a firm, clear voice.

Then Conar spoke to Melisande, and she could not find breath at all.

At her side, Conar grit his teeth hard, studying her. He had been stricken anew with his wife's incomparable beauty when he had first seen her upon Odo's arm.

They had dressed her in silver. A soft shimmering set of garments that both clung to her lithe and shapely form and floated around her with every movement. It was as fragile as precious metal, stunning. A veil of it, crested with a jeweled band, sat atop her ebony hair, and the inky darkness of her long locks contrasted hauntingly with the light silver. Her face, framed by the gossamer veil, was exquisite, her eyes alive, a deeper mauve than ever.

And now, while it seemed that all France waited, she knelt by him in silence.

His fingers curled around hers.

She gasped.

And the words tumbled from her mouth at last, the vows he had demanded spoken once again.

He slipped his old ring from her thumb, where it had stayed these many years, and put it back upon his own hand. He replaced this with a new band of etched gold, exquisite, upon her left center finger. His eyes met hers and perhaps there was something of his pleasure and triumph in them, for hers seemed to narrow and simmer.

He smiled, bowing his head, thinking of the night.

He had not begun to imagine what abstinence from her would do to him, and he had spent the days longing to hang Bishop LeClerc by his neck before that holy man could perform his holy deed.

But now that was past. He had only to wait for night.

He felt a tightening within himself, a longing so fierce, it was agony to remain still upon his knees. From the corner of his eye he looked at her again, and the force of her beauty swept him, along with greater emotions. He was possessive, she was his. They now had a long and curious history together. Naturally he cared for her.

Nay, it was greater, far greater.

He would never let her go, he knew, because he could not bear to do so. He couldn't think of her injured, or in the arms of another man.

Indeed, he could not imagine life without her. She created hell for him, she created heaven for him.

He was in love with her. She had set her claws into his soul all those years ago. Even when she had irritated him beyond belief, she had captured something of his heart with her spirit and with her courage.

Dangerous courage, he thought again.

But there seemed little to fear now. She was safe within the fortress, even if Geoffrey did prowl the woods. He'd try hard to see to it that he escorted her out often enough to make her feel a touch of freedom. And there would be times when they could sail away.

Time, he thought, they had time. Yet a shudder ripped through him, and he wondered why. She was his wife, had been his wife, and he would hold her forever. And he did love her.

One day, perhaps, he could even tell her so.

Melisande? Perhaps not. She was always so quick to seek her source of power. He dared never give her the upper hand in holding his heart.

She would rip it to shreds, he thought.

Yet he gazed at her with tenderness, longing for the feasting to be over now, longing for the night.

Would she keep her promise to him? In one way or another, for he could not keep his distance now. The dream had been with him through the long night, the desire, the aching, the anticipation.

A twinge of guilt assailed him. He had given her a promise that meant nothing, but it had been the one that she had demanded of him. And, her jealousy of Brenna had been surprising and pleasant to discover.

Ah, lady, he thought, meeting her violet eyes suddenly, feeling a stab of hunger so strong, it would have doubled him were he not upon his knees.

He realized that the ceremony was over at last. They rose, and to the great delight of the crowd, he appeased some of his hunger by sweeping her into his arms, bending her low, and kissing her with a taste of the long denied passion that roiled so furiously within his soul. Minutes passed, and still he tasted her lips, felt the desperate pressure of her hands. He lifted his mouth from hers at last, saw her dampened lips, her wide eyes. "Tonight," he whispered softly, and felt the force of her tremor.

But she ignored him, and they started from the altar, making their way through the guests, accepting the words of congratulations of friends and allies and, Conar realized, drawing together many of the great barons as Odo had been so determined would happen.

They were parted for a time, returning from the church to Odo's hall, where he found himself constantly surrounded by Odo's men, intrigued by his ships, by the way his Irish and Vikings fought upon horseback, by his instruction in various methods of warfare. Each time he looked up, his wife was likewise surrounded, for the barons were eager to come close to her, to gaze upon her, and as many had been good friends of her father's, they were eager to remind her that he had been a fine man. Sometimes Conar was close enough to hear her conversations, and he was intrigued. The barons assured her that they were still dependent upon the largesse and strength of the fortress. They were delighted that she had acquired such a husband, such a fine sword arm for their land. "Alas, we are oft on our own these days, lady, for there is little help in the weak king who sits in Paris!"

Melisande was gracious and knowledgeable, speaking with them about vulnerable points of geography, the history of Danish attack, the vulnerability of the rivers.

Later he saw her with Odo and Geoffrey, and he was stunned by the force of jealous fury that washed over him. She hated Geoffrey, he knew that. She greeted the man, for Odo wanted peace, yet Conar knew her freezing tones well, the imperious way she could lift her chin.

He was convinced anew that she despised the man with a greater animosity than she had ever borne toward him.

At last the evening meal came, and he was seated beside his wife at a place of honor. Still, they did not speak to one another much, for their attention was drawn to others. Odo had arranged for entertainment, an Irish seneschal to tell the tale of their combined families, a singer, jugglers, even trained bears.

Yet at last the time had come. Marie de Tresse paused behind her mistress's chair, and Melisande rose with her and left.

The other guests would notice her absence soon, and since he was in the mood for no raucous bedding as might occur tonight—with or without the approval of the church—he determined that he would not take long to follow her.

When he entered their room, it was cast in shadows. The only light came from the flickering fire.

She wasn't there, he thought, his soul sinking.

But he sensed a slight movement before the fire. She sat there, fingers closed over the arm of a chair, waiting for him.

He slid the bolt, announcing his arrival, and leaned against the door.

As he watched, she rose. She was still in silver, but different silver. This gown was just a glistening of color against her naked flesh. She paused a moment, staring at him across the room. It seemed that a tremor shot through her.

She arched back, lifting her hair. He watched the flawless display of her body as she pulled the cord at the throat of the garment and let it fall in an endlessly slow stream to the floor.

She stepped from it and slowly came his way, pausing just a step before him, then pressing her naked body to him, rising on her toes, touching his lips with hers.

He nearly burst into climax at that moment, yet fought against it, enwrapping her in his arms. She tasted like sweet, sweet wine.

His lips rose just above hers.

"How much did you have to drink to do this?" he whispered softly.

Her eyes touched his with a mauve sparkle. "Not nearly so much as I might have imagined."

"Pray, then, continue."

"Continue?"

"Disrobe me."

She paled slightly, but didn't back away. He decided that she needed a little help and stripped off his scabbard, mantle, and shirt. He collected her in his

arms again and felt the fierce burning as she shimmied
within them, freeing herself to press her lips to his
shoulders and throat, to rub her breasts erotically
against the breadth of his chest as she did so. His
breath caught, his heart hammered. He slid from his
boots and chausses at last. She paused before him.
"Bathed and perfumed. Eager. Seductive, arousing . . ." he murmured.

"I cannot—"

"Lady, you are that already!"

She stepped forward again, just a bit hesitantly. Her
fingers fell upon his shoulders with the lightest touch.
She brushed his lips hesitantly, his chest again.

Her fingers began to stroke his sides. Knuckles upon
his flesh, fingertips. She eased low against his body
again.

A low groan escaped him, a shudder seized his body
with a staggering violence as her fingers closed around
the engorged shaft of his sex. She started to release
him. "Jesu, no!" he said swiftly, and leaned against
the door for strength. "Jesu, no . . ."

Her ebony head bent low before him, and she went
down upon her knees. He gasped again, shaking as if
seized by lightning, when her lips closed hesitantly
around him, her mouth hot and liquid.

"God!"

His fingers laced into the silk of her hair. Her
hesitance faded. Her tongue flickered over the length
of him, stroked, laved.

Moments of sheer stunning ecstasy swept him. Then
the pleasure became pain, then an unbearable agony
of needing her. A hoarse cry tore from his lips, he
wrenched her from her knees into his arms, lifting her
high and swirling to lean her against the door. Her
eyes were wide upon his, somewhat frightened by the
wildness of his manner, then she gasped as he arched

her higher, and brought her down upon him there, commanding that she wrap her legs around his waist.

She did so . . .

In all his life he had never been so aroused. Never so hungry. Never so desperate to touch, to taste, to hold, to have. The fever that filled him was a tempest, blinding. He drove into her fiercely, having to fulfill the need she had awakened. A blaze burned, incredibly swift, incredibly high. He erupted in a climax more violent than he had ever known, holding her betwixt himself and the door, feeling the hot burst of his seed rush into her and over them both.

She clung to him in silence. He prayed that he had not hurt her and lifted her into the crook of his arm, carrying her to the bed. Her eyes were closed, her lashes over them.

"I will never again doubt your ability to fulfill a promise!" he whispered softly.

Her gaze touched his at last. "And what of you, milord?"

"I will fulfill any promise I give you, Melisande. I will never let you go."

Her eyes closed again. He thought the smallest smile curved her lip.

His lips touched down on hers. Rose above them. He wanted to whisper something.

I love you.

Nay, he might as well hand his heart to the Danes!

He couldn't speak. He touched her lips again, then determined that she would die a little tonight from his caress, just as he had died from hers.

And so he began to touch her. To stroke her. Slowly. Tongue teasing, fingertips just brushing. He left no spot upon her unadored, yet moved around the very center of her longing, creating spirals upon her belly with his tongue, caressing the soft inner flesh of her thigh. Suckling her breasts, stroking her thigh again . . .

At last he came upon his knees at the foot of the bed, caught her ankles, and brought her down hard against him. Parted her gently with his fingers, had her with his tongue. When she gasped and writhed and cried out softly, he still continued, until he rose over her, seeking one more thing tonight.

"Tell me that you want me, Melisande."

Her eyes fell upon his, damp, wild, filled with reproach.

"I—"

"You cannot!" he said harshly, for her. "Aye, but lady, you can!"

He rubbed his palm over her. His eyes demanded hers. With a startling fury she looked at him. "I want you!" she whispered.

"My name, Melisande."

"I want you—Viking!"

He laughed huskily at that, but brought his whisper low against her ear. "My name, Melisande."

She cried out softly, nails digging into his shoulders, face burying there. "I want you, Conar."

He rose above her.

"You have me, lady, you have me."

 **17**

Returning home was far more pleasant than riding to Rouen. Oddly enough, for all Conar's never-ending demands, something had changed between them, and for the better.

He was far more often with her, quick to urge her to race him to one hill or another, and he was even willing to call a halt to their entire procession one afternoon when she found particular pleasure in one of the streams where they had stopped. He sat with her by the water, his feet bared and cooled by it, as were hers.

Yet when they returned home, things were quick to change, fate was destined to step in upon them in a number of ways.

Melisande came down the stairs her first morning home to see that Brenna was slipping from the great hall. She followed her down the stairs to the courtyard below, wondering if Conar had really kept his word.

She shouldn't ask.

"Brenna."

The Dubhlain woman stopped, aware that Melisande had been following her.

She turned slowly. "Aye, milady."

Melisande discovered that she couldn't simply demand to know the truth.

"The runes," she murmured. "You plucked up the runes so swiftly the other day. Why? What runes were they?"

Brenna arched a brow to her. "Don't you know?"

Melisande frowned, shaking her head. "What were they?" she repeated.

Brenna paused a moment, looking at her. "Two runes, lady, Injuz and Jera."

Melisande shook her head blankly. "Ragwald knows the runes," she said. "He taught me some when I was young, but I'm afraid those elude me. What are you telling me?"

"You really don't know?"

"I really don't know!"

Brenna's golden lashes swept over her eyes. "Then count back, lady, and think carefully."

"I—"

"Milady, they are the runes for fertility."

"I don't—"

"You're expecting his child!" Brenna said impatiently.

Melisande felt as if she had been struck, she was so startled. And then she felt so incredibly foolish because Brenna had only to whisper a few words, and she realized how very late she was.

She shook her head. "I don't—I can't be! I don't feel anything."

Brenna shrugged, a small grin upon her lips. "Then you are lucky, and your labor might well be easy." She paused a moment. They were both silent. Brenna frowned, and Melisande realized that she must be very white, the blood having drained from her face.

"What is your distress? Your husband will be pleased. Indeed, Odo and half this land will be pleased, for a child is the mortar that holds close many a union."

"Does he know?" Melisande asked her suddenly. Was that the source of his sudden consideration?

Of the laughter that sometimes touched his hard features, of the tenderness.

"Well, it seems that you have not told him," Brenna said.

"But you!" Melisande cried. "You've known, and you serve him, and I'm certain you think he should know."

Brenna was quiet for a moment, studying her. "It is your place, not mine, milady, to tell him."

Melisande started, glad that the building of the keep was near where she stood, for she suddenly discovered herself leaning against it.

"You wouldn't do so?" she queried suspiciously.

Brenna sighed softly, looking to the ground. Then her eyes touched Melisande's. "I serve Conar," she admitted softly. "If you were endangered, or the life of the child were endangered . . ." She shrugged. She straightened abruptly. "I'm not your enemy, Melisande. I never have been."

Melisande bit into her lip, studying the beautiful blond woman she had avoided for so many years.

"Have you really . . ."

"Really what?" Brenna inquired.

"Ceased to sleep with him?"

"Ceased to sleep with him?"

Melisande let out a cry of exasperation. "You mean you've never slept with him?"

"Of course I have slept with him. I travel with him constantly. I have slept with him on ships on long sea journeys, beneath trees when we have traveled on land."

Melisande started to turn, afraid that she was going

to be ill after all. She had felt fine until this moment. She wouldn't have believed her feelings of dismay.

Now she felt desperately ill.

A small hand touched upon her shoulder. "Lady, I have slept with him. But you misunderstand the meaning of what I am saying. Swen has slept with him often enough, too, and I assure you, neither of them has an interest in other men or little boys! I have never made love with him. I cannot cease doing something I was not doing to begin with."

Melisande swung around again, astounded. "What?"

"Ah, don't look at me so! I would have done so, had he wished it. And should he ever seek me . . ." Her voice trailed away. "But that is unlikely. He has discovered what he seeks in you."

"Indeed," Melisande whispered softly. "He has discovered a fool!"

"Your pardon?"

"Never mind, Brenna." She stiffened, feeling wave after wave of fury sweep through her. His magnificent bargaining! Of all the horrid things to do to her. How amused he must have been! She had bartered herself to him in exchange for a promise that he sleep no longer with a woman he had never touched!

"Melisande—"

"Thank you for your honesty," she said smoothly. She turned back into the tower and made her way up the first flight of stairs. She found a chair in the great hall and sank into it, trying to remember everything he had said that night in Rouen. She had *demanded* he not sleep with Brenna anymore. And oh! He had sworn that he would not do so.

She had fulfilled her part of the bargain tenfold.

He wasn't sleeping with Brenna, *never had* slept with her.

He had taken Melisande again for such a fool. Even if she had walked right into it.

She would never, never tell him about their child. If it really existed. If Brenna wasn't taunting her even now.

But Brenna wasn't taunting her. All she had to do was look back and know that she hadn't had her time since Conar had come to claim her by that stream in Wessex.

She put her head down upon the table. It was what he would want. Exactly what he would want, what he would demand. And as usual, she would give it to him.

But not now, her heart cried out. Not now.

She tried to eat, but found she wasn't hungry. She reached for ale, then thought she should be drinking goat's milk. Marie de Tresse had always said it was good for women who were with child.

I don't believe this, she insisted to herself.

She rose and returned to her room, her father's room. Conar's room.

Mine first! she thought.

She lay down on the bed and stared at the ceiling. The child would be blond, she thought, despite her own ebony locks, despite Conar's mother's burnished black hair.

Blue-eyed and blond. His. For everything went his way.

No more! she determined.

She sat up. "I am going to have a black-haired girl!" she promised herself, but she found herself rocking and feeling within herself the first flurry of wild excitement and wonder.

A babe.

Hers.

Theirs.

His.

She stood and started pacing the room. Would she

tell him? Nay, her heart cried out. Not after that wretched trick he had played upon her!

The child would be hers as well. Her father's grandchild. If only Manon might have lived.

If Manon had lived, everything would be different.

She stood suddenly, eager to leave the place. Without thought she raced down the stairs and hurried to the stables, not seeking a groom, but seizing a bridle from a hook to slip over her horse's nose. In seconds she was leaping upon him. The gates were open, as there was no threat in the day and the animals were in the field, the farmers coming and going in their labors.

She rode hard, racing across the fields. She had no destination in mind. Still the spring beckoned to her. She forgot that Geoffrey had come there, she forgot everything.

Yet she had barely reached the water before she discovered herself rudely interrupted.

"Melisande!"

Conar had raced after her upon Thor and sat atop the stallion now, staring at her with a raw new fury. His voice shook with his rage. "Lady, you promised me you'd not put yourself at risk so foolishly!"

She stiffened, standing very straight, staring his way.

"You promised!" he thundered again.

She hadn't thought about breaking her promise, though what promise she really *owed* him, she didn't know.

"Jesu, lady, did you come here to meet that fool Geoffrey?"

She had never meant to break a promise, she hadn't thought about Geoffrey once, she had only longed to escape the tempest and fever in her heart.

"Leave me alone, you Viking bastard!" she cried out. She hurried toward Warrior, but Conar leapt down from Thor, accosting her before she could do so.

"What in God's name is the matter with you?"

"My promises! My promises! Oh, you bastard!" she cried, slamming her fists against him.

"What?" he thundered, confused. "What promise have *I* broken?"

"What promise did you ever need to make?"

"I—" he began, and realization dawned in his eyes, and he leaned back, crossing his arms over his chest. "You went to Brenna and asked her about my activities, milady?"

"Aye, I went to Brenna and discovered that you had played me for a complete idiot!"

"You are a greater idiot to ride here after all that happened!"

"Then I will ride back, and you may remain here!" she cried.

"Indeed, you will ride back!"

His hands upon her, he lifted her to Warrior's bare back. She kneed her mount, causing him to begin racing back toward the fortress before Conar could mount Thor.

It didn't matter. Not even Warrior's tremendous power mattered. Conar was right behind her.

She returned through the wall, leaping from the horse before the stables, tossing the reins to one of the boys. She ran up to her room and suddenly remembered the day he had threatened to take the beautiful gilded coat of mail from her, her father's gift.

She dived for the trunk, determined to hide it before he could come, yet even as her hands fell upon the gold emblazoned sword, he burst into the room.

He stood there, his brows arched. "A sword against me?"

"I am quite excellent with it, milord," she informed him coolly.

"Are you?"

He walked over to her. She had been hunched down by the trunk. She rose swiftly, the blade extended.

"I'll take it, Melisande."

She shook her head stubbornly.

"Don't come closer. You may be the great Lord of the Wolves, but you are flesh and blood, and I am talented with this weapon."

"You are talented with many weapons," he assured her swiftly. "All this!" he whispered suddenly, "because I *do not* sleep with another woman?"

"All this because you lie!" she cried.

"I never lied."

"Because you think to command me constantly, because your bargains are ruses, because—just leave me be!" she warned, waving the blade.

He shook his head slowly. "You'll never take such a weapon against me, Melisande. I swear it." He suddenly drew his own blade. She jumped back, stunned that he meant to battle her, here and now.

"Set it down, Melisande."

She could feel the blood draining from her face, but she was good, and she would not back down.

He took a step toward her, his steel suddenly and fiercely cracking down upon hers. She shuddered with the force of it but parried quickly.

She had practiced with his brother. She knew some of his moves.

She fought well, and she fought hard, leaping upon their bed to parry one blow, jumping to a trunk, finding the floor once again. She could combat him! But he was relentless, his eyes never leaving hers, his blows never ceasing.

She could feel the strain in her arms. The effort to keep lifting her sword was an agony.

"Surrender, lady?" he demanded coldly.

"Never, milord!"

There was a sudden pounding upon their tower door.

"Conar!" Swen cried anxiously. "Is all well within there?"

"Aye!" he cried. "We're fine."

"Melisande!" Ragwald called next.

She nearly missed the fall of Conar's blade. "I am well!" she cried swiftly.

"Leave us be!" Conar commanded fiercely. And he smiled, then began to come at her.

She realized that he had baited her all the while. She was good at defense, but he hadn't been sending his blows half as quickly as he was able.

Now he did so, coming at her with a sheer ruthlessness that was staggering.

She parried a blow, but he caught her sword and sent it flying. She clenched her teeth, staring at him, staring after the blade. He smiled and flicked his blade so that it nearly brushed her flesh.

But it did not touch her.

It rent her gown from her throat to her navel instead.

"Wretched Viking!" she swore, then dived suddenly to retrieve her own blade.

He let her find it, but then he was at her again, showing no quarter. He slammed his blade against hers and for a moment they were locked together.

Then his great strength showed. He forced her arm and blade to the floor.

"Let it go," he warned her.

At last her trembling, weary fingers lost their grasp.

He bent and picked up her sword, sending it flying toward the trunk. "No more, Melisande. No more swords, no coats of mail. And no more fights against me!"

She could scarcely breathe. She was heaving in great gulps. Her breasts lay exposed, rising and falling in wild beats. She hated him, hated him.

But dear God, she felt so alive! She wanted to keep fighting, pit herself against him, touch him . . .

She gasped as his sword rose again—she was certain he mean to cleave her in two.

But he only rent the rest of her garment. She backed away, glaring at him.

"It's a good thing you are the son of a wealthy king who has managed to make a very advantageous marriage, else your wife would walk about naked by now!"

"Naked is what I seek," he told her, eyes ablaze.

"Nay!" she cried, turning to flee. But his hands were wound into the torn fabric and it slipped from her shoulders. She ran to the door, yet paused, and he was behind her, suddenly laughing.

"Would my dear naked wife run so swiftly to Swen and the rest of that hall of Vikings?"

"Aye!" she cried, but she was going nowhere, and she knew it. And she knew when his hand came upon her that her anger, even her rage, meant nothing. She wanted him now as she had never wanted him before.

But tears welled in her eyes as he lifted her. She slammed her fists upon his shoulders. "Bastard!"

"Because I do not keep Brenna mistress?"

"Because you made me a fool."

"Should I sleep with you to appease you?"

She tried to slap his face but he caught her too quickly, sliding her down his body. She strained to free herself from his grasp.

He started to kiss her.

"Nay, not this time! Not this time!"

Yet she was already afire. His touch was swift, and it was magic. In seconds they had fallen back upon the bed, and she was impaled with him.

And it was later, far later, when she lay exhausted against him, that she even remembered there was something that she might tell him.

Nay.

Never after today.

He sat up by her side, stroking her hair. His eyes were suddenly hard and concerned and very serious. "Be angry with me, Melisande. Hate me. Loathe me. Call me what you will. But you cannot ride out alone. No matter what other promises we have made and kept or not kept, you must not ride out."

"Geoffrey was there at the service! He knows that I am your wife, that he cannot seize the fortress," she protested bitterly.

"Geoffrey is dangerous."

"How can he still be so?"

"I know that he is."

She turned away from him. He touched her shoulder. His voice was suddenly soft.

"Melisande."

"Leave me alone, I implore you!"

"Melisande—"

"I've nothing to say to you. You made a fool of me, milord—"

"There was no evil intent—"

"Ah, and what if I had played you, the mighty lord, the same way!" she demanded. she swallowed hard and continued. "What if it were the other way, milord? What if you wondered with whom I slept? Ah, pray forgive me! I may sleep with whomever I choose. There is a difference between sleeping and making love!"

He was up at her side. She was startled when he suddenly swung her around violently, the tip of his sword landing upon her flesh.

"Lady, don't test me. I would slay any man and would consider the same with you!"

He whirled away from her, reaching for his clothing, pulling on his chausses and then boots in what seemed like a singular motion. She watched him, her heart in a tempest. "Aye, leave it to a Viking!" she cried.

"Aye! Leave it to a Viking." He pulled a long-sleeved linen shirt over his head.

It was then that a thunderous knocking sounded on their door.

"Go away!" Conar cried furiously.

A small voice sounded. Brenna's.

"I cannot, milord. Ships have arrived from Dubhlain."

Conar frowned. Melisande pulled the covers to her chin, aware that he was about to throw open the door.

He did so. Brenna stood there with two tall men behind her. They were not Vikings, she didn't think, but dark-haired Irishmen. She flushed as they glanced her way, respectfully inclining their heads. She wished she could crawl beneath the bed, yet realized they thought little of her position. If Lord Conar desired his wife by day, it was his right.

Brenna's eyes remained upon hers for a moment.

"What is it?" Conar demanded.

"Your father sends for your help, milord," the younger of the two said, bowing deeply. He hesitated. "Your uncle Niall has disappeared in the north, and the kings are gathering at Dubhlain to ride in force to demand his return from Maelmorden, the west coast king who has taken him hostage. He prays that you can sail quickly."

Melisande watched as Conar stared at the man, inhaling deeply.

"My uncle lives?" he asked softly.

"So your mother believes."

"And mother?"

"She is strong, she has your father. She watched warfare all her life as the daughter of the Ard-Righ. She is Niall's sister, and your father must ride in his defense."

"And so shall I," Conar said softly. "So shall I."

"The king will be grateful," the messenger said.

Conar nodded and closed the door. He stared at her, but absently. "So we shall sail again," he murmured.

She sat up, holding her sheets tightly. "We? I should remain at home, Conar," she replied swiftly.

"You will come with me."

She couldn't bear to leave home again! She had only just returned!

"I loathe you, remember?" she demanded miserably. Tears were stinging her eyes. They were going to fall again.

She didn't want him to go. But she didn't want to spend endless days waiting in Dubhlain again. Not that she didn't love Erin. Not that she didn't care.

It was just that home mattered now. The Irish were always at war. She and Conar needed to be here! Odo needed Conar; surely that was evident!

But Conar leaned low over her. He touched her chin, wiped a tear from her eyes. For a moment, just for a moment, it seemed that he might soften.

Then he swore an impatient oath. "Lady, I dare not leave you here, I dare not! Can't you understand that? You will come with me! There is no choice in the matter."

He spun away from her. The door slammed, and she was left alone.

 **18**

There was no time for long good-byes when she left. And this time it seemed that there would be an even split of the households.

Swen and Brenna sailed with them. Ragwald, Philippe, and Gaston stayed home, as did Marie de Tresse, though she had sworn to Melisande that she'd gladly come with her.

As good as it might be to have one of her own people with her, Melisande had decided she wanted to accompany Conar alone. If she decided on any reckless action, she didn't want anyone holding her back—whatever she did once Conar rode into battle would be upon her own shoulders.

She wasn't planning anything. It was just that he had ridden away before. And she was older now. She had returned to her household. Even if Conar's presence was strong within it, there was much she had taken over. She had learned much from her years spent in distant lands. In Dubhlain she had learned the warmth of Irish hospitality and the laws that demanded kindness to strangers and travelers—

When those traveling strangers weren't ravaging their coastlines, of course.

With Rhiannon she had learned that graciousness

could exist during a time of peace. She had learned how to use beautifully crafted tapestries to keep away the harsh chill in an estate that had been ruled far too long by a lord alone.

She'd also learned to hold court to settle petty disputes among the villeins and tenants, to award repayment to those who had been wronged, to chastise those who wronged them.

She didn't want to leave her home. Her heart belonged there, her soul yearned to stay.

Nor did she want Conar riding off to a foreign war.

It was not a foreign war to him, she tried to tell herself. His father had summoned him, his uncle was the Ard-Ri. She loved her mother-in-law dearly, and cared for her happiness.

But she ached with the thought that Conar would ride away again.

Ride away, leaving her behind.

She couldn't manage to say any of these things to him. In fact, she had avoided speaking with him since the summons had come, packing what belongings she would take, then spending the early hours of the night on the fortress parapet with Ragwald, staring up at the stars that dotted the heavens. Ragwald pointed glumly to the haze about the moon and told her that it would rain in the morning.

"I will not be gone so long again!" she promised him. "I will not be gone so long!"

He held her close, and she stared out into the darkness that covered the land around them, so dimly illuminated by the hazy moon. She bit into her lower lip. If she was going to have a child, it would be born here. If Conar left her too long, she would come home without him. And if he came after her in a fury, well then, so be it.

Yet if he turned from her . . .

She remembered with an aching heart that Brenna

had warned her she was ready to serve Conar in any way that he asked.

She lay with her back to the center of the bed when Conar came to join her late that night. She kept her eyes closed and did not speak. He stood by the bed for a long time, as if he would do so himself.

Then he sighed and walked away and doffed his clothing. Yet when he crawled into the bed, he did not touch her.

Morning came too soon. It was miserable and wet, just as Ragwald had predicted it would be. She heard the drizzle of the rain long before she opened her eyes, before she realized that Conar lay awake, staring at her.

"What?" she murmured, unnerved, and so, biting into her lower lip.

He touched it with his thumb lightly, studying her face. "Nothing," he said quietly. "I was just wondering if I was going to have to roll you in a sheet again."

She curled away from him, staring over to the trunk with the gilded mail in it, the trunk that seemed now to contain her childhood.

But the sword atop it was a real sword. The mail would fit her still. It was surprising that he had not seized both mail and sword from her.

He would not leave her. She knew that.

"There is no need to roll me in a sheet," she said wearily.

She felt his finger draw an arch down her spine, and she trembled despite herself. How strange. That touch suddenly made her feel as if she quickened inside with a strange warmth, a strange longing. She wanted to turn against him, hold on to him, keep him close. She knew now that she would hate it when he went away because she would hate being without him. She would miss his touch in the night. Miss his strength, his warmth. Miss that wonderful way of sleeping, knowing that she was held.

She didn't turn against him. No matter what she said or did, he would ride away to war. And he would not bring her—as he brought Brenna. He would leave her alone in a household that was not her own, no matter how gently she was treated within it.

"Some wives," he told her, "might be glad to be with their husbands."

"But I will not be with you."

"Aye, you will until we ride north."

"And then you will be gone."

"And will you miss me now, my love?"

She was silent. He answered for her in a mocking tone. "Ah, indeed, you will. You will sleep with any demon or devil just to come home! You will be counting the hours until my safe return—just to come back here." He rolled away, rising to his feet across the bed. Melisande turned, seeing the magnificent structure of his back, the breadth of his shoulders, the ripple of them, the sleek line to his hip, the hard, tight curve of his buttocks, the hard length of his legs.

"And what happens if you do not come back?" she whispered.

He spun on her. "Does it concern you?"

"It is a reason not to go," she murmured stubbornly, her lashes falling.

He walked around the bed again, coming beside it, lifting her chin. "Would you have me turn my back on my father, Melisande?"

She didn't answer him at first. Then she sighed, twisting from his touch, her lashes falling over her eyes.

"No. But you risk yourself, you risk me—"

"Ah, indeed, if I were to fall, lady, what then? Would you mourn? Or quickly cast off the chains that have so tightly bound you and sail home to rule here with supreme power and pleasure?''

She met his gaze, her lashes sweeping over her own eyes swiftly once again. ''You are cruel to suggest such a thing, milord. I have never wished any man's death.''

''Any man's? I did not see you mourn Gerald's passing!''

''Well, perhaps not Gerald's—but only because he murdered my father,'' she said.

''Then again,'' he murmured, ''you have taken a sword against me yourself . . .''

She rolled away from him, rising from the other side of the bed. She stood and started to walk away, but he was suddenly behind her, pulling her around to face him again. ''I don't care to discuss this!'' she told him.

''But I do.'' His hands rested upon her shoulders. ''Perhaps there's nothing to fear. I will return, Melisande. I swear it. I will not die. I will never let you go, remember?''

''My father never meant to leave me!'' she assured him softly.

A golden brow arched her way, blue eyes, fire and ice, sizzled upon her.

''Does this mean that you've come to care for me in some small way?''

''Don't mock me, Conar!'' she charged him.

It seemed a strange shield fell over his expression.

''I do not mock you,'' he told her.

''What of you? Has the tyrant come to care for his ward—in some small way?''

''I have told you several times—and meant it more deeply each time—that there was nothing I wanted so much as you.''

''Wanted,'' she murmured, her eyes falling.

His fingers tightened upon her arms. ''I will return!'' he promised her again. ''I swear I'll never leave you to Geoffrey. And I'll not die until we've a child to keep any seekers at bay!''

Tell him, a voice cried within her.

But she could not. She still had only Brenna's words and a suspicious passage of time as any proof. She didn't feel ill. She hadn't gained an ounce.

By next week, she realized, she would have missed two months. And then she might be certain. Reasonably so.

He had promised to return. When he brought her home again, she would tell him.

''What is it?'' he asked her softly.

She shook her head.

''Melisande! I beg you, don't spend your life hiding from me!'' he entreated. She stared into his eyes and saw fever there, passion. Did he care?

He wanted her, aye. Unless he tired of her . . .

His mouth slowly descended upon hers. His kiss was provocative, tempered, his lips forming gently upon hers. She found herself upon her toes, arms slipping around his neck, fingers moving into the golden length of hair at his nape.

There was a sharp rapping on their door. They pulled apart, staring at each other.

''Milord!'' It was Swen. He cleared his throat uncomfortably. ''We must hurry and take the tide.''

''Aye!'' Conar called.

Melisande had already turned. She washed and dressed quickly, not speaking with him again.

At the shore he offered to have Warrior brought with them. She shook her head. ''This is his home,'' she told Conar. ''He is not accustomed to your curious manner of transporting horses.''

An unease filled her. She didn't want Warrior with her, because she didn't want to have to try to get him home later.

When they sailed, when they waved good-bye to

Ragwald at the beach, she realized that she had no intention of waiting for Conar.

She'd be home long before him.

She would pray for his safe return—and would do so from here.

The seas were rough, but Melisande still did not feel a twinge of illness. She wondered if Brenna could be mistaken, if the tempest of her life lately hadn't caused her to miss her time.

Indeed, she felt Brenna staring at her now and then, and once, when their separate ships were near enough, Brenna asked Melisande how she fared.

They stopped for water and supplies briefly off the southern coast of England, then made straightaway for Dubhlain.

It would have been good to come here if she hadn't felt such a great concern for her own home. Erin greeted her affectionately, demanding to know everything that had happened since she'd seen her last. Even Rhiannon and Eric were there, for Eric, too, had answered his father's summons to come and fight for their uncle.

Their first day in the walled city of Dubhlain was a wonderful one, but an exhausting one, and no matter how sweet the reunion with people she loved, there was an edge to it all, for they all knew that as soon as everyone had gathered, the men would ride out.

Eric spent the day closeted with his father, brothers, brothers-in-law, and various cousins and uncles. Melisande spent the afternoon with Erin, Rhiannon, and her sisters-in-law in the grianon, or ladies' sun room, a handsome long room, well ventilated, that the Viking Olaf had built in to his home in honor of his wife—and his adopted country.

Rhiannon was anxious, pacing the floor, and Daria, was, as ever, in constant, supple motion. Yet Erin and her older daughters sat calmly, working upon fine needlework. Katherine, Conan's wife, read aloud from a beautifully crafted manuscript about the ancient peoples of Eire, about the formation of their social structures. She read about Saint Patrick, who had brought them Christianity and ordered all snakes from the island.

Melisande listened awhile, but her mind wandered. She discovered Erin's still beautiful emerald green eyes upon her.

"How do you do it?" Melisande whispered softly. "Sit so calmly when they all ride away?"

Erin smiled and passed her a needle. "Thread this for me, please. My eyes are not what they were."

"Your eyes are excellent, Mother!" Daria charged her.

"Melisande, as Daria is behaving like uppity baggage, would you please be so good as to thread my needle?" her voice remained soft. Daria stood behind her, linking her arms around her mother's neck. "Take care, Mother. I am the most like you, so they say!"

"Heavens! Was I ever so wild?"

"Wilder, they say!" Daria replied sweetly.

Erin shrugged. She looked at Melisande and smiled. "I am calm because I have watched them ride away so many times. I am blessed, for they always return. Mostly . . ." she murmured, then shrugged. "I have lost those I loved, too. And every time I have seen milord Olaf ride away, I have died a bit inside. Leith, the eldest, was the first to ride to battle with his father, and I thought that I could not bear it if he did not return. I was blessed. He did return. A little life goes out of me each time I watch a son ride. But I learned long ago that I could not protect the men in my life by forcing them to be weak. You see, my father was able to hold most of this island because he had the strength of my brothers, because he forged tight alliances

among the people. When he could not rid the island of
Olaf—he wed me to him. We will remain strong as
long as we remain united." She leaned close to Melisande, her eyes gentle. "Conar will return, you
know."

"So he has assured me," she murmured.

He would come back—because he had not left her
with an heir.

"Do you resent his being called here, when you
have so recently returned to your home?"

"No!" she said swiftly. But she wondered if Erin
saw the lie. She lowered her lashes quickly. She knew
that even if she were expecting a child, there could be
no motion within her as yet.

And still . . .

There seemed to be a fluttering. What of their child?
Would it be a boy, would he be loyal, determined to
fight for his father and home at all costs? She would
have fought for her father, given everything for him!

She looked at Erin and repeated her protest. "No,
really. I—I am grateful to see you again, for I never
really said good-bye."

Erin smiled and set her sewing down. "You are
always welcome here. You are nearly as much mine as
my own blood." She stroked Melisande's cheek. "I
did raise a beautiful child!" she said softly. Then she
spoke to them all. "Pardon me, for the house is full,
and I must see to our meal this evening."

The house was full and lively. Bryan and Bryce
were eager to see her, and she was glad to see them
both, finding herself lifted off the ground and spun
around by them one by one. There were so many
people to greet. All the children of the king and queen
of Dubhlain were here, and they with their children,
and there seemed very little space to even walk.

But the young ones were sent to bed by mealtime,
and the hall was extremely well organized as the family

took their seats. Food was ample, consisting of steaming summer vegetables, dozens of fowl, boar, deer, fish, eels. Plates were brought to the table and passed around. Wine, ale, and mead were served.

The food was rich, but the entertainment that night was kept to a minimum. A lone musician played a lute while they dined, and Melisande quickly discovered why.

She and Conar had been the last to arrive. The men would ride in the morning, and they would retire early tonight.

Olaf himself was the first to rise, reaching down a hand to his Erin. The years had treated them kindly, touched them hardly at all. They were still a beautiful and glorious couple, he so golden, she so dark.

Erin's hand fitted into his, her gaze met her husband's. Melisande found herself looking away, for she was suddenly certain that even after bearing all these children, after the passage of all these years, the two would retire tonight and hold each other passionately and tenderly through the long hours until the sun rose.

"Melisande?"

Conar was reaching down to her. She hesitated just a moment, feeling a fierce ache streak through her. She wanted something she could nearly touch, but not quite.

She wanted what a Viking held.

What the king and queen of Dubhlain shared.

She bit lightly into her lower lip, then curled her fingers into his.

Leaving the hall was not so easy with all those who were within it. There were all his sisters and brothers and their mates with whom to exchange good nights.

As they left the hall, Conar had a final word with his brother Eric. While she waited for them to finish, Melisande noted a familiar figure she had not seen before.

Mergwin.

She cried out gladly, hurrying to him, throwing her arms around his neck. "I didn't know that you were here!"

"I will not stay long," he told her. "I am too old to ride to war these days. Brenna sees with keener eyes than I now the warning signs that God allows us to see. But I had a craving to come home and so sailed here with Eric and Rhiannon. We'll have time together," he promised her.

She kissed his cheek. "I'm glad."

"Your husband summons you," Mergwin said, and she looked back. Conar did await her, sending a salute to Mergwin, and she realized that Mergwin had surely been closeted with them all day.

"Good night, then. I'll see you tomorrow," she said.

He held her just a moment longer. "Conar will return," he told her.

"So he says."

"It is true. The runes say so."

"Are the runes ever wrong?"

"When I cast them? Seldom."

She smiled. "Thank you."

"Melisande," he murmured, just as she turned away.

"Aye, Mergwin?"

"It's a boy."

"What?"

"Your child. It's a boy. Have you told him?"

She paled. "I'm not even certain!" she exclaimed. Then she added softly. "Do . . . you intend to tell him?"

"Nay, lady. It is—"

"Aye, my place!" she interjected. Once more she started to turn.

"Melisande," he murmured again.

"Aye?"

"Wolves tend to mate for life."

"Pardon?"

"Wolves," he repeated gravely. "And their cubs. And the cubs of their cubs. They mate for life."

She smiled and wondered how he could so easily read her heart, and prayed that others could not do so.

"I ramble now and then," he said.

"Umm!" she replied. But she smiled and kissed his cheek again and fled. She accepted Conar's hand again as he escorted her to the room they were to share.

It was large enough. A window opened to a view of the moon, which had diminished in the night sky. She fumbled with a tie at her back, then felt his hands there. She went still, allowing him to loosen her garment.

"I know that you are angry," he said softly. "But do you fight me tonight?" His mouth touched down, a liquid breath of fire, upon her bare nape.

She held still for a moment, then turned in his arms. Her eyes met his. "No!" she told him softly. "No."

Tonight, nay. When she would lie alone so many nights to come.

When she planned to defy him.

When he would ride away with Brenna.

Nay, not tonight. Tonight she would love him with all that he had taught her, with all that God had granted her. She clung to him, returning his kisses with hot, open-mouthed fire, disentangling herself from him to nuzzle against his body, brush it with the silk of her hair, tease and caress with her lips, teeth, and tongue. Sink lower and lower against him.

His fingers wound into the ebony tangle of her hair and he let her have her way, his breathing ragged and heavy. She worked her way around him, on her toes to press her lips to his shoulders, sliding against him again with her body and breasts, pressing her kisses lower and lower. Sliding against him still, touching him, tasting him, having him.

Indeed, he let her have her way, until the point when he lifted her up and bore her to the bed, his eyes locked with hers. Yet despite the searing heat and energy within him, he did not take her then but made love to her very slowly.

Tasting her as if he could never taste enough. Stroking her flesh as if he could memorize its feel with his fingertips. And finally, when she tossed upon the bed with a wild frenzy, he came to her, joined with her, and rose with her until the tempest swept them both.

Later they met upon their knees. Their fingers laced together, their lips met endlessly. The fire built slowly, exquisitely.

Then it raged again, and left them curled together, shaken and exhausted. Melisande could barely move. Yet she was glad of his touch. Glad of the arm that held her close, of the strong leg that lay haphazardly draped over her. She closed her eyes.

When she awoke, Conar was nearly dressed. She could not imagine that she had slept so late when the courtyard was filled with such a din below, so many horses, so many men.

"Hurry," he urged her, "they are all but ready to ride."

She jumped up quickly, washed with a dab and a promise for later, and dressed.

When she turned, he was completely outfitted for battle, mail upon his chest, sword at his hip, helmet in his hand. Still he drew her against him and drank deeply of her lips once again.

"I will return. Wait for me but briefly, and I will return."

A shivering seized her. She stared into his eyes and

nodded. He touched her cheek, as if marveling at her, then demanded, "Melisande, do you heed me?"

"Aye! I must wait for you."

"Obey me in this."

"Aye!" she cried.

"Is it passion—or hatred—that burns so fiercely within your eyes?" he demanded.

She lowered her lashes, but he jerked her hard against him. "Melisande!"

"I beg you—"

"I beg you, lady. Heed my warnings."

"What choice have I?"

"None," he assured her curtly. And he turned to leave.

She followed him. He paused, turned again, and took her hand. She walked out below with him where he found Swen awaiting him, Thor behind his own horse. Conar took the stallion's reins, then paused, and drew Melisande into his arms once again. She grew breathless, afraid that she would not be able to stand when he released her.

He steadied her before doing so. She felt tears spring unbidden to her eyes. "God go with you!" she whispered suddenly. "I pray, God go with you."

"Aye, lady. And with you." His palm cupped her face, but briefly. He mounted Thor. She felt a hand upon her shoulder. Rhiannon. They backed away from the horses, and Melisande watched as the family grouped together.

They were splendid and terrifying. They stretched out in a formidable line that seemed to go on forever. There sat Olaf, and at his sides, his golden sons, Eric and Conar, tall and striking in their Viking helmets, their eyes glittering their Nordic blue, even at a distance. There were the others, Conan, Bryan, Bryce, and Leith. Michael and Patrick, sons-in-law, were in the line. And several of Erin's brothers and cousins, another Eric, pure Viking, brother to Olaf.

For a moment they were enchanting, incredible. Then the earth began to tremble, for they were moving.

In vast, great waves, they disappeared beyond the gates of the walled city.

Melisande remained in Dubhlain as the weeks passed, wondering when news would come.

Messengers rode in daily. But as yet, there was no news. They negotiated with Maelmorden for Niall's return, demanded it. Erin read each message aloud in the grianon, and then they all waited again.

As the days went by, Melisande still didn't feel in the least ill, she didn't suffer any symptoms of anything different.

Yet she had now passed by two full moons, and still there was no sign of her flow.

Despite herself, she began to dream about having a child. And it did not seem so terrible that it might be a boy, and that it might resemble its father.

Letters also reached her from home, and those were distressing. Ragwald wrote her of strange happenings. Riders appeared on the ridge some mornings and stared down upon the fortress. Again, again, and then again.

"Trouble?" Erin asked her.

Aye! she longed to cry. But she didn't dare be honest with her mother-in-law, because she was so desperately trying to find a way to await Conar at home, rather than here.

"Nay, nothing," she said. "Just news of people, births, and deaths, I'm afraid. We lost a sheepherder, so Ragwald tells me, to a fever. But things go well, they are peaceful!"

One week later Rhiannon informed them that she

was going home, that Alfred had sent ships with trade, and she intended to return to Wessex.

It seemed Melisande's golden opportunity.

"Perhaps I will come with you," she murmured.

"You would all leave me?" Erin asked. She was watching Melisande. "Should you sail with Rhiannon?" she asked.

Melisande had the greatest difficulty lying to Erin. Her lashes fell.

"Wait another week," Erin suggested.

She waited. And Rhiannon waited with her. But more dismal news came from Ragwald, frightening news. Ragwald urged her to beg Conar to come back.

The Danes were amassing near Bruge, as well as other places. Odo had come by, he was eager to see Conar return.

Melisande sat down that night and wrote to Conar, telling him that she understood his obligations, but that they were desperately needed at home. She implored him to come back and take her there.

She waited again. Days passed.

Then his curt message came back to her. He could leave soon, he was certain, but not now.

She was to wait.

That evening she told Rhiannon that she would sail with her. They left the next morning.

She lied to Erin, stating that she wanted to see Rhiannon's children, that she knew she would be safe, for Rhiannon was under Alfred's protection, and few men dared cross the king of Wessex.

When she reached Wessex, she knew that she had planned well. She had written to Ragwald again, telling him that Conar's ships were detained because of the state of warfare in northern Eire.

A sleek ship arrived in Wessex for her.

It was not hard to convince Rhiannon that it was all right for her to go home. She had never let her sister-in-law know that anything was amiss, and Rhiannon was distressed to see her leave, but understood how eager she was to go home.

A little after a month since she had set sail, she managed to come home. Yet sailing in, seeing the sky, the water, the beach, nothing gave her the feeling of contentment that should have been hers.

Indeed, as she neared the beach, she felt sick at long last. Wretchedly sick to her stomach.

He would be furious when he discovered what she had done. He would turn against her, despise her. Perhaps find solace in the arms of another woman, the ever willing Brenna.

She stepped upon the shore. Half the fortress had turned out to greet her again, Philippe, Gaston, Ragwald, Marie, milkmaids, sheepherders, farmers, men-at-arms. She was welcomed by them all.

Honored by them all.

She had returned to lead them in her husband's absence.

She greeted everyone, dined with Ragwald, Philippe, and Gaston, and heard more frightening news about the number of Danes arriving on nearby shores. She settled a dispute that had come up between two villeins over a cow that had sickened and died. She dealt with letters to Odo and other barons. Finally her first night home grew late, and she returned to her room.

Their room. Where they had slept together. She stretched out to sleep.

In a way she had bested him at last. She hadn't fought a single battie. She had taken leave of Dubhlain and then of Wessex. And she had come home.

Her stomach continued to churn. Tears ran down her cheek.

She suddenly felt as if she were choking on them.

She jumped up and found her wash basin just in time. She was miserably, wretchedly sick.

Her first night home. She was the countess. Taking power over her destiny within her own hands.

She had never been in such anguish before.

And she had never felt so alone.

Nor had she ever ached for him so fiercely, knowing just how great his anger would be.

And perhaps his retribution.

Home! She had longed for it so desperately.

She had not slept with a demon to achieve it. She had merely sold her heart and soul instead.

19

They had gathered a great army, but for the most part the army sat.

Negotiations with Maelmorden stretched on endlessly, with a few minor clashes occurring between various troops.

They had Maelmorden well outnumbered, but Maelmorden had his uncle Niall, the Ard-Ri now, and if he were to die under such circumstances, Maelmorden might well claim the title. Though the son of the Ard-Ri frequently took the title from his father, it was not necessarily an inherited title. A man had to prove his worth to be the Ard-Ri.

Niall's sons were young—they had been kept home from the fighting.

In the Christian world it had become customary to pay danegeld, or bribe money, to send Viking invaders on their way. But though Maelmorden had called on their ancient enemies, the Danes, to do his fighting, he wasn't after a prize of gold. He wanted the lesser kings to accept his authority, to bow down before him.

Long weeks into the campaign Conar stood once more with Leith, Eric, his father, and his other brothers on a field, with Maelmorden and his berserkers standing before him. Again Olaf set before him the demand that Niall be returned. He would never accept Maelmorden, nor his son after him. The king of Connaught cried out behind Olaf, and the other kings raised their voices.

Again Maelmorden went into a fury, swearing that Niall had little time left before his untimely demise.

In the end they all left the field. Tempers flared, skirmishes broke out. But there was no real fighting, and they returned to their encampments.

Conar slept that night right beneath the open sky. Watching the stars made him think of Ragwald, and then he thought of Melisande, though she was seldom out of his mind. He knew damned well that their position was precarious, and everyone knew that the Danes were amassing along the Frankish and Frisian coasts.

He wondered if there might have been some better way to answer her letter, then realized that there had not been.

He missed her incredibly. For all that so frequently rose between them, he missed her with an aching sense of loss that stayed with him night and day.

Night was worse, of course, because when he closed his eyes, the endless fields of men seemed to disappear, and he could hear her whispers again, see her as she walked to him across the room, naked. He could almost reach out and touch her.

In the long emptiness of the nights, when he reached over, his hands touched dirt where his wife might have lain.

There were women in the camp, but no matter how hotly his body burned, he had been startled to discover that he had no desire for simple appeasement; the little witch who had stolen his senses had also stolen his soul. He loved her. It was a strange emotion, not always so sweet, for it brought with it torture. He dreamed of her, he craved her, he thought of her by endless night and endless day.

Usually his dreams were sweet, but this night he found himself racing through the darkness, knowing he had lost her. He could hear the fierce pounding of his heart. His breathing was ragged and loud, his muscles ached and burned. He called her name and ran more quickly, and he heard her cry out in return, but he could not see her.

There were waves of the enemy before him. He stopped and suddenly became part of an ancient tree that stood beside him. As the tree he could move through his enemies. He sought her again, searching high and low. He heard her voice.

They had buried her. She was deep in the earth. Her voice cried out to him softly now. Melisande . . . there were tears in it, she wanted to come home to him.

He was so close to reaching her. He heard her voice. Heard it again. He would reach her, no matter how the enemy surrounded him.

He awoke with a start, banging his head on a tree limb. Thor was at his side, gazing down upon him. He groaned and sat up, cradling his head. Nearby, his brother Leith stirred, having chosen to sleep under the stars as well, his saddle pack his pillow. Eric lay just beyond.

"Conar!"

He turned. Leith, grown into a serious man, no longer a boy who would tease a brother by seizing a play sword, was studying him with a puzzled frown. "What is it? Are you all right?"

Conar nodded, studying his brother in return. "Why?"

"You've been tossing and turning, moaning in your sleep."

He didn't flush easily, but he felt a seeping of color

rise to his face. Damn her! His wretched dreams about her were even visible ones.

He hesitated a moment, standing, listening to his body creak as he stretched out the night's stiffness. Leith and Eric both rose as well, still watching him. Eric, more familiar with his life, asked him, "Are you worried about the situation at home?"

"I am always worried about the situation at home," he agreed softly. He shrugged and grinned. "And when I am there, I worry about the situation here." He paused a moment. "I had an interesting dream. That might stand us well."

"What?" Leith demanded.

"We keep meeting them, army to army. What if we were to find out exactly where Niall was . . . and simply release him."

"How?"

"One man slips in. One man, invisible when the enemy is looking for many."

"Perhaps . . ." Leith said, looking at Eric.

They summoned their brothers and others in the family circle, then went to Olaf. Yet even before they spoke, they had sent spies out to the fringes of the enemy groups to learn where Niall was being kept.

"One man definitely risks his life. Perhaps capture, perhaps torture. Perhaps such a thing will cast us into further negotiations—" Olaf began.

"Father! How much longer can this go on!" Conar protested.

Olaf looked about. "Leith?"

"I believe my brother has a sound idea. Father, they keep us here endlessly, baiting us. We cannot rush them, fight them as we should, for if we were to slay Maelmorden, the Danes would slay Niall in retribution!"

"Who would go?" Olaf demanded.

"I would," Conar said, dismayed by the chill that settled over him. "My dream, my thought. I must go."

"How?"

"Monastic robes," he said.

"My brother the monk!" Eric murmured, and there was a snort of laughter that broke some of the tension among them.

"Ah, but his habits have changed greatly as of late, haven't you noticed?" Leith murmured. "What magic could have done this?"

"I believe she is tall, raven-haired—"

"And extremely willful and disobedient," he replied, eyeing them one by one. "If we may get back to this?"

"Ah, of course. Back to business," Leith stated.

"Father, I'd need to have secrecy to a certain point, then I'd need the whole of the army. I could get so far alone, then I would need help."

"Niall is probably well guarded."

"At the outer defenses. Within, I imagine he is watched by one or two men at a time. Yet his disappearance would soon be discovered, and that's when the army would be so dearly needed."

"What if Niall is injured, crippled?"

"It's a chance I am willing to take, Father."

"We'll wait," Olaf said. "We'll wait until our people return and tell us what they know. Conar, stay a moment. I would have a word with you."

The others departed, and Conar was left alone with his father in the swiftly built wooden long house where they centered their command. Olaf strode some distance from him, then turned.

"Have you heard from your wife?"

A cold wave, like a wall of ice, seemed to fall over him. "No, I have not," he said. "Not of late. She wrote when she had received a message from Ragwald about the number of Danes arriving, and I answered her. I have not heard from her again. What is it?''

''Nothing, perhaps. Erin has written that Melisande sailed with Rhiannon for Wessex, that is all. I had thought she might have written for your permission.''

His temper soared, and his anger was doubled by fear. His mouth went dry.

''You're free to return home, Conar. Someone else can carry out this plan. If—''

''No, Father. I will carry out the plan. Today. Then I will be free to leave.''

After a moment Olaf nodded. ''Perhaps you are right. If you carry out this plan today, then we are all free.''

Their spies returned shortly. Niall was being kept in Maelmorden's house, just behind the lines they had set for themselves. There were numerous people coming and going, indeed, members of the clergy, merchants, servants. The line of defense around the manor was all that protected it.

Niall and Eric were Conar's escorts to the outer defenses. He left Thor in their care and knew that they would be waiting for him, that they would not fail him. Then, in his monk's cape and cowl, he walked toward the enemy line.

They stretched out before him, Irishmen, Danes. Some in loose trousers, some in knee-high pants, their hairy legs bared. Many wore furs against the chill, all carried their battle-axes.

He was approached at last by a one-eyed man in a massive coat of bearskin. ''What do you do here?''

''I've come to tend to the soul of one you keep behind this line.''

''Niall?''

''Indeed. As you would seek to reach the halls of Valhalla, milord Niall seeks a different heaven, and might need guidance at this time.''

The man grunted and told him to wait. In a while he was back, saying that Conar could go through. Maelmorden hadn't given a damn about a black-cowled friar entering his domain.

Conar swiftly walked the distance from the lines to the manor, which stood far back from them. Chickens and pigs blocked his way, even here, at a king's house. It was the least well kept Conar had seen. His father's Dubhlain was great with its walls, and his own fortress . . .

This manor was little more than wood and thatch, with strange additions built of wattle and daub.

He passed through the yard unmolested. A wide-eyed child greeted him.

The doorway was low. There were but two men before it. They ignored him, parting to let him enter, then continued with their conversation.

He ducked beneath the low frame of the doorway and entered the main room of the manor. There was a peat fire burning, and a veil of smoke filled the place, stinging his eyes. The floor was raw earth and rushes. Dirty, half-clad children scrambled about.

At a table in the center of the room Maelmorden sat, pointing out places on a rough map to the men who stood at his rear. He paused, looking up, when Conar entered the room.

Maelmorden was a tall, husky man, well built, with a wild mane of reddish brown hair and dark eyes. Conar had despised him from the moment he had first seen him—there was a flaw in his eyes, they were small, set too close together. They glinted quickly with greed.

Maelmorden looked up at Conar and grinned broadly. "You're not one of mine, Brother, nor do ye have the look of a man of the cloth. But I hear you've come to tend to the Ard-Ri, and I'd not be denying any man his right to absolution."

Conar bowed. "No last rites, Maelmorden. I'm a monk, not a priest. I've come only to give him company, spiritual guidance in these great days of travail."

"He needs a priest," Maelmorden said, and the men behind him burst into laughter.

Conar wondered if he hadn't come just in time, if they weren't planning his uncle's murder even now.

"If he desires one now, I will send a man in my stead." Conar assured him.

Apparently Maelmorden had given the matter enough time. He waved a hand in the air and beckoned to a thin, dark-haired woman who hovered in a corner of the room.

"Bring him to our—guest," Maelmorden commanded.

He was taken down a long, dank hallway. A huge Viking sat on the ground before a heavy wooden doorway.

"The friar would enter," the woman said.

She left him. The flame-haired Dane seemed completely uninterested in him. He grunted and shoved the door open. Conar entered a small, drafty, peat-filled room with no windows. In the darkness he could barely see. He realized a man sat upon a bed of rushes on the floor, leaning against the wall.

"Welcome, Brother," Niall said softly after a while. "Take your time entering. I have been here long now, and my eyes have grown accustomed to this darkness."

Conar quickly made his way to his uncle, hunching down beside him.

"Have you come to raise my spirits, man? They have never fallen, and what comes will come, as is God's will. Maelmorden will kill me, but he will never win. If my life no longer stands forfeit, my family will crush him." His uncle sounded amazingly like his grandfather. Aed Finnlaith had been such a man, to calmly curl his fingers around that which he could hold—and defy fate when it could defy him.

"Aye, Ard-Ri!" Conar said softly. "But your family does not intend your life to be forfeit!"

"Who is it?" Niall whispered.

"It is I, Conar."

He felt his uncle's fingers touch his face. "Dear God, Conar! You've come alone? What foolishness! I have aged, my boy, my death would not be such a tragedy. You are young, with life stretched out before you!"

"Uncle, we haven't the time to discuss that at the moment. I have to know, can you stand, can you walk?"

Niall was quickly on his feet, not unsteady in any way. "We risk all the fury of the gods!" Conar muttered.

"God, son. God. One God. This is Eire. Your father has turned Christian!"

Conar sighed. "Uncle—"

"Aye, time, time! What is the plan?"

Conar was pulling off his robes. "Put these on."

"But you—"

"I slay yonder dragon, lying at the door, seize his armor, and escort you out. Do you see?"

"Aye, it could work, it could work . . ."

"It has to work!"

Conar left him and returned to the door. He watched the man and slowly drew his knife from his calf.

He threw open the door.

The Dane saw him, his eyes widening with shock. He scrambled to unsheath his sword, but even as he drew it, Conar's knife found its mark on the man's throat.

He caught the massive Dane as he fell, then quickly divested him of his mail and horned helmet, knife, mace, and sword.

He hurried back into the room. There was no going back. Speed was everything.

Niall was clad in the robes. He silently accepted the weapons his nephew offered him, then studied Conar. "Aye, you'll pass for him!"

"Then we move now."

Conar took his uncle's arm and led him down the long hallway. They came into the center room, where Maelmorden was still complaining about the strength of his enemies.

The Norse languages were nearly the same, yet there were subtle differences in the words spoken by Danes and Norwegians, and Conar was careful to guard his tongue as he grunted out the statement that he was seeing the friar out.

"His soul's a loss, eh, brother?" Maelmorden said, and burst into long spates of laughter. Conar pressed his uncle's arm, and they started out together. They quickly walked the long distance from the house to the line of guards surrounding it.

His father, his brothers, the other allied Irish kings, could see them now. They would know that the plan had been successful thus far.

He had only to cross the line.

Then came a wild cry of fury from behind them. Conar swung around. Maelmorden was bursting from the house, his teeth gnashing, his mouth near foaming. He drew his sword, racing forward with his men behind him, yelling in a dark rage for his men to slay them both.

But there was a cry from the fields as well. His father's forces came bursting out of the trees, riding down thunderously upon the line of defense and the manor. He saw his brother Eric sweeping toward him and thrust his uncle toward him. Eric reached for Niall, and Niall shed the monk's robes, reaching for his nephew, leaping up behind him on his horse, the sword Conar had given him from the slain Dane held high in his hand.

It was well Niall had reached his family, for the enemy was upon them. Eric and Niall hacked and slashed from atop Eric's horse.

Conar met the men who charged him from the ground, swinging in a broad arch that silenced several in one sweep, keeping his back to his brother's horse.

A second later a known enemy pit himself in fury against him.

Maelmorden himself.

The rebellious Irish king was a battle king, well trained, hardened, and in a rage. Conar thought back to all his training as Maelmorden faced him again and again, as their swords clashed and shuddered, as they broke away from each other. Maelmorden was smiling, displaying broken teeth. He fought like a berserker, foam forming upon his lips.

Never lose your temper in battle . . .

So had been his father's warning when he had been a child. He remembered it now.

When the powerful Maelmorden rushed him next, he simply moved aside. And when the man passed him, he drew up his sword and slashed it down.

Maelmorden fell before him. The small eyes looked at him once again. The man smiled. "Would that it were to your Valhalla, where battles are fought daily, that I might go!"

His eyes closed. Blood bubbled from his lips.

He died.

"Conar!" Leith was riding in hard, leading Thor. Conar leapt atop his horse and rode into the rest of the battle.

There was not much more of it. With Maelmorden gone, the backbone of the resistance was broken. With Niall freed, order was restored. Most of the Danes fled. The Irish cast aside their weapons and bowed low in fealty to Niall on the battlefield where their comrades lay dead.

At long last it was over.

They ate in Maelmorden's house that evening, and Conar was honored by his father, uncle, brothers, and the other kings.

"What boon would you ask of me, nephew?" Niall asked him.

"No boon, Uncle. Except to give me your blessing to sail. I wish to reach my own land as soon as possible now."

"Melisande has gone to Wessex—" Eric began, frowning.

"No. Melisande used Rhiannon to reach Wessex, and from there, sent for her own ships. I am deeply worried about things at home."

"You've more than my blessing, Conar. You've my full support," Niall promised him. "You've this land in Maelmorden's stead, awaiting you always, should you choose to return."

Conar thanked him and retired. He awoke Swen and Brenna and the rest of his men early, riding hard for Dubhlain, where his ships waited. He forced them to travel hard, covering more than fifty miles a day.

In Dubhlain he discovered what he had expected.

Rhiannon had written Erin to tell her Melisande had chosen to go home.

Melisande had written that times might soon be desperate.

Erin had just told her that the men had not returned from the north, that Niall was still hostage.

"I'll write again immediately—" Erin said.

"Nay. I sail now. For home. And my wife."

"You must long to hold her—"

But his eyes were cold. She had cut him deeply, and he determined that he would bury his heart against her.

"To slit her throat!" he swore to his mother, and Erin fell silent. She kissed his cheek.

"Give her a chance—"

"Mother, I only pray that I arrive in time to do so!"

He sailed immediately, heedless of the tides. He did not need Brenna or Mergwin to warn him that time was of the essence.

The days seemed to pass endlessly for Melisande. She was most concerned with the wall of the fortress, which still seemed to have weaknesses. She sent men to acquire stones to repair it from the Roman ruins and gathered them inside the fortress, not certain as yet just how she wanted it repaired.

She heard frequently from Odo, who seemed concerned for her safety. She also heard from Erin and knew that nothing had changed in the north.

She felt as if she had been away from Conar forever. She ached for him, yet at times he even became vague in her mind, for he was so far away and so distant. She had not heard a word from him, and she knew that he was probably coldly furious, and that he might well despise her all the more for what she had done.

Maybe he would never come, she thought. He was too fiercely loyal to his homeland. That was what he didn't understand. This was her homeland. She had to care about the fortress, had to defend it. Even at risk to herself.

To their child.

Eire was vast. Conar would always have his place within it. This was her land, and she had to fight for it.

She was called upon to do so when she had been home scarcely three weeks. Philippe came to her in the great hall to tell her that a group of raiders were pillaging a fishing village just to the north of them. She had been studying a letter from Rhiannon, reading to see if Eric had mentioned his brother or her, when she heard his breathless arrival and looked up.

"What do we do, milady?"

She hesitated a moment. "We defend them," she said. She stood. "I will ride with you."

Philippe gaped at her. "Milady, do you think that wise?"

Ragwald came thundering into the room. "It is not wise indeed! The count would be furious!"

"But the count is not here," Melisande said coolly. "I will ride with you."

She hurried to her room and opened the trunk with the gilded mail. She quickly donned the armor, then lifted the pretty sword.

Her fingers trembled when she remembered the last time she had wielded it. A sudden, anguished longing swept through her. She fought it.

He would have to have known that she had come here. And still he hadn't come. Yet he had always sworn that he would never let her go.

But she had left him, and perhaps now he had decided that she and her fortress were not worth the effort. What difference did the anguish in her heart mean now anyway? If he came here, he would be ready to kill her. Aye, as fearsome as any enemy.

She shook off the tremors that had seized her and hurried down the stairs. Ragwald and Philippe remained there, worriedly discussing her actions.

"Do I ride alone?" she asked from the bottom of the stairs.

Philippe hastily joined her.

They rode hard upon the enemy, and Melisande knew that she drew her people's loyalty and that riding at their head, she gave them strength.

They were quickly victorious, for the small party of Danes that had set ashore had done so for rape and plunder, they quickly discovered, with no intent to stay. Even as the invaders saw the horses sweeping down on them, they cried out, seeking their ships.

Philippe managed to save a pretty child from being kidnapped, grasping the babe from a fleeing Dane and returning it to the outstretched arms of her wailing mother. Gaston, the old but talented fellow, managed to slay their leader, ducking the man's battle-ax, catching him in the midriff with his razor-edged sword.

Melisande watched it all, hating it, feeling ill. Yet she felt that she'd had no choice but to ride.

Conar would never see it that way.

If he ever found out.

If he lived.

If he returned.

Days later an Irish player arrived on their shores. He came to her and sang, setting a recent poem to music, explaining that she would enjoy the words.

It was about the great fight in the north, its having just been won. Niall was freed. The player knew only the message in the poetry, for details were still not known, all that passed south like wildfire had been that the Ard-Ri lived, the Irish forces had tricked Maelmorden, Niall had been taken, and Conar had slain their enemy and received titular head as king in Maelmorden's stead.

Melisande thanked the player for coming to her.

"He will come now," Ragwald told her.

She shook her head. Would he? If he did, she must fight against him. Nay, they needed him.

But what would he do to her now?

"He will not come. They are eager to make him a king in Ireland."

"He has a wife."

"In Eire a man may set his wife aside if he so chooses!" she said softly.

"He will come," Ragwald insisted.

Yet the next morning, when she awakened first, it was not Conar who had come.

Gaston rushed in upon her. "Jesu! Jesu! You cannot imagine! It has come at last, Geoffrey's attack. Lady, they are lined upon the ridge, lined there endlessly!"

She was freezing. Oh, so stiff! It was damp and miserable and dark in Geoffrey's awful prison beneath the earth.

She had fought against her fear, remembering.

All those men lined there! And that just this morning!

Thus had begun her day. She had donned her gilded mail again. She had fought Geoffrey, and then Ragwald had been right—and she had been wrong.

Conar had come in his magnificent ships. Beaten back Geoffrey's troops, thundered through the wall.

Come to her, claimed her anew, spoken to the people with her.

And she had fought him. She had told him that she loathed him when she loved him.

He had touched her again. Taken her to heaven, no matter what the tempest. He had made love to her.

I will never let you go. Aye, he had said it time and time again. But what chance did he have now?

Melisande pulled the cloak more tightly about her shoulders as she sat in the dank prison so deep in the earth, where Geoffrey had cast her. She fought tears, fought screaming. But who would see her tears, or hear her screams?

She closed her eyes, praying that it would take Geoffrey a long, long time to come back for her. If he touched her, she would want to die.

She couldn't die. She was expecting a child.

Should she tell Geoffrey that? Would that keep him away from her?

Nay, he'd be convinced he needed to slay her quickly.

She rose, but the darkness was complete. She hugged the cloak to her and tried to move. Her feet were bare, blistered, bleeding. She trod carefully.

She heard the squeal of a rat, and her breath caught, and she jerked her hand back.

She had to escape. If God ever gave her a chance again, she would . . .

What?

Ah, indeed, what? she mocked herself. Tell him that I love him, that we are to have a child. That I was hurt and willful most often because he did not understand that I needed to fight with him, I thought that I battled alone, but I needed him.

She thought of his tenderness, thought of the way that he touched her.

If Geoffrey came, she would die, by his hand, or by her own.

What a fool! she cried to herself. She had to keep fighting, she had to escape, find the door . . .

But she went dead still. She could hear the ancient door creaking. She could feel things, sense them in the darkness, she had been here so long.

She stood on her toes, flat against the damp wall, listening. She held her breath. Her heart hammered furiously.

She was no longer alone.

Someone had entered into the stygian darkness of the room with her.

Someone who closed the door quietly in his wake, locking them in together.

A silent scream welled in her throat.

After . . .
A Siege of Hearts

 **20**

Spring, A.D. *885*
The Coast of France

The wall had taken the greatest extent of the damage today, Conar decided, surveying it in torchlight against the darkness that had fallen.

The wall, and our lives, he thought wearily. Dear God, but it had been an awful day. The fear that had gripped him when he had seen the fortress under assault had been horrible; he'd never known such anguish.

The fear had fueled his anger.

He'd been so damned furious. Ever more so when he came here, when she had so nearly fallen to Geoffrey, as wretched a traitor as his father had ever been.

What if Conar hadn't arrived when he did?

The thought caused a cold sweat to break out on his forehead, and he closed his eyes momentarily, praying for the tension to ease from his body. And his wife! How great the distance that lay between them now!

He gave orders that the stones be shored up for the night, and he started to turn from the damage. He felt a presence behind him and turned to find Brenna watching him with large, soulful eyes.

"What?" he demanded, crossing his arms over his chest.

Brenna shook her head slightly. Inhaled and exhaled. "You should not be so hard on her."

He arched a brow. "Brenna," he said very softly, "she defied my orders and came here, and there was nearly disaster."

"But she knew she would be attacked—"

"And what is this fortress except for wood and stone?" he demanded. "Had it fallen, we would have rebuilt."

"There are her people," Brenna reminded him.

He turned his back on her, having little answer for that. "She defied me. I don't know why you speak on her behalf—the lady remains highly suspicious of you."

Brenna smiled. "Only because she is blind to one truth. She does not see that you don't allow her to travel with you because you are so deathly afraid that some danger will befall her. I am more expendable."

"Brenna—"

"I serve you, as do Swen, and the others."

He fell silent, waiting, knowing Brenna, knowing she intended to say more.

"You haven't—done anything to her, have you?"

"Done anything!" he repeated, then his voice took on the edges of a growl, though it remaind soft. "How long have you known me?" he demanded. "What do you think I would have done?"

"I have never seen you so angry." She hesitated. "Nor so hurt."

He sighed. "No, I have not beaten her, nor caused any injury to her! I confess, I'm at a loss. What do I do? Lock her within her tower? I must find some way to make her understand how reckless she is, how much she risks!"

"How much she risks . . ." Brenna murmured.

"What are you talking about now?" he asked in exasperation, suddenly frowning. "Why your worry about what I might have done? What else does she risk?"

Brenna's lashes fell quickly, but too late.

"I want to know now," he urged softly.

"She's told you nothing?"

He threw his arms up in frustration. "Brenna, she did not welcome me with open arms—"

"And I'm sure that you did not greet her with a tender kiss."

"She defied and disobeyed me, Brenna—"

"Yet she tried to tell you it was desperate you come home."

"I couldn't leave my father, my uncle, my brothers."

"She couldn't leave *her* people."

"All right, Brenna, I want to know what you are trying not to tell me, why the concern, why the worry? I still might flay her to within a half inch of life. If there's some reason that I should not—"

"She's expecting your child."

His breath left him. He was so stunned, he might have been blown over like a leaf. Aye, he'd always wanted a child, it was natural. And aye, children certainly did come from the one very thing that he and Melisande seemed to do so well together.

But he hadn't even begun to hope that she might be expecting. Perhaps because she battled him so, because she did not want it, did not want him.

He swallowed hard. Nay, she had not told him, had not mentioned a word to him.

Brenna seemed to read his mind. "Perhaps she does not feel certain as yet, perhaps she wants to assure herself that she will not lose the babe—"

"And perhaps she simply hates me so deeply that she has no intention of telling me."

"She doesn't hate you."

"Hate, loathe, despise—I think those are her words."

"And hatred, milord, is very close to love—and passion is readily its bedfellow!"

Did Brenna know his own feelings when it came to Melisande? Aye, surely she did, even if others did not know how deeply his Frankish beauty ruled his heart.

"You needn't fear anything," he said at last. "I never intended to beat my wife. What to do with her, I do not know. But I never meant to strike a blow against her. And now . . ." He paused, for a deep trembling filled him. A child. A babe. A handsome lad like his brother's Garth. A beautiful girl like Eric's infant babe.

But his own . . .

His own to raise, to teach. A child with so rich a heritage! One to touch, cradle, love.

"What do I do with her?" he asked Brenna.

"Love her?" she suggested.

He grinned slowly, then slipped an arm around her. "I've tried . . ." he murmured, then shrugged. "Perhaps, who knows? Perhaps this great breach we've created now can be healed. We've the future, we've . . . a child!" His fingers closed, his hands formed white-knuckled fists. What were her thoughts on the matter? Why hadn't she told him? She loved children, he knew it well enough, he had seen her with his brother's offspring, with other nephews and nieces and cousins.

But this was his child.

"A Viking child," he murmured. "Will she want it?"

"Only a fourth Viking, milord," Brenna reminded him. "A fourth Irish, and a full half Frankish."

"Indeed?"

"On the other hand . . ."

"Aye?"

"The child I am about to have with Swen will be half Viking from both of us, and half Irish—from both of us."

"You and Swen . . ."

"We'd like to wed. Have we your blessing, Conar?"

He kissed her cheek, holding her to him. "Indeed. Blessing! I shall insist upon the marriage. My heartiest best wishes to you both."

"Thank you, milord. Mergwin will be disappointed, of course." She wrinkled her nose. "He always thought my powers would be greater were I to vow myself to a life of chastity."

"Ah, but that old scoundrel gave no thought to the powers of love!"

She smiled. He slipped an arm about her shoulders and led her back into the fortress. Swen was in the great hall drinking ale, talking animatedly with Philippe and Gaston. Conar immediately poured himself a goblet of ale and then poured more for those in the hall, passed the drinks around, and offered a toast to Swen and Brenna. Their health was drunk all around.

Conar sat at the table, half listening as the men spoke about the situation in the Frankish kingdoms.

Melisande lay above him. He wanted to go to her, shake her, demand to know why she denied him so much. He wanted to hold her tenderly against him as well, he wanted to touch her again, make love to her again, feel the fiery heat and vibrant force of her body against his, feel the desire, the exultation, the simple comfort of sleeping beside her.

She had threatened that she would not be there. She had not come down to the hall. Did she fear him so at last then? Melisande . . .?

Did she pace the floor, waiting? In anger, dread . . . Anticipation?

"Ah, but Swen!" he heard Gaston murmur. "Your

troubles in Eire are vast, I agree. But look at our
recent history here! 'Twas just 860 when Vikings set
upon Jeufosse, an island in the Seine a bit north of
Paris. Charles the Bald tried to dislodge them, his
brother Lothar fought with him to remove the menace.
Then Charles's other brother, Louis, invaded from the
southeast, Charles had to leave to fight his brother,
and the Vikings were entrenched. But the Vikings are
enterprising, eh? Another group offered Charles to rid
the isle of the wretches—for a mere five thousand
pounds of silver! Plus food and sustenance, of course,
the finest wines available, if you please! Charles was
not fond of paying this danegeld, and so he began all
that you see here, what you will see dotted over the
countryside—fortresses such as this! The Vikings do
not like to attack fortresses.''

"Aye,'' Philippe agreed. "You have your woes, and
ours grow worse. When Alfred won his great victory
in England in 878, the Vikings set to attack him, then
set their eyes upon us! And Lothar's kingdom was
divided between one King Louis and another King
Louis. Our King Louis of the western Franks went on
to win a great battle at Saucourt, near the Somme, but
went on to kill himself in the pursuit of a young girl!
His brother, Carloman, died just last year, and so we
are left to the mercy of Charles the Stout, who has
already sold out to the invaders again and again. Only
Count Odo stands strong against him, and so we stand
strong with Count Odo!''

Conar smiled a moment, curious at the manner these
Franks had of referring to their kings. There was now
Charles the Fat, before him there had been Charles
the Bald. He was glad it was not so with his family.
His grandfather had been, if anything, Aed the Fair.
His father, and his father's father, always the Lord of
the Wolves, as he himself was called.

Thank God. He would not want to be titled for his

shortcomings. He smiled inwardly, thinking of a few Viking titles he knew. Rodir the Hairless, Hak the Limper. Raup the One-legged.

Perhaps none of them was too kind. He would have to be careful not to lose his hair.

And just what did Melisande call him in his absence? he wondered.

The *Viking*. He would always be the *Viking*, he thought, and he could disavow his heritage, or a father he loved. Yet it seemed that he could not teach her that no matter what a man's heritage, he had to be judged for himself, for the life he had come to live, for the ideals he embraced himself. Maybe it was too much to ask of a woman from a world that had been too long terrorized by a certain people.

Ah, but he did ask it! He demanded it, he craved it! She had to be made to see, to meet him halfway, to obey him, aye, for she was in such great danger if she did not! She had to be made to . . .

Love him? Did Brenna have the simplest answer of all?

He realized suddenly that Philippe was looking at him, and that he had spoken. "Your pardon, Philippe. I'm sorry, I'm weary, and my mind wandered."

"We're glad to have you home, milord. We have missed you sorely. All of us, as well as milady Melisande."

"Thank you. I am glad to be here," Conar said. His lip curled. These men were not fools. They had to know that though Melisande might of necessity have been glad of his arrival, she must have dreaded it as well.

"It's true, milord," Gaston told him. "She has walked around here like a pale ghost these many weeks. I know she is glad you have come home."

Home. Aye, this was to be his home now. It was

difficult to be torn so, to feel the bind to his native land, and now to this one.

Melisande's land.

Nay, their land.

Yet perhaps she had her point. If he was to claim it, then he needed live on it. He prayed the future would allow him to do so.

Ragwald entered the room, looking strangely uncomfortable.

"What is it?" Conar demanded, then sighed inwardly. Surely if Brenna was concerned about his treatment of his wife, Ragwald would be doubly so. Yet Ragwald had been glad of his return, Conar was very aware of that.

Ragwald was glad of the firm grip he had upon Melisande—when he actually had that grip.

"I don't know . . ." Ragwald murmured, then shrugged. "Nothing, something. I don't know, aye, there is something! It has haunted me for hours now!" He hesitated, then frowned. "Milord, where is Melisande?"

Just then Brenna gasped and doubled over. Swen leapt toward her, as did Conar, anxiously.

"Are you all right?" Swen cried.

"Is it the babe?" Conar asked.

She shook her head, her hand on Swen's reassuringly. He sat, drawing her to his lap. "I'm fine, it was a feeling, a feeling such as Ragwald's . . ."

Suddenly the silence from the floor above seemed to shriek a warning to Conar. He leapt up and tore for the stairs, bounding up their length. He burst through the door to their room.

And found it empty.

Empty. Damn her! She should have been here! He had told her that he would come back, and she had said that he must not count on her being there.

"Damn her!" he breathed. "Damn her . . ."

He felt as if a knife pierced his heart. Jesu, had she really tried to flee him again?

"Nay, nay, Conar!" Brenna cried. She had followed him frantically up the stairs. "Look at the bed, it is torn about, there was a struggle."

He strode swiftly to the bed and saw the truth of Brenna's words. He wrenched the remaining sheet into his hand. His head fell back. "Melisande!" It was a cry that seemed to rip the night, to cause the very fortress walls to shudder and quake.

He staggered back, sick with rage and fear. For a moment he didn't feel he had the strength to stand, his terror for her was so great. He had to find strength. He could not falter now. Yet how? How had he come just in time. How had he bested his enemy, fought so long, so hard, touched her, held her again. He had feared that he would never do so, but she had been in his arms, fragrant, wild, sweet silk, Melisande.

How . . .?

Ah, just as he had tricked Maelmorden in Eire, someone had tricked them all here. A single man. No, more—no one man could have taken Melisande from here! She would have fought like a wild thing.

"She did not leave here of her own free will, I swear it!" Ragwald said passionately, his voice trembling with emotion.

Conar lowered his head, fighting to control his fear and his rage, all dangerous when it was imperative now that he keep a clear head.

"Geoffrey," he said.

"But how . . .?" Philippe questioned.

"The battle was over. People were milling about, the wall was broken, everyone was busy. He watched me leave the tower. And he went for Melisande."

Gaston crossed himself, tears in his eyes. "How do we fight him, how—"

Conar whirled on Swen. "Get someone down to the

Danish prisoners. Find out where he might have taken her. Slip someone in among them, someone who can be one of theirs. Quickly, now!''

Swen hastened to do as he was bidden. Conar could not bear to stay in the room.

To stare at the bed where he had so recently loved her.

From where she had so recently been taken.

Had Geoffrey touched her as yet? The rage swept through him. Nothing that the man could do would change his love for Melisande, but if he hurt her in any way, Conar would want to kill him slowly, painfully!

His eyes fell upon the gilded mail. Upon her delicately engraved sword.

He could not stay. He left the room and paced the hall below as he forced himself to patience, forced himself to wait for word to come.

It did, quickly. His man Jute arrived soon with Swen, bowed, and spoke quickly.

''The Danes will soon lay siege to Paris,'' he said swiftly. ''Their numbers here are huge, and they have been paid in silver by Geoffrey Sur-le-Mont to fight with him as well. They camp by the old Roman ruins, from where Melisande was taking her stones. Geoffrey has taken her there. There are foundations there, with deep hallways and pits in the earth. There are burial chambers, too. The place is quite a maze and does not need so many guards.''

''I will go for her then,'' Conar said.

''Have we the numbers?'' Philippe demanded.

Conar shook his head. ''I will go for her alone.''

Philippe gasped. ''What insanity, milord! Brave insanity!'' he added quickly. ''But to what avail?''

''Geoffrey came for her alone, and so walked through us all. It is a ploy we quite recently used in Eire, and I don't think Geoffrey will expect it to be used against him now. I do know something of these ruins. I met Count Manon there with my uncle when I was very young and have ridden near them since. I remember the layout . . . and the look of the land.''

He strode to the table, knocking goblets from it with a sweep of his arm, then quickly replacing them to show landmarks. ''The old tower lies here. There is a passage below, and it enters the burial vaults. There is another here, ending in what must have been a storage vault.'' He paused and placed a goblet flat upon it. ''Here!'' he exclaimed. ''Here is where they will have her. And here''—he paused, placing another goblet on the table—''is where his men will be gathered, behind this broken rubble of wall. They can camp and still keep their eyes upon the road. And there, my fine friends, is where you must wait for me with our numbers. When I appear with Melisande, you must be ready to charge.''

''If you can appear with her, dear God, we will still be so outnumbered!'' Gaston worried.

But there was suddenly a loud exclamation. Conar turned to see Ragwald standing in the entry. He was breathless, and Conar realized that he had not followed them at first. His hair and beard were windblown. The old man had been outside. ''Nay, Count Conar, nay! I do not believe we are outnumbered!''

Ragwald turned and started up the stairs again. Curious, Conar and the others hurried behind him. He came to Melisande's tower and hurried after Ragwald.

The night was dark. They could still see the sea. It was dotted with torchlight.

The torches illuminated a great army of ships.

''Jesu, more and more Danes!'' Philippe cried.

But Conar smiled slowly. ''Nay, friends. Ragwald is right. We no longer lack numbers!''

''But what—?'' Philippe began.

''My family!'' Conar said softly.

When Maelmorden was beaten, his father had told him, they would all be free.

And so they were.

And just as he had always answered a call for help, now he was being answered, when he had not even thought to voice the call.

"Aye! My family!" he repeated. "They have arrived!" He pointed to the ships, growing more and more visible as they drew closer.

Again, as if he had asked the sky for help, the clouds lifted away from the moon.

Aye, they came. Eric, his father, Leith. Bryan, Bryce, his brothers-in-law, cousins, uncles, cousins-in-law.

He swung around suddenly. "Swen, greet them. I must make haste to reach Melisande before she does herself damage in her fear of Geoffrey." Or of me, he added silently. "Tell them what I have told you. They will know what to do. They have done it once."

He spun around, ready to hurry down the stairs.

"Conar!" Swen called.

Conar waited.

"How will you slip through them, what disguise will you use?"

He grinned. "One that I am very adept with. One that will blend in."

"Aye?"

He sighed. "I will go as a Viking, Swen. I will go as a Viking."

He turned and left them once again, and in minutes he was riding into the darkness alone, even as a vast army arrived on his shores to help him.

He was grateful. He needed help now.

But he also had to reach her. Quickly. Alone.

It was the only way to save her. He could only pray that they would follow.

21

Melisande could see nothing, not even a form in the darkness. What little filtering of light that had come when the door opened left as soon as it had closed. She stood dead still, listening.

She could hear it. Deep, ragged breathing.

Geoffrey? Had he come back?

No, he would have brought a torch—he'd want to see the dismay on her face when he returned for her.

The person who had come now brought no light. He had come furtively.

"Where are you?" The soft question came in the Norse language, and she felt a cold wave of dread slip over her. Geoffrey had played with rapists and thieves. Now his thieves were wishing to steal the prize he had plundered himself.

She remained perfectly silent, then felt movement from the door. The Dane had entered, come down the steps, and was now swinging heavily muscled arms from side to side to try to trap her.

She ducked low just in time, feeling the whir of air as the hand struck the air, inches from her face. He crossed the room and started back.

A rat squealed, just at her feet. She bit her lip as her

blood raced, ducking and fleeing across with only a breath to spare when he started back again.

The man laughed softly, a husky, chilling sound in the darkness. "Stay still, girl! Lady Melisande. Lady, lady, lady!"

She inched back against the wall. For a while it seemed that he pressed his hands against the dank stone on the opposite wall. She held her breath again. He was coming in a circle. She would have to move again, or he would find her.

She did so. He did not hear her, as his hands were slapping against the stone.

It went on.

She began to wonder desperately just how long she could hide from the man in the darkness. Could this game go on forever?

She thought about seeking the doorway. Perhaps he was the man sent to guard her.

And perhaps he was not. Perhaps it was another Dane, and if she dared touch the door, she would find herself trying to elude two. Should she move for it?

But then he swore softly, and heavy, impatient footsteps took him across the floor once again.

He was opening the door himself, up the steps, not far from where she stood, just cracking it to allow some of the torchlight from the underground hallway to leak in upon them. There was still little to be seen, except for silhouettes and shadows.

Her silhouette, a clean dark shadow upon the wall.

"Ah!" The man cried.

He bounded for her. She gasped and evaded him, sweeping by him. She tried for the door. He reached her on the steps, dragged her back. She beat her fists against him, she started to scream. His hand fell upon her mouth, and she was shoved down to the floor. She twisted and bit into fleshy fingers. He swore and cuffed her cheek, stunning her. The cloak, her only garment, was slipping away, and she could feel the rough texture of his clothing biting against her tender flesh, feel his hands, his weight.

Tears sprang into her eyes. He lifted his weight for a moment to free himself for his purpose, and she slammed her foot up against him with all of her strength.

A gasp escaped him, and then a bellow. Melisande rolled swiftly, leaping to her feet again. He was behind her, seized her, threw her back. She felt the hiss of his breath as he came close again.

But then he was suddenly lifted off her, thrown across the room. He fell hard against the wall, swore, leapt to his feet.

There were two men in the room, two Danes, Melisande thought. One lunged at the other now, and they were on the floor, dark shadows, wildly tearing at one another. She heard the sounds of blows, but then, in the darkness, she heard something more.

Knives. Knives met and clashed. And now flailed in the darkness.

She began to inch for the doorway but then went still, hearing a different sound.

That of a knife sinking into flesh. She held her breath. The two men had been standing.

Now one sank slowly to the floor.

She paused, barely breathing. The victor turned his eyes toward her.

She made a desperate leap for the door.

"No, Melisande!"

She couldn't comprehend her own name at first, she was so terrified. She was trying to run until she could run no more.

But once again fingers wound into her cloak. She was dragged back hard. She kept fighting. "No, no, no . . .!"

She found herself spun around, pressed to the wall, a hand falling over her mouth once again.

"Melisande! It is me!"

Conar!

She went still, limp, disbelieving. Her teeth began to chatter. She was shaking so badly that she could not stand. She started to sink to the floor, and he caught her, lifting her into his arms, carrying her to where the greatest filtering of light from the cracked doorway now offered some dim respite against the shadows. With her in his arms, he went down upon his knee.

Indeed, it was him. Wolf skins covered his chest and shoulders and buffered his tunic of mail. His conical helmet, allowing only his fierce blue eyes to show, covered his head and nose. He stared down at her, seeing the rough borrowed cloak, the dirt that smudged her body, the tears in her eyes. His voice was suddenly impassioned, whispered, but filled with rage. "By the gods, if they've hurt you—!"

She shook her head wildly, fighting for reason. In all her life she had never been so terribly frightened, nor had she ever felt so keenly her own weakness. But he was here now. He had come for her after all.

She fought for words, trying to still her shaking, trying to stop the tears that dampened her eyes, slid to her cheeks. "The ride was rough. This hole is damp and chill, but Geoffrey threw me here and left, and you—you came before this man could do me much ill."

His hands moved upon her suddenly, covering the length of her. Stroking her cheek, assuring himself, she realized, that she was well and whole. They moved over her nakedness, and she curled against him, her arm around his shoulder, and a ragged sob escaped her.

"Melisande . . ." For a moment his hand stroked

the tangled black fall of her hair. But then he pulled
her away, his touch firm. He met her eyes. "Can you
walk, can you stand?"

Her eyes widened on his. She realized that he was
here, alone, dressed completely in Viking attire.

There had been so many Danes when she had arrived, littering the rocks and ruins beneath the moonlight.

"Can you stand?"

She nodded, bracing herself against his shoulders,
managing to stand.

She was shaking still. But she released her hold
upon him, standing of her own accord, the cloak falling
back in place to cover her.

He stood before her.

"How did you get here?" she whispered quickly.

There was a fiery glitter in the blue eyes that gazed
at her. "I told you, I would never let you go."

Her fingers curled into fists at her sides, nails digging
into her palms. "I didn't try to leave, Conar, I didn't
run. They came. They came into the keep, up the
stairs . . ."

"Shh, shh! I know! But stay quiet. We've got to get
out of here for now."

"You're going to fight all those Danes out there,
alone?"

He shook his head slowly. "I am going to walk right
through them, just as I did coming here. Now listen.
You must pretend that I am one of them. An awful
enemy. Maybe that won't be so hard."

She winced inwardly, her lashes low. "Conar—"

"My apologies, lady. We've no time for recrimina-
tions. It must appear that you are the prisoner still,
that I just escort you from one place to another. Do
you understand?"

She nodded. Conar opened the heavy door. The hall
was empty.

Her only guard had been the one who lay dead just behind her.

She inhaled, feeling Conar's hand upon her arm. "Swiftly," he warned her.

She ran down the hallway, clutching the cloak tightly to her throat. As they neared the end of the hallway, where the ancient, uneven stones reached back up to the cool air and soft blanket of night, they were suddenly challenged.

"Who's there?"

A man in leather sandals, short trousers, and skins hurried down the steps. "Where are you taking Geoffrey's woman?"

"Friend, I am taking her out," Conar said smoothly.

"Wait!"

The Dane drew a sword. "Taking her where?"

"Home!" Conar announced. The strength of his arm propelled her behind him, and instantly his sword was drawn. The Dane lunged, Conar lunged in return, his sword entering the man's belly. "Home, friend," Conar repeated as the man fell, and he withdrew his sword. "She is not Geoffrey's woman but mine!"

The Dane was dead, and Conar stepped around him. Melisande stood still, stunned, staring at the man.

"We must move," Conar told her.

She started for the steps.

"Nay, not these. Take the corridor there."

Melisande paused. Her gaze met Conar's and his hand gripped hers again. She had scarcely seen the near black opening to a further hallway.

But now he led her along it. At first she could see nothing. Then, barefooted, she tripped upon something on the ground. She staggered, for the object had pierced her flesh. She reached down, trying not to step upon it again.

She lifted a bone. A human bone.

A shriek rose in her.

"Shh!" Conar swiftly silenced her, taking the offending femur from her hands and tossing it aside.

"What is this place?" she cried.

"A Roman burial chamber. Come, let's go. It lets out far closer to the woods."

She inhaled. She stepped carefully again, yet a gasp left her lips, for the floor here was littered with bones.

As were the walls, she realized.

Row after row of bodies lay in perfect symmetry to her left. Some nothing more than bone, some still clothed in ancient costume, some in shrouds, and some left to rot with no gentle gauze to cover the ravages of death . . .

"Oh, my God!" she whispered. "You've brought me through a city of death!"

"Milady, I am trying to rescue you!" he reminded her, sweeping her off the floor as she gasped at another sharp fragment in her way. His eyes touched her. "You are not supposed to complain about the method."

She was still terrified, yet his words made her smile. "Your pardon, milord. I will take care that should I be abducted in the future, I will do so with shoes."

"And clothing!" he reminded her curtly.

"You had just left me," she said softly.

They were far from safe as yet, Melisande knew. But as those eyes touched her, she felt a furious trembling begin again within her. She felt amazingly secure at this moment, protected, warm, safe.

Incredibly happy.

He had come for her.

The strength of his arms was around her. The heat of him filled her.

Why had she ever sailed away?

Because he had ridden off to war.

But she had been wrong. No matter how great her passion for home, she had been wrong. She wanted to tell him so, but he moved too swiftly, it was not the time, or the place.

Yet would they ever have the time, or the place?

He fell silent, his long strides carrying them quickly through the hallway of corpses. She lay against the cool metal of his mail, her eyes closed.

Then he set her down again, pulling on her arm so that she followed him. She saw there was another set of white stone steps just ahead of them, steps that led back up to the moonlit night.

"Up the steps, quickly," he commanded, and she scrambled up, nearly slipping on their lichen-covered slickness.

Then they were out in the moonlight. Her breath caught.

The Danes were everywhere. Clumped in groups by rocks and boulders, resting on the remnants of ancient stone walls.

Fires burned.

Melisande closed her eyes for a moment against the things the fall of night could not hide.

Vikings could be so coldly, brutally cruel. They sometimes played with their captives before killing them.

They sometimes killed them very slowly, binding them to trees, cutting out their entrails, and letting them die thus. They were known to cook their meals in the stomachs of their slain enemies.

There were bodies tied to trees. Sagging bodies. The scent of blood was rich on the air.

And they were alone amidst all of this. If they were captured again, Geoffrey would only take her back.

He would kill Conar in the most hideous way possible.

Her knees grew weak. His hand was upon her elbow again. "Nay! Don't fail me now!"

She shook her head. "Walk. See the rise of wall

there? Let's keep to the rear of it. And hurry along. It must seem that I am escorting you as I have been commanded.''

She nodded and began to walk. They covered some fair distance. She realized that Conar was trying to reach a place where the Roman wall had ended, where the forest still claimed the land.

They had traveled some distance before Conar was suddenly tapped on the shoulder. He paused, turning back swiftly. Three men stood behind them.

''Where are you taking the woman?''

''He has sent for her.''

''He has sent for her? You are going the wrong way.''

Conar started to shrug. Then one of them laughed. ''Ah, it's not like the lovely countess has no knowledge of a man, eh? There's nothing to be saved for his fine Frankish pleasure!''

''Being wed to a Viking,'' another agreed. ''She'll be craving more than his poor sword!''

''We take her out, share her, return her,'' the third said, ''and no one is the wiser!'' He bellowed out a laugh. ''And if anyone is the wiser, then damn them, for he does not pay us enough to keep us from such a tempting morsel.''

''Share her . . .'' Conar murmured. Melisande's eyes widened on him, but he wasn't even glancing her way. ''The clump of trees yonder, behind our lines. Let's take her there.''

Melisande opened her mouth to protest. Conar's hand slammed down upon it, and the other men quickly formed a guard around him, hiding the fact that he now dragged her along. She struggled against his hand, for she couldn't breathe. He lifted her off the ground, and her toes dangled just above it.

They passed by the rocks where the Danes lay and

drank and kept a casual guard. They passed the end of the broken wall and entered the trees.

"Here!" Someone commanded.

"Deeper!" Conar said, "We cannot afford for others to hear her screams."

"Aye!" came a simultanous cry.

And so they moved deeper into the woods, into darkness. They came at last to a cove with pine carpeting. They could still see the fires, but they were some distance away.

"Here!" the biggest of the men demanded again. Like Conar, he was clad in mail. His helmet was winged, with no nose guard. He was heavyset, and not as well muscled as many of his fellows. The man behind him was shorter, but square, stout, and heavy-muscled. The third was slimmer, well built.

"Aye . . . here . . ."

Her eyes widened with alarm again as he brought her forward, dropped her instantly, and unsheathed his sword, swinging on the others.

"What—" began the heavyset one.

"Friends, she is mine!" Conar said quietly.

"By all the fires of a bloody Christian hell!" the heavy one exclaimed. "By the rood, man, she is ours!"

He, too, drew his sword, lunging forward quickly. Conar waved a hand to Melisande, and she leapt behind a tree trunk, her heart in her throat as she waited.

"Take her then!" Conar commanded.

The first man fell to his goading and rushed forward. There was no real clash of swords. He lunged wildly for Conar's throat, and Conar instantly parried the blow, then drove his blade homeward at the man's nape. He fell with a loud whooshing sound.

It had all happened so fast. His two companions instantly drew weapons, the one a mace, the other a sword, and began to circle Conar. Conar crouched low, watching them both. They rushed him. He parried the mace, but the sword slashed across his chest. He grunted with the force of it, yet his mail kept the blade from piercing his flesh. He staggered back and shoved his foot against the chest of the first man to come for him again. The man fell back, stumbled.

The other waved his mace in the air and brought it crashing down. Conar moved with seconds to spare. The heavy steel ball of the weapon crashed into a tree trunk when it might have cleaved his skull.

He swung around swiftly, catching the sword wielder in the side. The man screamed, staggering backward. Conar inched for him, trying to retrieve his weapon. He drew it back, but the last man slammed his weight against his shoulders just then, and the weapon flew.

Melisande cried out in horror, watching as the man swung again and again, as Conar leapt and ducked, watching him, fighting for his life.

The sword!

She left the tree trunk and dived for the silver weapon shimmering beneath the moonlight.

The man had left Conar, he was fast approaching her. She leapt to her feet, waving it before her.

"Melisande! Give it to me!"

The mace swung toward her blade. The strength of it was shattering. Conar was circling around. She tossed the weapon to him swiftly. The Dane lunged. Conar stepped before her, shoving her back again. The mace swung. Conar ducked. He swung his sword. The blow was good. He caught this opponent in the throat as well. Blood spilled out as the man sank to his knees.

But Conar sank down, too. He fell back, flat upon the ground. His eyes closed.

Melisande leapt beside him, tapping his cheek beneath the steel of his visor. "Conar!" she cried with alarm, her heart seeming to shatter. How had he been hurt? When the blow? She hadn't seen it. Did he bleed, did he lay dying? "Conar!" she cried out again, touching his throat, seeking the beat of his life.

His eyes flew open, shattering brilliant blue upon her. "Winded, tired. It took you long enough to go for that sword!"

"Oh!" she cried out. "You're all right—"

He sat up.

"Aye, for the moment."

"How dare you scare me so!"

"Lady, I but fell for a moment! Those fellows were heavy, not to mention that I just carried you down the length of that full corridor!"

"My feet are grievously torn!"

"Aye."

"You offered to share me with the three!"

"How else escape them, Melisande? Have you ever known me to share something so thoroughly mine as a wife?"

Of course not. She had just been so riddled with fear.

"Nay, you do not share such things!" she agreed softly.

"Alas, the sword could have been gotten a shade sooner!"

"You told me to get behind the tree."

"You've decided to obey me now?" he queried.

"Nay, I just—oh!" she cried out, flushing, but he smiled, then his smiled faded, and he pressed a finger to her lips. "I have brought us too far to the east now. We must make our way back through the woods. Quickly. Before our trail of dead men is discovered, and Geoffrey realizes that you are gone." He came to his feet and reached for her hand.

She took it quickly, yet pulled back a moment. She

felt a sudden rush of tears to her eyes. "Conar, I know we haven't time, but there's something I must tell you. We—we're going to have a child. I realize that makes it worse that I donned mail and led the men, but I was desperate, you were not here, you have so much across the sea. Yet this is all that I have, my father taught me a great responsibility to the people—"

"Melisande—"

"Mergwin told me that it is going to be a boy," she finished, eyes downcast.

"I know."

Her eyes flew open. There was so much hidden against her when his helmet covered so much but eyes and mouth!

"Mergwin told you?"

"Brenna."

"Oh . . ."

"Melisande, she told me just tonight. Because she knew how angry I was, and she was worried that I might hurt you, or be too rough with you. She demanded I be gentle."

"Oh . . ."

He caught her arm. "Come. I would live to be a father."

They started through the soft pine trail again. "She is expecting her own child," he said.

Melisande froze, causing him to misstep. He pulled back, staring into her eyes.

Brenna had told her that she and Conar had not been lovers.

Brenna had also told her that she would always be there for Conar. To serve him as he might wish. In any way. Brenna rode with him, fought with him.

Melisande had left him. Brenna had stayed.

And so much time lay between them now, no matter how tempestuous their meeting.

He had come for her tonight. Risked death and terrible odds, torture, things he knew all too well.

She lowered her lashes quickly, fighting tears.

Conar suddenly lifted her chin. "What is it? Ah!" He shook his head, a smile curving his lip. "The child she carries is Swen's. They plan to wed soon."

Melisande bowed her head, determined he would not see her swift smile, nor realize just how deeply her emotions had been running.

His hand was upon her arm again. "Come, hurry."

She hurried. She followed him blindly, trying not to wince as her feet fell upon sharp twigs and stones.

"Almost there!" he whispered.

Where? Where was there?

What help was there for them?

Suddenly they burst out into a clearing. Conar stopped so abruptly that she slammed against his back. Stunned, she braced herself against him and looked around. Her breath caught in her throat, and her heart leapt to meet it there.

Geoffrey stood before them, surrounded by bearded, bearskin-covered berserkers. At least ten men, equipped with swords, maces, battle-axes.

Geoffrey smiled slowly.

"I think that the odds are mine at last, Viking," Geoffrey said softly.

"Are they?" Conar inquired in turn.

"Indeed. You shouldn't have come for her."

"You stole my wife. I had to come."

"She should have been mine. This is not your country, or your place."

"As your father murdered hers, she was never very fond of you!"

"She will be. I will see to it. When you are dead and gone, Conar—which will be shortly, though I do intend it to take time—she will be glad enough of me! You will simply be out of the way."

She found herself slipping around Conar's side, choking with her fear and fury. "Never!" she cried. "Never, you daft fool! Do you think that you can slay the years that have passed between us, do you think that you can slay love?"

"Melisande!" His hands were on her; she was placed firmly behind him.

"Slowly," Geoffrey promised. "Would you like to know what I've planned? Four of the swiftest horses, each wrist tied to one, and each ankle as well. Then a whip will lash across their haunches and the mighty Lord of the Wolves will be ripped. Ah, but first, I think, we will slash your stomach and let your entrails hang. When you are split into the proper pieces, we'll have a great fire and roast what is left of you!"

Conar didn't even flinch. He drew his sword, still pressing her around his back. "Only in your sweetest dreams, Goeffrey! Only there!"

Geoffrey swore. "Fool. Even as you face death—"

But he broke off. From far to their left, where the forest broke off and the remnants of the Roman wall stood, she suddenly heard motion.

She turned.

And her breath caught anew with the greatest pleasure. With awe.

They were there. It was incredible, it might have been a dream.

But it was real. They were all there. Conar's family. His father in the center in the line that seemed to stretch forever on the horizon of the night. Their men—so many of them—stretched out around and behind them.

They sat atop their horses, great beasts that pawed the air, that snorted out gray steam beneath the moonlight. They sat in their armor, mail and helmets that glittered against the soft glow.

They sat, formidable, invincible. She could see Olaf, Eric, Bryan, Bryce, Conan, and there—dear Lord—at the end of it all, Mergwin! She could not believe it; it had to be a trick of the misty night and the moonlight.

But then they began to move, and they were, indeed, awesome. Their great horses plowed over the walls and began to tear up the earth as they thundered down upon the enemy.

For a moment there was chaos. Conar was dragging her back, and they were watching the pounding horses arrive together.

"I must get you out of here!" Conar whispered fiercely.

"Nay, don't make me leave you, I'll be quick now to retrieve your sword, I swear it. I can wield one nicely enough myself, even though I cannot best you, I can—"

"Lady! Be safe that I may fight with a clear mind, I beg of you! Jesu, Melisande, obey this one time!" She had little choice, so it seemed. Suddenly he was thrusting her forward, crying out, and someone was reaching toward her.

"Father!" Conar called, and she was looking up into Nordic eyes, cool blue, so like her husband's. Then strong hands clamped around her, and she was lifted up, swept away from the clash of steel and the thunder of men and beasts.

Someone attacked from the rear. The great white horse she sat atop reared high. The king of Dubhlain slashed down on his enemies and nudged his mount, and they were away. They came some distance and the horse rose again on its haunches, spun, and fell down flat. They looked back. They could see the battle now. Men fighting fiercely. Norse against Dane, the Frankish troops, Odo! Count Odo was there. Her own Philippe, dear Gaston. They were all assembled, and in such fantastic display, with such an advantage. They were all mounted, while only part of Geoffrey's mercenaries were so prepared, and even those who had seized horses to ride, or who had been given them by Geoffrey, had not time to reach them.

Geoffrey had imagined that he would bring his ten men to capture Conar in the woods, seize her, slay Conar.

It wasn't to be. Atop the white horse, the calm strength of her father-in-law behind her, she felt an amazing burst of warmth.

Aye, Conar had come home when he had been called. Yet tonight . . .

"Lady, are you well enough?"

Her trembling had caused the question. She turned to see what she could of Olaf's strong features, fine eyes.

This would be Conar in time. He would so age, nobly.

She nodded slowly, biting into her lower lip. "I am merely thanking God, milord . . ." she hesitated just a moment, then added, "for the Vikings in my family!"

Olaf smiled beneath the steel of his visor.

"It is nearly ended!" he said softly.

The fighting suddenly seemed to cease. It had not really stopped, she realized—men had simply given way. Looking through the sea of men, Melisande could see that a small clearing had been formed.

Within it Conar now faced his enemy alone.

They walked a careful circle.

Men began to shout.

Conar and Geoffrey . . .

"Why do they fight further?" Melisande cried with alarm, afraid. Conar was whole, he was in one piece.

He was weary. He had battled too many men. Brought her so far . . .

"They must end it," Olaf said.

"But—"

"They must," Olaf repeated, and fell silent.

And so there was nothing for her to do but watch through the veil of fear and tears that had so swiftly seized her.

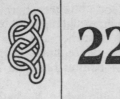 **22**

A greater space was cleared around the two men.

Geoffrey lunged instantly and wildly. Conar immediately parried his blow.

Geoffrey fell back. He turned around and faced those grouped around. "A champion. I demand a champion. You, Horik!" he called to one of his men. "Jon, send that berserker forward! Let one teeth-gnashing sea raider fight another. Winner takes all, Conar of Dubhlain, the woman, the land, the battle."

Melisande's eyes shot to the one they called Horik. He was nearly as tall as Conar, heavier, bulkier. She felt fear streak into her system. "No!" she whispered.

But to her astonishment Horik was shaking his grizzled, platinum head. "This is your battle, Geoffrey. The fight is yours and—his."

Geoffrey started to walk from the circle in a rage. "You've been well paid, you bastard—"

"Paid to fight a battle with men. Not to stand in your place against such a man as this Norse wolf."

"He killed your companions—"

"He came for his wife. It is your fight."

Geoffrey looked wildly from one man to another. He suddenly seized a knife from his ankle—Melisande saw the motion.

"Conar!" she cried. "Conar! He has a knife!"

In time, in time! Pray God! The treacherous Geoffrey was just turning, hurtling his missile expertly toward Conar's eyes.

Conar ducked, and the knife sailed past his head. He stared at his enemy and drew his sword.

"Come at me, wolf dog!" Geoffrey shout d in a rage. His own sword at the ready, he ente: :d into battle. He was not a weak swordsman.

But he did not compare to Conar.

Melisande remembered the way she had fought her husband, how he had kept her moving.

He fought Geoffrey just so now.

He calmly parried each blow that fell his way. He struck again, and again, and again. Geoffrey's blade met his, clashing, clanging in the moonlight. That was all that could be heard, the awful sound of steel screeching against steel.

The circle widened and widened. Conar leapt backward over a tree stump in his way, Geoffrey nearly fell over it in his haste to reach Conar and offer another blow.

He was weakening, weakening fast, Melisande realized.

"Please . . ." she whispered in a soft sigh to heaven—or Valhalla.

The warrior gods were with him, great Wodin, mighty Thor. Conar raised and lowered his sword again in a mighty sweep. It caught Geoffrey's. The man's weapon flew.

And Conar's blade rested against his throat.

"Kill him!" went up a cry.

From the Danes. From the man's own allies.

Merciless when their leader proved his weakness.

Conar kept his blade tight against Geoffrey's throat. "If you ever glance her way again, Geoffrey Sur-le-

Mont, I will slice you like a spitted boar, dismember you piece by piece, and feed you to the vultures.''

He turned, and seeing his father and his wife, started in that direction.

Melisande saw his eyes. His incredible blue eyes, impaling as they settled upon her. Her heart seemed to cry out.

But then, from the corner of her eye she saw Geoffrey begin to move once again. Hunching down at his ankles, reaching to the tight sheath above his left boot.

There was a second knife inside it. Within seconds his fingers had fastened around it.

And once again Melisande saw it coming.

"Nay!" she shrieked. "Nay!" Not now, not after all this.

"Conar, he has another knife!"

This time when Conar flew around, he reached down to his own ankle and drew his knife.

And threw it with an even swifter speed.

Geoffrey's blade just grazed Conar's shoulder and neck, with little space to spare.

Conar's blade found its mark, flying straight into Geoffrey's heart. The man stared at him for one moment, then keeled over in a smooth motion, dead before he hit the ground. His eyes remained open. He stared at Conar even in his death.

But Conar turned away. The battle was over for the evening. The Danes would go off on their own, with Geoffrey no longer there to guide them. Some might join up with other groups terrorizing the people here.

Some might sail home.

But the battle was done for the night. Conar's numbers were the superior ones, the Irish line of the house of Vestfold had linked its mighty arms together.

They had left many slain and injured. They had done their damage.

Even Odo could be pleased with the night's work.

For Conar it was time to go home. He slowly approached the line of horses, reaching up to grasp hands with each of his brothers. Only Leith had not come, for someone must remain behind. Eric had been safe enough to leave Wessex, for Alfred's law extended well over his land.

He came to Mergwin and shook his head with slow astonishment. "You've mounted a horse to ride into battle."

Mergwin shrugged. "I try to read the future for you and your siblings, I cast runes, I foretell great things. Once I have done so," he said with a deep sigh, "I find that I must sometimes give destiny a hand."

Conar smiled slowly.

He came to his father at last. Melisande still sat before Olaf on the great white horse.

"It seems the trial is over here, as well," Olaf told him.

Conar nodded.

"And you are free."

Count Odo had ridden up from behind. "The trials here are just beginning. The Danes sail the rivers, they head for Paris, for Rouen, for Chartres. Our fight goes on!"

"Aye," Conar agreed softly. "The fight goes on." For him it would. Eric would sail back for Wessex, his father, Conan, Bryan, and Bryce would return to Eire.

For their fight never really ended either.

But tonight's battle was over.

"Thank you," he told his father. He felt Melisande's eyes on him, felt the tears within them. Had she cared so much, then? She might have saved his life twice tonight—her cries had alerted him to Geoffrey's treachery each time. She looked so beautiful before his father, even if dirt smeared her cheeks and her ragged cloak. Her hair fell around her like ebony rain, waving, curling. The cloak draped around her slender form. Her eyes, their huge violet depths so haunting, remained steady upon him.

"I believe I've something of yours here?" Olaf murmured.

"Aye, indeed," Conar agreed.

He stepped forward, stretching his arms up, reaching for her. He was careful to keep the cloak about her as he lifted her high, then slowly down against him.

"What a husband!" Olaf murmured. "Is that the best you can do in gowning your wife?"

Conar smiled slowly, looking back up to his father. "No, milord, I swear, I customarily keep her clad in a finer style!"

"We shall see," Olaf said. "There stands Thor. Perhaps you would be good enough to mount him and escort us all to your home. We've come a long way, it's been a wearying night, and we're most eager to sample your hospitality."

"Aye, Father!" Conar agreed.

Eric, smiling, brought Thor forward. Conar deftly wound Melisande in the cloak, set her atop the stallion, and leapt up behind her.

The remaining Danes watched as they turned and rode away.

Melisande closed her eyes, leaning back against her husband's chest. Her heart had not ceased its frantic beat. She had never been so exhausted.

Nor so awake . . .

So weary yet . . .

So very alive. They were going home.

Together.

The ride took time, but it didn't matter. She was content to remain against him, feel his heartbeat, his warmth, his arms around her once again as they rode, tight, secure.

"So you keep me finely clad!" she murmured to him, as they rode.

"I don't?"

"Nay, milord, it seems to me that you are forever making havoc of my clothing!"

His lips nuzzled her ear as he spoke. "Then we must thank God that the fortress can be filled with able seamstresses!"

She leaned back again, smiling. They rode in silence.

In time they came to the fortress.

Melisande was newly amazed to discover that Erin and Daria had come as well.

There was complete chaos when they returned, so many people filling the hall, so many people demanding to know everything that had happened. Erin had been quick to remind them all that Melisande had endured a great deal through the night, it was daylight now, and surely she needed a long bath and a cup of warm sweet wine.

And perhaps something more substantial than the cloak to wear.

It was with Erin that she came to her room, and though Marie was there to cast soap and oil into her bath, to enclose her fiercely in her arms and whisper her delight that she was back, Erin was the one to stay with her, to warm the wine over the fire and pour it into a chalice for her.

Sinking into the hot water and sipping the wine felt delicious. Knots eased from her body, she seemed to wash away some of the terror of being with Geoffrey.

Geoffrey would never bother her again.

Erin stood across the room, and Melisande saw her studying a trunk. The gilded mail lay across it.

Erin lifted it and brought it to the foot of the bed. "I had mail like this once . . ." she remarked. She looked over to Melisande, smiling. "In fact, I still have it."

"You?" Melisande murmured.

Erin nodded, lifted the garment, folded it over her arm, and returned it to the trunk.

"Was it a gift?" Melisande asked her.

Erin shook her head. "I was very determined to fight the Vikings," she said. "So I did it in disguise."

Melisande found herself hugging her knees to her chest, staring at her mother-in-law. "You fought the Vikings?"

"I fought Olaf."

Melisande gasped. Erin came around the tub and began to work suds through Melisande's hair. Melisande tried to twist to look at her, but Erin commanded that she stay still, in the same voice she might have used when Melisande had first come to her house as a child.

"But then—"

"But then I found myself wed to him."

"But . . ."

"Aye?"

"You're so happy!" Melisande exclaimed.

Erin tapped her head, and Melisande ducked beneath the water, rinsing her hair. She emerged again, staring at her mother-in-law. Erin nodded, a small smile curving her lip. "Indeed, if I could wish a blessing on any lass, it would be to live as sweet and rich and full a life as I have shared with him. We have had our times of tempest. To this day we are both willful and stubborn, and he does have a fearsome temper. As do my sons . . . But, as Mergwin will tell you, wolves are wild creatures. They hunt, they thirst, they prowl restlessly in their quests. But most often . . ."

"They tend to mate for life," Melisande filled in. "They are fiercely loyal. Creatures who band together, care in a strange way for one another." She looked up at Erin, and Erin smiled again. Melisande

felt a snowy linen towel set atop her head, felt it
rubbing her hair. She felt a gentle kiss upon her cheek.

"I'm very glad that one of my wolves has you,
Melisande. His growl is rough, but remember the
creature beneath!"

Erin left her then. Melisande stepped from the tub,
rubbing her body dry. She found a soft clinging gown,
and sitting before the fire with her brush, finished
drying her hair and easing the tangles from it. She was
thus engaged when she heard the door open again, and
when she turned, Conar stood there.

He leaned against it, watching her. She paused,
watching him. He crossed the room, his hands falling
upon her shoulders for a moment. "Continue, my
love, I like watching you so."

She tried to continue, but she discovered that her
fingers were trembling, and she didn't want him to see
that it was so. He stood by the mantel, stripped of his
helmet and mail, striking in his linen shirt and tight
chausses.

"Conar," she murmured softly.

"Aye?"

She looked up at him, suddenly fighting a wealth of
tears again. "I'm sorry that I came here. I never did
so just to defy you. I truly felt that one of us must be
here; the Danes were ravaging us as well as Eire."

He came to the chair where she sat, lowered himself
to one knee, and stilled her hands in her lap. "Melisande—"

"I was wrong."

"Aye! You were wrong, and I was wrong. And I
was furious and acted like a wild dog. But it doesn't
matter now. When I discovered you missing, I had
never known a greater fear. When I thought of Geoffrey with you, I wanted to rip him to shreds with my
bare hands and teeth."

She shook her head, her eyes wet. "I was so afraid

that you wouldn't come for me! That you might think that Geoffrey made the mistake, seizing me."

He laughed softly. "Nay, lady, never. But come to think of it now . . ."

She lifted the brush as if she would give him a good whack. He snatched it from her, coming behind her to pick up long tresses and pull the brush through them.

"The Irish put aside their wives if they choose to do so," she reminded him.

"Ah, does that mean you recognize I've Irish blood within me?"

"A trickle."

He grunted. She fell silent for a moment, feeling the gentle luxury of his hands upon her hair. "Conar, they were wonderful!" she said suddenly. "They sailed here, all of them, coming to our aid."

"Aye."

She turned and met his eyes. "Your father is quite incredible."

"Aye."

"Of course, so is your mother.

"Of course."

Again a silence fell. She could hear the sound of the fire crackling and that of the brush moving through her hair.

"Odo wants you to ride with him again immediately," Melisande told him. "We won tonight, Conar, but you cannot imagine. The Danes cover us, seeking Paris, invading the rivers, the isles. We are in dire trouble here."

"Aye, I know."

"I don't want you to go with Odo."

"I will have to," he reminded her.

"And I—"

"You will be an obedient wife for once," he told her.

Her heart skipped a beat. "You'll send me away again—"

"Nay, not if we shore up the walls to an extent where I am happy and if the fortress can be made battle-ready. I don't believe the Danes will tarry with such a difficult position now. Geoffrey is gone." He was silent a moment. "And my son should be born here."

She felt a burst of happiness within her. Her fingers were trembling again. She knotted them in her lap.

"Hmm," Conar murmured suddenly.

"What is it? Are you thinking of the battles to come?"

"Nay, lady," he said softly. "I was thinking of this ebony tress of hair. I was thinking of stroking it over my own bare flesh, watching it create a tangle of black silk around us both . . ."

Once again her heart seemed to skip a beat. She inhaled sharply as he came around, dropping down on one knee before her.

"Does such a sweet vision have possibilities?" he inquired, eyes as endlessly blue and piercing as a sunlit northern sky, a gentle curve to his lip.

"You're asking?" she whispered.

The smile deepened, and he shrugged. "I'd hate to give up all my Viking tendencies, but aye, love, at the moment I am asking." His voice went hoarse. "You did have a difficult evening. But then again, so did I, come to think of it. Imagine, my mother worries so about you! Does she give a care to what injuries I might have sustained in the rescue?" He sighed. "The world is not always fair."

She laughed. "Milord, I could have told you that years ago!"

"Well, milady?"

She rose smoothly, drawing him to his feet before her. "Bathed and perfumed," she whispered softly,

and she brushed his lips with a kiss, then walked
before the fire. In an easy movement she loosed her
gown from her shoulders and let it drift to a soft white
puddle at her feet, then stepped from it.

"Charming," he murmured.

"I am running out of clothing."

"How intriguing."

"Your shirt, milord."

"Pardon?"

"Your shirt."

"Oh." Swiftly it was over his shoulders, tossed atop
her gown.

"The rest."

"As you wish it."

In seconds he was naked. Golden, gleaming muscles
rippled handsomely in the firelight. She surveyed him
fully, her breath catching at his loin, finding it just a
bit difficult to force her eyes to rise coolly to his once
again.

Arms crossed over his chest, arrogant in his nakedness, he watched her now with keen interest.

"And now?"

She came toward him. He would have caught her,
but she eluded his arms. She came behind him, palms
working over his back, lips delicately falling upon old
wounds and scars. "Bathed and perfumed . . ." she
repeated. She came on tiptoe, kissed his neck, teased
his earlobe. "And ready and willing . . ."

Her hands brushed upward over the hard muscles of
his buttocks. She pressed against him, the tips of her
breasts rubbing erotically against his back, the ebony
hair at her triangle mercilessly teasing his flesh. Then
she slipped around him once again, arms rising around
his neck, body flush to his, lips just a breath away
from his.

"Ready, willing . . . hungry, aching, eager . . ."

His mouth ground down upon hers, his tongue

plunging, plundering, seeking, passionate, fierce. She found herself swept up into his arms, both weak and exhilarated with excitement. She met his eyes again as he carried her to their bed, kept her gaze locked with his as she landed hard, he atop her.

"Dying!" she whispered. "Entreating, needing—"

His kiss cut away her words. His fingers curled into hers, driving them high against the bed. The length of his body seemed to meld to hers, then his hands were over the length of it, large, bold, creating fierce blue fires where they would roam. His palm ground against the downy triangle, fingers slipped in it, found its cleft, rubbed, stroked. She moaned, twisting, crying out his name.

Again his mouth covered hers. Then rose just above it.

"No sane man, Irish or Viking, would ever set aside such a wife!" He assured her passionately.

Her eyes widened. She laughed at the teasing smile that curled his lip.

Then her laughter was cut short, her breath stopped, for he was suddenly plunging within her, deep, deeper. A gasp escaped her, she shivered and trembled with the sweet impalement of her body. After a moment he began to move, and in time the movement became a wild ride, rocking her, sweeping her. Her arms clamped around him, his hands were upon her buttocks, kneading, rousing her to greater heights. She arched, writhed. His mouth closed over her breast as he loved her, his hand slid down to press against her mound even as his body thrust hard with hers.

Her climax swept her, sweet and shattering. She clung to him, lips upon his shoulder, teeth lightly biting. A low moan escaped her even as rigor seized him and he held himself fiercely above her, then thrust so deeply, it seemed that they must indeed be one, the liquid mercury of his body searing and sweet as it entered hers.

He fell to her side. Seconds later she felt the light, tender touch of his fingers moving gently over her arm. "Could I possibly hear those words once again?" he murmured. "Eager, hungry. Wild. Indeed, and all from the same lovely witch who loathed me not a full day's time ago!"

"You test your luck, Viking!" she warned softly.

"Ah! And there's my vixen again."

She rolled, straightening upon her arms, to stare into his eyes. "Truly, Conar, for many things I am sorry."

His hands slid along her arms. "Truly, Melisande, you must not be. I would not love you so deeply were you any other than the vixen you are!"

She gasped, lowered her lashes in a great sweep over her cheeks, and met his eyes again. "You . . . love me, milord?"

"Only a blind man could not see it," he answered solemnly.

"Nay, my lord! You might have deceived the most far-seeing of men—and women!"

"Do you think so?" he inquired lightly, lacing his fingers behind his head to study her.

"Indeed. Perhaps . . ."

"Well, you have never spoken those words before. You are surely aware that I sometimes need to hear things more than once!"

He rose, sweeping her into his lap and stroking long damp strands of ebony hair from her face. "I love you, Melisande. Deeply, dearly. I thought that if I were to lose you, I would long for death, for the sweet harbor of a Christian heaven, or the halls of Valhalla. I was never quite sure where it all began, for you were so wild and independent and hostile—and disobedient! Yet always there was within you that sweet simmering of courage, that endless spirit, that sensual beauty, sweeping around me, seducing me, capturing my heart. I love you. Have you heard me now?"

"Oh!" she breathed softly. She touched his cheek, the hard, handsome planes. "I've heard you."

"And what of you, milady?"

"I love you!" she whispered.

"Ah, so simple! After such a declaration!"

She smiled, a small smile at first, then a sweetly wicked one. "Nay, never so simple!" she cried. And she pressed him back upon the pillow, her lips touching his, his throat, his fingers, his chest. "I love you . . ." She inhaled deeply. "Need you, crave you, seek you, adore you—"

"Ah, lady!" he cried, and took her into his arms.

The day had dawned, yet those gentle words were repeated over and over again, and day or night did not matter, for there, then, in that room, they clung together.

And loved.

Epilogue

Fall, A.D. *887*

The days were growing cool. By sunset on a night like
this, the air had true crispness to it, and the water at
the stream was actually cold. Melisande didn't mind.
She loved the chill feel of it against her feet, for her
feet always seemed to be uncomfortable these days.

She lay back against a tree with gnarled old roots
that stretched right into the water and stared up at the
dipping branches. The leaves were beautiful. The dying sun touched them with a brush of fire, and the
colors were radiant, orange and gold, yellow and red.
Soon they would begin to fall as winter came, die
along with the waning year. But what a year it had
been.

The Danes had set forth upon an astounding invasion as summer came. They came by the thousands—
some estimated as many as thirty thousand invaders,
though their numbers were multiplied by mercenaries,
Swedes, Norse, any who would join them. They
choked the rivers, they came up the Seine, they laid
siege to Paris.

Three times assaults came against the fortress.

Three times the invaders were swiftly repelled with bombardments of oil and arrows.

Melisande governed the defenses along with Bryce, for her brother-in-law, so like her own blood and so very loyal to her husband, had chosen to remain with her, a self-appointed protector for those times when Conar must be about on other business. Conar had carefully planned their defenses, taught and advised her, and stressed the importance of every action. But Conar had not been there only once when they assaulted, and that upon the morn of the last attack, for he had ridden at Odo's side, and it was well that he had done so.

Louis was not in Paris when the siege was laid. The Vikings had devastated Rouen and then moved in upon Paris. There Count Odo, Bishop Joscelyn, Conar, and perhaps another two hundred barons defended Paris against seven hundred Viking ships and their numbers. Paris burned, orange clouds touched the skies. But the defenders held the city. The Danes went on to ravage much of the countryside, and Paris lay under siege for a year, but Odo and his men turned them back each time they might have taken the city. The warfare was endless, yet despite it, and despite the dangers, Conar did manage to come home. And when he did, it was always a heart-stopping occasion for Melisande. Even as time went on, she discovered that her heart still beat too quickly each time she saw him riding home to her, the sweet fire of Wodin raced through her limbs, and she would die to be in his arms.

He always managed to find a way to come home when it was really important. He was there in the late fall of 885 when his son was born, and he was the one to insist the boy be another Manon, for her father, Manon Robert, and yet somehow the babe came to be known to them all as Robbie.

Her son was all that she had expected him to be, all
that Conar might have commanded he be.

His eyes were sky blue, his hair a deep, rich, sun
gold. He was a big baby, hale and hearty from the
beginning, and the strength of his lusty wails kept
them all laughing within the household. Conar had
been there through all her long hours of labor, down
in the hall—drinking with his father, for Erin and Olaf
and Daria had also managed to return for the birth,
along with Mergwin. In the midst of absolute chaos,
happiness had managed to reign. Conar was determined to be at her side, even when she had called him
every dastardly name that would come to mind, and
Erin had assured her that it was quite all right, it was
the one time she could call him anything she desired
and be immediately forgiven for all.

She did call him many, many things. He nodded,
agreed with them all, and allowed her to curl her
fingers around his knuckles so hard that they might
have shattered. He held her when she cried out, when
she struggled. He held her even when she swore that
he should let her go.

And he smiled and reminded her that he would
never, never let her go.

And in due time, with him holding her still, the babe
was born.

To Melisande, every unhappiness in the world was
forgiven, everything became a taste sweeter, a bit
more beautiful, the moment Robbie entered her life.
The family doted over him; poor Marie de Tresse was
distressed to find that she never had the babe to
herself.

Conar adored the lad, and the most wonderful times
of all were those precious moments when they would
lie with him, together on their bed, marvel at his
fingers and toes, and weave their own tales for his
destiny.

Sometimes Melisande almost felt guilty for finding

such sweet happiness when so much of the country
suffered. Hers was a wonderful home, where Ragwald
and Mergwin sat for hours discussing the sky and the
stars, chemistry and medicine—and the future. Everyone enjoyed Robbie, and the household was filled with
life and warmth. Not even Melisande could remember
its being so before.

She wished her father might have seen his fortress
now.

The terror that ravaged France did intrude, however,
for Conar would come home and ride away again. But
by the end of 886 Louis the Fat managed to return to
Paris, and though Odo demanded the king take a
strong stand, Louis paid the invaders danegeld for
promises from them, and they turned around and
devasted the countryside further.

Count Odo was hailed for his actions, as was Conar.
From being a foreign prince, he became one of the
most popular of the Frankish nobles, known the countryside over as the Lord of the Wolves. Odo granted
him further tracts of land, and though the Danes
remained to plague them, their Danish power was
disbanded, and they knew the strength of the fortress
and kept far from it.

Erin and Olaf had not stayed with her too long when
Robbie had been born, but they were back now, and
Olaf was out riding with his grandson, a lad now nearly
a full two years old. He was not far, Melisande knew.
Even now, she didn't dare stray too far from home
unless she knew someone was near. Conar had been
gone several days now, in deep consultation with Odo
and other barons, and she missed him dearly and
yearned for his return. Her father-in-law, knowing her
love for the stream, and fully aware that winter would
soon keep her away, had suggested he accompany her
and Robbie here. They had carried bread and cheese

and skins of goat's milk and wine to enjoy beneath the trees.

But now those two had gone, and she was alone, able to stare up at the branches, to cool her feet, to doze, to dream beneath the glorious blaze of colors.

It had become a good life for her. Rich. Still such a tempest at times, and still richer for that tempest, for their feelings always ran deep, their tempers, their opinions and their love.

She thought she heard a slight sound and looked up.

He was there, returned.

The Conar she knew so well, seated so expertly and casually upon his ebony Thor, shoulders so broad, chest clad in mail, a fiery red mantle cast over his shoulder. His helmet sat atop his head, for these could still be treacherous times for travel, and his eyes were shimmering, brilliant sky blue, searing out at her from the slits within the visor of his helmet. He seemed so indomitable there, a warrior.

A Viking. Golden, towering, striking, compelling. And as always now, a sight to create a stream of joy within her.

"Conar!" she cried softly, and tried to struggle up to reach him.

"Wait, lady!" he commanded, and slipped swiftly from Thor, tossing his helmet carelessly to the ground as he came to her. He helped her as she flailed, for she was sadly out of balance now, nearly nine months gone with their second child.

"I can rise—" she began.

"Stubborn," he chastised. "As always. I'm here to help you. Be still."

Despite her cumbersome weight, he quickly had her plucked up in his arms, and he sat against the trunk of the tree, cradling her in his lap.

"Will this suffice?"

"Oh, Conar!" she clasped his cheeks within the

delicate embrace of her hands and kissed his lips. She did so in a long and leisurely fashion, trembling just to feel his warmth, his vibrant touch once again. She lifted her lips, and he groaned softly, eyes sparkling as he ran his hand over the huge cup of her stomach.

"Ah, my love! Have mercy on a husband gone too long—yet too soon to be a father again!"

She wrinkled her nose at him. "Fine. Scold me for being so very delighted to see you!"

"Never," he promised. Then he asked gravely, "How are you, well, I pray?"

She smiled, stretching back contentedly in his arms. "Very well, thank you. And Robbie—"

"I saw him with my father. They are both quite well. I saw that myself."

Melisande smiled, then grew grave. "And what of our world, Conar? What is going on?"

Conar sighed. "They intend to depose Louis. The barons are set upon it, and how can one defend such a weak king for whom we have fought so hard, only to be undermined by him so continually?"

She stroked his cheek, knowing that he was still bitter over what had been done in Paris. "What will happen then?"

"Charlemagne's old empire will be broken up, my love." He studied her eyes. "Odo will become king of the West Franks, and we will continue to give our fealty to him."

"That should please you."

"Aye, it does." He fell silent for a moment. "Geoffrey's lands have fallen to us, and we have been granted still further land to the east. Does that please you?"

She shuddered. "Aye, and nay. Nothing to do with Geoffrey pleases me greatly."

Conar shrugged. "Aye, that is one way to see it. There is also another."

"Aye!" she asked curiously. And he smiled, tracing his finger over her lip.

"Were it not for Gerald's treacherous determination to have you for himself or his son, I'd not have acquired my beautiful child bride to begin with. And then again, if it hadn't been for Geoffrey's abducting you that night, I'd have never believed that my hostile, disobedient—yet exquisite—wife, turned to a woman then, might love me."

"You knew before I said the words," she told him.

"But you did say the words, right before Geoffrey, don't you remember? He wanted to have me drawn and quartered, fed to vultures. And you threw yourself in front of me and told him that he could never slay love."

"Umm! And you threw me right behind you again!"

"Ah, but the words burned fiercely in my heart!" he assured her. She stared into his eyes and couldn't help smiling once again, couldn't help kissing him, hungry for his lips, for any touch at all.

Ah, it was so sweet. Every time she kissed him, she felt such wondrous things. A tempest, a turmoil. Fever in her blood, knots in her stomach.

She broke away from him, ruefully realizing the sudden knots in her stomach were not from his kiss.

"Conar?"

"Aye?"

"Nothing. Nothing. Never mind." She kissed him again.

The knot tightened, harder and harder. Her breath caught. She drew her lips away.

"My beloved wife," he whispered, "what sweet effect you have upon me as well . . ."

"Conar?"

"Aye?"

"'Tis not your kiss."

"Nay?"

She wet her lip and smiled. "Still your effect, milord, I do assure you."

"Then—"

"The babe!" she whispered softly.

He was up, swiftly, carrying her with him. Long strides quickly brought them to Thor.

"Milord, it may take a long, long time."

"And this is a second child, and he may come quickly as well."

"It is not a he, Conar. Mergwin has told me that we are to have a daughter."

"Then she may come quickly!" he said with exasperation, and leapt up behind her.

In minutes they were back at the fortress. And she was incredulous—and just a bit annoyed—to discover that he was right. Their daughter was born within a matter of hours, and she didn't call him half so many names as she did the first time.

This baby was beautiful, too. Her hair was neither blond nor dark, but a fiery red, and there was a startling wealth of it. Her eyes were as blue as a summer's sky, even deeper perhaps.

"Violet," Conar determined, inspecting the babe. He sat at the head of the bed, inspecting the baby as Melisande lay with her in the cradle of her arms.

Melisande was sweetly exhausted, and her eyes started to close. Erin was swiftly there to scoop the newborn from her arms. Half asleep, Melisande felt Conar shift, and her fingers wound around his hand again.

"Nay, milord, don't leave me!" she whispered.

He sat at the top of the bed, shifting her weight so that she rested curved into his shoulder against the carved headboard.

And she heard his soft, tender whisper. "Nay, my love. I shall never let you go."

She smiled, and her eyes closed, and she lay there exhausted, but so content.

For she knew that it was true.

Viking, Irishman, tormentor, demon, friend, warrior, protector.

Husband.

Lover.

He would never let her go.

And she would love him forever, her Lord of the Wolves. For life, for all eternity.

Time was theirs now, life was theirs now, and the sweetest of all, love was theirs, always. The years stretched out before her with wonder. It was incredible now to remember how she had fought him, how she had hated him, tried to hate him.

Loved him, and feared that love.

Ah, but they had come far! They had paid with times of anguish for the joy they shared now. They had so very much. One another, Robbie . . . this little lass!

She wondered what Mergwin would have to say of their new daughter, of their future.

Held securely within her lord's arms, Melisande smiled and, at long last, slept.

And began to dream anew, sweet, sweet dreams.

About the Author

New York Times and *USA Today* bestselling author Heather Graham has written over one hundred novels and novellas, including category, romantic suspense, historical romance, and paranormal. Married since high school graduation and the mother of five, her greatest love in life remains her family, but she also believes her career has been an incredible gift. Romance Writers of America presented Heather with a Lifetime Achievement Award in 2003.